CAUGHT BY THE SCOT

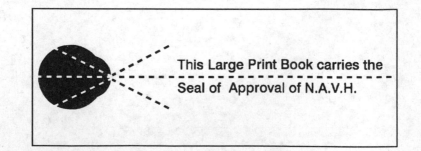

MADE TO MARRY

CAUGHT BY THE SCOT

KAREN HAWKINS

THORNDIKE PRESS
A part of Gale, a Cengage Company

Farmington Hills, Mich • San Francisco • New York • Waterville, Maine
Meriden, Conn • Mason, Ohio • Chicago

Thorndike Press® Large Print Romance.
The text of this Large Print edition is unabridged.
Other aspects of the book may vary from the original edition.
Set in 16 pt. Plantin.

LIBRARY OF CONGRESS CIP DATA ON FILE.
CATALOGUING IN PUBLICATION FOR THIS BOOK
IS AVAILABLE FROM THE LIBRARY OF CONGRESS

ISBN-13: 978-1-4328-4417-2 (hardcover)
ISBN-10: 1-4328-4417-2 (hardcover)

Published in 2018 by arrangement with Pocket Books, an imprint of Simon & Schuster, Inc.

Printed in the United States of America
1 2 3 4 5 6 7 22 21 20 19 18

For my beloved Cap'n Hot Cop, whose technomagick keeps my printer printing, my computer computing, and my "smart" phone smart. If I didn't have you in my life, I'd have to hire a 24/7 techie and, while I'd make sure he looked like Hugh Jackman (I mean, the cash picks the stash, am I right?), I'm sure he would never satisfy my many tech issues with your calm demeanor, sparkling wit, or devilish sense of humor.

TAI, my love.

ACKNOWLEDGMENTS

Big hugs to my longtime editor, Micki Nuding, who retired and rode off into a much-deserved sunset. Enjoy your perpetual holiday!

And huge thanks to Marla Daniels, who stepped in to answer my thousand and one questions and help in so many ways. I owe you major margaritas!

1

Conner Douglas slammed his glass onto the heavy oak table. "Bloody hell, *nae!* I will nae do it!"

Lachlan Hamilton, the Duke of Hamilton and Conner's brother-in-law, stared out the castle window at the rocky cliff overhanging the cold, gray sea. " 'Tis nae a question," he said shortly.

Conner knew what lay on that cliff. Under a giant oak was a grave, the dirt freshly turned from the burial they'd attended not an hour ago.

Och, Anna, why did you leave us? A wave of grief hit Conner like a hammer and he had to swallow twice before he could even breathe. His only sister, gone. "Hamilton, 'tis too soon. You cannae expect us to —"

"I do and I will," Hamilton snapped with a look of blazing fury. "You and your brothers will find wives within the next three months or you'll nae touch a penny of your inheritances."

"You've nae that authority." Jack's voice was heavy with rage.

Conner eyed his oldest brother with unease. Jack was not called "the Black Douglas" for naught; his temper was as dark as his midnight hair.

"I am the executor of your sister's will," the duke said grimly. "Do as Anna wished and find wives, and I'll grant you each your portion of the inheritance. Guid wives, too — nae tavern maids, nae actresses, and nae soiled doves, but women of quality like your sister."

Conner ground his teeth in anger, not just at the terms of the will, but at life. One week ago he, Declan, and Jack had sailed here, to the Isle of Arran, in high spirits after receiving word that their sister Anna was delivering her baby. They'd expected to be met at the dock by their brother-in-law, jubilant with news of a bonnie lad or lassie. Instead the butler awaited, his pale face and trembling mouth delivering his wretched news for him.

Conner curled his hands into fists and pressed them into his thighs to stop the pain. Anna, who had raised all three of them when their parents had died eighteen years ago in a carriage accident, was gone.

God, Anna, what am I — we — to do without you? His eyes burned and he swiped at them with an impatient hand. He and his brothers had been blessed with a strong, capable sibling who had become more mother than sister. And even though he'd been on his own for years, without her, he was as lost as a ship without a rudder.

Declan scowled at Hamilton. "Three months to find a wife? 'Tis nae long enough."

"Then make it four months, but nae a day more. And dinnae argue, for I'm being generous in giving you that." The duke turned from the window and planted his feet, facing his three brothers-in-law. "So go. The lot of you. And dinnae come back until you've properly wed."

"Nae," Jack snapped. "You're trying to force us to bend to your wishes, nae Anna's."

The look Hamilton gave Jack was as bleak as night. "You think I give a damn aboot any of you? If I had my way, I'd give you your blasted portions and send you off so you'd bother me nae more. But Anna wanted you settled and thought this would serve." He glowered at them all. "Do as your sister asked, or the family fortune will be distributed to others."

11

Conner picked up his glass of whisky. "I've never wished for the damned money, anyway. Keep it."

Jack's dark look disappeared at Conner's words. "We've made our own way withoot it. Why would we wish for it now?"

Hamilton's brows climbed, and he said in a suddenly silky tone, "Indeed? You'd have the Douglas fortune gifted to the Campbells, then?"

Conner choked on his whisky. "The *Campbells*? They're our greatest enemies!"

"Are you daft?" Declan demanded.

Hamilton fixed a frosty gaze on them. "I'm doing as Anna asked, unpleasant as 'tis. She was tired of your spendthrift ways —"

"We pay our own way, and always have," Conner protested.

"Aye, through pirating and thievery and smuggling," the duke snapped, his jaw set. "Nae to mention the gambling and whore-mongering and scandals. Nae wonder Anna despaired of you."

A twinge of guilt hit Conner. Anna had always worried; but wasn't that what sisters did?

"Come, Hamilton, dinnae be hasty," Declan said in a soothing tone. "Anna's death is —" His voice broke, but he swallowed hard, and added in a husky voice, "None of us are oop to facing life right now. Let's nae make any decisions whilst we're struggling to catch our breaths. Give us a few months to think aboot this, to find a way to answer her wishes."

"She said three months, and oot of respect for your grief, I've added a month. But that is all I'll give you and it's bloody well all I'll say aboot it." Hamilton waved a hand. "Go. And dinnae return until you've done as Anna wished."

Declan spread his hands. "Hamilton, be reasonable. We just need —"

"Reasonable?" Hamilton's voice was quiet, yet it thundered through the study. "I just lost my wife, the only woman I ever loved, or will love, and I'm left with a babe to raise on my own. Right now, the whole world is cold, cruel, and bloody unreasonable." His gaze flickered over all of them. "Now go. Dinnae marry and I'll give your funds to the Campbells. I dinnae care who has it."

"Hell will freeze before a Campbell touches Douglas gold!" Furious, Jack started forward, but Declan grabbed his brother's arm and jerked him back.

Hamilton's mouth had gone white. "Dinnae test me. Today of all days, I'd like nothing more than to stomp the life oot of

13

someone. Fate owes me that satisfaction, if nae else."

Jack made as if to rise to the bait, but Declan said sharply, "Whatever Anna wished for, it was nae an argument. She hated it when any of us disagreed."

There was a moment of heavy silence, emotions too raw to ignore thickening the air. Somewhere in the distance a door slammed, followed by the faint cry of a baby.

The duke turned toward the cry, all color draining from his face. His shoulders sank and he took an involuntary step back, as if struck by a sword's blow.

As the baby's cry was hushed by the soothing voice of a nanny, the duke leaned heavily against the wall, his head down, his breathing harsh.

As if the wind has left his sails. Conner cleared his throat. "Perhaps we should go to the babe and —"

"Nae," Hamilton said harshly. "He is with the wet nurse. She will care for him."

Jack's brows lowered. "Hamilton, dinnae hold the lad at fault for Anna's death. He did naught but be born."

"Of course I dinnae blame him," Hamilton snapped, his voice raw. "If anyone is at fault for Anna's death, 'tis me."

The words hung in the room.

14

Conner shook his head. " 'Twas the cruelness of nature, Hamilton, but nae more."

Hamilton slowly gathered himself and turned back to the window, his expression hidden from view. "Leave. Now."

Conner exchanged looks with Declan. What did it bode for Anna's babe if his father could not even bear to hear his cries?

Jack's eyes were now dark with sadness instead of fury. Silently, he crossed the room to where the duke stood slumped against the wall. After an awkward moment, he placed his hand on Hamilton's broad shoulder.

The duke bowed his head, but did not move. It wasn't an encouragement, but neither was it a rebuff.

Declan cleared his throat and went to stir the fire, as if to give Jack and the duke a bit of time in silence. Conner looked out the door to the broad stone staircase that led to the nursery, his heart aching. Anna had wanted to have a child so badly. Now she'd never have the chance to hold the baby in her arms, never know the pleasure of being a mother, never see her baby grow and laugh and — The burn of tears threatened to escape his control. *This will nae help anyone. But there is one thing that will.*

He dashed his hand over his eyes and

sighed. "Fine. I will do as Anna wished."

Declan and Jack turned surprised faces his way.

"She was right and 'tis time. 'Marry, settle doon, be at peace with your life.' " Conner managed a faint smile. "How many times did she tell us that? A hundred?"

"At least." Declan's smile carried regret, and after a quiet moment, he nodded. "I will agree, too. I will find a wife, and soon."

Jack's face hardened, and he dropped his hand from the duke's shoulder, but didn't argue.

The duke pushed himself from the wall and turned to face them. "Thank you."

"We should nae tarry. Come." Conner went to the door, his brothers following. Once there, he turned to say good-bye, but Hamilton was already looking back out the window, his gaze locked on the grave.

Declan jerked his head toward the hallway and the three of them left, softly closing the door behind them.

Jack scowled as they headed to the front door. "Much as I loved our sister, I'd go into this more willingly if I knew there were benefits other than honoring her memory."

Conner accepted his coat from a footman. "If we marry and settle doon, it will silence society's chattering. 'Twas that which ir-

16

ritated Anna."

Jack glowered. "All I want is to howl and stomp like a madman."

"As do I." Declan gave a humorless laugh. "Perhaps we need wives to soften our angry hearts."

Conner wondered what he would do with his inheritance. He'd never thought about it before; he'd been too busy with his shipping and privateering interests, which had proven wildly profitable. Truly, he had no need of these funds. *But, then, neither do the bloody Campbells.*

The butler opened the door. Conner sent a final glance up the long stairway where his nephew was now sleeping. Should he visit the lad? He shook his head; he'd just wake the babe. The lad was better left in the care of the nurse Anna had chosen before her lying in.

With a reluctant sigh, Conner followed his brothers outside. They stood in the cold, the wet, gray day suiting their moods as they waited for the carriage.

Conner turned up his collar against the wind. "We might as well make the best of this. Think, lads: had we received our inheritances withoot the security offered by a marriage, we'd be the targets of every matchmaking mama in Scotland."

Jack looked appalled. "You're right."

Declan grimaced. "We would nae be able to go oot in public withoot being mobbed by crazed mamas and their wedding-hungry daughters."

Jack nodded. "By Zeus, that's true. We must find pleasant, malleable brides and quickly."

Conner added, "A lass with the guid sense nae to try and change us. Someone nae demanding. A woman of calm disposition, nae given to dramatic scenes or possessive tantrums, who —" Good God, he knew a woman like that. Only one, but one was enough. *Thea.*

Theodora Cumberbatch-Snowe was the sister of one of his best friends. She was well born, practical, and pretty enough, although rather quiet. The daughter of a diplomat, she knew her way through life, plus she was well past society's declared marriageable age, which would make her grateful for his offer. Flooded with relief, he announced, "I know the lady I'll marry. My friend Derrick's sister, Thea. I'll go to her and tell her what's toward with the will. She'll marry me and be glad of it."

Declan shook his head. "Conner, lad, you're a bloody fool if you think Miss Cumberbatch-Snowe will entertain such a slapdash suit. I've met the lady, and she dinnae strike me as the type to accept a half-baked proposal."

Conner grinned. "I'll wager you a hundred pounds she'll take my offer withoot question."

Declan looked intrigued. "You'll tell her flat oot you're desirous of marrying her for nae other reason than to attain your inheritance?"

"And that you think she'd nae be a bother as a wife?" Jack added.

Conner scoffed, "I'd never lie to Thea. She knows me and accepts me as I am." She liked him well enough, he was certain of that. She always seemed pleased when he visited, and she couldn't wish to spend the rest of her days at her parents' house. Who would?

Jack snorted in amusement. "Fool. I accept your offer of a hundred."

"Count me in," Declan said. "That's a hundred each, nae a hundred split between us."

"Done. You two are making an error; I know her weel. I've been friends with her and her family since I met her brother at Cambridge."

Declan snorted. "Friendship is one thing, wiving another."

"I'll enjoy spending your funds, both of you." He wouldn't enjoy being wed, but perhaps with Thea, marriage would at least be bearable. He was fortunate Thea's father was between assignments now, or Conner might have had to sail to a foreign clime to find his intended bride. As it was, she was safely docked at Cumberbatch House, a mere week's travel away, ready and waiting. *As if it's meant to be.* He grinned at his brothers. "You'll see how right I am. In a month or so, I'll make my appearance at Cumberbatch House and walk away with the perfect wife."

Declan's eyebrows rose. "You're nae going straight there?"

"We've four months, so there's nae rush, and the lady's father is awaiting orders that are nae expected for two months or more, so she's going naewhere soon. I might as weel enjoy the time I have left as a single mon."

Declan didn't look convinced. "You're taking a lot for granted."

"Never take a woman for granted," Jack added in a grim tone.

Conner waved them off like pesky flies. "You'll see. Meanwhile, what will you two fools do? Any likely candidates in mind?"

"Bloody hell, nae." Jack raked a hand

through his hair. "I want a wife like I want a shot in the arse. I've nae idea who I'm to marry; I dinnae care overmuch for respectable women."

"They are boring," Declan agreed.

The coach rattled around the castle and stopped before them, two portmanteaus strapped to the back. As the footman hurried from the castle to open the coach door, Declan frowned. "Where's my black trunk?"

The footman blinked. "I'm sorry, sir, but these were the only bags in the foyer."

"Dammit. That fool valet must have forgotten to send it doon." He turned to his brothers. "Go ahead. I'll meet you at the ship."

"Dinnae be late." Conner climbed into the carriage and took a seat, Jack joining him. "With this wind, we cannae wait."

Declan stepped back from the coach. "If I'm nae there when the tide turns, leave withoot me. I'll catch another ship in a day or two."

Conner banged on the ceiling to signal to the coachman to head to the port, anxious to leave. These next few weeks would be his last days of freedom, and he was determined to wring every possible ounce of pleasure from them. But in the meantime, he could relax, for his path — and Thea's, though she didn't yet know it — was set.

2

The door of the coach swung open, spilling bright sunlight inside. Conner threw a hand over his eyes as shards of pain splintered through his aching head. "Bloody hell, Spencer, close the damned door!"

"We have arrived, sir."

Vaguely surprised, Conner squinted past the tall, slender footman to the building behind him. Of drab gray stone, the two-story manor house was kept from blandness by a profusion of deep green vines that climbed up its stone walls. Most likely one of Thea's additions — no matter what climate or country her father set up house in, the woman was forever planting greenery.

It had been five weeks and two days since his brother-in-law's ultimatum. A prudent, careful man would have rushed to secure his bride, but Conner had never been prudent, and he damned well wasn't about to start now. Besides, he knew he had time as Derrick had mentioned casually in one of his many letters that their father was awaiting orders and thought they'd be in residence for at least two more months.

Conner rubbed his face and sat up, the carriage blanket falling to his lap. "I suppose I should climb oot and get this over with."

"Indeed, sir," Spencer said in a repressed tone. The footman served as bos'n's mate on ship, but made an excellent footman/valet when on land. Tall and brown haired, he sported a round face sprinkled with freckles that made him seem far younger than his thirty-odd years.

"Indeed," Conner agreed and fumbled with the buttons on his shirt, noting that while he still wore his boots, his nether regions had no covering. He found his kilt flung over the opposite seat and picked it up to reveal a nearly naked woman.

Ah yes. He'd almost forgotten.

The female who'd been sprawled under his kilt was dressed only in her chemise and she cradled a bottle of his best whisky like a doll. He reached over and raised her arm from the bottle, then uncorked it and lifted it to his dry lips. It was empty.

Of course.

He sent her an unforgiving scowl, dropped the bottle to the floor, donned his kilt and pinned it in place, and then tugged his coat over his shirt. As he did so, he untangled her red silk gown from about his boots and spread it over her. She continued sleeping heavily, her long brown hair flowing over the edge of the seat to the floor like a muddy waterfall.

He rescued his cravat from where it hung from the ceiling strap, and grimacing against the throb in his head, he climbed out of the coach and into the harsh daylight, where Spencer waited.

Conner tucked in his shirt and adjusted his sporran, hoping Theodora wasn't watching from a window. "Did you bring a fresh shirt? This one reeks of Lady Winstead's perfume."

"I suggested you bring a new set of clothing, but Lady Winstead dinnae wish to wait whilst one was fetched."

Normally, Charlotte was a jolly, enjoyable companion, but this time her company had palled after a day or so. Most likely because he was still torn by grief over Anna's death, irritation at the demands of that blasted will, and fighting a growing reluctance at the thought of giving up his precious freedom.

He caught Spencer's observant gaze and noted the frown lines between the footman's eyes. "Oot with it. You'll rip a seam like a too-full sail if you keep your thoughts bottled oop."

"Sorry, Cap'n, only . . . I hope you will nae hurt Miss Cumberbatch-Snowe's feelings."

"Feelings? How would I do that?"

"By appearing as you do, and asking her to marry you for nae better reason than to gain your inheritance."

Conner wished he hadn't shared the purpose of his errand with his footman, but such was the cost of drinking such an amount. "Come, Spencer, 'tis nae so ugly as all that."

Spencer held his ground, his round face pink with outrage. "I dinnae blame ye for wishing to find a malleable, agreeable wife, nor for drinking like a fish since your sister's funeral. The first is the dream of all men, and the second —" Spencer's face fell. "Och, Cap'n, Her Grace will be badly missed. I never knew a kinder soul."

Conner's throat tightened, his chest aching as if he'd just this moment walked away from Anna's grave. He'd been unprepared for the way grief snuck up on him and crashed over him like ocean waves. One moment, he'd be close to fine, and then next, sadness would dig her cruel claws into his heart and drag him so low, he feared he'd never surface. He forced a smile. "I miss her, too." *But now is nae the time to think of Anna. I need to start thinking about Thea.* "Rest easy that I know what I'm aboot."

Conner raked a hand through his hair and smoothed his wrinkled coat. "After all, 'tis just Thea, nae some grand lady."

At Spencer's surprised look, Conner waved a hand. "I mean, she's a lady, but she's also my friend, and she'd never want poetry nor flowers nor such flippery nonsense."

"If you say so, sir."

"I do. You can trust me on that, for I've known her forever." Just as he knew her brother Derrick. When Conner and Derrick had first met at school, they'd engaged in a relentless battle to see who was the better lad, and after many battles, tricks, and pranks had finally decided they were tied, and became best friends. Anna used to complain that Conner had spent more Christmases with the Cumberbatch-Snowes than with his own family, which was a fair complaint, he had to admit. But then at the holidays it was always easier to be a guest than to be a family member, wasn't it?

27

The sound of a female yawn made him move away from the coach and say in a low voice, "Return Lady Winstead to the ship and have MacDougal take her home. Meanwhile, you and Ferguson return with the coach and bring my luggage and horse."

"Aye, sir. Will we be heading for Gretna Green once you've spoken to her ladyship?"

"Guid lord, nae! Why would I run for the border? Miss Theodora and her parents will welcome me. We'll post the banns this coming Sunday and marry as soon as we can after that. It'll take three weeks at the most, I should think."

Spencer blinked. "Three weeks? To plan a wedding?"

"I dinnae wish for a large event, and neither will she." Spencer was beginning to sound annoyingly like Conner's brothers. Conner wished everyone would quit acting as if they knew better than he what Thea would want.

"Verrah weel, sir. If you say so." Spencer turned toward the house and frowned. "I wonder where everyone is? Nae a single porter nor footman has greeted us."

"Most likely they are busy elsewhere. Miss Cumber-batch-Snowe is forever appropriating the household servants for her gardening projects. Her mother complains aboot it

28

frequently." Thea would be glad to get away from her mother, he was certain of that. Kind as Lady Cumberbatch-Snowe had been to him, she was a bit of a termagant when it came to Thea, ordering the poor lass aboot as if she had no other purpose in life than to be of service to her family.

Soon she won't have to worry about such things. There had been a garden of sorts at Dunskcy House when he'd bought the ancient manor, but he hadn't bothered doing anything with it since he was rarely there, so it was now more a jungle than else. But Thea would soon set it to rights. They'd need more servants at Dunskey now that Thea was to live there, and he'd set aside a handsome fund for renovations so she could garden and decorate to her heart's content.

He looked at Spencer now. "Off with you, before my guest awakens. I've nae wish to hear her lamentations when she discovers she's to be sent home to her husband."

"Aye, aye, Cap'n." Spencer bowed and returned to the coach, clambering into his seat. With a lurch, the equipage turned toward the drive.

As soon as it disappeared from sight, Conner strode to the front door and grasped the heavy brass knocker. The second his hand closed about the ring, the door moved.

29

It's ajar. That's odd. He pushed it open and waited for a footman or the butler to greet him, but the foyer was empty.

The hair on the back of his neck tickled as a sense of foreboding pressed upon his shoulders. Frowning, Conner walked through the foyer, his footsteps echoing in the silence.

An hour and a half later, Conner hurried up to the coach as Spencer leapt down, looking surprised to find his master waiting in the courtyard. The footman looked past Conner to the house. "Where's the miss?"

"She's eloped."

Spencer blinked, looking as if someone had kicked him in the gut. "She did *what*?"

Conner knew the feeling well, and he answered through clenched teeth. "She eloped, dammit!"

"The devil she did!" Ferguson, Conner's first mate at sea, and butler when on land, tsked loudly. He'd left Coxswain MacLeish at the reins and had clambered down on hearing Conner's loud denouncement. A wiry, bowlegged man with a red face and a wisp of white hair combed over his shiny pate, Ferguson was a marvel at organizing both crew and ship. "With what scalawag?"

"Some bloody squire." Conner untied his

horse from the back of the coach. An hour and a half ago he'd entered the house to find it in an uproar, the servants clustered about the doors of the drawing room where Thea's mother sobbed upon the settee, while Thea's father paced the thick carpet like a caged lion, a note crushed in his hand. Derrick, who'd been trying to console his mother, had taken the time to explain to Conner the events leading to such a tragic scene — he and his parents had returned home a week early from a short visit to the capital only to discover Thea gone, leaving nothing behind but a note announcing her elopement. From what Conner had been able to surmise, she'd left for her misadventure several hours before he'd arrived.

How in the hell had this happened? Dammit, I shouldn't have tarried.

But who could have foreseen this? Never in a million years would he have thought quiet, demure Thea Cumberbatch-Snowe capable of doing anything so scandalous.

Furious, Conner swung onto his horse.

"What are you going to do, Cap'n?" Spencer asked.

"Find Thea and bring her home."

"So you know where she is?" Ferguson asked eagerly.

"Nae, but I'll find her. She's eloping, so

she's bound to be on her way north to Gretna Green." Conner ground his teeth. "She's to marry *me,* dammit, nae some country bumpkin who'll do naught but bury her in the countryside."

As soon as he said the words, Conner realized he'd planned on doing the very same thing. But somehow it was different. He would have left her well taken care of, with a generous allowance, a house full of servants, all the books she might care to read, and a garden that cried out for her. Conner clenched his jaw. *It's not the same. Not even a little.* "I'll overtake the misdirected couple and convince Thea to abandon her plans, return home, and have a proper wedding — to *me.*"

Ferguson scratched his chin. "Forgive me, Cap'n, but does Miss Cumberbatch-Snowe's parents know you mean to marry her yourself? Or do they think this is a rescue mission?"

Conner let loose a long string of curses that made both of his men blush. When he could contain his temper, he snapped, "Follow the North Road; I'll ride ahead. Once I've located Thea, I'll send a courier to meet oop with you and bring you to us. And dinnae tarry. The sooner we bring her back, the less damage there'll be to her reputation."

Without waiting for another word, Conner turned his horse and cantered down the drive. As the trees blurred by, he wondered where Thea might be and how far she and her ridiculous squire had gone. *Bloody hell, Thea, what's gotten into you? When I find you, I'll not let you out of my sight until we're married.*

The thought felt almost like a vow, and he realized how furious he was — which was rather surprising, now that he thought about it. Thea hadn't known he was coming for her, so her elopement wasn't a personal insult, although it felt like one. Somehow, in the time between his decision to marry Thea and arriving at her house, he'd come to think of her as his.

He set his jaw. She *was* his. All he had to do was inform her of this new development, and turn her from the ridiculous path she'd chosen for herself. With any luck, he'd have her back in the arms of her waiting family by dinner. And without it — well, he'd think about that when the time came.

Jaw set, he urged his horse to a faster pace, the dust flying.

3

Never had an elopement been so poorly planned nor so shabbily executed. Huddled in a wooden chair pulled up to the fireplace in the parlor of the Wild Boar — a rather depressing inn miles and miles yet from the Scottish border — Theodora Cumberbatch-Snowe pressed her hand to her uneasy stomach and hoped she wouldn't worsen an already horrendous day by retching.

Though her fiancé, the esteemed Squire Lancelot Fox, possessed many admirable skills, driving a carriage safely was *not* one of them. When not racing haphazardly down the straight portions of the poorly maintained roads, he oversteered the ancient curricle, leaning wildly through every corner, causing Theodora to hang on for dear life, her stomach protesting the sickening sway while the wheels groaned in protest.

Which explained why they were not traveling at this moment.

She'd first suggested and then demanded that Lance slow down, or better yet, allow her to drive. He had refused, saying that while he acknowledged her greater skill with both horse and carriage, he was determined to sweep her away "in the most romantic way possible."

Theodora should have held firm, but the squire's undeniably romantic and noble intentions, as well as her own deeply in-grained training as an ambassador's daughter to always be polite no matter the circumstances, had left her with a forced smile and an increasingly ill stomach as she endured the squire's terrible driving.

However, while she had been willing to endure the squire's ham-fisted efforts, the antique curricle had not. One of the wheels gave way during a misjudged corner and sent them tumbling head over heels. Lance and the curricle had ended up sprawled topsy-turvy in the middle of the muddy road, while Theodora and her portmanteau had landed in a water-filled ditch.

She kicked at her wet gown where it clung to her legs, wincing when her swollen ankle protested. Why oh why had she allowed herself to be talked into eloping?

She sighed. She knew exactly why: for the longest time, she'd been yearning for a change, a new beginning. And along had come Lance, who had claimed eloping would be romantic and thrilling. His excitement had been contagious. Although she was well past the age of foolishness, she'd been seduced by the exhilarating thought of flinging propriety to the winds and experiencing a real-life adventure before she settled down.

"Stupid, stupid, stupid," she admonished herself, and reached for the glass of whisky she'd demanded when they'd reached the inn. She and Lance had arrived in the most ignominious way possible — muddied and bruised and in the back of a farmer's hay-filled cart. It had taken the better part of ten minutes to get all the blasted hay off her wet skirts.

Of course, Lance had done what he could to smooth the situation over — bespeaking the parlor, pulling a chair to the fire for her, and pressing the demanded glass of whisky into her cold hands. He'd then hired three of the innkeeper's strongest postboys to accompany him to the overturned curricle to see if it could be righted and brought to the inn for repairs.

"This is not how elopements occur in novels," she muttered, shoving a wet curl from her cheek, and wincing when her fingers brushed the scrape on her jaw.

She took a sip of her whisky, the smooth tones soothing the ire bubbling through her veins. Finally relaxed a bit, she took off her half-boot and put her injured foot upon the footstool, her heel catching in the torn flounce. As she struggled to free it the material rubbed her scraped knee, and she bit back an unladylike urge to curse.

That's another reason to drink. She took another sip and leaned her head against the high back of the chair. "That ridiculous curricle," she muttered. It had belonged to Lance's grandmother, and for some odd reason he'd thought the lumbering, faded orange, silk-lined contraption would add a romantic cachet to their flight to the border.

Sadly, he hadn't taken into account that the main springs were completely ruined, so that each bump in the road had been more of a thud, while the cracked leather seats reeked of hen droppings and moldy hay. Lance had unwittingly explained these unfortunate circumstances when he'd mentioned that the creaky contraption had been abandoned in the barn "for some time" until he'd "revived" it.

Judging from the odor wafting from the seats, Theodora could only imagine that "for some time" was well over a hundred years, and his "reviving" had not included a thorough airing out.

Yet another reason to drink. She took a bigger sip and realized she was already woefully low on whisky. If she kept this up, she'd have to fetch more from the decanter across the room, which would make her ankle ache even more. *Besides, if I continue to drink, I'll be too bosky to walk out of here on my own.*

As kind and well meaning as Lance was, there were times when he seemed oblivious to simple comforts. *Conner would never be seen in such a curricle. He would have brought his new cabriolet, or that sleek blue coach he bought in Bristol just a year ago —*

She caught her thoughts with a grimace, her heart sinking. *As if he would ever plan an elopement. He'd abscond with someone's wife without a thought, yes. But marry? Never.*

Which was why she was here now.

Though Conner came from one of Scotland's leading families, by the time he was twenty he'd already established himself as a societal outcast. Theodora wasn't certain which escapade had finally stricken his name from the eligible bachelor list for most of England's acceptable families. She'd heard whispers of scandalous affairs, misty-dawn duels, outrageous wagers, bare-knuckled brawls — the list was long. One of the more repeated stories held that, recently returned from a privateering mission and punch-drunk over an outlandish haul of casks of jewels and silks, he'd seduced a popular, sought-after actress who'd been under the protection of the Marquis of Cheswick. Cheswick had naturally taken exception to such an insult and, in the middle of the Duke of Devonshire's ball, passions had flared. Impervious to propriety, the two men had fought a duel right there in the Grand Ballroom much to the delight and dismay of onlookers. The Marquis was injured (although not fatally), a mirror shattered, and a precious antique suit of armor dented, with ladies fainting at the sight of Cheswick's blood. It had been an unmitigated disaster.

Naturally, Cheswick was soon forgiven, for he had the superior title and birth, while Conner — his position marred by his Scottish name and his scandalous endeavors — was banned from most guest lists forthwith.

There were countless other stories, even wilder than that, and none to Conner's credit. If only half of them were true, she didn't wonder that society had struck his name from their invitation lists. To them, he was a complete rakehell.

But to her, Conner Douglas was her brother's best friend — and the man she'd been in love with since she'd been a young, starry-eyed girl of fourteen.

They'd met when her brother Derrick had brought Conner home as they'd traveled north to a prizefight. She had been a leggy, flat-chested, awkward girl, while Conner had been a twenty-year-old, handsome, athletic, piercing-gazed rogue. She'd been lost the second he strode into her mother's sitting room — his dark hair falling across his brow, ice-blue eyes framed by thick black lashes, a lithe grace as intriguing as his smile was charming. He'd bowed over her hand, murmuring a polite greeting. She'd been mesmerized, and her heart had jumped when he'd brushed his lips across the back of her fingers.

Sighing, she curled her fingers into a fist. *That is how a young girl falls in love — instantly, and with no more reason than a handsome face and broad shoulders.* Of course Conner never paid her the slightest heed, for he never saw her as anything more than his best friend's young sister. She saw him often, for he visited her family at their various posts in Europe and he spent many holidays with them. Sadly, she didn't see him often enough to tire of him or grow disenchanted, so her feelings had grown, unchecked by reality. Truly, it had been the worst of all circumstances. Over time they'd gradually fallen into a casual friendship, which she treasured far more than she should have.

Oh, how she'd dreamed of him, and the what-ifs and perhaps-could-happens. But by the time she was twenty-five, Theodora had reluctantly realized that their friendship would never be anything more than platonic. Their casual closeness had slowly ended any hope of a romance, foolish as the idea had been to begin with. Yet the realization had done nothing to alleviate the strength of her feelings, and she'd had to fight to free herself from their grip.

It had taken her time, but over the last two years she'd ruthlessly tamed her unruly sentiments, and now she could firmly say that she saw Conner as a friend and no more. And if her heart sometimes fluttered a little too much when he looked at her, well, that could be explained by the unconscious sensuality of the man. It was a simple fact of nature that couldn't be changed.

And so time passed, but no other man caught her attention with the same fervor, and she hadn't felt the slightest inclination to marry, perhaps longing for the same heady reaction she'd had whenever Conner was near. Lately, she'd realized she'd been foolish to hope for passion. At her age, compatibility and the ability to hold pleasant, reasonable discourse were reasons enough to marry.

Thus last week, when Squire Fox had surprised her by dropping to one knee and in the most romantic way imaginable, begged her to elope, she'd found herself tempted. The squire was a worthy man, his affection genuine, his character flawless. She could do worse.

Much, much worse.

Feeling fluttery over the idea of breaking free from the constraints she'd always lived under, and giddy as a romantic miss of seventeen, she'd accepted. And now, here she was — wet, bedraggled, bruised, and well on her way to being bosky.

The best reason of all for another sip. She finished the glass and then sourly eyed the distant decanter and wished her ankle didn't ache so much.

The worst outcome of this horrible day was that after such an uninspiring start to her elopement, Conner seemed more attractive than ever. Perhaps she'd been foolish in expecting that to change. He was one of those rare men who could just walk into a room and every woman would turn his way and *wonder.* It wasn't just his looks. No, it was something dark and dangerous, a *make your heart pound until you beg for me* sort of thing. He was the kind of man women dreamed about, but never admitted to.

Even now, as she stared out the window, Theodora could almost imagine that the gentleman who'd just ridden into the inn yard was Conner. He swung down from his horse, a big black gelding with a long, flowing mane. The man was every bit as tall as Conner, his shoulders just as broad, his hair the same deep chocolate brown and slightly long. He was even dressed in a kilt — though kilts were probably to be expected, as they were traveling the North Road.

As she sighed, the man raked a hand through his hair and turned, the afternoon sun touching his handsome face —

Her empty glass dropped from her suddenly nerveless fingers as she jerked upright. *"Conner?"*

4

Theodora bolted to her feet, grimacing as her ankle protested the sudden move, her gaze locked on the man outside. *What is* he *doing here?*

It had to be an unfortunate coincidence, since her parents wouldn't know she'd eloped until next week, when they returned home and found her letter. She couldn't let him discover her — he'd want to know why she was here, and she had no plausible story to cover her elopement and precious little time to think of one. But he was already striding toward the inn door, the sun limning his shoulders as if the sky were happy to see him. Heart thundering, she looked frantically around the small parlor to find a place to hide — but the sound of his deep, lilting voice in the hallway put that faint hope to rest.

She'd have to face him. Cursing feverishly, her heart sinking, she limped to the mirror, horrified to see the bloodied scrape on her jaw and the way her thick, light brown hair, only partially dry, had curled in a horrifyingly Medusa-like manner. *Good God, where is a comb when one needs it?*

Before she could do more than pat her curls one quick time, the door flew open and Conner strode into the parlor escorted by the maid, a young lass with red hair who couldn't stop staring at the Scotsman, her eyes full of longing.

Theodora couldn't blame the poor girl. The striking Douglas looks were hard to resist. Broad-shouldered and startlingly handsome, with dark brown hair that curled about his neck, a piercing light blue gaze that changed with his moods, and a smile as blinding and wild as a pirate's, he was the stuff of fairy tales and dreams.

His gaze flickered over her, taking in her wet, muddied gown, her bedraggled hair, and then the scrape on her jaw. His gaze, so bright on seeing her, instantly turned icy. "If that fool has laid one finger on you —"

"Don't be ridiculous!" Her voice was sharper than she meant it to be and she took a second to calm herself, realizing with a sinking stomach that, judging by his comment, Conner must already know of her elopement. *At least now I don't have to hide*

45

anything. "We had an accident — the wheel on our curricle broke, and I was thrown out."

Concern darkened his eyes. "Bloody hell. Are you injured elsewhere, lass?"

She thought of her knee and ankle. "No."

His eyes narrowed as if he knew she was lying. "You're soaked. Have you nae dry clothes?"

"My portmanteau was thrown into the same ditch as I. My gowns are being cleaned and dried, but it will be hours before one is ready."

"What a mull! I'm glad you were nae seriously injured." His gaze moved over her in a way that felt as intimate as a touch, and she couldn't hide her shiver.

His expression softened. "Puir lass, you're cold." As he spoke he stalked across the room, tugging off his overcoat. He swung it about her shoulders, instantly enveloping her in warm wool and the heady scent of his sandalwood cologne.

She tried to push off the coat. "Please, I don't —"

"Pssht." He tugged it back in place. "Wear the damned thing; you're shaking from the cold."

It wasn't the cold that was making her quiver, but she didn't have the energy to argue. She pulled the coat more snugly about her, and was instantly warmer. While the long woolen coat only reached Conner's calves, it pooled at her feet.

The soothing warm weight comforted her, and as her shield of irritation eased, the stressful events of the morning hit with fresh vigor. Theodora had to swallow the desire to both burst into tears and throw her arms about his neck.

To prevent herself from doing either, she turned to the maid, who watched with palpable interest. It took several hard gulps, but Theodora managed to say in a voice that only trembled a little, "We would like some tea, please."

The maid struggled to rip her gaze from Conner, who was oblivious as usual to the attention being paid him. With a lingering sigh, the maid bobbed a curtsy. "Yes, miss. We've lemon cakes fresh from town just this morning. Shall I bring some for the squire, too?" The maid sent a secretive glance at Conner to see if he was surprised to hear Theodora was not at the inn alone.

Conner's scowl deepened the faintest bit.

Thea wet her bottom lip nervously. *Why is he so upset? He wouldn't care if I eloped, I'm sure.* She said to the maid, "The squire is seeing to the curricle; I doubt he'll return anytime soon."

The girl looked disappointed at Theodora's aplomb but bobbed another curtsy and, with a last longing gaze at Conner, left.

You poor girl, Theodora thought. *He looks like every hero you've ever imagined, yet he's far, far from it.*

"You dropped something, lass." Conner nodded to the floor near her chair.

She looked down and saw her glass lying on the rug. Irritated, she scooped it up. "It must have fallen when I stood. The coach ride made me ill, and I was trying to soothe my stomach."

His blue eyes, as changeable as the weather, flickered over her, resting for a long moment on her face. Without a word, he took her chin between his fingers and turned her cheek. He tsked and pulled a kerchief from his pocket and gently pressed it to her wound. "Och, Thea, what have you done to yourself?"

He murmured the words more to himself than to her, and his use of his pet name set her heart aquiver. The agony of the day, her disappointment in an event she'd secretly hoped would prove romantic, and her frustration with the squire not heeding her advice, along with the plethora of aches and pains stabbing her, threatened to overwhelm her.

She desperately longed to lean into Conner, but she wasn't so foolish as that. *I must remember why I'm here; I'm starting anew. Putting wasted feelings behind me while eagerly embracing my future.* She straightened her shoulders and forced a smile she didn't feel. "I'm quite all right, as you can see. Just wet and chilled, but the fire is quite warm."

He took in the grass stain on her skirt where it showed between the folds of his coat, concern darkening his gaze. "You said you were nae injured elsewhere."

She started to shrug, but the ache on her left side forbade it. "A few scrapes and a sore ankle, that's all. A soak in some hot water and a good sleep, and I'll be as good as gold."

"Or too sore to walk." Conner's brows lowered. "Had you been seriously injured by that fool's ham-fisted driving, I'd have killed him."

"How do you know he was driving?"

Conner's expression softened. "Over the years I've seen you drive many a cart and curricle. You'd never take a corner on a wheel like a greenhorn."

She had to agree. "Though I'd never

49

admit it to the squire, he's a sadly wretched driver."

"And you're an exceptionally guid one."

There was no ignoring the admiration in Conner's gaze. Warmed by it, she found herself smiling. "I was much more ill from the swaying of the curricle than I was bruised by the fall. Which is why I helped myself to the whisky."

"Did it help?"

"It was beginning to." She eyed him curiously. "Why are you here?"

"Ah, yes. That. I'll tell you, but first return to your chair. 'Tis closer to the fire and will burn away some of that chill." He tucked a hand under her elbow and assisted her to the chair she'd left.

Her ankle already protesting how long she'd been standing, she sat down with a grateful sigh and placed her empty glass back on the table.

Conner pulled a chair close to hers. "Your boot is off. Let me see that ankle."

"There's no need. Lance — Squire Fox offered to send for a doctor, but I didn't think it necessary."

Conner bent, lifted the edge of her skirt, wrapped his hand about her calf, and lifted her foot so that it rested on his knee.

He did it so quickly, all she could do was

gasp. "Conner! I said —"

"I heard you." He kept a firm grip on her calf so she couldn't move, his fingers strong but gentle. "I'm going to move your ankle. Tell me when it hurts."

Slowly, ever so slowly, he turned her ankle in a circle.

"It's fine, just a little — OW!"

He stopped. " 'Tis only a sprain. But you should have it oop." He pulled the footstool closer and gently rested her foot on it. "There. Now dinnae move it."

Her ankle was instantly cool where his warm hands had left it, and she tugged the coat more closely around her. "How did you know I'd —" *Eloped.* The word stuck in her throat like a two-day-old piece of toast.

His clear blue gaze rested on her face, questions lurking. "I stopped by your home earlier today. Your family had just read your letter."

"Family? Derrick was there, too?" When he nodded, she grimaced. "My parents were supposed to be in Edinburgh until Friday. They must have returned early." She bit her lip. "I hope they weren't too upset. I take it they sent you after me."

"Nae one sent me. I came on my own."

The blackness of his gaze made her say sharply, "You shouldn't have bothered. It's a good match. The squire is kind and good and —"

"Do you love him?" Conner asked abruptly.

She blinked. "That's not —"

"Do. You. Love. Him." Conner's gaze locked upon her face with an intensity that made it hard to breathe.

Don't mistake friendly concern for love. You've done that far too many times before.
"Love has nothing to do with it."

Conner's expression eased, and he leaned back in his chair, steepling his fingers under his chin. "Which means 'tis a marriage of convenience."

"What else could it be?" she asked crossly. "If you spoke to Derrick and my parents, then you must have heard I've only known the squire a short time."

"Aye. Why *did* you do this, lass? If 'tis nae love, then what did you hope to gain?"

"I'm ready for a change, and this seemed the best one available." She was seeking more than a mere change, but she couldn't tell him the truth — that she wanted her own home; one where she was free from the constraints of being an ambassador's daughter whose every word was weighed for meaning. But even more than that, she wanted freedom from the hopes she'd held out for winning his love.

But she could say none of that to Conner, so instead she shrugged. "I wanted an adventure of my own."

"Adventure? You've done naught but travel your whole life."

"Which was more of a chore than else. I'm done with changing houses as if I were changing into a fresh gown. I want —" She looked down to where her hands were clutched together in her lap so tightly, her fingers ached. She loosened them and said carefully, "I want my *own* life, my *own* adventure."

"You are tired of your family and their travels. That's understandable, to be sure. 'Tis boring as hell to be tied to the same people, the same faces, all the time."

Her heart sank, although she wasn't surprised to hear him utter such an inane stupidity. It was further confirmation she'd made the right decision in attaching herself to the squire. "I fear our ideas of adventure differ."

"Perhaps." His gaze flickered over her face, and he stood so suddenly that she blinked up at him. "We need whisky." He went to the sideboard and poured himself a generous measure of whisky, then returned with the decanter and refilled her glass.

"You're still pale, and nae wonder. You always get squeamish when you travel. Dinnae your mon know that?"

My man. She'd never thought of the squire in those terms and it made her oddly uncomfortable. "He's aware of it now."

Conner grinned with the mischievous expression that always made her want to flash an answering smile. "I'm glad you're nae holding back with your intended."

She had the glass halfway to her mouth, but at this, she lowered it. "Holding back?"

"You're too polite, lass, and have a tendency to nae say what you think. Nae with me, of course, but with others." He placed the decanter on the table and settled back in his chair, unaware he'd left her gaping. "Your thoughts always show in your eyes."

And all this time, she'd thought she'd hidden herself and her thoughts from him. Good God, what had she revealed? She wished she could ask, but was afraid she wouldn't like the answer. *Besides, whatever he thinks he's seen in my expression, it hasn't made any difference.* More dispirited than ever, she took a generous sip of whisky.

He watched her over his glass. "I was shocked to find oot you were eloping. It dinnae seem like something you'd do."

She fought the urge to tell him that he

didn't know what was or wasn't something she'd do. "The squire is kind and a gentleman. He's well established and has much to offer. And I've no wish to spend the rest of my days doing nothing more exciting than organizing for yet another move to a state post, or sitting at some dull function, pretending I am enjoying myself. And I'd like to have a family if the fates permit it —"

A shadow crossed Conner's face, so dark and nakedly painful that she blinked. What had caused that? She'd said something about the fates and family — She caught her breath, then leaned forward and gripped his hand. "Oh no. What's happened?"

Conner had spent the last month and a half trying to get used to life without Anna. Until she'd gone, he'd had no idea how much he'd relied on simply knowing she was there and would always be there. Thea's concern, so genuine and unexpected, hit him like a hammer, shattering his thin hold on his composure.

His throat tightened into a noose and wouldn't let a single word slip free. *Bloody hell, how did she know? I spent a half hour with Derrick and her parents, and they never noticed a thing.*

Emotion pressed against him until he

couldn't breathe, so Conner took a large gulp of the whisky, forcing the fiery liquid down his throat. After a long moment, he managed to rasp out, "Anna."

"She — no!" Thea's eyes filled with tears and her hand tightened over his. "Oh, Conner, no."

He nodded, fighting a swell of emotion as big as the inn itself.

"I'm so, so sorry. What — when —"

"Six weeks ago." *And two days, three hours . . .* He clenched his jaw against the tears.

Thea's soft sigh washed over him. "Anna was expecting a child. Was that . . . was that what happened?"

He nodded miserably, his gaze dropping to where Thea's hand covered his. To distract his mind from his painful thoughts, he looked at her hands — *really* looked at them. They were surprisingly beautiful — long and slender with tapered fingers, like an artist's. Somehow, he'd never noticed them.

"Oh Conner, if only there was something I could do. I know this is hard for you."

He ran his thumb over her soft skin, wondering when it would feel normal to say aloud that he'd never see Anna again. He still couldn't say it, his soul obstinate and aching and refusing to accept his loss. The thought beat him into yet more of a bloody pulp each time he faced it.

"The baby?" Theodora asked softly.

"A beautiful lad. He's well." *But Anna will never see him grow up.* Conner took another desperate gulp, determined beyond all else that he would not weep. Not in front of Thea.

People assumed that her brother Derrick was his closest friend, and at one time that had been true. But after Derrick married, Conner found himself seeking out Thea more. She was delightfully levelheaded, had a dry wit, and was always honest, at least with him — he valued her opinion more than anyone else's.

Of all the women he knew, Theodora was the easiest to talk to. In some ways, she was the only woman he trusted.

Which was why he was here now, he reminded himself.

He freed his hand from hers under the pretext of refilling his glass, unable to handle more sympathy.

As if understanding, she pulled back. "I know how much you loved her. Is there anything I can do?"

Conner replaced the decanter on the small table, and sent her a straightforward look.

"You would help me if you could?"

"Of course." Thea's clear gaze met his, questioning but unflinching.

"Thank you, for I've need of you. It's why I came."

Her brows rose. "Oh? This . . . isn't about the baby, is it? I'm not certain I'd be able to — But if there is need, of course I'd —"

"Nae. Anna's husband has hired a squadron of wet nurses. 'Tis something else. 'Tis the reason why I went to your house to begin with." He rubbed his chin. Where to begin? " 'Tis a bit complicated. There's some history I must explain first."

She cupped her glass with both hands, her eyes locked on his face, a hint of wariness now in her gaze. "Yes?"

"You know my parents died when I was but a lad, but I dinnae think I ever mentioned the Douglas lands and fortune."

"Lands *and* fortune?"

" 'Tis a guidly parcel in the north — over a thousand acres, and quite a bit of gold and silver, as well. It was placed in my sister Anna's care until my brothers and I were ready to assume our responsibilities. She turned it into far more than it was; she has a knack for such things." He stopped short. "Had. I cannae seem to remember that."

Thea's warm brown eyes darkened. "It

will take time."

He rubbed his neck, wishing his throat weren't so tight. "Anna watched over our inheritances, waiting for the time when my brothers and I were ready to claim them."

Thea frowned. "You say that as if none of you have done so."

"Aye." He didn't like the disbelief in her eyes.

"For the love of heaven, why not?"

"We do fine withoot it. Besides, Anna got to be such a stickler over it. She said that in order to take our portions, we had to prove our worth and settle doon. None of us wished such a thing, so . . ." He shrugged.

"Fools, the lot of you!"

He raised his brow, astonished to hear her speak so sharply.

She didn't flinch from his surprise. "Your brother Declan is besotted with horses and racing, which is hardly a firm foundation for running an estate. As for Jack, they don't call him Black Jack for nothing. He's even more of a pirate than you."

"I'm a privateer, love. 'Tis nae the same as a pirate. I've a letter of marque that spells it oot to anyone who might claim otherwise. I've made a guid living at it, too, so I've nae apologies to make."

"Anna didn't think so, or she wouldn't

have put stipulations upon you claiming your fortune."

"You think I should claim it, then."

"Of course. I don't understand why you haven't."

"Guid. Because that's why I'm here today." He finished his drink, oddly hesitant to continue, now that the time had come. Which was ridiculous, because he knew Thea, and knew she'd help him. She'd just said as much. "According to Anna's will, I and my brothers must marry, and soon, or the Douglas fortune will go to the Campbells, our blood enemies."

"Why would Anna do such a thing?"

"Because she knew us weel. Had she left our estate to charity, we would have gladly let it go. Who needs the burden? But the Campbells? That is nae acceptable."

"I see." Thea's gaze never left his face. "So . . . you must marry. All of you."

"We've only a few months to do so. And it must be to a lady of quality." Conner rested his elbows on his knees and leaned forward. "And that, Thea, is why I came. As soon as I found oot aboot the will, I thought of you."

"Of me." She said the words flatly, as if she couldn't believe them herself.

"Of course you," he said impatiently. "You know me, and you're a sensible sort, so we'd

60

do well together. We'd have reasonable expectations of one another, with nae silly drama. Surely that is a guid foundation for a marriage."

"No. You can't be —" She stopped, took a deep breath, and placed her whisky glass at the table at her elbow. Then she said in a slow, calm voice, "Conner, you're not *proposing* to me while I'm *eloping* with another man."

His smile slipped. It sounded rather poor when she said it that way. "Lass, I'm nae disparaging your decision. I'm sure this mon is a fine choice, for a squire. But I am making you a better offer, a step oop from your current path."

She stared at him as if unable to grasp his meaning.

With an impatient sigh, he took her hand where it rested on her knee and pressed a kiss to her fingers. "Come, love. Say aye, and let's have a wee dram in celebration —"

"No." She tugged her hand free and stood, pulling his coat from her shoulders and dropping it onto her chair. Bedraggled and damp, her hair curling about her face in a thousand rebellious curls, she glared at him.

Conner stood. "Wait, lass. I was a bit overbold, I know it. Let me explain."

"No. I don't want to hear another word."

"But —"

"Not. Another. Word." Theodora turned to leave.

Conner grasped her wrist and turned her back so he could explain himself, but her wet skirts became tangled around her legs and she fell.

He caught her against him, her chest to his. She looked up at him, her eyes wide, her mouth parted in surprise.

Because it seemed the most natural thing in the world, and because he wanted more than anything to keep her from leaving, Conner kissed her.

It was a gentle, *because you are here* kiss, the kind he'd shared with a hundred women before. But the second his lips touched hers, a blazing shock of passion shocked his entire body to life, his senses floundering in surprise.

She must have felt it, too, for she went still in his arms, her hands tangling in his lapels where she gripped him as if suddenly afraid of falling from a great height.

Her passion ignited his own, but he moved slowly, as it was obvious she had little experience. She was awkward and uncertain, her lips pressed together, her eyes tightly closed, her expression tense with yearning. Gently, he kissed her, tracing the captivating line of her lips, feathering soft nips until she gasped with want. He instantly captured her mouth and deepened the kiss. She stiffened, but he continued, stroking her back, holding her close.

Slowly she softened, accepting his kiss, and when his tongue brushed hers, she moaned in pleasure. He released his passion, plundering her mouth, teasing her tongue as his heart thundered in his ears.

She was so warm, so soft in his arms, her body fitted to his as if made for it. God, why had he not kissed her before? He slid his hands down her back and held her closer —

She turned her face away, breaking their kiss. "No," she gasped, her sweet breath brushing his cheek.

He almost groaned, and he rested his forehead against her temple, struggling to find his own breath, his body stiff with desire.

"We cannot." She pulled away.

Though it cost him greatly, he released her. "Thea —"

"No." She turned and limped toward the door as quickly as her injuries allowed.

He took a step toward her. "Wait!"

She stopped, although she didn't turn to

face him.

His mind still whirling from their stupefying kisses, he managed to say, "I'm sorry. I should nae have kissed you; I did nae think. But . . . I asked you a question, lass, and you've nae answered. I asked you to marry me."

Thea stiffened, her hands at her sides tightening into fists. After a second, she faced him, her face pink, her mouth set in a mutinous line. "No."

"But you havenae thought aboot it! We're perfect for one another — even more than I'd realized, judging by the passion of those kisses."

"We're not even *close* to perfect for one another. And even if we were —" Her eyes blazed anew. "I would not marry you, Conner Douglas, were you the last man on earth."

With those damning words, she turned on her heel and limped out of the parlor.

5

Muttering curses that no well-bred woman should know, Theodora limped up the stairs and into the bedchamber, where her empty portmanteau sat drying in the sunlight. Tears blurring her vision, she slammed the door and headed toward the faded brocade-covered chair that sat beside the narrow bed.

"Fool!" she snapped at herself as she stormed past the mirror. "That's what you get for speaking to that man at all! What was I thinking?" She brushed her trembling fingers over her lips, still swollen from their kiss. Why, oh why, had she allowed him to kiss her? And worse, why had she kissed him back?

She couldn't allow it to ever happen again. *Ever.* She'd make certain she was never again alone with him, even for a second. He challenged her self-control in ways she'd never thought possible.

She was done with Conner Douglas.

D-o-n-e.

She dropped into the chair, revealing one booted foot and the other covered with just a wet stocking. *Blast, I left my boot in the parlor.* For some reason the sight of her lonely, bootless foot made her eyes fill with tears.

The entire day had been a disaster; one deep disappointment after another. The elopement was a shambles and now, after that silly kiss, she was beset with fresh doubts about her venture. Was she doing the right thing? This morning, marriage had seemed like a practical path to ensuring her future. But after that kiss, she found herself wondering about Lance . . . In all the times they'd been together — while courting, planning their elopement, and even while traveling alone here — he'd never once attempted to kiss her. She'd ascribed it to his innate politeness, but with the memory of Conner's passionate kiss warm on her lips, she now found herself wondering why Lance hadn't done the same. Didn't he *want* to kiss her? Was there no passion between them at all?

Though her marriage to Lance would be a marriage of convenience, that didn't mean she didn't want passion. She'd always assumed that would develop naturally after they grew closer. But try as she could, when she thought of careful, cheerful Lance, she couldn't imagine the instant, raging heat she'd experienced with dashing, dangerous Conner.

She brushed her lips with her fingertips, amazed they still tingled. She wanted —

No. Don't think about that. Conner is not good for me, and his actions today proved it. How could he be so cruel, asking her to marry him just to gain an inheritance he didn't even want? Meanwhile, Anna —

Theodora stifled a sob as without warning, the deep shock she'd felt on hearing about Anna's death returned. From their first meeting, she and Anna had liked one another. Distance had kept them from becoming fast friends, for they'd only met whenever Anna happened to be traveling with Conner, which happened less and less once she'd married. But Theodora had always hoped that if she and Conner marr—

And there I go again, blast it! Conner and I will never *marry. If we did, it would be a disaster for us both.* Theodora pressed her fingers over her hot eyelids and remembered how he'd thought her decision to change her life had been based on the desire to avoid living with her own family because it was "boring" being tied to the same people all the time. *Damned by his own words. Why, oh why, did he have to show up at my elopement like this? I will not allow his presence to make me question my decision to find a future with Lance.*

But as irked as she was with Conner, she was far more upset with herself. When he'd kissed her, her body hadn't been the only thing to react. Her heart had leapt with blinding joy, and hope had flared to life. He *wanted* her. So many of her daydreams had been centered around exactly that scene: where Conner rode hell for leather after her, threw himself before her, declared that he wanted to marry her, and swept her into his arms.

Of course, in her dreams, he'd done so out of love. *Never has anyone received a more selfishly motivated and ruder proposal! I deserve better.*

But that was apparently far more than Conner could give, and Theodora was left feeling as if she'd lost something yet again. Her eyes burned as she fought the urge to give in to a good, solid cry.

She sniffed and lifted her chin. She was through crying over Conner Douglas. But his appearance had made one thing very clear: if she wished her arrangement with Lance to succeed, she would have to guard her heart much, much more closely. *I can do that,* she told herself firmly. *It'll be easier once Conner's gone.*

Her only regret was that she wouldn't be nearby as he attempted to deal with Anna's death. Even when he wasn't speaking of his sister, Theodora could sense his sadness, and her heart ached for him. *Anna would hate to see him so . . . Oh Anna!*

The tears finally came, running down Theodora's face and blurring her vision. Unable to fight it any longer, she dropped her face into her hands and wept. She wept for what had been, for what would never happen, for the new baby without a mother, and for the desolation she'd seen on Conner's face.

Finally her tears subsided, leaving her with a sniffly nose and burning eyes. Sighing, she arose and washed her face in the water from the flowered pitcher on the washstand near the window. She patted her face dry, and took the opportunity to undo her hair and tug a comb through it.

She'd just finished pinning it up when the sound of the inn's door made her peer out the window. In the inn yard below, Conner was motioning for a postboy to come over. He engaged the youth in earnest conversation, pointing down the road in the direction he'd arrived.

The postboy nodded eagerly, and Conner placed a coin into the lad's open hand. Obviously elated, the lad pocketed the coin, set his hat more firmly on his shaggy head, and then took off, loping down the dirt road.

What's that about? Theodora watched the lad until she could see him no more, and then returned her gaze to Conner. He was walking back to the inn, a thoughtful expression on his face.

He disappeared as she heard the door open and then close yet again, although she could see him plainly in her mind's eye, walking down the hallway, entering the parlor, his broad shoulders filling the doorway, his pale blue eyes deepened with his thoughts as —

She closed her eyes and leaned her forehead against the window, the smooth glass cooling her heated skin. *Why, oh why, does he affect me so?*

She tried to focus instead on Lance, how polite he always was, how enthusiastic he was about their coming marriage, how involved he was with his sisters and mother — all the things that had convinced her to accept his proposal. It took several minutes, but slowly her confused feelings for Conner untangled a bit. They didn't disappear, but they eased until she could almost pretend they didn't matter.

She was just about to turn away from the window when the heavy creak of a wagon caught her attention. Lance was returning, and behind him in the wagon bed were two stable boys holding on to the broken curricle wheel. The wagon came to a stop and Lance jumped down. He spoke to the stable boys, and one of them scrambled into the seat and drove the wagon toward the stables. The innkeeper came outside and judging from the way Lance gestured toward the wagon, they were talking about the needed repairs. Then Lance turned toward the inn door.

The door Conner had just walked through.

Her heart leapt to her throat. *Lance will go to the parlor looking for me, and find Conner instead!*

She bit her lip. Surely Conner wouldn't say why he'd come . . .

Or would he? She pressed her fingers to her temples. When had Conner ever needed a reason to do anything outlandish or unexpected? No one enjoyed shocking people more. *Blast it, I was never going to speak to him again.* She scowled. There was no help for it.

Muttering about uppity Scottish pirates, she limped toward the door to confront the damned lout once again.

Conner leaned his arm against the mantel and stared at the crackling fire, wondering what he should do next. He wasn't used to not having his direction in a mission, and he couldn't quite shake the feeling that he was sailing with a broken rudder. Should he send word to Thea that he wouldn't leave until she came downstairs and allowed him to explain things? Or should he wait for the squire and set the man straight about what would *not* happen? The only thing Conner knew was that there would be no elopement, not while he had breath left in him. He owed it to her, if not her family.

And perhaps to himself, too. He rubbed his mouth, remembering their unexpected passion. Thea was even more suited to be his wife than he'd realized, which made her flat "no" all the more regrettable.

What a blasted coil! One he'd made himself. Had he been a few days earlier in delivering his proposal, he'd have been able to prevent Thea's precipitous elopement and none of this would have been necessary.

His jaw tightened. He couldn't change the past, but he could certainly change the future. If only he knew what had led Thea down this crazy, unlikely path to begin with. What was she really after? She'd said she'd wanted her life "to change," but in what way?

Frowning, Conner kicked absently at an ember that had fallen from the fire, sending it back into the flames. She was not a romantic, nor was her situation at home so dire that she would have felt compelled to marry a lowly squire she barely knew. Whatever her reason was, she hadn't been inclined to share it with him. In fact, judging from her expression when she'd quit the room, she was of a mind to never speak to him again.

He rested his elbow on the mantel and placed his chin in his hand. Perhaps it was something as simple as boredom. He understood the emptiness that could leave; he always felt adrift if he were too long away from the sea. Even now, he longed for the roll of a ship's deck under his feet, the feel of the fresh sea breeze rather than the stuffy confines of an antiquated inn. Poor Thea had been becalmed all of her life. She'd traveled, aye, but as she'd pointed out, never to a place of her own choosing. She'd been moored by the expectations of her father's position, and landlocked by her mother's oversight.

Perhaps Thea's motives were as simple as the fact that she yearned for the freedoms that came with being married. Although that didn't explain why she'd accepted a man who was likely tied to his farm and lacked the social connections that could give a woman those freedoms. That would be changing one prison for another, and Thea was too smart for such a move.

Conner frowned. It had to be something else, then. But what? "Women!" he grumbled. " 'Tis easier to read the intentions of a nor'easter than it is to follow a woman's thinking. They never go from one point directly to the next, but wend their way through so many thoughts, back and forth, oop and down, that they drive a man mad."

All he knew was that his offer had missed the mark. Perhaps it was the way he'd worded his offer, but how else could he have said it? He would never tell Thea falsehoods, even if it was for his own benefit. She deserved the truth. Besides, she knew this wasn't a matter of the heart, and had he pretended it to be so, she would have seen through him in an instant.

No, he was here with a business proposition, one they'd both benefit from. And if she'd given him a chance to explain those benefits, he was certain she'd have accepted his proposal.

Perhaps his error hadn't been in the tone of his offer, but in his timing. She'd been exhausted, bruised from the hardships of her botched elopement, aching from her injuries, and cold and dirty from being dunked in a ditch.

That must be it. He sighed in relief that the answer might be something so simple. *I was a fool to bluntly tell her my errand right away. I should have waited until she'd recovered from her journey. Worse, I added to the situation by telling her about Anna.*

His chest tightened at the thought, and he took a deep breath in an attempt to wash away his pain. *I can see why a person may nae be in the mood to hear a proposal of any kind hard on the heels of such a dreadful announcement. Bloody hell, I have botched this proposal weel and guid.*

He had to give Thea time to recover her usual calm. Meanwhile, he would stay nearby so that when the time came, he could present his offer again, but in a more well-thought-out manner.

Hmmm. What reason could he make for attaching himself to the elopement party?

With the squire's coach wheel broken they would be stuck at this inn for a while, perhaps even days. Conner could make use of that. Good use.

Conner glanced around the unsatisfactory parlor and shook his head. Thea deserved better than this. If he'd been forced to bring her to such an unworthy inn, he would never have left her alone, wet and bedraggled, bruised and ill, while he went out to oversee the repair of the curricle. There were servants for that, and she shouldn't have been left to nurse her pain alone.

He would have stayed with Thea. He'd have sent for a physician to see to her bruises and wounds, made sure she was warm, and ordered her some hot tea and a nice luncheon. Then he'd have had the landlady find a local laundress to clean and press at least one of Thea's gowns so she'd have something warm and dry to wear. *Oh squire, the opportunities you've missed.* No wonder Thea had been so irritated by the time Conner had caught up to her.

Which gave him hope. Not that he would ever give up; he was a Douglas, by God, and the family motto wasn't *Jamais Arriere* for nothing. He'd be damned if he'd walk away while Theodora blithely raced to her doom.

A wagon rumbled into the inn yard and Conner turned toward the window. Seconds later, the innkeeper hurried down the hall ordering one of the servants to rush below stairs and tell Cook to ready the meal as "the squire has returned."

Conner adjusted his cravat, and then heard someone hurrying downstairs. *Ah, Thea. That's drawn you out, has it?* The sound of her footsteps caught him, for she was still limping, but there was something else, too . . . was she wearing only one shoe? Surprised, he looked at the chair beside his and caught sight of Thea's boot, which made him smile.

Yet even limping and one-booted, she was rushing. *You dinnae wish me to have a moment alone with your intended, do you? What is it you fear, wee one?*

Thea limped through the doorway.

He bowed, noting that she'd managed to put her hair somewhat in order, although it made the scrape on her jaw more visible. "I'm glad you returned. I'm —"

"We will not discuss what happened," she announced coolly, although her cheeks were flushed. "It was a mistake, and we will never mention it again."

"Lass, we cannae pretend it never happened. I still wish to marry you and —"

"*Don't!* If you continue like that, then I must ask you to leave immediately." Her head up and her shoulders back, she looked as spirited as a frigate dancing before a storm, but there was a brittleness to her expression that gave lie to her stern gaze. Worse, now that he saw her in the light, there was no mistaking the faint redness to her eyes. *She's been weeping.*

Regret caught him and his boldness sank beneath a wave of concern. "Fine. As you wish. I will nae say another word aboot this . . . nae today, anyway."

"Not *ever.*"

"So you dinnae wish your squire to know aboot my proposal." He raised his brows. "That's why you came limping so quickly doon the stairs."

She flushed a deeper pink. "There's no need to tell him about this nonsense."

"Och, lass, and you walked on that hurt ankle, too." Conner grimaced. "I truly dinnae wish to cause you discomfort. You've had enough trouble today withoot me adding to it."

Her eyes darkened, her expression losing some of its rigidity. "Thank you. This day has been —" Her eyes shone with fresh tears as she shook her head. "I'm sorry if I made a scene earlier; you surprised me, that's all.

And Anna was always —" Thea's lip quivered.

He had to fight himself not to go to her and capture her in a hug. His heart ached with hers, but if he touched her now, she would give in to the tears that threatened, and — worse — as fragile as his own hold over his emotions were, he might join her. "I should nae have told you when I did; 'twas thoughtless. 'Tis been a long few weeks for me. That is my only excuse." He wished he could say more than that, but he was no match for those puppy-brown eyes, especially when they were filled with such sadness. "Lass, I —"

Firm boot steps came down the narrow hall toward the parlor, and Thea whirled toward the door, smoothing her gown.

Conner faced the door with smug certainty. Finally, he would meet this portly squire and put the man on notice, although quietly, without upsetting Thea. The footsteps drew close to the door and then the squire walked into the room. Conner started to take a step forward, but at the sight of his rival, froze in place.

Conner looked. And then looked again.

In his mind, the squire was about forty years of age, slightly balding and a touch pudgy, with bad teeth. But this . . . *Bloody hell, the man is an Adonis.*

While Conner was two inches over six feet, the squire beat him by an inch, perhaps more. The man was built on massive lines, too, with powerful forearms and thighs like tree trunks. No doubt the lout could rip a spar in two with his bare hands.

Worse, he was handsome of face and possessed white teeth, a blinding smile, and a full thatch of russet hair. *Bloody hell.* Where on earth had Thea found such a specimen? *It's no wonder she decided to elope with this man, he's a bloody paragon of male beauty.*

Conner realized Thea was watching him, smiling faintly as she savored his surprise, and he instantly schooled his expression to one of polite interest. He'd be damned if he'd let her peer into his soul any more than he already had. He'd just been so shocked to discover that he might be facing a worthy opponent.

Is this why she refused me? Was it possible Thea was in love? She'd denied it, but . . . *was* she?

His spirits lowered and he covertly examined her expression as she greeted the man.

To Conner's relief, there was no obvious softening in her expression, no cow-eyed longing in her thickly lashed eyes, no sap-filled emotion in her clear voice. Still look-

80

ing amused at Conner's initial reaction, she greeted her intended with the fondness one might have for a well-thought-of acquaintance. *Or a lapdog.*

Good. Conner turned his attention to his nemesis.

Thea might not be head over heels in love, but it was instantly obvious the squire was. His gaze locked on her face and he hung on every word that passed her lips, which Conner found as annoying as having to sail through thick fog. Thank God Theodora didn't return the man's passions for it allowed Conner to bare his teeth in a smile as he stepped forward. "Squire Fox! Finally, we meet."

The man's gaze hadn't left Theodora since he'd entered the room, and he reluctantly turned Conner's way, looking vaguely surprised to find someone else there. "Why, yes. And you are . . . ?"

Conner arched an eyebrow at Thea.

With obvious reluctance, she made the introductions. "Squire Fox, this is Mr. Conner Douglas, a friend of my brother's." She turned to Conner. "And *this* is Squire Fox, a friend of *mine.*"

There was no denying the emphasis of her words. The squire clearly noticed, a flash of surprise crossing his face before he turned a happy pink.

Conner was not amused. His smile firmly tacked to his face, he held out his hand. "Pleased to meet you, Fox."

The squire gripped Conner's hand. "And you, Douglas. I've heard a lot about you."

"Indeed?" Conner kept his smile, but increased the pressure in the handshake.

"Oh yes." The man didn't seem concerned by Conner's overly firm handshake, but merely matched the pressure.

Conner tightened his grip to a point where a normal man would protest.

The giant didn't so much as flinch, but returned the hard pressure and then some.

Pain shot through Conner's hand as the squire rumbled amiably, "Any friend of Theodora's brother is a friend of mine."

Conner gritted his teeth. *Bloody hell, he'll break my fingers!* With no other choice, he loosened his grip.

As if unaware he'd even been challenged, the squire released Conner's hand and then smacked him on the shoulder in a way that nearly made Conner stagger back a step. "This truly is a pleasant surprise! I feel as if I know you; Theodora mentions you often."

Thea blinked. "Do I?"

Conner supposed that was something. He tucked his hand behind his back and flexed it gingerly, keeping his smile in place. Good lord, the man had hands the size of ham hocks. If Conner wished to win the day, brute strength was a losing strategy.

Fortunately, there was more than one way to scale a rigging. He turned to Thea and smiled fondly. " 'Tis nae surprising you may have mentioned me, lass, seeing as we've known one another for such a long, long, *long* time."

Thea's brows lowered. "So we have," she said in a flat tone.

"And we know one another better than most. We're close, we two. Verrah close."

Her gaze narrowed on him in warning.

"Like brother and sister!" the squire said politely, although some of the brightness of his smile had left.

"Och, nae," Conner said just as Thea blurted out, "Exactly."

She blew out her breath in an annoyed puff. "Blast it, Conner! You are the most pestilent and annoying acquaintance I've ever had."

Ah, that was more like the Thea he knew. He laughed at the squire's shocked expression. *She's been playing the shy maiden, has she? Just as I suspected. You, lad, don't know Thea.* Conner spread his hands wide. "Ah, squire, I am found oot. My ability to annoy is a gift, one my brothers can vouch for."

"And my brother, as well," she added, a defiant sparkle in her gaze. "He calls you the Great Inconvenience."

"Aye, well, he calls you the Greater Inconvenience, so I would nae be announcing such things."

She choked back a sudden laugh, his joke disarming her as he'd hoped it would. Thea's temper was always short lived and could be turned with a smile. It was one of the things he most enjoyed about her.

Still, in some odd way, he was surprisingly relieved to see her reacting in her usual manner. She was rarely furious with him, and he now realized how concerned he'd been about it.

"We should sit," Thea announced and then limped toward the chairs by the fire. "My ankle demands it."

The squire was instantly all concern, a contrite expression crossing his face. "Your poor ankle. How is it? I wish you'd allowed me to call for a physician."

"I've no need of a physician; 'tis naught but a sprain." Theodora sank into her seat and realized with a sinking heart that Conner's presence complicated things much more than she'd realized. Even if he didn't reveal his purpose in following her here, she now had a secret she had to keep from Lance, and it hung between them like a wet sheet.

Should she go ahead and tell him all? No, in doing so, she might accidentally reveal her conflicted feelings — it was better to keep the truth tucked away. But she was less comfortable with Lance now, and she hated it. *It's a good thing Conner will be leaving soon. He is ruining everything.*

"We should all sit and have a wee chat." Conner stepped past the slower-moving squire and adroitly reclaimed the only remaining chair, which left poor Lance with no place to sit.

She glared at Conner, who merely said in a mockingly concerned tone, "I'm glad you sat doon. You should nae be standing on that injured ankle."

The squire looked guiltily at Thea's foot, and she said, "Pssht. It will be fine by morning." Poor Lance hadn't meant to hurt her. His ineptitude was only due to a lack of instruction, which wasn't surprising given his upbringing.

Lance's father had died when he was only four. Left in the care of his strong-willed mother and five older sisters, he'd been the darling of the family and had received no encouragement to stand on his own, even after he'd reached an age to set up his own household. He'd admitted that at one time he'd been interested in courting the vicar's daughter, but although his sisters had supported the match (less than enthusiastically, of course), his mother had had a fit of the vapors every time the poor woman was around. The relationship didn't make it past that.

Theodora was fairly certain he'd shared that story as a warning, and she'd assured him she was prepared for any theatrics his mother might throw their way. So long as the rest of the members of his family were welcoming, she was more than willing to soothe his mother's understandable fears of losing her son.

It explained why Lance had remained single for so long. He felt responsible for his mother, and Theodora honored him for it. Truly, he was the kindest man she'd ever met.

He shook his head now. "Perhaps we should have a physician look at your ankle."

Conner said in a cheerful voice that belied the evil he was trying to perform, "Och, squire, you need nae worry; 'tis nae broken. I know for I examined it myself."

Theodora stiffened.

The squire's polite smile wavered. "You

examined her ank—"

"Fox, fetch a chair," Theodora announced hurriedly. She warmed the abruptness of her words with a smile. "I'll get a crick in my neck if I have to look up at you, for you are so very tall. There should be more chairs in the common room."

He hesitated a moment, but after she sent him a pointed look, he flushed and then nodded. "Of course. I'll be right back."

As soon as he was out the door, Theodora whirled toward Conner and hissed, "I know what you're doing and it will not work!"

6

"Me?" Conner feigned an innocent look. "I'm being pleasant."

"*That's* being pleasant?"

A smile twitched his mouth, and his blue eyes twinkled with humor. "Considering the circumstances, aye. At least more pleasant than I wish to be."

"I would not call it 'pleasant,' and neither would anyone else. First, you try to squeeze poor Lance's hand off — Oh yes, I could see what you were doing. We *all* could. And then you blurted out that you had been looking at my ankle, as if it were the most natural thing in the world."

"It felt natural to me."

It had felt natural to her, too, blast it. For the hundredth time that day, Theodora had to swallow the temptation to curse. "Stop trying to shock him."

Conner looked thoughtful, as if he were truly considering her words. "That was a bit much, eh?" He leaned back in his chair and looked her up and down. "Such a fine-looking couple. The two of you match in looks, as handsome as galleons in full sail. But lass, I can already tell he's nae your equal elsewise."

She stamped down a traitorous trill of satisfaction at Conner's "handsome" comment, and said in a firm, cool tone, "You know nothing of the man. You've just met him."

"I've heard enough. And I know you better than you know yourself. You need a man strong enough to sharpen wits with you — otherwise you'll lead him by the nose, and neither of you will be happy."

"You don't know what I need, and I will not 'lead him by the nose.' I'm not that sort of woman."

Conner's brows rose, but he wisely didn't respond.

"Besides, Lance is —"

"Lance. I meant to comment on that earlier." Conner made a face. "What sort of name is that?"

"A good one." She narrowed her gaze on Conner. "I'm warning you — don't start. Whenever you don't like something, you mock it in that odious manner you have, sneering as if you knew something no one else does, when in fact you know nothing. I won't have you doing that to either of us!"

Conner's smile fled and he leaned closer, his knee now against hers. "Thea, I'd never make fun of you. Nae in earnest. I respect you more than any woman alive."

His deep voice rippled across her, as delicious as sinking into a hot bath on a cold winter day. "You tease me all the time."

"Nae in a cruel way. But Lance? That is completely different." Conner shrugged. "If he warrants teasing, I'll do so."

She shifted in her chair, moving her knee away from his and wishing her skin hadn't warmed at that small touch, reminding her of their kiss. Suddenly, the day seemed too long to bear. She sighed, sinking a bit in her chair. "Conner, please. Just stop."

"I dinnae know, lass. He seems to be a verrah easy target. I may nae have the strength to resist the temptation to fire a few warning shots over his bow." Conner shrugged. "If he wishes me to quit, he'll let me know. He's nae a child."

Conner absently flexed his fingers as he spoke, and she couldn't hide a smirk. "He squeezed your hand back, didn't he?"

Conner stopped flexing his hand and sent her a sharp look. "Nae too much."

"He should have crushed it, as impertinent

as you were, but he's too much a gentle-man."

"Is he, now? Obsessed with the niceties, I've nae doubt." Conner leaned back, his elbows resting on the chair arms as he templed his fingers and rested them against his chin. "I wonder what the guid squire would say if he knew I've seen his intended bride wearing naught but a sheer, seductive nightgown?"

"Oh!" Her face heated. "It was not sheer, and you know it!"

He sighed. "True. 'Twas a heavy fabric, and had enough ruffles to make a sail. Frankly, I've seen nuns wear less to bed."

How had he seen nuns — No. Don't ask. You don't want to know. "You swore you'd never say anything about that." Indeed, in all these years, he'd never mentioned that night years ago when, frightened out of her wits by a crashing thunderstorm, she'd run from her room at Cumberbatch House and down the gallery hallway toward her parents' room.

The storm had shaken the house, the windows rattling as if ready to shatter, and at seventeen, she'd been so crazy with fear that she hadn't seen Conner standing in the hallway until she'd run straight into him.

He'd been on his way to the guest bedchamber that was always kept ready should he happen to visit. As it was so late, none of the lamps were lit, and the hallway was dark when Theodora had burst from her room. Conner hadn't hesitated a moment, but had pulled her hard against him as she shook, the storm raging overhead.

She never knew how long they stood there, her cheek pressed to his broad chest as he whispered against her hair, telling her over and over she was safe and that the storm would pass.

Eventually, the thunder had lessened and the rumbles grew quieter. And during that time, Theodora had burrowed against him, breathing in the seductive scent of his cologne, soaking in the strength of his arms, and — second by second — falling even more deeply in love with him.

And as the storm had slowly abated, the air about them had grown thick, as if charged with electricity left from the storm. She'd grown aware of his closeness in a new way, enjoying the warmth of his hands as he slowly stroked her back, the scent of his cologne lingering in the softness of his silk waistcoat where it rested beneath her cheek, the sheer headiness of his closeness — every delicious detail enveloping her like a warm blanket.

As the seconds grew, her erratic breathing had grown more so. Her legs had grown heavy, her skin prickled with awareness, and her heart thundered in her ears. She'd thought Conner had felt the same, for his breathing had increased with hers, and for one startled moment she'd thought she'd felt his lips brush against her temple.

She'd wanted to lift her face to his, rise up on her tiptoes, and kiss him — a wild and bold thought that had made her tremble anew. But while she was gathering her courage, Conner had dropped his arms and stepped back, leaving Theodora suddenly alone and quite cold.

Worse, as she stared at him, filled with longing and desire, he'd chucked her under the chin as one would a child and then said with cool indifference, "Off to bed with you, lass. You look a mess."

The words had crumpled her soul even as she faced the shocking realization that not only had she clung to a man who didn't want her, but in her haste she'd forgotten her robe and wore only her night rail, her hair unbound and tangled.

Embarrassed and flustered and in a true *oh God, what have I done* panic that only a brokenhearted seventeen-year-old could feel, she'd mumbled something about nightmares that had made no sense and bolted back to the safety of her room as if the hounds of hell pursued her, slamming the door behind her with enough force to knock a vase off a table.

Once safely alone she'd thrown herself on her bed, embarrassed and yearning, his cold voice echoing in her overactive imagination. She hadn't been able to sleep for the rest of the night, dying a thousand deaths of mortification.

The next morning had found her bleary-eyed and anxious, wondering how she'd come to make such a fool of herself. And things had gotten worse when she'd gone downstairs to find Conner alone in the breakfast room.

He'd looked less than happy to see her, which had flamed her insecurities to wild new heights. In an attempt to save face, she'd awkwardly demanded that he never tell a soul about their brief encounter. She'd sworn it had meant nothing to her, and how she desperately wished to forget it. To her deep disappointment, he'd merely said sharply that of course it had meant nothing, and it would be impossible to tell anyone about something he'd already forgotten. His slightly bored air had furthered her agony and she'd returned to her room even more mortified than before. It had taken her weeks before she could think of those moments without wanting to burst into tears.

Shaking off the memory now, Thea said, "I'm surprised you remember anything about that night. I barely do."

His brows went up. "Forget the time a lovely woman threw herself into my arms and begged me to save her? Never."

Her cheeks couldn't get any hotter as she fought a wild trill of triumph that the long-ago moment had stayed in his memory after all. "I didn't beg you to do anything except forget the entire incident, which you promised to do."

"So I did," he said gravely, though his blue eyes twinkled anew. "Which I said merely to protect the obvious embarrassment of a young, tender lass."

She searched his expression. "You were protecting my feelings?"

He shrugged. " 'Twas obvious you were distressed by the incident. I thought it best to put your mind at ease."

That was kind. If she could believe it. "So I can count on you not to mention it now."

"Sadly, nae. You're nae longer a lass, and this is a special circumstance."

"Oh yes, you need to marry someone — *anyone,* really — so you can keep your inheritance from the 'bloody Campbells.' *That* 'special circumstance,' " she said bitterly.

His gaze darkened, the humor now gone from his face. "This is nae just aboot me. 'Tis for your own benefit, as weel."

She gave a short laugh. "How in the world would marrying you benefit me?"

"Och, there are many benefits, and you know it." His gaze caressed her and left her short of breath. "But more than that, it would prevent you from making the greatest mistake of your life."

The words hung over her head, and her throat tightened as if he'd suddenly jerked a noose about it. And she realized that she was terrified of that very thing. Is *this the biggest mistake of my life? After I marry, will I wake up and wish for something else . . . Someone else?*

Her gaze met Conner's, and for a horrified second she wanted to blurt out everything: how much she'd loved him, and how he'd never once even noticed, and how she now desperately wanted to find her own way, her own life, without living under his shadow.

Her thoughts all tumbled from her lips in one breathless question. "Would you care?"

"If you married the wrong mon? Of course I would. Your brother is one of my oldest friends."

"We're not talking about my brother. And forget your inheritance for a moment, and answer this." She leaned forward, committed to hearing the truth, however unpleasant it might be. "*Why* would it matter to you if I married the wrong person?"

He looked uncomfortable. " 'Twould take a hard-hearted mon nae to be concerned aboot that, especially if it is someone they cared for."

"So you care for me."

"Of course I do. I've known you far too long nae to."

Don't ask. He'll say something you don't want to hear. But the words flew from her lips like an arrow shot from a bow. "In what way?"

He shifted in his chair, looking so ill at ease that she knew she'd hate his answer before he even spoke. "Are there different ways to care for someone? You either do, or you do nae. And I do."

She was already too far gone to let it go. "But *how* do you care for me?"

"Dammit, Thea, what do you want me to say? I would watch oot for you, and make certain you are weel. You can always count on me, as you know." He seemed to sense that what he'd said wasn't enough, for he added in a tight voice, "You are my closest and best friend. Surely that's enough."

But it's not. Her disappointment was so deep, it was as if he'd stomped on her heart. She shook off the bitter taste of his rejection, and managed to say in a colorless tone, "You are my closest friend, too."

But I cannot settle for being just friends.

To her relief, Lance's footsteps sounded in the hallway and he appeared with a large chair.

Looking as pleased as if he'd found a treasure, he carried it to where she sat and plunked it down at her side. "There. I'm sorry that took so long, but most of the chairs in the common room were mere stools. The landlord kindly allowed me to bring this chair from his own bedchamber." Lance sat, the large chair creaking. "Now we may all be comfortable."

"So we may," Conner agreed, as if he were somehow responsible for that comfort.

The squire placed his hands over his knees and smiled. "So, Mr. Douglas —"

"Please. Call me Conner, as Thea does."

"Thea?" The squire looked at her, a question in his eyes.

"Theodora is too big a name for such a wee thing," Conner told the squire.

Lance looked at Theodora as if he were

only now seeing her. "So she is."

"I'm over average height for a woman." Most of her friends were inches shorter than she. "The term 'wee' is incorrect."

Lance chuckled and patted her hand. "But we're talking as men. To us, you're quite delicate in size."

Theodora had just opened her mouth to flash her answer to that pompous statement when she caught Conner's pleased expression. There was nothing he'd like better than to see her argue with Lance.

It was difficult, but she swallowed her retort. "Of course." *Later, you and I will have a good discussion about this.*

Blithely unaware he'd barely escaped a precarious moment, Lance said in a playful tone, "I believe I will call you Thea as well."

"No. 'Thea' sounds like a pet's name." She sliced a look at Conner. "Which I've said before, although *some* people don't listen."

"I listened," Conner protested. "I just dinnae agree. Besides, you dinnae have to answer to it." His eyes glinted wickedly. "But you always do."

She did, blast it. Over the years she'd gotten used to it, and now it was second nature. She sniffed.

The squire chuckled. "I have nicknames

for all of my sisters. The oldest we call Teapot because she was obsessed with having tea from the time she was a tiny thing, barely able to walk. And the youngest we call Duckling, as she made a pet of one of the ducks and refused to allow it to sleep out of doors, so it nested at the foot of her bed for years." Lance turned politely to Conner. "Mr. Douglas, I believe you have siblings as well. Two brothers and a sister, I was told."

Theodora caught the frozen look on Conner's face. *Oh no. Anna!* Theodora turned to Lance. "I'm sure Conner doesn't wish to discuss his family right now. He's been away for a while, and surely he'd rather discuss something more interesting like — like the weather or — or —"

"Thea."

She met Conner's gaze, his pale blue gaze was warm with appreciation. "It's all right, lass. I have to get used to it."

The sadness she saw in his eyes made her own fill with tears.

Lance looked from one to the other, clearly confused. "I'm sorry. Did I misspeak?"

"Of course nae," Conner said. "Recently, my sister, she —" He stopped, his mouth parted, though no words passed his lips.

100

After a moment, he cleared his throat and said, "She left us."

"Dear God!" Lance's face folded with genuine contrition. "I'm so sorry. Forgive me; it was impertinent to mention so personal a topic."

Conner took a drink of whisky, and Theodora noticed his hand was tight on the glass. After he'd swallowed, he managed a faint smile. " 'Tis naught. I must get used to saying it aloud. Meanwhile, you've enough sisters to fill a crew and sail for India. Tell me, is it madness at your house?"

"At times," Lance admitted. "Especially at dinner."

"I daresay that explains why you're running away, to escape the female chatter that must attend such a household."

"Ah! You're out there." Lance claimed one of Theodora's hands. "I had many reasons for this adventure, but none of them had to do with running away." He lifted her hand and pressed a kiss to her fingers. "Indeed, I am running *to.*"

Theodora's face heated. "Lance, there's no need for —" She untangled her hand from his.

The squire instantly looked contrite. "I should not have been so forward in front of Mr. Douglas." He turned his attention back to Conner, allowing Theodora time to collect herself. "So, Mr. Douglas — Conner — what brought you hither? It could not be mere coincidence you stumbled upon us."

Conner sent Theodora a look under his lashes, and she found herself holding her breath. *Please don't say a word about the ridiculous errand you came on. Please.*

It would just make things awkward. Lance would never understand her relationship with Conner. She wasn't sure she understood it herself.

Conner shrugged. " 'Twas pure happenstance. I was driving through and found myself parched. Imagine my surprise on finding Miss Cumberbatch-Snowe sitting here in the parlor."

Lance chuckled. "I'm glad you weren't sent here by her parents or brother, as I would hate to have engaged you in a duel."

Conner's smile froze, a hard look entering his eyes. "Oh?"

A clatter arose in the hallway, and the maid finally arrived with tea and cakes. Theodora had never been happier to see a tea tray in her life.

The girl set down the tray but made no move to serve the tea, merely gazing at Conner with a *come hither* look until Theodora snapped out, "That will be enough. I will pour."

The maid dragged her gaze from Conner. "Oh. I'm sorry, miss. I can pour. I was just —"

"No, thank you." Theodora picked up the pot. "You may leave."

The maid sent a final glance at Conner from under her lashes and, with a reluctant curtsy, left the room.

Theodora looked at the three cups. "Who would like some tea?"

Conner held up his whisky glass. "Nae for me, thank you."

"I'll take some," Lance said.

She handed him a cup of tea before filling her own, the steam carrying the scent of bergamot and cinnamon.

Lance started to take a sip, but then paused. "We should have told the maid to set another place for dinner."

Theodora almost choked on her tea, managing to croak, "Conner is not staying for dinner! He — he is on a family errand, and cannot stay." She pinned him with a stern look. "Aren't you?"

"I am," he said promptly. "Fortunately, my errand can wait, and I would be happy to stay for dinner."

She glared at him over her teacup.

Blissfully unaware he'd just been visually fried, Conner stretched out his legs, looking even more relaxed. "I can stay even longer than dinner, too —"

She smacked her cup into the saucer, tea splashing over the cup lip. "No, you cannot."

His brows rose, humor shimmering in his gaze while Lance looked at her with a startled expression.

She refused to back down. "Perhaps you've forgotten, but you have an *important* errand. I'm sure we'll miss you, but never fear, we'll see that you've some dinner to take with you." To keep Conner from refuting her yet again, she turned to Lance, a smile plastered on her face. "What is the word on the wheel? You returned faster than I expected."

"Ah. Yes. That's because I rushed like a madman; I hated leaving you here alone."

"She was nae alone," Conner pointed out.

Lance's smile slipped a bit. "So it appears, but I wasn't aware of that." After an awkward moment, he turned back to Theodora. "I do not have the best of news on the wheel. It can be repaired, but the closest wheelwright is located in Sheffield."

"Sheffield? Good God, that's at least three

days from here. Surely there's someone closer!"

"Sadly, there is not. All in all, it could be a week or more before we're back on the road."

"No!" At this rate, she'd never be married! It seemed to Theodora that her boring, staid past had just reached through time to hold her in place. "Surely there's a wheelwright closer than Sheffield."

"I fear not. To be honest, we're fortunate there's one as close as that. There are no large towns in this area." Lance smiled encouragingly. "Come, Theodora, a week is not so long. At least we're at this delightful inn and not stranded upon the road."

She glanced about the common room, noting the threadbare curtains and the lack of cushions on the chairs, which hinted at very poor conditions for the beds. She wished she'd examined the one in her room, but her mind had been elsewhere.

Disheartened, and far too aware of Conner's intense gaze, she forced herself to swallow her disappointment. "You're right, of course. We'll be fine here." She collected herself a bit more. "Better than fine. I'm sure we'll be quite cozy."

Conner's gaze swept the room, lingering in the same places Theodora's had. "It's quite a rustic inn, is it nae? But then, that is what makes it romantic."

"Exactly!" Lance beamed. "It has its own brand of charm."

Theodora found herself saying with far more enthusiasm than she might have otherwise, "It will be an adventure of sorts."

Lance smiled proudly. "That's my girl!"

Conner's brows rose at the "girl," and Theodora, avoiding his gaze, busied herself by refreshing her cup of tea. "I can use the extra time to get my clothing back in order. Everything I have is wet."

Lance made a face. "I wish my sister Arabella was here to help. She is especially talented at organizing clothing and mending and such."

At the word "sister," Theodora slipped a glance at Conner. His gaze was locked on his whisky, a bleak expression in his eyes.

Theodora's throat tightened yet again and she wasn't the least surprised when Conner set aside his glass and stood. "Pardon me, but I just realized I must see to my horse."

Lance looked at him in disbelief. "Right now?"

"Aye. He gets a wee bit nervous around people he dinnae know."

Lance put down his cup as if to rise, but Conner threw up a hand. "Dinnae get oop.

'Twill nae take me long to see to the animal. It'll be easier once my coach arrives and brings my servants to —" His brows knit. "Hmm." Conner didn't say anything more but rubbed his chin as if he'd been struck by a thought.

Lance politely asked, "Yes? What is it?"

"It just struck me that as, er, romantic as this inn is, I know neither of you are eager to stay whilst the wheel is being repaired. If you'd like, you could use my coach to continue to Gretna. It's coming doon this very road as 'tis following me. In fact, it should arrive tomorrow."

"You don't plan on riding in it yourself?" Lance asked.

"Och, nae. I dislike being shut oop in a coach. Besides, I have my horse and as I've said, I'm in nae hurry." Conner nodded as if it were decided. "You will use my coach to continue your trip."

Theodora said "No!" even as Lance exclaimed, "Of course!"

Her face hot, she sent a hard look at her intended.

He looked confused. "Theodora, I don't know how we can say no, unless you want to wait here while our wheel is repaired."

"We couldn't possibly importune Mr. Douglas in such a way."

"Och, I've nae plans to use it, so you may as weel take it. You may return it later, once you've married your squire."

Lance couldn't have looked happier. "By Zeus, that would be just the thing. Are you certain you wouldn't mind?"

"Not at all. In fact" — Conner's gaze slipped to Theodora — "I insist."

Lance stood and grasped Conner's hand in both of his and pumped it heartily. "Thank you! It's most generous. I can see now why Theodora is always talking about you."

"It's nothing. Now, if you'll excuse me, I'll have a word with the innkeeper to bespeak a bedchamber."

Theodora had just taken a sip of tea to calm her sinking heart, but at Conner's words, she looked up, her mind racing. *Stay? Why?*

As if he could hear her question, Conner added, "The weather's looking a bit grim and I dislike riding in the rain. I caught the ague once from such a turn of weather, and I've avoided it since."

She gritted her teeth. *What are you doing?* The inn was so small, and had so few rooms, that only a narrow hallway or a thin wall would separate her from Conner. The last thing she wanted was to spend the night within feet of where he was to be sleeping.

Yet despite her irritation at his machinations, her heart fluttered at the thought of being so close to him, and her mouth felt oddly dry as the memory of their kiss flickered through her.

Was it wrong that she had no reaction about the nearness of her fiancé, and was all too aware of Conner's? *I'm sure it's perfectly understandable,* she told herself firmly. *Conner is unprincipled enough to take advantage of that nearness, while Lance would never do so. Yet another reason why Conner is not the sort of man one should marry.*

The wind lifted a bit and rattled the windows, as if in cahoots with Conner.

That seemed to decide Lance, who said, "The wind is lifting. Douglas, you were wise not to continue today."

"I'm fairly guid at reading the weather." Conner walked to the door, looking far too pleased with himself for Theodora's peace of mind. "If you'll pardon me, I will give you two lovebirds some privacy while I speak with our host aboot a bedchamber."

"But —" Theodora began.

"I insist." He bowed, sending her a particularly winsome smile as he left, whistling a

109

merry sea ditty as he disappeared out the door.

Theodora's eyes narrowed. She couldn't shake the feeling that she and Lance had just walked into a trap of some sort, one too complex for her to see. *Blast it, Conner, what are you up to? What can you hope to gain through this?*

Whatever it was, she'd figure it out and whoa betide the man then!

7

Much to his amusement, the rain Conner had fictitiously predicted arrived during dinner. He made certain to say several times how glad he was he'd decided to stay, which the squire readily agreed with, making Thea glower.

Dinner had been every bit as awkward as Conner had expected. Thea was quiet and taciturn, while her beau attempted to pull her from her obvious doldrums by expounding on his latest plan for crop rotation, a subject Conner found painfully boring. Even the green-thumbed Thea couldn't seem to muster a hint of enthusiasm. After dinner she'd abruptly excused herself, saying she was tired from the day's events, and limped from the room.

The good squire had tried to excuse her behavior, which had bothered him far more than it had Conner. Thea had good reason for her irritation, although he was more than willing to risk her ire in order to make his point.

Still, Conner hadn't minded the time alone with Fox. A toasty fire, a bottle of good whisky, and two hours of jovial story-telling had given Conner the opportunity to explore his enemy's weaknesses.

Thus this morning, even though Conner had awoken with a fuzzy head, he was well satisfied that he'd not only gained the squire's trust, but had also planted a few seeds of future discord. Conner went down-stairs and found that breakfast had been set up in the empty parlor, but the fresh breeze outside offered some solace for his heavy head, so he opted to take a walk instead. The rain had left the morning cooler, the leaves and cobblestones freshly washed, the roads newly muddied. It was a sun-drenched day, the sky a pure blue, and he felt more at peace than at any moment since Anna's death. His heart was slowly healing, and pursuing Thea was serving as a much-needed — and entertaining — distraction.

Turning his face to the sun, Conner leaned against the wall of the inn and mulled over his next move. He knew two things well — privateering and women. If he wished to win this game and have Thea to wife, then the decision to end her engagement would have to be hers — which meant he had to convince her that he was the far better choice of husband, and that could take some doing.

He'd picked up a few clues at dinner last night. The squire had been openly courting Thea, and her discomfort with that attention had been obvious, although the squire didn't seem to notice. She was a private person, not given to public displays, but the squire hadn't honed in on that yet. This lack of attention on the squire's part emphasized the differences between the couple, which showed promise. Unfortunately, it also showed the squire's commitment to wooing Thea, which couldn't be quickly dismissed.

On the surface, Lance seemed uncomplicated and straightforward. If he was happy, he smiled. If he was sad, he frowned. There were no shades of gray to be pondered, no hidden agendas, and thus far, no covert attempts to thwart Conner's presence.

Conner pulled a cigar from his pocket and rolled it between his fingertips, the fragrant scent lifting his spirits. This errand was proving far more difficult than he'd expected. Or rather, *Thea* was proving more difficult, and stubborn, and . . . He couldn't say disappointing, because she was being true to who she'd always been, strong-willed and calmly focused on what she thought to be right. It was what he'd always liked about her, but he now realized that it also meant she wouldn't be nearly as malleable as he'd rather foolishly imagined. Hmm. Was it possible his expectations of her as a wife were a bit off, too?

It was possible she wouldn't quietly sit back while he went to sea for months on end, or established himself in London for part of a season without her presence now and again. In fact, now that he was no longer indulging in the brotherly braggadocio that had first sent him on this quest, he had to admit that while Thea wasn't overly sentimental, neither was she without pride. She would demand a high level of respect.

He thought of the flash of her eyes when he'd blithely informed her of their impending marriage. While it revealed a large flaw in his earlier thinking, it hadn't put him off. Instead, he was intrigued and challenged. She'd surprised him, and it felt as if he were seeing her for the first time, *meeting* her for the first time. He supposed that made sense as before now, he'd always visited her while she was at her home, with her parents or brother. But here she was on her own, and he was intrigued at the difference. The new

Thea — or perhaps it was the more honest Thea — could not be easily won over, and he would have to adjust his plans accordingly.

He laughed softly and lit his cigar. Sparring with her was as exhilarating as a sea battle. He'd assumed he wanted a quiet, complacent wife, but he had to admit that he appreciated her spirit. She wasn't afraid to speak her mind, which added a layer of challenge he was enjoying far more than he'd expected. His wife would need to be independent if she were going to run Dunskey House while he was at sea. Of course, it might also mean she'd expect him to visit their home far more often than he'd imagined.

Home. It was a distant word for someone who'd lost his at such an early age. For try as she would, Anna hadn't been able to make any place feel the way their home had when their parents were alive. What would "home" mean with Thea? She was dashed good at organizing things; he'd seen the way she'd taken over the many, many temporary moves her family had undertaken. She was the one who evaluated their assigned living quarters and, when necessary, hired out a new one, decided which furniture (if any) would go, saw to the delivery of necessary items, made certain their travel arrangements were comfortable, oversaw the hiring of servants — the list was truly impressive. And she'd done this yearly, sometimes more often, depending on her father's assignments.

He imagined Thea at Dunskey House and had to admit that he could see nothing but good coming from it. Damn, it would be nice having a well-organized, smoothly running home to come to when his ship was in port. He could see himself sitting before a fire, dinner ready nearby, Thea at his side, smiling as she refilled his whisky glass — He snorted. *As if she'd refill my glass. It's far more likely I'll be refilling hers.* But there was a certain charm in that, too.

He was making the right decision to woo Thea; he was certain. His only other option was to leave and find another female to meet the requirements of the will, and he couldn't picture that. Although there were always plenty of women on the marriage mart who wanted money over all else, none were so interesting, so comfortable, so amusing, so . . . everything. Compared to Thea, the thought of marrying a stranger was distasteful.

He glanced up at her window, noting the lace curtains were still drawn against the morning sun. What would it be like to wake up in her bed, to roll over and pull her near? To place a kiss on her neck and warm her body to wakefulness —

His cock stirred, and he grinned. There were more benefits to be had by marrying Thea than he'd originally realized. Which was why he'd offered his carriage.

It would take time to dissuade Thea from her intention to marry Fox, time for Conner to convince her that he and she would make a better couple, so he had to slow the pace of their rather poorly planned elopement. The more time she spent in the good squire's company, the better. Meanwhile, Conner would find ways to subtly point out the differences between Thea and her beau, and if possible, exacerbate them.

It was unfortunate he couldn't race in and sink the squire's ship immediately in a glorifying blaze — which would be most satisfying, but would put Thea on alert. But Conner *could* make certain the winds weren't favorable for the eloping couple. If things worked as he hoped, the hapless squire's pursuit would founder on rocks of his own making.

Conner smiled, thinking of the suspicion in Thea's eyes when he'd offered his coach. *Och, you know me weel, my dear.* He'd have to steer lightly through the shoals of her suspicions and be careful not to throw up an alarm, but he was fairly certain he could do it — especially with such a rich prize awaiting.

Lance's voice came from somewhere inside the inn, raised as if in greeting. Was Thea already up? Conner dropped his cigar and ground it out with his heel, and then moved closer to the parlor window, remaining out of sight. Through the glass, he could hear Lance saying in a placating voice, "Theodora, pray reconsider!"

Well, that was promising!

"No. I cannot believe you made this decision without consulting me."

Oh ho, a fight! Conner leaned against the wall, crossing his arms over his chest, unable to keep from smiling.

"Theodora, you must understand. I thought of it late last night, and as I couldn't imagine you'd disagree, I saw to it first thing this morning, before you awoke. Once you've had time to consider everything, you'll agree I did what was best for us both."

"I doubt it." Her voice snapped like a cannon shot.

Thea was in rare form this morning — but then she was every morning. Everyone in her family knew that one never, *ever* addressed anything more than a calm "good morning" to Thea before she'd had her morning tea and toast.

Lance plowed on, unaware he was sailing straight into a storm. "You're upset. I understand that, but you are not thinking clearly."

Conner winced. *Och, lad, you're poking Neptune with his own trident this morning, aren't you? You're brave, I'll give you that.*

Apparently Thea's expression must have expressed just that, for the squire added in a breathless, rather pleading voice, "Even on a romantic venture such as this, we must not be blind to the proprieties. You need a chaperone."

Conner stifled a laugh. That was one of the many suggestions he'd made last night to the receptive, if tipsy, squire. It hadn't taken much   just a couple of comments about people's perception of Thea traveling alone for days on end with a single man, followed by Conner's instant reassurance that he knew her so well that *he* would never make such a scandalous assumption.

"Good God, Lance, I'm seven and twenty! I haven't had a chaperone since I was eighteen. And I'm observing the proprieties on my own, thank you very much. I had the landlady send a maid to sleep on a cot in my room. I *told* you I'd done that."

"Yes, but —"

"No buts! I didn't sleep a wink, for the girl snored as if she were sawing logs all night long. I don't need you, nor anyone else, doing anything more."

Och, Lance, that's a shot over the bow. I'd stand down if I were you.

But Lance continued as if Thea hadn't given him fair warning, saying in a stubborn tone, "If our trip is to be elongated and our marriage delayed, we need more than the services of the occasional chambermaid to protect your reputation."

"Lance, we are *eloping.* It's the nature of an elopement that one recklessly throws the proprieties to the wind, and embarks on adventure for the sake of it!"

"Good God, no!" The poor man couldn't have sounded more horrified. "Theodora, if at any time you thought my actions were colored by any sort of impropriety, I hope you'd tell me so that I may correct them immediately!"

"For the love of heaven, Lance! I —" She bit off the end of the sentence and took a deep breath. "When we first spoke of eloping, you said it was an exciting leap. If it wasn't a leap over the stifling bounds of propriety, then of what?"

120

"A leap toward marriage, of course."

"Oh."

Conner took hope in the disappointed note in Thea's voice. Like all women, she'd been hoping for a touch of romance. *Which I didn't consider either,* he realized with a grimace. *But now I know better.*

"Theodora, I would never be disrespectful or put your reputation in harm's way. *Never.*"

There was a long silence, and then another deep sigh. "That's very honorable of you. But I wish you'd asked me first. I'll admit I wouldn't mind having a lady's maid, but I do not see the need of a chaperone."

"I'm sorry. This elopement had been far more complicated than I anticipated. It's a wonder you don't demand I return you home."

Conner leaned closer to the window, unable to still a flash of hope.

To his disappointment, Thea gave a gurgle of laughter. "Oh Lance, you cannot be *pouting.*"

"I'm not pouting! I am disappointed, but who would blame me? I hate seeing you upset."

"You're very kind." Her voice was calmer now, and warmer, too. "I'm sorry if I took your head off. I don't do well in the morning."

"I'm shocked to hear that, for you look beautiful in that blue gown."

Conner rolled his eyes. *Good God, man. She will not fall for such a blatant maneuver as —*

"That's far too kind of you."

Dammit, Thea. Conner's earlier humor had fled.

"It's true," Lance persisted. "You are a lovely woman, Theodora. I've thought so since the moment I laid eyes upon you."

Conner had to give the man credit; he was a fount of compliments.

Thea sighed. "I still wish you'd spoken to me beforehand."

"I'll do so next time, I promise. Just don't give up on us."

"Of course I'm not giving up on us."

"Then you'll still marry me?"

"I don't make promises lightly. When I say I'm going to do something, I do it."

"Theodora, you *dear*!"

Silence answered this, and for a wild moment, Conner wondered if the two of them were embracing. The image burned like hot tar, and he scowled fiercely and started toward the window. He'd think of a reason to explain banging on it later; he had an embrace to stop, b'God! But then he heard Thea's cool laugh and she said in a calm voice, "I'm hardly a dear; I'm merely being practical."

"So you see why a chaperone is necessary. It'll answer the calls of propriety." He hesitated, and then said in a less enthusiastic tone, "Plus, if you decide at any time that you've changed your mind and no longer wish to go through with our marriage, then you will go home with your name unsullied. It is because of that, more than Mr. Douglas's suggestion, that I was determined to find a proper —"

"Wait. *Conner* put you up to this?"

Conner winced. He'd hoped Lance had been too tipsy to remember exactly who said what. *The man has a stronger head for drink than I gave him credit for.*

"No! Not at all. Getting a chaperone was entirely my idea."

"But apparently Conner said something that made you think of it. What did he say?"

"It was nothing. We were talking last night and I can't remember how it came up, but he mentioned quite innocently how glad he was there were so few people at this inn, as they might assume things if they saw you traveling alone with me."

"That arse!"

"Theodora!" Lance couldn't have sounded more shocked if she'd announced she'd killed her own brother with a dinner knife and had found the experience invigorating.

"I'm sorry. But I should have known he was behind this."

True, Conner decided. She *should* have known he wouldn't sit idly by while she ran off with the wrong man.

"Theodora, you greatly mistake. Mr. Douglas wasn't behind anything. In fact, he never mentioned hiring a chaperone. That was *my* idea."

Thea gave a very unladylike snort, and Conner choked back a laugh as he imagined the squire's shocked expression. *Oh, how I wish I could see that.*

He moved closer to the window, his elbow bumping the shutter. He froze in place. *Had they heard that? Surely not. It was a small noise and —*

"Lance, you're right. I *do* need a chaperone."

Conner frowned.

"Theodora!" Lance couldn't have sounded more pleased. "You don't mind, then?"

"No, I'm flattered you went to such trouble. In fact, I'm looking forward to meeting her."

Blast it. Conner scowled. This was not what he'd hoped for.

"You'll like Miss Simmons," Lance was saying. "I visited her this morning before you came down for breakfast, and thought her delightful. She's the youngest sister of the local vicar, and until recently was a governess, but was let go when her charge came of age for her season in London. Miss Simmons is pleasant without being forward, kind, and very eager to be of use. I was quite impressed with her."

"Wonderful. I will thank Conner for his fortuitous suggestion, although I daresay he was three sheets to the wind when he offered his assistance. He frequently is."

What?

There was a surprised hesitation, and then Lance said in a cautious voice, "He didn't seem drunk."

"Was there whisky in the room?"

"We both had a glass or so, but he didn't seem unduly affected."

"He's good at hiding it," Thea announced. "Did you know he is also afraid of heights?"

Conner stiffened. Perhaps when he was younger, but not now. Hell, he climbed the rigging without even thinking about it.

"Strawberries make him break out in a horrible rash, too. And he cannot *abide* mice. He screams like a little girl every time he sees one."

Ah. He gave a reluctant smile. *So you know I'm here, and will tell faradiddles as punishment for my manipulation of your squire. Fair enough.*

Thea wasn't finished. "He wears only silk waistcoats, even when at sea, and he reads all of Miss Compton's racy novels. In fact, he *wept* when the heroine died in *The Evil Duke.*"

His smile left him. She'd gone too far with that one, for it was the one truth she'd spoken, something only she knew, and an embarrassing moment for him although he'd been quite young at the time.

The jangling of an approaching coach pulled Conner's attention from the couple inside the inn. He pushed himself away from the rock wall and sauntered toward the gate, crossing in front of the window. As he did so, he glanced into the parlor. As he'd hoped, although the squire's back was turned, Thea faced the window.

Unable to resist, Conner stopped and made a bow so elaborate, it wouldn't have been out of place in the French court.

Thea's gaze narrowed, a flash of disapproval crossing her face. With an obviously deliberate move, she turned her shoulder to him and continued speaking with the squire, no doubt heaping more character flaws on Conner's hapless head.

Grinning, Conner reached the gate just as his coach appeared, splashing through puddles as it turned from the road into the yard.

MacLeish was handling the reins, with Spencer and Ferguson perched beside him on the high seat. They brightened on seeing Conner.

The coach clattered to a halt, and Ferguson and Spencer hopped down, the younger man calling for a postboy to hold the team.

Spencer grinned. "Here we are, Cap'n! Fresh as the wind and ready to see you married." He peered past Conner. "Where's Miss Cumberbatch-Snowe? Is she ready to return home?"

"Sadly, 'tis nae going to be as easy as that." Conner glanced at the sun. "You're late. I expected you an hour ago."

"We had word from the ship. After we left yesterday, Lady Winstead refused to evacuate your quarters. She caused quite a ruckus, she did."

"She's still there?"

"Och, nae, Cap'n," Spencer said fervently.

"But apparently 'twas an unruly scene."

MacLeish, a great bear of a man with thick curly brown hair and a full beard, nodded solemnly. "She threatened to burn the ship, she did."

"They said 'twas ugly, as she'd decided you'd sent her home as you'd found a more pleasant companion to replace her."

Ferguson nodded. "From what we were told, she threw a tantrum fit for any three-year-auld."

"I'm sorry the men had to deal with such," Conner said, faintly surprised. He hadn't thought Charlotte would care that he'd decided their liaison was over. She was married, for God's sake, and should be concerned about a scandal, which would hurt her far more than it would hurt him.

Ferguson grinned. "Aye. MacDougal threatened to tie her to the mast whilst he sent for her husband."

"That clipped her sails," Spencer added with glee.

"Guid." Conner wished he'd never wasted his time with the woman. "I hope you found a decent bunk last night."

"Ferguson refuses to call it an 'inn,' though 'twas warm and dry. We cannae ask for more than that."

"Dry?" The First Mate looked offended.

"Parts of it were until it rained," Spencer said. He cocked a brow at Conner. " 'Tis fortunate you sent the postboy yesterday to let us know you wished us to hold until you sent word, for we were almost here when we met him."

"I worried as much. I'm glad you waited."

"I'm nae sure why that helped. Did you nae find her ladyship?"

"Aye. She's here, but so is her beau."

"Beau?" Ferguson looked intrigued. "You dinnae talk her oot of that little obstacle, eh?"

"Nae yet. I fear it will take more effort than I'd first envisioned."

MacLeish, who'd been following the conversation closely, crossed his arms over his broad chest, his expression one of lively interest. "What's toward, Cap'n? Spencer said we're on a mission of the heart."

"So we are, and I've a plan, but 'twill require patience. For now, take the coach and the horses to the stables."

MacLeish looked surprised. "You dinnae wish to leave now?"

"Nae. The horses will need to rest first."

"But we only drove a few miles here and the coach was nearly empty. The horses are plenty fresh enough to —"

"MacLeish!" Spencer said sharply. "The

cap'n is scheming, he is."

"Aye, we're on a quest," Conner agreed. "And the prize is grand." Grander, perhaps, than he'd admitted to himself when he'd first begun.

He'd need his men's help. The more they knew, the more he could count on them to assist him. Most men of fashion surrounded themselves with servants who were often far more snooty and class-aware than their masters, and who refused to cross the line in the sand society drew between servants and masters. But life on a ship was more egalitarian and it served Conner well to have his crew about him, whether they were on land or sea, especially now, when he had a treasure in sight. "We've an adventure to plot, men. And 'twill take all of us to ac-complish it."

"You can count on us, Cap'n," Ferguson said solemnly, as if taking a vow.

"Aye," MacLeish agreed.

"Guid!" Conner gestured for his men to move closer. "As you know, I had planned on asking Miss Cumberbatch-Snowe to wife yesterday, but when I arrived at her home, she'd mistakenly eloped with Squire Fox."

"Hold there, Cap'n!" Ferguson scratched his chin. "*Mistakenly* eloped? How does that happen?"

"It dinnae matter. What matters is that I've now met the mon and he is nae her equal. 'Tis to her benefit, and mine as weel, that she wed me instead of this squire."

"Och, a *squire.*" Ferguson spat the word as if it tasted of rotted wood and vinegar. "Who'd wed a lowly squire when she could have a cap'n?"

"Did you explain that to her, sir?" Spencer scrunched his nose. "Mayhap she dinnae understand that you outrank this mon."

"I'd mention the fortune you stand to inherit, too," MacLeish added. "You know how women are when it comes to gold."

"She has her own funds and is nae impressed with mine. Nor does she care if I'm captain or cabin boy."

"Pardon me." MacLeish flushed when Conner looked his way, and then said hesitantly, "Forgive me, Cap'n, and I may be oot here, but since the miss is on her way to wed another mon, perhaps 'twould be best to find another woman to wife?"

Spencer gaped. "MacLeish, do you wish the cap'n to give oop withoot a fight?"

"The cap'n's honor is at stake!" Ferguson added in a fierce tone.

Spencer added, "They've been friends for years. 'Tis a prodigious match for them both."

131

"She's fortunate the cap'n has picked her, she is," Ferguson agreed.

MacLeish had been looking from one of his shipmates to the other as if he were watching them play a vigorous game of tennis, but now he eyed Conner with a confused look. "But . . . she's eloping with another mon."

"Aye," Conner said shortly.

"Would nae that remove her from the 'Available to Wed' column, and instead place her in the 'If Only I Had Asked Sooner' column?"

"If I dinnae care aboot her future, it would," Conner said curtly. "What I've seen of this squire tells me they will nae last a month."

Ferguson leaned forward, the breeze lifting his hair. "Is this squire an upstart, then?"

"I would nae say that," Conner admitted.

"He must be a rummy fool," Spencer offered.

"Nae exactly."

"A curmudgeon given to yelling and such?" MacLeish offered.

"Or an auld mon, aged and decrepit?" Ferguson threw in for good measure.

"Nae, nae, and nae. He's pleasant-spoken and young."

MacLeish's thick brows lowered. "He has

some bad habits, then? He gambles, or womanizes?"

"Nae. He's thoroughly decent. All taken, he's a guid enough mon."

Everyone stared at him.

Conner said sternly, "But he's the wrong mon for Miss Cumberbatch-Snowe."

Everyone but MacLeish looked convinced. He asked in a cautious voice, "Did you mention this to the lass?"

"Aye," Conner said grimly. "I asked her to wed me, instead, which was an error, for the timing was ill and she was nae in the mood to hear me oot."

"I can see that," Ferguson agreed. "What with her being on an elopement with another mon and all."

"I will nae let that deter me," Conner said firmly. "I'm nae courting her. I'm *saving* her."

Spencer's eyes widened. After a stunned moment, he said in a fervent tone, "Why, that's the most romantic thing I've ever heard."

"Aye," Ferguson agreed. " 'Tis like one of them famous poems where the hero rides into the wedding, yanks the heroine o'er his saddle, and they gallop off, happy ever after."

It was exactly like that, Conner decided.

"I've a plan to fix this and win the lady. But first, we must slow things doon a bit. So, heave to, lubbers, and put the coach and horses away. We will delay our trip until tomorrow."

"And after that?" Spencer asked.

"After that, we will see. MacLeish, how long would it take to drive to Gretna Green from here?"

"If we drive at a goodly but comfortable pace, stopping at night, and changing the horses at least once —" MacLeish squinted into the distance. "Two days, mayhap three."

"I want a week. You must drive slowly. We'll say the coach is heavy and the horses must rest often."

Ferguson rubbed his hands together. "We're flying under a false flag, are we?"

"Aye. The more time Miss Cumberbatch-Snowe spends in the company of her squire, the more she'll come to realize he's nae the paragon she thinks. So while you're putting the horses away, be sure to tell everyone who will listen that you've come a long way already this morning and the horses need rest. Just to be certain our story holds water."

"Aye, aye, Cap'n," Spencer said. "Anything else?"

"For you, aye. Once you're done in the stables, come find me in the inn. I've one more task just for you."

Spencer looked intrigued, and agreed quickly. Soon the men disappeared with the coach into the stables.

Smilwing to himself and satisfied he was well on his way to repairing his situation, Conner returned to the inn.

8

Theodora picked up the gown and shook it out. It was one of her favorites, a blue traveling gown of light wool trimmed with pale green piping, with a double row of delicate flounces decorating the hemline. Or it *had* been one of her favorites.

One of the inn's few maids had supposedly cleaned the gown and laid it out to dry in front of a fire. A smoky fire, from the smell of it, for it reeked of damp ashes. Worse, though the maid had sworn she'd washed the gown thoroughly, there were still large, muddy stains, and the bottom ruffle had come loose and hung limply.

"Ruined." Theodora looked from the smoky gown to the one she wore, which was the same one she'd worn yesterday. It was hideously wrinkled and just as mud stained. "At least the one I'm wearing doesn't smell like the bottom of an ash bin." Sighing, she carried the dress to the window, hoping some fresh air might eliminate the smoky scent. She stepped gingerly, although her ankle barely ached as she walked now, which was a relief. *At least that's better.*

She pulled back the lace curtains and opened the window latch and spread her gown over the sill, anchoring it in place with a heavy, pewter candleholder. The fresh breeze stirred the gown as well as her hair as she looked at the inn yard below. Conner's coach, gleaming and impressive, had arrived not a half hour ago. It was a truly beautiful equipage, pulled by four matching gray horses. *Now, that's the sort of coach one should elope in.*

But why *had* Conner offered them his coach? "It's a trick, I'm sure of it," she murmured. "But what could he possibly hope to gain?"

Whatever it was, it wouldn't work. She wouldn't let it. Lance was the kindest, gentlest man she'd ever met, worth a dozen charming, brown-haired, blue-eyed almost-pirates, who knew how to look at a woman as if she were his to claim, and whose heated, head-swirling kisses made her —

She clamped a lid on her thoughts. *That's what got me into this mess to begin with. He's an impudent, disrespectful mess of a man. He even eavesdropped on my conversation with*

Lance! Had Conner not made a noise, she'd have never known it. And his graceful bow and twinkling grin on being caught had done nothing to soothe her ire. *I hope he heard all the faradiddles I told Lance. It would serve Conner right if he were embarrassed and —*

A soft knock sounded at her door. *Ah, my tea at last!* "Come in!"

The door opened, and someone, a male by the sound of it, cleared his throat.

She dropped the curtain and turned.

An awkward-looking youth stood in the doorway, and she recognized him as Conner's footman. "Oh! You're Spencer, correct?"

The young man flushed a bright pink, as if she'd just paid him the highest compliment possible. "Aye, miss. The cap'n sent me. He suggested I might be of some use."

"Oh, he did, did he?"

She hadn't meant to sound ungracious, but her sharp tone made her visitor flush an even deeper red. He backed away. "Och, perhaps now is nae a guid time. I can come back when —"

"No, no! I'm sorry. I was just in a foul mood. It's kind of you to offer to help, although I'm not sure what you could do."

"The cap'n said your clothing took a

spill." The young man's gaze moved to the gown now fluttering in the open window. "I might be able to set your gowns to rights."

"Could you?" She couldn't hide her hope.

"Och, miss, I'm the bos'n's mate." He straightened, obviously proud of his position. "I take care of the equipment on ship, including the sails, which is why I'm rather handy with a needle. When we're on land, I take care of the cap'n's clothing, too."

"Ah, so you're the one responsible for Mr. Douglas's starched cravats and silk waist-coats."

Stewart grinned. "Aye, and his linens, fine breeches and kilts, and the like. I polish his boots, too, and see that everything is mended and pressed. He's a bit of a beau."

"That must be a lot to keep up with, in addition to your other duties."

"Och, I dinnae mind, miss; 'tis the cap'n. And when the cap'n looks guid, we all look guid. I daresay that's why he sent me to you. He knows the value of such things."

As do I. "I must warn you, it will take a lot to repair and clean my gowns. If you cannot, I fear I will just have to make do."

The man's expression grew solemn. "Making do is never pleasant, is it, miss?"

"Never," she agreed. "Sadly, it seems I have been doing a lot of that lately."

"Then you will nae be oot if you allow me to try." Spencer nodded to the gown fluttering in the open window. "May I?"

Theodora hesitated. She desperately wanted to accept Spencer's help, but feared that if she did, she would end up owing Conner even more than she did now.

The smoky scent of the gown wafting on the breeze made up her mind for her. She crossed to the window and gathered the offending garment, and handed it to Spencer. "Yes, please. The maid swears she washed it, but there are mud stains, and a tear, and — Well, you can see for yourself. My other gowns are still in the kitchen, most likely spread before a smoking fire."

Stewart carefully folded the gown over his arm as if it were made of gossamer. "Never fear, miss. I will do what I can."

"Thank you. I wish you had more time, but as the captain's coach has arrived, we'll be leaving soon."

Stewart's expression froze a bit.

"We're not leaving?"

He hesitated, then said in a guarded manner, "The horses must be rested before we leave, so 'twill most likely be tomorrow before we leave. But that's a guid thing, for 'twill give me more time to see to your gowns." He smoothed a hand over the gown she'd given him, looking at it with an expert eye. "I could have this one ready in aboot two hours, mayhap three."

"Really?"

"Aye. I'll work oot the stains, then wash and rinse it again. After that, I'll use an iron to dry it." He examined the torn ruffle. "And this will take nae time at all. All told, three hours at most."

"Thank you. I would be most grateful."

"My pleasure, miss!"

As he turned to go, a thought hit Theodora. "You said we would leave after the horses rested. Who is 'we'?"

The look on the footman's face told her everything she needed to know. So *that* was Conner's plan. "Mr. Douglas is planning on going with the squire and me."

Looking miserable, Spencer backed up. "I would nae know, miss. The cap'n dinnae always share what he's planning."

She followed the footman into the hallway. "But you must know where he will be tomorrow."

Spencer gulped, holding her gown in front of him as if it were a shield. "I cannae say, miss."

"Cannot or will not?"

"I cannae," he repeated stubbornly. "Mayhap you should speak to the cap'n."

She would indeed. Borrowed coach or no, cleaned gowns or no, he was *not* going to intrude on her elopement any further.

But her fight with Conner had nothing to do with this poor young man, so she smiled and said, "You're right; I'll speak with him. Meanwhile, whatever you can do for my poor gowns will be most appreciated."

"Very good, miss." The footman bowed and, looking as if he'd been released from a lion's claws, hurried away.

Theodora closed the door, and leaned against it. So *that* was why Conner had offered his coach — as an excuse to accompany them! She could only imagine how awkward that would be; it had been difficult enough having to face him at dinner last night. She'd been so aware of his intense stare that she'd scarcely been able to eat. Well, she had a surprise for Mr. Conner Douglas — she was onto his tricks and stratagems, and she would not fall victim to them. Her only concern was that his actions indicated that he believed there was still some hope she would eventually accept his suit, a sad misconception she needed to quash immediately. There was no future for them, and the sooner he accepted that, the better for everyone.

But first . . . she looked down at her

rumpled frock and thought of the clean, repaired gown Spencer had promised. She'd confront Conner after she'd bathed and was properly attired. She'd need all of her wits sharpened and ready before she undertook the impossible: convincing Conner Douglas he was wrong.

Two and a half hours later, Theodora felt far more herself, having scrubbed away the grime of the trip in a tub so small, her knees had almost touched her chin. But the water had been hot and clean, and the innkeeper's wife had miraculously produced a bar of lavender soap. The scent had soothed Theodora's worn soul.

To her pleasant surprise, Spencer had done much more than wash, mend, and press her gown; he'd also prepared a chemise, a petticoat, and her best stockings. His repairs had been faultless, too, his stitching so tiny she could barely see it. For the first time in two days Theodora was freshly and properly attired, luxuriating in the newly laundered muslin against her skin as she pinned her almost-dry hair in place.

She eyed herself in the mirror, pleased to note that, except for the scrape on her jaw, she no longer appeared so abused by life. Now all she had to do was put Conner firmly in his place and send him on his way, and her life would be back on track. Once he was out of the way, she would press Lance to leave immediately.

Wishing her heart didn't race at the thought of confronting Conner, she straightened her shoulders, ready to fight the good fight. She opened the door and turned into the hallway — and walked straight into his arms.

Conner couldn't believe his good fortune. Still preoccupied with his conversation with MacLeish on ways to lengthen their journey to Gretna Green, Conner hadn't been paying the least heed to his progress down the hall. Peering at tiny roads on faded maps did that to a person. After much discussion, he and MacLeish had decided that instead of going directly north, they would turn west and take the spider's web of roads up the coast. It would add at least a week to the journey, and Conner was confident that would be enough time for him to convince Thea she was making an error in marrying the squire.

He'd been returning to his room to change for dinner when Thea had thrown open her door and rushed straight into his arms.

She looked far more like her usual self now that she was in a freshly laundered and pressed gown, her hair upswept and silky. He took a deep breath, tightening his arms as he inhaled the beguiling scent of lavender soap and newly ironed muslin.

Thea stared up at him, her eyes widened, her lips curved in a shocked "O."

God, but she had the most delicious lips, plump and pink, and he fought the powerful desire to kiss her thoroughly. *How in the hell have I resisted her all these years? It's as if I've been completely blind to her.*

Their gazes locked, and her lips parted, and he found himself bending down to taste those lips, to savor their softness and —

She gasped and jerked free, pressing back against the wall. Had the hallway been wider, that might have been a significant step. As it was, all he had to do to close the gap was place his palm on the doorframe behind her, and lean forward. He smiled, his body humming with awareness, and he wondered if hers was doing the same. "If you wished for a hug, you had but to ask, lass."

She sent him a black look, rubbing her arm as if his touch had burned her. "I wasn't looking for a hug or an embrace or anything else. But . . . now that you're here, we need to talk."

"I'm listening." He shifted the slightest bit

forward, his knee only an inch from hers.

She moved a little to one side, away from him. Her cheeks were deliciously pink as she said in a breathless tone, "I'm glad I found you alone, for I don't wish Lance to know of this."

Conner was glad she'd found him alone, too. *Very* glad.

She took a deep breath, which had the fortunate effect of pressing her breasts into the pleated front of her gown.

Conner had always considered Thea attractive, and he'd been surprised to learn from kissing her that she was damned sensual, as well. He looked at her with fresh eyes, noting that her figure was lushly curved, her shoulders delightfully set with the most intriguing hollows that cried out for further exploration, while her breasts were the perfect size to fill a man's hands. His palms itched to —

"I'm not sure where to begin, but . . ." She wet her bottom lip as if nervous.

His gaze locked upon her generous mouth. It begged to be tasted, and he fought to keep from leaning in to do just that.

But now was not the time, he reminded himself with regret. He needed to assuage her suspicions, not add to them. So with great disappointment, he dropped his hand back to his side and shifted to give her more room. "Oot with it, then. What has you racing from your bedchamber to find me?"

Her jaw firmed and she suddenly looked like the Thea he knew well. "I know why you offered your coach to us. You think to use that as an excuse to join us on our trip."

"Join you on your elopement? I'd nae thought of that, but if you want me to join you, odd as that seems, I suppose I could —"

"No! Of course I don't wish you to travel with us!"

Conner had to fight to keep from grinning. "But you said —"

"That's not what I meant, and you know it."

"Fine, I will nae travel with you. I had nae intention of it to begin with. Are you happy now?"

"No." Her gaze narrowed. "There's one more thing. And I need to make this very clear to you, so there can be no question. No matter what you do or say, no matter what schemes you have planned, I am going to marry the squire. And if, by some unforeseen happenstance, I do not, I *still* would not marry you. If you want your family fortune saved from the Campbells, then you'd best find another woman to wed."

He raised his brows. "Guid lord, that's a bit harsh, lass."

"It's honest."

Even though she said all the right things to send him away, her gaze kept resting on his mouth as if she was remembering their kiss. *Aye, lass, I cannae forget it, either.* "Verrah weel. If this is how things are to be, then I suppose there's nae need for me to continue scheming, as you call it."

"Exactly. Lance and I will depart first thing in the morning. You will not."

"Fine, but I'm nae staying here in this pitiful inn. You would nae be so cruel. Have you seen the tub? 'Tis made for bathing small dogs, and perhaps a chicken now and then."

Her lips quirked and he thought he'd won a laugh, but she fought it off to say in a severe tone, "Don't be ridiculous. You don't have to stay here, and you know it. I don't care where you go, as long as you don't go with us."

He sighed. "Fine. I'll go my own way. But I should point oot that it would be safer if I rode along, in case there are brigands."

"No, thank you. We'll be fine without your help." Her gaze narrowed and she tapped his chest. "Admit it: you lent us your coach just so you could manipulate us."

He captured her hand and pressed a kiss to her fingers, his eyes twinkling warmly. "I'm admitting nae such thing." He turned her hand over and kissed her palm. "But neither am I denying it."

Theodora yanked her hand from his grasp, her skin tingling from his touch, her heart thudding wildly as her fingers curled over his kiss. "You don't need to say a word, because I know what you were doing. Lance will feel beholden to you for allowing us the use of your coach, and then you'd suggest traveling with us, and he would feel obligated to agree."

Conner threw up his hands. "You found me oot, lass, but I'm a mon of my word. When you and the squire leave tomorrow morning, you'll do it alone."

She eyed him suspiciously. "And you won't attempt to win an invitation from poor Lance to join us?"

"I will nae."

"Oh." His capitulation threw her off balance. "Good. That's — I appreciate your cooperation. Thank you."

"Of course." His vivid gaze brushed over her face, lingering on her mouth. "Which means I've a huge task ahead of me."

"A task?"

"I must find a lady to wife before the clock

strikes the magic hour and the Douglas fortune ends up in Campbell coffers."

She blinked. "Is there no other way to meet the conditions of your sister's will?"

"My brother-in-law was most definite aboot it. We do this to the letter, or the funds are gone. And if 'tis nae you I'm to wed, then 'twill have to be another."

She hadn't thought about that. She should say something comforting like *I know you'll find a wonderful wife,* or *Best of luck,* and return to the safety of her room. But somehow the words that tumbled from her mouth were, "Do you have someone in mind?"

"Nae yet. I'll have to think on it." He sighed heavily. "I only hope you've nae ruined me for the lot of them. I'll be constantly comparing them, and they will fall short." He returned his hand to the wall near her head, and leaned forward to whisper in her ear, "Especially when it comes to kisses. There, you exceed all dreams."

God, he smelled so good, of sandalwood and fresh pine trees. She tried not to breathe more deeply than usual, and failed.

" 'Twill be a difficult task to find a lass like you." His warm breath brushed her cheek. "But if I must settle, then settle I will."

Settle — how I hate that word. She closed her eyes, trying hard not to hear the worries whispering in the back of her mind. *Careful; you're weakening.*

She slipped her hands behind her back and clasped them together tightly, then said as coolly as she could manage, "I can't imagine it is a good thing to settle in marriage. You could end up with someone quite unacceptable."

His blue gaze moved over her face. "You've settled. Why should nae I?"

How dare he! Why, Lance was — *Not Conner.* The words froze in her mind. *Good God, have I* settled *in marrying Lance?*

"Och, dinnae look so oopset. I'll find someone. There are plenty of women who'll welcome marriage with a privateer, so long as he has a guid name and a large fortune."

True — she could think of four well-born ladies right now who would jump at the chance to wed Conner. All of them had tossed lures his way over the years, though she doubted he'd noticed.

Two of them were decided flirts, and though they'd profess lasting love, they were sure to wander the first time he sailed over the horizon. The other two were of such pallid intelligence that he was sure to lose interest in them before the end of the wedding service.

None of them boded well for Conner's future happiness.

And she cared about his happiness. No matter what, he'd been her friend for a long, long time. "Surely you have *someone* in mind?"

He shrugged. "It dinnae matter. If 'tis nae you, then a wife is a wife."

She couldn't disagree more. He wasn't the sort of man who would be happy with a meek, mild woman, nor a shallow, silly one. He needed someone who would make him laugh at life's ironies, who would force him to face his own ridiculousness, who would show him that there was more to life than sailing away from it.

When he found that, he would fall in love deeply and forever.

And forget me completely. Her chest tightened, and she swallowed an uncomfortable lump. *It's good that I'm facing the truth. He will never fall in love with me; he's had plenty of opportunity and nothing happened.* She said in a tight voice, "I'm sure you'll find the right woman for a wife. Just . . . do not make the decision lightly."

"Och, Thea, if only —" His lashes lowered slightly, and he leaned forward until his face was even with hers.

For a startled moment she thought he would kiss her again, and a surge of shocking wildness raced through her, making her ache for his touch.

But he moved past her lips to her ear, where he whispered, *"Suirghe fada bhon aigh, 's posadh am bun an dorais."*

She turned her head, her eyes meeting his, her lips so, so, *so* near his. "What does that mean?" she whispered huskily.

His eyes darkened, and his gaze dropped to her mouth. "It means, 'Go courting afar, but marry next door.'"

"I don't understand."

He didn't answer, but shifted away, the humor gone from his face. "Rest assured I will nac embarrass myself in my choice of wife. Whomever I marry, 'twill be someone you dinnae mind seeing at your family's house on the holidays."

She gaped at him. "You'd . . . you'd bring your wife to our house?"

"Nae yours, for you'll be with the squire. But to your parents' house? Of course. I'll nae break that tradition and they, as weel as your brother, are still my dear friends."

Her heart sank. Of course he'd bring his new wife to Cumberbatch House, or to whatever embassy her father happened to be attached to. Conner had only missed two

Michaelmas meals in the last twelve years, joining them even when her family had been overseas.

She tried to imagine Conner at her family dining room table, where he'd been so many times before, but this time with a wife, someone he would gaze at in adoration.

Theodora found no comfort in the thought at all, and she was left with the horrifying realization that although she didn't dare risk marrying Conner herself, neither did she wish someone else to have him.

Aware that he was watching her, her heart beating sickly, she took a step toward the landing. "I should go now. Lance will be waiting."

"Thea, I —"

"No. I've — we've said enough." She dipped her head and hurried to the stairs, her heart dragging behind.

9

The next morning, Lance opened the door to the coach for Theodora's inspection.

She sighed happily when she saw the thickly padded seats, the heavy lap rugs, and the shiny gleam of brand-new foot warmers. She reached inside and rubbed her hand over the plush, soft velvet. "I've never seen such a luxurious coach."

Lance said in a wistful tone, "It's much better than my previous effort, isn't it?"

"Very much so." She caught the regret in his eyes and added quickly, "Not that the other carriage didn't have its charm, too. It was far more historical."

He chuckled. "That's kind of you, but the seats were deuced uncomfortable. Stuffed with horse hair, I've no doubt, which over time can pack down until a rock feels comfortable by comparison."

"It wasn't that bad."

He sent her a rueful look. "It was, and

you know it."

She laughed and stepped back so Lance could close the door. She tugged her gloves back on. "I wish we could have left yesterday."

He nodded in agreement. "So do I, but the horses are magnificent and we dared not overtire them. Luxury often carries certain responsibilities."

"At least we'll be on our way today." *And leave Conner behind.* After spending several hours last night watching him charm Lance into a sense of camaraderie that she was certain was false, she'd expected to be more than ready to leave Conner in her wake. Instead, she felt anxious and unsure.

Stop it! That's exactly what Conner wants, and I will not give him the satisfaction. She lifted her chin, pasted on a smile, and asked, "When do we leave?"

"I'm to fetch Miss Simmons soon. Once I bring her here, the servants will load our luggage and we'll be off."

Theodora nodded, wishing they didn't have to wait for the chaperone. But there was nothing to be done for it; Lance was decided. And, even though it had been Conner's idea originally, perhaps Lance had a point. This was no longer a simple overnight elopement, but a journey of several days.

The inn door swung open on its creaky hinges and Conner stepped out, the wind ruffling his hair as he approached. He examined her in that deucedly uncomfortable way he had, his hot gaze lingering on her hair, her mouth, and then moving to the lace at her bosom. Instinctively, she tugged her pelisse closed and buttoned it to her neck.

But that didn't stop the slow, steady flush that traveled across her, prickling the skin on her neck. She bit her lip in an effort to stop the sensations, wishing he'd stop looking at her like that. But it wasn't in his nature to hide his desires. She wondered if that boldness had come from spending so much time at sea, unfettered by society and as free as the wind to go where he wished.

"Your equipage is beyond compare." Lance, still looking at the coach, nodded his approval.

"So it is." Conner's gaze never left Theodora, and his eyes glinted with humor.

She frowned at him. "Your *coach* is beyond compare."

Lance gave a surprised laugh. "Theodora, I just said that."

"So you did." Conner grinned and turned to the squire. "I trust you find it sufficient to carry you on your journey."

"I cannot imagine a more well-equipped coach. I'm tempted to take a nap in it right now."

"Feel free. When one is used to being at sea, travel on land seems unnecessarily harsh, so I spend a wee bit extra on my conveyances. The true genius in the design is the suspension."

"I look forward to testing it. I'm off to fetch the chaperone soon, and will return with a report."

"I await your verdict." Conner slid his gaze back to Theodora with a smile. "You must be well pleased. Soon you will feel a maiden of fifteen again, shadowed by a chaperone, your virtue protected by hawkish eyes."

Truth be told, Conner's hot stare already made her feel like an uncertain miss. She ignored his words and said in a bland tone, "Thank you for offering your coach. I wish we could leave this instant."

"Eager to be wed, are you?"

"I am!" Lance took Theodora's hand and pressed a fervent kiss to her fingers. "I'd fly if I could."

Conner's faint smile disappeared and his lashes dropped to obscure his expression. "You are valiant, Squire."

Valiant — as if it took bravery to fall in

love with her? She sniffed her disapproval as she reclaimed her hand from Lance.

Conner's gaze met hers. "And you, Thea. Are you ready?"

Ready. Such a simple word, and yet it meant so many things. The word hit her like a wall collapsing upon her head. *Was* she ready? She found herself looking at Lance, who blandly smiled, unaware of her turbulent thoughts. She couldn't ask for a kinder husband . . . but was that enough? What *was* enough?

While Lance seemed unaware her thoughts were in turmoil, Conner's brows had lowered, a question in his eyes. "Thea?"

She collected herself. "Of course I'm ready. Spencer ironed my last gown this morning. He's been performing miracles."

"Spencer?" Lance asked.

"My footman and bos'n's mate," Conner said. "Yesterday, I sent him to assist Thea with her wardrobe."

Lance looked surprised.

"He's extremely talented," Theodora assured him. "My gowns have never looked so well."

"Then that's another note of thanks we owe you, Douglas. That was quite kind of you."

Conner shrugged. "It was nothing."

But in a way, it was. Conner evaluated everything with a pragmatic eye for comfort, ease, and convenience. Things that she and he both considered important — like the quality of a coach's suspension or the seats, or whether one had proper clothing to wear and if it was warm or dry enough — Lance never gave a thought to. She was beginning to realize that even though he was quite well off and enjoyed all the advantages of that, life was only about expedience for him, while quality and comfort were much less so. Today Lance would enjoy riding in Conner's luxurious coach, but sometime during the course of their travels, the squire would also decide that such luxury was unnecessary and frivolous.

Lance turned to her now. "I must fetch Miss Simmons, but I will return soon."

Theodora murmured her agreement, and he climbed into the coach and tapped the ceiling to alert the coachman. The restless grays began to move, and the coach rolled smoothly out of the inn yard.

As soon as the coach was out of sight, Conner faced her, a mischievous twinkle in his eyes. "Alone at last." He stepped toward her.

She threw up a hand. "Stop right there."

A challenge warmed his smile yet more.

"What's the matter, Thea? Afraid?"

"Of you? Never." *Always.* As she spoke, the inn door opened and, to her intense relief, Spencer appeared.

"Dammit," Conner muttered. "Am I to never have a moment alone with you?"

She sincerely hoped not.

Spencer joined them. "There you are, miss! I oversaw the proper packing of your portmanteau and small trunk, so everything is ready."

"Thank you; I don't know how I'll get on without you. I don't suppose I could hire you away from the good captain?"

Conner snorted. "Belay, lass! You're nae trying to steal my men right in front of me, are you?"

She looked at him with raised brows and he gave a sheepish grin. "I suppose I've been guilty of worse than stealing a servant, havenae I? But all's fair in love and war." The twinkle remained in his eyes and it both unsettled her and drew her closer.

She was glad when he turned to Spencer. "Do nae let this woman convince you to abandon your post. She's a siren, she is, and will make you do things you'll regret."

"Aye, aye, Cap'n!" The footman grinned. "And, miss, as I'm traveling with the coach,

I'll still be available to assist you during your trip."

"You're going with us?"

"Aye, miss. The Cap'n thought it best if you and the squire had the benefits on your journey of what servants are available."

"Meanwhile, I'm left withoot." Conner sighed as if plagued by the thought, although she knew better. "By the by, Spencer, did you find time to pack my bags, or am I to do it myself?"

"I packed your things early this morning, sir."

"Excellent. I'll save the cat o' nine tails for another day, then."

The footman chuckled. "I will fetch the bags." He bowed, and then left.

Theodora watched him as he disappeared back into the inn. "Spencer's a good man."

"Verrah. Sometimes I think he believes me a bit of a loose cannon."

"You *are* a loose cannon."

"Only with you, love."

Her cheeks heated. He tossed out the word "love" as if it meant nothing, and although she knew better, she couldn't stop a tiny trill of happiness from racing through her. She hated that, even as she was unable to stop it.

Well, if she couldn't stop her reactions,

she could at least put some space between them. "I just remembered that I left my reticule in the parlor. I must fetch it." She headed for the door.

To her chagrin, Conner fell in beside her.

Protesting would reveal her weakness, so instead, she asked in what she hoped was a casual tone, "Where will you go once we leave?"

He opened the door and stood to one side. "I've an inheritance to win, remember? So I must marry."

She stepped inside the hallway and walked toward the parlor. "Do you have someone in mind yet?"

Conner followed her inside. "Aye."

Theodora continued to the parlor even as her heart gave a sick thud. "Already? That was quick."

He shrugged. "You ordered me to find another."

She had, hadn't she? She just wished he hadn't told her about it. In less than an hour, he'd be off to make this woman, whoever she was, his wife. Theodora decided that the less she knew, the better. But as if her brain and head were no longer connected, she heard herself ask, "She is beautiful, I suppose."

"Of course."

"And well bred?"

"Naturally. And one of the most intelligent women I know," Conner added, watching Thea's ever-changing expressions.

Her brows drew together, and she looked less than pleased. He hid his smile. He'd been thinking of Thea when he'd described his phantom intended, and it was gratifying to detect a bit of jealousy in her gaze.

Hmm, perhaps I should pursue this. Sometimes we don't appreciate what we might have until the choice is gone. It's true of how I feel about her. Would she feel the same about me if I were no longer available? He made his way to the fireplace, his gaze never leaving her. "Soon, we will both be wed."

Thea picked up her reticule from a table beside the fireplace. "Do I know her?"

"Oh yes. Very well."

"What's her name?"

"Och, I'm nae one to flash a lady's name aboot until I've a reason. If — *when* she agrees to wed me, I'll introduce you."

Thea didn't look pleased with that announcement. "I'm sure that would be lovely."

"Aye. I'll be off to make her mine as soon as you and the squire leave."

"I — I hope you've thought this through."

"I've given my coming marriage as much

thought as you have yours."

She flushed, and said in a brittle tone, "Our cases are not the same."

"They are exactly the same. We decided we needed to marry, and whilst our reasons might be different, our methods were equally quick. Besides, I'm only doing as you asked, although it goes sorely against my principles."

"Your principles allow you to seduce a woman already engaged to another man. I hardly feel they will suffer should you decide to become a respectable husband and a more worthy member of society."

"Lass, you know how to put the worst light on things when it comes to me."

"I know you, and you never do anything unless it benefits you."

Conner's smile slipped. "I dinnae deserve that."

Her eyes blazed, and he thought she would argue. Then her shoulders slumped and she grimaced. "I'm sorry — I'm just in a quarrelsome mood this morning. You've been everything kind. You gave up your coach, and sent Spencer to assist with my wardrobe, as well as offering up your other servants. You've been kind. I'm just . . ." She shook her head. "I'm suspicious. You're not one to give up on something, and this seems like a sudden reversal."

"I'm nae happy with your decision, as you know. I still think you would be the best wife I could wish for. But you've said nae, so there's nae much I can do aboot it, is there?"

"No."

There was uncertainty in her brown eyes, and more than a little worry. *Which that fool of a squire didn't even notice. The man is blind.* Frowning, Conner captured her hand and held it between his own. "What's wrong, lass? You dinnae look happy."

She flushed and pulled her hand free. "I'm fine."

"Come. We've never held back from one another. Why would we start now?"

"Because things are different now."

The words sliced him and he found himself blustering. "Nonsense. Things are nae a bit different and —"

"They are," she said sharply. "And you know it."

The finality of her words sent him reeling and he felt off balance, as if he were trying to keep his footing on a storm-wet deck, but he couldn't refute the truth she'd spoken. *Bloody hell, things have changed between us, and they will keep changing.* God, he hated that.

Her lashes lowered and she looked at her clasped hands, her expression hidden. "Sadly, the time for us to share secrets is long gone."

"But, Thea, who else can you talk to, if nae me? There's nae one else here."

That seemed to catch her, for she paused, her gaze searching his face. Finally, she shook her head. "No. It's not wise."

"Perhaps nae, but 'tis all you have." He softened his voice. "Come. Tell me what's wrong."

She bit her lip. "You'll keep this in confidence?"

"Always." He would never betray her — not if he were flogged and keelhauled within an inch of his life. The strength of his feelings surprised him, though they shouldn't — as she'd pointed out, they'd known one another for a long time.

"I . . . this whole thing is . . ." Emotion caught her, and she took a deep breath before she whispered, "I wonder if I know what I'm doing."

Conner fought the urge to sweep her into his arms, though it cost him sorely. She was like a fawn in the woods, and he knew better than to move too quickly or risk startling her and sending her fleeing. He had to proceed carefully, or the moment — and she — would be gone. Perhaps forever.

The thought burned like acid and he had to clear his throat before he said in a careful tone, "How so?"

She clutched her reticule tighter, as if afraid it might disappear. "This elopement, Lance — all of it! I was certain I knew what I was doing, that this was what I wanted, but . . ."

"Now you're nae certain?"

"I suppose everyone has such moments before they wed. And Lance is a stalwart, trustworthy man — and more. He cares for me, or seems to, and that's a good beginning. But then things went wrong with this journey — the carriage, the accident, and then you showed up . . . and now I wonder if I should be here at all?"

Hope warmed Conner. "So my coming here made things worse?"

"Of course, because I —" Her gaze locked with his as the words froze on her tongue.

"Because why?"

She shook her head, her thick lashes lowering to obscure her gaze.

She's not telling me something. "Come, Thea. How did my arrival make things worse? Is it because we kissed?"

A deep flush rose to her cheeks, but she turned her gaze to her reticule, nervously sliding her fingers through the fringe. "The kiss wasn't — I'm not — You don't need —" She shook her head. "It's nothing. Forget I said anything."

He moved closer and placed a finger under her chin and tilted her face to his. "Tell me, Thea. Please. Why did my coming here make things worse?"

She met his gaze, and something flickered in her eyes. She looked — What? Before he could fathom it, she mumbled, "No. No," shifting as if to move away.

He couldn't let her go. If he did, she'd leave, and this delicate moment would disappear like foam upon restless waves. Without another thought, Conner bent and captured her lips with his.

For a long second, neither moved. A jolt of heat sizzled through Conner as he savored Thea's warm, soft lips. He kissed her again with more urgency, slipping his hand about her waist.

She shivered once, and then melted against him, her reticule dropping to the floor as she slid one arm around his neck and grasped his lapel with the other.

He deepened the kiss, teasing her lips over and over until, with a moan, she parted them. Her sweetness tormented his senses, awakening every fiber of his being. He plundered her mouth, tasting her, his body afire with each new discovery.

Why had he never thought to kiss her in all the years they'd known one another? So many wasted, wasted years. Her kisses were tantalizingly delicious and now she was kissing him back, her tongue brushing his, rousing a passion so blindingly hot that he could only react. She took every act of his and reflected it back, with a thousand times more passion and sensuality.

With her hand pressed to his chest, she had to be aware of his thundering heart. Surprised at the strength of his own reaction, he pulled her closer, and kissed her with every iota of his being.

To his delight she pressed back, her body molding to his, her mouth opening greedily, her tongue touching his —

She broke the kiss with a gasp. Flushed, her lips damp from their kisses, breathing hard as if she'd been running, she backed away, shaking her head. "No! This is wrong! I swore I'd never do this again and I — I can't. I just can't."

"Thea —" He stepped toward her, determined to get her back in his arms.

"Stay where you are."

He did as she asked, although it went against every instinct he had. "Thea, please.

That was —"

"A mistake." Her voice shook, as did her hand as she brushed her fingers over her lips, a stricken look in her eyes.

Her reaction cooled his passion instantly. "Lass, please. I dinnae mean to oopset you. 'Twas just a kiss —"

She stiffened. "*Just* a kiss?"

"Aye. And a damned guid one, too." His body was still afire, his brain muddled by the kisses, the softness of her lips, the look he thought he'd seen in her eyes — God, what had just happened? "Your kisses are as beguiling as the sea, unlike any I've ever had, and I've had a guidly bit of experience."

He regretted the words as soon as he said them.

Displeasure flashed through her eyes. "*Oh!* So not only was it *just* a kiss, but now you're bragging that you've kissed so many *other* women."

Good God, had he said that? She had him so muddled! "That's nae what I meant."

"But it's true, isn't it? You've kissed dozens, perhaps hundreds of women. Haven't you?"

How did he answer that? If he said nae she wouldn't believe him (and with reason), and if he agreed, he looked a loose-moraled

171

fool. Best to proceed cautiously. He spread his hands wide. "I've kissed my fair share, but —"

"Your fair share." She looked disgusted with herself. "What was I thinking? I'm a fool."

"You're nae such thing, and you know it. Lass, you're making much oot of nothing. What's important is what just happened; we've fire between us. Admit it."

She straightened her shoulders. "It doesn't matter; I'm engaged. I made a commitment. That may not mean anything to you, but it does to me and I cannot — will not — allow this to happen again."

"You said you were having second thoughts," he hurried to point out.

Her face pinkened yet more. "I was a fool to admit that to you. But it's only normal, I'm sure. And that — that kiss just confirmed it. Lance is the right man for me."

"Bloody hell!" Conner raked a hand through his hair. "Thea, that kiss dinnae prove a damn thing aboot you and Lance. 'Twas aboot you and *me*. And you have to admit 'twas worthwhile. To be honest, I dinnae expect you to be so guid, nae after the last time —" Her expression froze his tongue in place, and he could have kicked himself. *Guid lord, that kiss has turned me into a bloody pumpkin.*

He threw up a hand before she could speak. "I worded that poorly. I just meant the first kiss — while excellent — was nae as guid as these last ones. You were a bit new then, but you're a quick learner and —" He winced at the fury he saw in her eyes. "Och, I'm making a mess of this." He shook his head helplessly. "You set me afire, lass. I dinnae expect that."

"You should stop talking."

He nodded, unable to disagree. Yet he couldn't stop looking at her with a new awareness. Had her brown eyes always been so thickly lashed? Her mouth so beguiling? Her hair so silky soft that he longed to unpin it and sink his fingers in those golden brown strands?

Her eyes flashed as if she'd like to strike him, yet all he could think about was how delectable she looked. "I vow, it's as if I never knew you," he said softly.

She sent him a flatly irritated look. "You knew me; you just didn't pay attention. I was like a — a piece of furniture. You never really *looked* at me, did you?"

"I paid attention to you," he protested, a little surprised by her vehemence.

"Really?"

How could any man answer such a disbelieving look? "Aye. And I've always been there when I knew you needed it. Did I nae come to you in Italy when your mother was so ill that you and Derrick thought her as good as gone? And what aboot the time Sergeant Tibbs died? As soon as Derrick told me what happened, I traveled three hours in the rain to come and help."

A flicker of sadness crossed her face. "He was the best cat ever."

"He was. And it was an honor to be the one to bury him for you."

"Under the yew tree in the garden." A sad smile softened her expression. "You gave a lovely eulogy."

"He deserved one. He was a guid cat, even if he did bite."

Her lips quirked. "He never liked you."

"I liked him in spite of that," Conner admitted grudgingly. "I've never seen a cat fetch before or since."

She started to reply, but caught herself and instead turned away, her shoulders sagging as she dropped her face into her hands. "Oh, Conner, what are you doing?"

"I think you know."

"I do know. And it's wrong." She dropped her hands to her sides, facing him with grim clarity. "You must leave. Go, find this woman you were telling me about, and settle your inheritance."

"And you?"

"I'll marry Lance. It's what I'm meant to do. I'm certain of it now."

Dammit, how had they gotten to this? He'd thought she had changed her mind, but now she seemed firmer than ever in her resolution to marry the squire. "You have doubts about Lance."

"I did, but no more. I will not hurt him." She crossed her arms, almost hugging herself, her eyes soft with regret. "If only you hadn't come. Having you here is — difficult."

"Why?"

"I don't know. But I wish you hadn't found me. Lance is my future. I must embrace that fact."

"Your future? Then what am I?"

"The past."

The words struck him like a ship's bow, ramming straight through his heart. He looked at her mouth, still damp from his kiss, and he firmed his jaw. "Present or past, I'm here now. And it would be wrong if we dinnae discover why we react so strongly to one another."

"I will not hurt Lance. I cannot."

Dammit, she was so bloody stubborn. And if he kept pressing, it would only set her more firmly in her decision.

Gritting his teeth, he threw up his hands. "Fine! If you'll nae have me, then I'd best return to thinking of someone else."

Her gaze narrowed suspiciously. "Was there someone else? Or did you just say that to get me to lower my guard?"

"Lass, as beautiful as you are, if you say nae, then nae it is." He rubbed his neck, thinking quickly. "If you'll nae have me, then I'll go north to . . ." Bloody hell, who lived in the north? He only knew a few families in that direction with marriageable daughters and — Ah. "Wentlow Manor."

She blinked. "Wentlow? The Lambert family?"

The Lamberts were friends of the Cumberbatch-Snowes, and during some of Conner's visits he'd met the family — a son Derrick's age and four daughters, all a bit younger than Thea, and quite pretty in a vapid sort of way. At the time Conner had thought them just a pack of gigglers, but they were well born, and not unpleasing. It was the best he could do, considering the circumstances. "Aye," he repeated grimly, "the Lamberts."

"I see." She pressed a hand to her stomach as if to still a sudden roil. "Which daughter will you court?"

"Whichever will have me."

Thea gaped at him. "You don't have a favorite?"

He thought about it. "I suppose the tall one would be a guid choice. She dinnae talk as much as the others."

"That's — I can't even — Conner, that makes no sense. You'd pick a wife based on her *lack* of conversation?"

"Why nae? If I cannae have you, I dinnae care who I wind oop with. But I dinnae wish to listen to idle chatter all day, so a woman who'll nae talk would be best."

"Conner, no! You don't know the Lamberts, *any* of them, not really."

"You are marrying someone you barely know."

She flushed. "I know Lance better than you know Letitia." She rubbed her temples as if they ached. "I cannot believe this. You're going to offer for *Letty*?"

"Why nae? She always flirted with me — they all did."

"The Lamberts are known for that."

"So she'll be guid at it, if she's been practicing. And as her family is in need of financial assistance, they'll welcome my suit." Eagerly, which is why Conner had vowed to never cross the threshold of Wentlow Manor without a guard.

But all Thea needed to know was that he had his sights set elsewhere, which should assuage some of her fears. "I'm sure this Letty and I will make a decent marriage, if nae the best. She seemed very biddable, which is guid, too."

Theodora felt as if someone had punched her in the stomach, removing the last lingering bit of passion that had roared through her at Conner's kisses. "I'm surprised you've singled out Letty. She may not chatter like her sisters, but you said the hair on her chin was unacceptable."

Conner frowned. "I dinnae remember any of them had hair on their chins."

"Letty did," Theodora said firmly, wondering if she should feel remorse for telling lies about people she barely knew.

He shrugged. "Then I will go for another one. The buxom one, what was her name?"

"Lenora."

"I'll court her, then."

"You used to call Lenora 'Loud Lenora,' I remember that, for I begged you not to do so within her hearing."

"Och, so I did. She talked as if her words were afire and she was trying to outrun them. That will nae do." He grimaced and rubbed his neck. "Och, this is a pain. What aboot the short one?"

"That's Lydia."

"Lydia, then." His smile didn't reach his eyes. "I'd best remember her name, or I'll end oop with the wrong one and find myself shackled to a chatterbox or worse." His gaze dropped to Thea's mouth. "I wonder how Lydia will kiss? Nae matter. If she does nae do it weel, then I'll teach her."

A hot flash of jealousy sucked Theodora's breath away. The strength of it shocked her, making her wonder how she'd ever thought she could easily purge him from her life. She should have been relieved that he was setting his sights elsewhere, but all she could muster was a brittle, "I hope you'll be happy."

He lifted a shoulder. "I will have kept the Douglas fortune from the Campbells. That will have to be satisfaction enough."

"Yes, but —" The sound of the coach rattling into the inn yard made her glance at the window. "There's Lance." She and Conner were out of time. She wished miserably that she knew what to say to turn him from his disastrous path, but she had no words. Nothing but a nauseous certainty that he was about to make the biggest mistake of his life.

Conner's gaze swept over her with obvious regret. "That's it, then. Good luck,

Thea. I wish you the best."

She struggled to find words, but none would come. After an awkward moment, Conner bowed and — with a final lingering look — left, his steady footsteps fading as he walked down the hall and went outside.

Theodora went to the window and watched as Conner greeted Lance and the new chaperone, a small woman so enveloped in an overly large pelisse and bonnet that it was impossible to make out her features.

Theodora's mind raced, her heart sick. What a coil! She'd expected to be happy and excited about her elopement, but all she could think about was Conner's error in marrying one of the Lambert chits. And added were those tempting, forbidden kisses. Why didn't she feel that same passion with Lance?

But I haven't kissed him. Perhaps that is why. Whatever the problem was, she had to figure it out soon, or there would be no turning back.

Sighing heavily, she picked up her reticule from where she'd dropped it on the floor and made her way to the inn yard.

10

Lance brightened as Theodora joined him by the coach. "There you are!" He lowered his voice. "Miss Simmons seems charming."

Theodora's new traveling companion stood by the coach talking to Conner, peering up at him with a mixture of awe and amazement. Dressed in a faded pelisse with a straw bonnet that framed her pretty face, the chaperone was much younger than Theodora had expected. Small and wrenlike, with dark brown hair that curled about a heart-shaped face and soft blue-gray eyes, she wore a perpetually startled expression, as if she expected harshness from the world at large. "Miss Simmons appears quite young. She can't be more than eighteen."

"She's twenty-three, although I would not have credited it when I first saw her, either. She seems younger because of her mannerisms." Lance watched Miss Simmons a moment, his expression softening into a smile as he confided, "She reminds me of my sisters, who've had such sheltered lives that they seem younger than their ages."

Theodora added drily, "Unlike me, who seems much *older* than my age because I've never been 'sheltered.' "

He flushed. "No, no! I never said —"

"Oh, Lance!" She laughed, amused at his obvious alarm. "I was only teasing, although I'm sure I was never young for my age. With Papa dragging us from one end of the world to the other, and Mama always too ill to tend to things, I undertook a lot of responsibility at an early age. But I enjoyed it."

Lance nodded thoughtfully. "Meanwhile, the opposite seems to be true for Miss Simmons. She was thrust into the world before she was ready. From something she let fall when she introduced herself, I believe that while her brother would like her to remain with him, his new wife is determined that should not be the case."

"No! And that wretched woman has pushed the poor girl out of the house?"

"The sister-in-law was almost gleeful when she discovered I'd come to fetch Miss Simmons. It was deuced awkward."

"Oh dear." Aware that her own favorable circumstances were a matter of chance and birth, Theodora was always sympathetic to the plight of single women who'd been forced to find a position in order to make their way. There were so few respectable jobs available to women, and even fewer where they were not improperly importuned by their employers. "I was so dreading having a chaperone that I never thought if the position would be advantageous for the lady in question. I feel quite selfish."

"You're far from being selfish. I *knew* you'd feel for her once you realized her circumstances." Lance captured Theodora's hand and pressed a fervent kiss to it. "You are truly the kindest, the most giving woman I've ever met. You are perfect, truly perfect."

Except she wasn't. She was sometimes impatient and impetuous — and far, far too attracted to someone who wasn't her fiancé. Her cheeks hot, she freed her hand. "You think too well of me. If you knew me better, you would never say such things."

"I don't hand out compliments easily. I mean what I say, and you are a good, caring woman. Indeed, your comportment is almost angelic."

"Good heavens, Lance! Next you will be pinning wings on me in the mad belief I can fly! I'm no paragon of virtue — far from it." Seeing his crestfallen look, she slipped her hand into the crook of his arm, although

183

she wished he saw her more realistically. "See, I've managed to make you miserable with just a few words. It would be my fault if you decided to leave me here to elope alone."

He gave a reluctant laugh. "You do not count yourself highly enough. But I see it makes you uncomfortable when I mention such things, so I will say no more."

"Good! Introduce me to this young girl you've hired. I fear I shall forget who is chaperoning whom."

He chuckled, patting her hand as he led her forward. As soon as they reached Miss Simmons, the chaperone dipped a quick curtsy.

Lance smiled. "Miss Simmons, allow me to introduce Miss Cumberbatch-Snowe."

"Oh! I'm so pleased! I cannot thank you enough for this opportunity, although I'm sorry to hear you were tossed into a ditch. How awful for you."

Theodora caught Conner's amused gaze. "Ah, so Mr. Douglas has been spreading tales, has he? Let me assure you that I'm perfectly fine now."

"If that had happened to me, I don't think I would ever get into a coach again."

"But how would you travel?"

Miss Simmons shook her head. "I

wouldn't. Not even if the coach were made of gold and had diamond wheels. If one threw me into a ditch, I'd never set foot in it again."

"We'll hope you never end up in a ditch, then. Fortunately for us all, this new coach is more stable."

"It's a wonderful conveyance," Lance said. "We will be most comfortable." He turned to Conner. "Those grays are magnificent. I've never seen such a set."

Conner eyed the horses with a satisfied air. "I paid far too much for them, but I cannae regret it."

"Were they purchased from Tattersall's? I so longed to go there when I was a youth, but sadly I never made it to London. Thus, I was left with the guidebooks that made the auction house seem like a heaven on earth."

" 'Tis a place like no other. And yes, that's where I found them. They were the Duke of Devonshire's. You'd never know him to be the wealthiest man in England, the way he bargained."

That led Lance into recalling a spirited haggle he'd had over a pair of lumbering yard horses, and he described the exchange with enthusiasm.

While Lance talked, Theodora was aware

of Conner's gaze, which rested on her frequently. Her body quivered every time his attention turned to her. As difficult as it was, she made sure she hid every tremble and every flash of remembered passion, longing for the privacy of her room to indulge in a spate of deep, deep sighs. Things had changed so much in the last few days, and it had all begun with that first blasted kiss. Her feelings were so different from when she'd silently longed for him and he'd remained blissfully unaware.

Now, she longed for him in a new, even more devastating way. He was just so blasted appealing, with that direct gaze that made her shiver as she imagined —

"Theodora?"

She blinked and discovered Lance looking at her with an odd expression. She smiled apologetically. "I'm sorry. My mind wandered."

Conner — blast him — smirked as if he knew exactly what she'd been thinking.

"Mr. Douglas and I were talking about horses and Miss Simmons said she did not ride, so I asked you the same."

"Oh, I love to ride."

"Thea is a capital rider," Conner added.

Lance said, "I should have known you were a good rider. You're good at everything you put your mind to."

Miss Simmons appeared envious. "My brother has only two carriage horses, both so slow that my sister-in-law is forever vexed. I wish I knew how to ride, but frankly, horses frighten me. They're just so *large.*"

Theodora tsked. "You've just never met the right horse. Once this journey is done and we're home at Cumberbatch House, you may ride Dumpling. She's a small, gentle mare."

Lance laughed uneasily. "Theodora, we will not be going 'home' to Cumberbatch House, but to Poston."

His words stopped her. "Oh — yes. Of course. I don't know what I was thinking." Somehow in the excitement of her elopement, Theodora hadn't really thought about the specifics of what would happen afterward. About *his* home now being *hers.*

I'm never going home again. The thought was as final and heavy as a huge rock, and her heart squeezed unexpectedly. She loved Cumberbatch House and would miss it.

Conner's eyes narrowed in concern. "You and the squire will visit Cumberbatch often," he said softly. "Is it far away? I dinnae suppose it was."

She grasped his words with relief. "No.

187

It's not far at all. An hour, no more." Yes. She would visit Cumberbatch. She could indeed go home whenever she wished.

But it wouldn't be the same.

"Of course you'll visit." Lance looked surprised she'd thought anything else. "I have a carriage, and Old Markham will be your driver. He's not fast, and our set of grays not nearly as pretty as these, but they suffice. Naturally you can visit however often you wish. Although —" He smiled. "I will hope it will not be too often."

"Of course!" She glanced up at the sky. "Oh, my. There are clouds to the north. It looks as if it might rain soon."

"We should be on our way, then," Lance announced.

"Here come the postboys with my trunk." Theodora turned to Miss Simmons. "Let's make sure they lash it on correctly; my clothes don't need any more experiences with ditches."

Conner watched as Thea led the chaperone away. The two of them made a pretty pair. Whereas Thea was tall, fair, slender of build, and exuded a natural confidence, Miss Simmons was tiny, brunette, and had a pretty but anxious face. He couldn't imagine two women more different.

"Theodora will enjoy having a female to

talk to." The squire said it as if it were a fact merely because he'd announced it to be so.

"Hmm. Does Miss Simmons read?"

"Read? I don't know. But she knits; her basket is in the coach."

"Thea dinnae knit, nor does she embroider. Perhaps Miss Simmons gardens?"

"Not that I know of."

"Then hopefully Miss Simmons has an excellent sense of humor. They will get along famously if she does."

Lance's brows drew together. "Theodora knows Miss Simmons is in an awkward position, so I'm sure they'll deal just fine."

"Thea is always polite," Conner said far more sharply than he intended. At Lance's surprised look, he added in a milder tone, "I hope Miss Simmons and Thea have something in common. Otherwise, they will chaff at being within the close confines of a coach for hours on end."

"You need not worry about such." Lance turned a fond glance to where Thea stood. "Theodora's kind heart will never allow her to be small-minded or ungenerous. She is a paragon of feminine virtue."

Conner frowned. While he knew better than anyone else that Thea was a remarkable woman, she wasn't some dull portrait of impossible perfection. "I've known Thea for a long time, and while I appreciate her good qualities, she is nae a paragon, nor would I wish her to be."

Lance's gaze remained on Thea and he said with a decidedly proprietary air that irked Conner nigh to death, "My intended is a marvelous example of womanhood even though she may need coaching in some areas, which is perfectly understandable when one knows the deficiencies of her upbringing."

"Deficiencies?"

"She has lived abroad much of her life and has become a bit more independent than is attractive. But I'm certain that once she's settled at Poston House under the tutelage of my mother and sisters, Theodora will blossom into her true potential."

Conner fought to contain his outrage over the man's smug determination that Thea needed "coaching" of any kind. While she was far more colorful and much too lively to meet society's narrow definition of "feminine virtue," she didn't need "coaching." She had a sharp wit and a clever tongue, and although she struggled at times to curb them both at the same time, she was without question the kindest, most caring person he knew.

Obviously Lance did not feel the same

way, which made Thea's determination to marry him even more alarming. Worse, that determination seemed to grow by the minute. A chilling thought struck Conner. *Bloody hell, am I pushing her toward a man who can't understand her uniqueness, who would try to change her? Is my pursuit chasing her into the squire's arms?*

Conner's gaze went to Thea and his chest tightened. She was beautiful, and fascinating, and intelligent, and Lance was a damned fool to not see and appreciate her as she was.

The trunks now secured, Thea and Miss Simmons rejoined the men.

Miss Simmons smiled at Conner. "Mr. Douglas, if we have your coach, how will you get on?"

"By horse. I'm headed to Wentlow Manor, which lies north of here."

Lance looked surprised. "North? We are going the same direction, then."

"So we are, although you will nae be going as far."

"You're more than welcome to accompany us —"

"*No.*"

Lance and Miss Simmons looked astonished at Thea's outburst. She flushed and said in a stubborn tone, "Mr. Douglas is on

191

a romantic mission and will not want us around. In fact, he's on his way to visit a young lady, a mutual acquaintance of ours, and offer for her hand in marriage."

Lance eagerly turned to Conner. "And you never said a word! Congratulations. I hope you will be quite happy."

Conner shrugged. "I have to ask her first, although there are signs she'd nae refuse. She has indicated more than once that she'd welcome a relationship."

"Ah, how we look for those hints. I was quite uncertain how Theodora would receive my offer of marriage. She never seemed anything more than fond of me." The squire beamed at her. "Fortunately, she accepted my humble offer quickly and I was not left in agony for long."

Thea flushed. "Yes, well, it's getting late and we should be on our way." For the first time since he'd come outside, she faced Conner, holding out her hand.

He took it in his, her fingers cool between his own. "I hope your journey will be pleasant and give you time to reflect —"

"I'm sure it will. Good-bye and good luck with your endeavor." Stiff with haste, she pulled her hand free and hurried to Spencer, who waited by the coach door, ready to assist the ladies into their seats. He opened the door and pulled down the steps, and Thea disappeared into the coach.

With a breathless good-bye, Miss Simmons hurried to follow.

Lance tipped his hat. "Best of luck on your venture, Douglas."

"And you." Conner stepped back as the squire joined the ladies in the coach.

Spencer closed the door and, exchanging a knowing look with Conner, scrambled up onto the seat next to MacLeish, who set the horses in motion. Prancing, the team pulled the coach out of the inn yard.

Ferguson led Conner's horse from the stable and came to stand with him, watching the coach lumbering down the road. "I thought for certain you'd have convinced the lass to accept your proposal by now."

"She's as stubborn as the Horn," Conner returned tightly, taking the reins from Ferguson. "But I'll fight this battle to the ends of the earth and back."

"Guid for you, Cap'n. Show nae mercy! I'll fetch the cart and we'll be off."

"Be quick aboot it. We've a distance to travel." Conner couldn't fathom it; how in the hell had a stiff-necked prosy bore like Lance worked his way into Thea's good graces? Conner didn't know. All he knew was that for a man supposedly taken with

193

her, Lance knew damned little about her. Wouldn't a man who was truly in love, not merely infatuated, accept his beloved as she was? And wouldn't he learn everything he could about the woman he adored?

Wouldn't he know her well enough to know she'd be insulted if he'd hired a chaperone or a servant of any kind without discussing it with her first?

Wouldn't he know what sort of acquaintance his intended would converse comfortably with, and as an equal?

Wouldn't he notice when she grew flushed in the presence of another man?

Wouldn't he be tempted to watch her, to catch every nuance of her expression, to see when she was happy or worried or — Good God, *everything*?

Conner found himself doing those very things, and he wasn't in love with Thea, nor promised to marry her.

It made no sense unless . . . was it possible the squire valued Thea not for her specific person but for some sort of abstract, romanticized concept of femininity? If so, the man was a bloody fool. Thea would never be comfortable being defined in such a way.

It boded ill for their marriage, and while Thea was beginning to share Conner's concerns about her plans, she (and her pride) wasn't yet willing to give up her elopement. It was good she was going to be shut up in a coach with the man — chatting chaperone, bad roads, and all.

Anna had always said that if you wished to truly know someone, travel with them. Flaws were amplified, nerves strained, luggage lost or forgotten, rains came and went — that was a true test of a relationship. He could almost hear Anna saying it now and he smiled wistfully at the thought, wishing for the thousandth time that he could ask her advice. But it was not to be.

Still, he thought his sister would agree with his plan thus far, or most of it, anyway. Thea had to make this decision herself, and all he could do was make sure she had the time to consider it from all angles. Whether she knew it yet or not, there was only one man she would be comfortable with, whom she could be herself with — and that was *him*.

Conner watched the coach taking the final turn and he realized he could no longer hear the horses' hooves. He had to fight a very real desire to leap onto his horse, chase down the coach, plant a facer on the squire, throw Thea over his shoulder, and ride away with her into the sunset like a scene in an overly romantic play. *She would kick and scream and call me a thousand ill names. Patience will win this, not drama.*

The coach disappeared from sight, and Conner's heart sank. He'd never felt more alone in his entire life.

11

"Is it still raining?" Miss Simmons asked for at least the eighth time.

Repressing a sigh, Theodora turned from the window. "Yes. It's still raining." The gray afternoon matched her mood. She was unexpectedly low.

The chaperone smiled brightly. "I do love a rainy day. It's so cozy!"

Theodora smiled blandly and turned back to the window. Jane, as she'd asked to be called, was a sweet creature who was obviously addicted to knitting, working at a rate guaranteed to catch the wool on fire. Unfortunately she seemed to find companionable silences oppressive, for she often blurted out random thoughts all said in a breathless, hopeful voice that made Theodora grind her teeth. Meanwhile, Lance seemed enchanted by the chaperone's little-girl voice, and encouraged her by laughing in an obnoxiously indulgent manner at most of her senseless comments.

Twice now Theodora had imagined kicking open the coach door and jumping out to escape her chaperone's empty chatter and Lance's increasingly stifling presence. Such unworthy thoughts made Theodora wince at her short temper, for Jane seemed to be a genuinely *good* person, sweet tempered and as pure in intentions as driven snow, while Lance was — Well, he was still Lance, and Theodora had no reason to wish him to be otherwise.

No, the problem was with *her.* She was in an unexpectedly foul mood, and for no reason she could think of. She sighed as rain streaked across the window in oppressive bars that made her think of locked cages, and she remembered yet again her last sight of Conner.

A hollow sensation had settled in her chest at seeing him there, his feet planted as if he were on the deck of a ship, a lone figure at the wheel. Despite her irritation with him, Conner was still her good friend, so it was only natural that it had lowered her spirits to see him looking so alone.

Then again, he was often alone — except for his servants and Derrick, he had few friends. He was alone when he traveled, alone in the way he'd chosen the wild sea over a safe life on land, alone in all of his pursuits. He seemed oddly unaffected by his aloneness, and for some reason it made her wish to show him the value of being a part of something bigger. Something more lasting. Theodora suspected his sister Anna had wished the same, and that was the real reason behind the conditions of her will.

Conner was far more vulnerable than the bold face he presented to the world indicated. To someone who didn't know him, he appeared implacable and hardened, glib and always in control, but under that shell, she knew him to be warm and caring and capable of great love, which was proven by his deep affection for his siblings.

It was only when it came to romantic love that she was left wondering. She obviously wasn't the woman for Conner, but somewhere out there, some woman was. What sort of woman would it be?

She rubbed her arms, feeling as gray as the day. The coach swayed gently, the rain drumming lightly on the roof, the wheels splashing through deep puddles. Jane was right about one thing; it was cozy in the coach. The squabs were thickly padded, and warm woolen blankets were spread over their laps as their feet rested on foot warmers that had been refilled with hot coals at every stop.

She should have been chatting happily with her companions, enjoying the beautiful countryside that seemed greener and lusher with each passing mile, or dozing in a corner, oblivious to all of the world's discomforts. Instead she was restless and anxious, as if she'd left something behind. Something necessary.

She sighed. At least they were still able to travel despite the weather, although they'd had to stop twice now, once because Jane had pleaded motion sickness, and another time to rest the horses. At the last stop Lance had decided they might as well have tea, too, so they'd ended up spending almost an hour at the inn. *At this rate, I'll be a hundred years old before we reach Gretna Green, far too crotchety to want to marry anyone.*

The coach slowed, and Theodora looked out the window as they turned into a large inn set at the crossway of two roads. "Why are we stopping?"

"Because we're here," Lance said simply, as if that explained everything.

"Where's 'here'?"

"I hope we can importune the staff for some refreshment." Jane put her knitting back into the basket. "I could use a cup of hot tea to settle my stomach."

"Must we stop again?" Theodora asked.

"The horses must rest," Lance said.

"They've already been rested twice!"

Lance's mouth tightened. "I agreed to take care of Mr. Douglas's team, and I cannot risk them by pressing on without reason when —"

Spencer opened the door and let down the steps. Theodora, seeing Lance's unyielding expression, realized they'd get back on the road faster if she acquiesced. With a frustrated sigh, she climbed out of the coach and listlessly followed Lance and Jane into one of the inn's private parlors. She had to admit, it was a lovely inn, with large windows and red velvet curtains. The inn boasted two private parlors, a large and airy common room, and acceptable refreshments. Still, even fortified with hot tea and offered a piece of delicious lemon cake, her spirits remained low.

A short time later, she poked at her piece of cake with her fork while Lance — seemingly intent on cheering her up — pointed out that each turn of the wheels took them closer to Gretna. He then waxed eloquent about how he looked forward to "wedded bliss" and "the eternal promises of a happy home and hearth." The romantic-hearted

Jane thought it sigh-worthy and was clearly charmed by Lance's enthusiasm, while all Theodora could dredge up was a faint smile and an "Indeed."

Under normal circumstances she would have appreciated his attempts to paint their irksome travels with a romantic air, but the entire effort rang hollow and irritated her. She stared at the cake she'd just shredded with her fork. What *was* she so irked about? Why wasn't she happy to be heading into this fresh new phase of her life? She was certain it had nothing to do with Conner, who would now be on his merry way to Wentlow Manor. *As he should be.*

She put her plate on the table. "We should get back on the road."

Jane hesitated and then put down her cup of tea. "Of course."

Lance lowered the forkful of cake that was halfway to his mouth.

Theodora forced a smile and stood. "It was a lovely tea, but we should continue on."

"Not today," Lance said.

"Why not?"

Lance placed his fork on his plate. "We're staying here tonight."

"What?" Theodora couldn't keep her astonishment from her voice.

Even Jane looked surprised.

Lance frowned. "It's a very tidy inn, and I was told the food is exceptional, which this cake proved."

"The cake was delicious, but we've traveled less than half a day!"

"The next inhabitable inn is miles away and we couldn't possibly reach it tonight, so this is our best option."

"Who told you that?"

"Douglas's coachman, MacLeish." Lance added with enthusiasm, "The man is a gem! He has everything planned out. He has a complete itinerary with the distances we're to travel each day, which inns we're to stop at, where to find a decent tea — It's quite impressive."

She'd had no idea. "When did you see this itinerary?"

"This morning, after breakfast." He frowned. "Didn't you see it? I could have sworn Mr. Douglas said it had your approval. But perhaps he said he hoped it *would* have your approval. I should have mentioned it to you."

Theodora didn't trust herself to answer as a horrible suspicion began to raise its head.

Looking nervously from Theodora to Lance, Jane said in a bright tone, "It's quite thoughtful of Mr. Douglas's coachman to go to such lengths."

Theodora said tightly, "Isn't it?"

"Oh yes! My brother uses a travel book to plan his trips, and it does the same — lists the distances between small towns and where there are lodgings to be had, and such. I prefer to have that sort of knowledge when I travel, so there are no unpleasant surprises."

Yes, well, Theodora would have done so, too, *if* she could have trusted Conner and his servants. Sadly, she wouldn't put it past the wretch to slow their progress as much as he could, if for no other reason than to put his stamp on their journey. Blast that man! She turned to Lance. "We should go, itinerary or not. So long as we rest the team properly, it would do them no harm to pull the coach another ten or more miles today. As to restricting ourselves to only the inns on this list, I'm sure we can find others that are equally sufficient for our needs."

Lance didn't look convinced. "A bang-up team cannot work the same long hours as common job horses. We've been traveling so much faster than we might have been, that I'm sure we've covered the same distance, even with the reduced travel time. Besides, we're in no hurry; we've a chaperone now, so the proprieties have been seen to."

"Lance, please. We could make much better progress than this."

"Perhaps, but I've no desire to return Douglas's horses to him in less-than-perfect condition." Lance smiled and stood, taking her hand between his. "Come, Theodora. Enjoy the journey! Don't you find it exciting to be traveling in such a luxurious coach through the countryside, on our way to Gretna Green? It's the stuff of all romantic plays!"

So far, the trip had been more a bumbling comedy than a romance, but she wisely held her tongue. "I'm enjoying the trip," she lied. "But I'm anxious for it to be over with, so that the coach can be returned to Conner with all possible speed."

Jane sent Theodora an understanding glance. "You dislike borrowing Mr. Douglas's conveyance."

"And his servants. It was kind of him, but — it may sound odd to you, but it feels as if we're burdened with his presence because of it."

"I understand completely." Jane sighed in sympathy as she picked up her knitting basket and began to look through the contents. "It is sometimes a burden to be beholden to someone, even when their intentions are noble."

Theodora had to bite her tongue to keep from announcing that Conner was far from noble. She couldn't tell them she suspected him of slowing their trip without also explaining why the lout might wish to do so, which left her with no way of explaining herself.

"Come, Theodora," Lance said in a faintly pleading tone which irked her nigh to death. "We must stay here tonight. I already asked Ferguson to unhitch the team and have them fed and brushed. It would take an hour or more before he could get them ready again. By then, what's left of the afternoon would be gone and we could easily get stuck on the road without proper lodgings."

There was no answer for it, then. Swallowing her irritation, she threw up her hands. "Fine! It appears we're staying the night. But only *one*."

Lance visibly relaxed. "Perhaps you should take a look at our bedchambers. If they're half as charming as MacLeish reported, you'll be quite happy we're staying here."

"Oh no!" Jane looked up from searching in her knitting basket. "One of my needles is missing. It must have fallen out in the coach."

Lance cast a regretful look at his half-

206

eaten cake. "I will go to the stables and look for it."

Jane set her basket aside, arose, and joined him. "I'll come with you. I might know better where to look."

"Of course." He looked at Theodora expectantly.

She had no desire to inspect the inn, but it would give her something to do. "I'll see to our rooms, but first I want to fetch my bonnet. One of the ribbons is coming loose." It would give her something to do while they waited for dinner.

"I can help you with that when I return," Jane offered.

"Thank you." Theodora walked with Lance and Jane to the front door, closing it behind them as they left for the stable. Once they were gone, Theodora looked about the hallway with a critical eye.

She reluctantly decided that MacLeish was right; it was a neat establishment, far superior to the last few they'd visited. The wooden entryway floor was polished to a warm gleam. A small table sat to one side, just the place for bonnets and gloves, while on the wall next to it hung a neat line of hooks where her pelisse hung. Under the hooks, some thoughtful person had placed a potted fern right where wet cloaks and coats would drip, effectively watering a pleasant bit of winter greenery.

She absently picked up her bonnet from the side table and began to examine the loose ribbon, noting that it was nicely warm here in the hallway, which meant a proper fire had been lit somewhere nearby. In the distance women chatted over the comforting clink of crockery, while the faint scent of plum pudding made her stomach growl. Perhaps it *was* best to stay here. And accepting a more leisurely pace would give her time to shake off the sense of impending doom that had hung over her since this morning.

Feeling more at peace with their decision, she had just taken a step for the stairs when a maid — a thin, brown slip of a girl — stepped out of a private parlor, balancing a tray of empty dishes. Overburdened, she left the door ajar behind her as she made her way down the hallway.

As she left, a faint whistled melody, nautical in nature, drifted out of the parlor door.

Theodora froze, her eyes widening. She had heard that melody more times than she could count.

No. Surely not . . . She found herself at the door, pushing it open. She took a step inside and came to a sudden stop, her bonnet falling from her nerveless fingers. *"You!"*

In a winged chair by a crackling fire, legs resting on a footstool, a glass of whisky in one hand, sat Conner.

"Och, there you are." He flashed a satisfied smile, his blue eyes crinkled with laughter. "I was beginning to think you'd gotten lost."

12

Theodora's hands clenched into fists. "What are *you* doing here?"

"Waiting. You took your sweet time." He nodded to the small clock that sat on the mantel. "The lot of you are a guid half hour late."

"We stopped for tea, and —" Her gaze narrowed. "What do you mean by 'late'?"

"You tell me; you're the one who stopped for tea." He tsked. "What sort of elopement is this, lollygagging at every inn along the way?"

"It would be a much better elopement if you wouldn't attach yourself to it!"

"I suppose 'tis fortunate you dinnae see roses from the coach window, or you'd have stopped for those, too." His blue eyes were alight with amusement. "Tell me, are you lingering in the hopes you'll find a way oot of your predicament?"

"I'm not in a 'predicament.' I'm eloping."

"With a chaperone."

She plopped her hands on her hips. "You know Lance doesn't wish to put my reputation in jeopardy. He's a good man."

"I never said the squire was anything else. I just dinnae think he's the mon for you."

That gave Thea pause. Too much, in fact. She wished she could ask Conner what he meant by that, but he didn't need more encouragement to flash his opinions.

She sniffed. "You don't know what's good for me and what's not."

"Och, Thea mine, I know you as weel as I know my own heart." He stood in a smooth, powerful movement, and his voice deepened with intimacy that instantly made her picture rumpled sheets and hot kisses.

She fought a shiver and wondered how he was able to make her think of anything so *decadent,* and with only a few words. "Sadly, you don't know me at all." She couldn't keep the bitterness from her voice.

"I know enough. You're nae the meek, mild sort, but are filled with fiery spirit. Which is how I know the type of mon that wild heart of yours needs."

Oh, she did have a wild heart. And it beat harder every time she saw Conner, which she hated. "It's not your job to know what's best for me, so I'd appreciate it if you'd stop thinking about it."

"I worry that you will nae consider what you're aboot until 'tis too late, and the knot tied. The squire is nae braw enough for a feisty woman like you."

"I'm not feisty," she snapped, and then bit her lip when he laughed.

"Lass, I would nae have you any other way."

If she could control her own emotions, he'd not have her at all, but it was harder than she'd imagined. He made it worse by constantly baiting her, too.

"Think on it, lass. 'Tis obvious you're nae in a hurry to reach Gretna. Why is that, do you think?"

"I asked that we go faster, but Lance felt it would be a strain on your team. He was determined to follow some itinerary Mac-Leish had set and —" *The itinerary.* She narrowed her gaze on Conner. "*That's* what you meant when you said we were late. It was *you* who made that itinerary. I suspected as much."

" 'Tis possible I knew of it."

"I'm sure you did," she said with awful scorn.

Conner's eyes twinkled at her over the rim of his glass. "Och, 'twas for the squire's benefit. At breakfast this morning, he said he was nae familiar with the way and seemed worried aboot it, so I decided to help the puir mon."

"Help him, or help yourself?"

"That's one and the same, love. I'm surprised he told you of the schedule; I expected him to take credit for knowing the guid inns and such."

"He's not that sort of man." She retrieved her bonnet from the floor and brushed it off. "I daresay every one of your servants are in this plan of yours to make our trip to Gretna last days, and perhaps weeks longer than it should."

"Weeks? Lass, I'm guid, but I cannae make the road longer. You'll be there before the week's oot, with my itinerary or nae."

"A week! Blast you, Conner!" Yet a voice inside whispered, *Only seven days and I'll be married. A few extra days would not be amiss . . .* Her throat tightened and she had to fight the very real desire to spin on her heel and run away from everything — the elopement, Lance, her chaperone, Conner, all of it.

Conner watched her, all humor gone. "Och, lass. You're frightened."

She was, but she could not — would not — admit it. Whether or not she married the squire, she could not succumb to Conner.

That would be trading one mistake for another. *Oh God — is marrying Lance a mistake? Do I already know it?*

Aware that Conner watched, she said with spirit, "I'm only annoyed about spending an entire week locked in a coach, traveling on heaven knows what sort of roads."

"It'll be guid for you. You'll be forced to spend the week with the squire and you'll soon realize how unsuitable he is for a woman such as you. The question is, will you be able to overcome that pride of yours and put an end to it? Or will you marry him just to spite me?"

"My choice of husband is no concern of yours."

His brows lowered. "You've been my particular concern for years; I'm nae stopping now."

"Me? You never paid the slightest heed to me before now."

"Of course I've paid you heed! We are friends, lass."

Friends. Never had a pleasant word caused so much pain. "That doesn't give you leave to interfere with my life. You have gone too far."

"You make it sound as if I had evil intentions, when I've naught but the best."

"Don't you?"

"Nae that I'll admit to," he retorted. A wickedly handsome smile touched his mouth as his gaze dropped to her lips. "I'll be glad to prove my 'intentions,' should you wish."

"No, thank you." Heart racing, she backed away a bit. She regarded him for a long moment, then sighed. "I'm through arguing about this with you."

"Guid, for there are other things we could be doing." He took a step toward her.

She threw up a hand. "Oh no, you don't! Tell me the truth. You never planned on going to Wentlow Manor, did you?"

"If you decide to have your squire at the end of this trip, then I'll be left with nae other choice."

"Then why are you here now?"

" 'Tis the best inn for miles. Besides, since I'm also heading north, I might as weel travel with you and your party as go alone. When I meet my wife-to-be, the lovely Lora, I will —"

"It's not Lora."

He pursed his lips. "Letty?"

She narrowed her gaze.

He sighed and rubbed his chin. "Lucille?"

She frowned.

"Lilah —"

"For the love of — It's *Lydia,* you fool!"

He shrugged. "One is the same as the other."

She hated hearing him say that. It was a pity he wasn't in love with one of the Lambert sisters. If he were, her own feelings would die a natural death.

Wouldn't they? Or would she be tormented by the thought of him in love with someone other than her?

The sudden ill feeling in the pit of her stomach irritated her, as did the realization that Conner was right: she was indeed questioning her decision to marry Lance. With each passing moment, once-quiet whispers of doubt grew louder, and she·was finding it hard to ignore them.

Restless, she moved to where the decanter sat on the tray. The tea hadn't warmed her as much as she'd hoped.

"Aye, a wee dram will hit the spot."

Conner's voice was so close behind her that she jumped and moved away, oddly uncomfortable in her own skin.

He poured her a finger's width of the amber liquid and handed her the glass. "Something to hold off a gray day."

She took the glass and sipped the whisky. Instantly, her throat and chest warmed. "Ah. It's good and smoky."

"So 'tis." He took a sip, satisfaction plain

on his face. "Just the way I like it — silky smoke, with just a hint of a bite."

She paused, her lips on the edge of her glass. Was he still talking about his whisky? Or something . . . else? Her mouth went dry, and she moved to the fireplace as if seeking warmth rather than running from it. "I cannot believe you followed us here."

"I did nae follow you at all; I've been here at least an hour, perhaps longer. I did nae meander on my way, as you've been doing."

"*I* wasn't meandering."

His eyes were the color of a flower she'd once seen on a mountainside in France, a pure, pale blue that could appear both icy cold and burning hot. Now, they burned, and she wondered if the whisky had added to it.

"Are you afraid of marriage?"

The abrupt question took her aback and she had to think about it for a moment before she answered. "I'm not afraid, no. Unlike you, I welcome the thought of marriage and sharing a home with someone who will make the same commitment. I'm sure that's something you would find onerous." She didn't know why she'd added that last bit, but it had slipped off her tongue as if waiting for the opportunity.

"I would like a home," he said, surprising

her. "Eventually."

She raised her brows. "And when will this magical 'eventually' occur? You're more at home on a ship than elsewhere."

He looked down at his glass and swirled his whisky. "Do you know why that is?"

She realized with surprise that she didn't. "Pray tell."

"When my parents died, we were living in our family seat, Lennoxlove House."

"Where Jack resides now."

"Aye. When he's home, which is nae often."

"None of you seem fond of staying in one place," she observed.

"We all had the same experience. After our parents died so suddenly, our lives changed quickly, too much so. Anna had just turned eighteen and she went from being a sister to being a parent, and the only one, too."

"I cannot imagine how difficult that must have been."

He took a drink of his whisky, his voice husky. "Anna decided we would stay at Lennoxlove, keep the same tutors, the same servants, and live as if things were the same."

Theodora saw the shadows in his eyes and said softly, "But things weren't the same."

"Nae, and my brothers and I, being too young to understand, were angry. We were angry at fate for stealing our parents, angry at them for leaving, angry with our lives for being less, and angry at Anna for nae fixing it." He grimaced, his tone heavy with regret. "We dinnae make it easy on her and became wild. And when she grew stern over our actions, it made it seem as if we had nae only lost our parents, but our sister, as weel."

"You were all hurting."

"We were raw, cut to the bone with sadness. The whole house seemed like a prison of memories that hurt, a sister who was forever unhappy, and the three of us lost . . ." He sighed. "It was a difficult time."

"Anna loved all of you."

"As we loved her, but we dinnae understand her anger. It was just so . . . big."

"She was trying to keep you safe."

"Desperately, but that never occurred to me, or to the others. And as soon as we were auld enough, we left one at a time, and never returned. I know now that broke Anna's heart, but all I could think was that finally, I could start anew, withoot being tormented by my sister's fury, or the weight of memories of those I'd lost." He sighed, long and deep. "I was a bloody fool."

His regret was so evident that Theodora

looked away to give him some privacy, dropping her gaze to her glass of whisky, the amber color reflected by the fire. In all the times she and Conner had talked, he'd never mentioned this, which had to have been one of the worst times of his life. She took a sip of whisky to loosen her throat. "I'm sure all of you did the best you could. It was a terrible situation. There was no making it right."

He finished his whisky, and his gaze found hers. "Perhaps. But now you know why I feel more at home on a ship. There are nae memories from the past lurking oot on the waves. Only the present and the future, for you're always moving forward. You cannae go backward in a ship." He flashed a lopsided grin. "At least, nae on purpose."

"So you ran away from home when you were a youth, and you've never stopped since. And now the worst place you can imagine is a home."

"Och, I would nae say that. The sea called and I answered. There is something glorious aboot sailing, Thea. Something freeing and —" He shook his head in bewilderment. "I cannae describe it."

"You would never be happy on land."

"Perhaps nae," he answered honestly. "I cannae imagine it, although there's something to be said for having a home port. Anna's death has brought that fact to light, among others."

"A home port is not a home."

"Nae."

Thea finished her whisky and held out her empty glass.

He fetched the decanter and refilled both of their glasses, putting a goodly measure in his glass, and a small splash in her own.

She might have protested, but then decided she would be foolish to drink too much while alone with Conner. She took a fortifying sip of the whisky, her chest tingling with the warmth. "We are a pair, us two. Opposites in many ways. You went to sea because your house no longer felt like a home; meanwhile my parents moved so often that while we had a house, we never stayed long enough to make it into a home. Not really."

"You've always enjoyed traveling."

"We didn't travel, we *moved* — sometimes for only five or six months at a time, depending on Papa's assignment. We always stayed in excellent hotels and apartments, as you know, but they were never home. We always had someone else's furniture, someone else's beds, someone else's gardens and curtains."

"I never thought of how disruptive it must have been — you always seemed to enjoy it."

"It was what we did." She gave a small laugh. "I carried just one picture from place to place with me. Do you know what it was of?"

He shook his head, watching her with an intent expression.

"Cumberbatch House."

"Ah. So you took your home with you."

"I tried to." A pang of homesickness made her sigh. "Whenever we were home for a month or longer, I'd plan the gardens, and — if it were spring — I'd put every spare hand to work at the planting."

"Derrick always complained about that. He said he was forced to learn how to starch his own cravat." Conner grinned.

She sniffed, unimpressed. "He never had to iron anything, and he knows it."

"He always complained a great deal more than was necessary." Conner took a drink of his whisky, watching her over the edge of the glass. "You said that you planned the garden every year. Even for years when you were nae home?"

"Even then. If I wasn't home, as was usually the case, I'd write instructions to the gardeners." She thought about all her garden plans, each one carefully drawn out so there could be no question. "Each year since I was seventeen, I've added something new to the garden."

"New flowers?"

She chuckled. "Nothing so mundane. New flower beds, of course, but also a new path, a folly, a fountain." She finished her whisky and put her empty glass on the mantel. "Do you know how many times I've seen my creations in full bloom?"

He shook his head, watching her with such intensity that for the moment, it felt as if the two of them were the only people in the world. "I've seen the gardens at Cumberbatch House bloom only twice. Twice, Conner. And one of those times, we came home in the spring only because Mama grew ill and couldn't stay in Venice because it was so damp."

He nodded thoughtfully. "That explains why you're so determined to have your own establishment."

"It's more than that." She lifted her chin. "I want a *home*. And a family, and children, two dogs, a cat — I want it *all*. I want to go to sleep at night in the same bed, and never wonder if tomorrow will be the day we must start packing to leave. I want comfort, and familiarity, the beauty of sameness each and every day, and most of all, I want a man who craves those same things."

"I see." He rubbed his jaw, looking both rueful and irritated. "We are somewhat opposite, are we nae?"

"Too much so. All the things you dislike, I want."

His brows locked. "Really? If that's what you want, this staid life with no changes, then why this leisurely elopement?"

She threw up her hands. "Why are you back on that? I told Lance we should travel faster."

"Pssht. If you'd wished to, you could have convinced him to forget the damned schedule and race to Gretna Green. He'd do anything you want, and you know it. But you dinnae try, lass. Admit it."

A vague disquiet held her tongue. Had she truly made an effort to hurry their trip, or had she merely fumed inside her own head? Was Conner right? Was she *glad* for the lagging pace of the journey? She grimaced. "Blast you. Stop trying to confuse me."

"There's naught confusing aboot it. You're lying to yourself aboot that lug of a squire. You may wish to settle doon and have a home and family, but nae with him."

Conner was right. But the man she wished

to settle down with had just explained to her all the reasons why he would never do so. Her heart felt as if a band had tightened around it, and her eyes grew blurry with tears. To hide them, she retrieved her glass and went to the decanter and poured herself another small measure. When she'd had a sip and trusted herself to speak again, she said in a cool tone, "I've made up my mind."

"Oh?"

"Marriage to Lance is the answer to everything." *Almost.*

Conner scowled. "Fine! Wed the lug. I've said all I will on it, since you will nae listen."

He stalked to the window, leaving a teasing trace of cologne in his wake, and she found herself breathing it in deeply.

She'd danced with most of London's eligible bachelors and had been exposed to a wide variety of colognes. But not a single soul had worn such a delicious-smelling cologne as Conner. It suited him — spicy and tantalizing, it drew one forward. She had but to smell it and her mouth went dry, and the most improper thoughts stirred. She gulped the final bit of her drink and set the glass on a side table, her gaze never leaving him.

What might he do if she followed him to the window and kissed him? Would it shake him as much as his last kisses had shaken her?

She had a sneaking suspicion he would not only welcome her efforts, but would willingly take them further. The thought left her as breathless as if she'd just run up a flight of stairs, and she found herself unable to look away from his mouth, shivers racing through her.

One step . . . and she would reach him.

Two steps . . . and she would be in his arms.

Three steps . . . and she would capture that fascinating mouth and kiss him as senseless as he'd kissed her.

Yet it would only make me more miserable than I am. He's not for me — not now, not ever.

Conner turned his head, surprising her. His gaze locked with hers.

For a moment, time stood still. Then he dropped his glass to the floor and strode to her, closing the space between them with impatient, furious strides. He reached her and stopped, his boots touching hers, her chest a mere inch from his.

He put his fingers under her chin, tilting her face to his, his blue eyes warm as he —

Lightning flashed, followed by a deep, long rumble of thunder. A hard rain burst from the sky and drummed against the roof and windows.

Conner, about to scoop Thea to him for the kiss she so obviously wanted, cursed as the inn door banged open and the squire's voice could be heard in the hallway.

Thea spun on her heel and hurried to the door, her face flushed in the most adorable way.

One more second and I'd have had her in my arms, and would have convinced her to wed me. One damn second! Conner clenched his fists against the ache of his empty arms.

Thea stepped into the hallway. "Oh no! You're both so wet! Come in here. We've a fire." She backed into the room, Lance appearing, his coat dripping on the rug as he assisted a sopping-wet Jane into the room.

The small woman hung on to his arm, her hair flat to her head, her soaked gown dragging about her feet, shivering as if she'd fallen into ice water.

"Jane, you poor thing!" Thea slipped an arm around the younger woman's narrow shoulders. "You're shaking like a blancmange."

The squire wiped water from his eyes, concern plain on his face. "The lightning frightened her."

"I-I don't know wh-why l-l-lightning af-
fects m-me so," Jane said piteously, her pale
lips quivering.

"It frightens me, too, when it is this loud."
Thea rubbed Jane's hands between her own.
"You're so cold! Lance, where's her trunk?
She'll need dry clothes."

"Spencer was unlashing it from the coach
when we were in the stables." Lance's gaze
fell to Conner, who was just retrieving his
glass from where he'd left it on the floor.
The squire gave a visible start. "Douglas?
Where did you come from?"

"Happenstance. We're both going north
and this is the best inn in this part of the
countryside, so —" Conner placed his glass
on the side table beside Thea's discarded
glass. "Here I am."

Lightning flashed, followed by a loud
crack of thunder. Jane gave a startled
squeak, and Lance's attention instantly
returned to her. "She's still shaking."

"Come." Thea led the poor woman to the
chair by the fireplace.

Conner said shortly, "I'll fetch my coat
from my room. It will warm her."

"My pelisse is closer," Thea answered.
"It's hanging in the hallway. We'll wrap it
about her until her clothes are brought in."

Conner moved toward the door, but

Lance was faster. "I'll get it." He strode out and returned with the wool pelisse.

Thea tucked it about the trembling young woman. "There. Let me stir the fire —"

Thunder crashed again, rattling the windows as lightning flickered wildly. Jane shrieked and clutched Thea close.

Thea put an arm about the girl's shoulders. "You're safe here." The thunder rumbled again, although not so loud. "This storm came so quickly! Did you see it roll up when you were outside, or were you surprised by it?"

"It came very suddenly!"

"Which made it all the more frightening, I'm sure. I used to be terrified of lightning."

Jane looked at Thea. "But no more?"

"Not as much, although loud thunder still makes me jump. Once, when I was living in Spain, a fierce storm came through town. It crashed and rumbled so loudly that the floor shook, and the spire on the local cathedral was struck twice."

"Oh no!"

"Oh yes! Once it was over, I was certain that when I looked outside, nothing would be left standing. But everything was still there — just freshly washed. Spain was like that, always unexpected. Have you ever been?"

"No, but I've wanted to visit."

"Oh, you should go one day — it's lovely." Thea began to tell tales of her time in Spain, her voice low and soothing.

Conner watched, admiring the way she distracted Jane from the storm. Thea continued talking over the thunder, wondering aloud whether a hot bath could be had from the inn, how lovely the lemon cake they'd had earlier had been, and other inane comments.

Jane shivered less and less, while the squire hovered nearby looking concerned.

Conner added wood to the fire, thinking regretfully of the kisses he'd been denied because of the blasted storm chasing Lance and Jane indoors. With a sigh, Conner shoved his uncharitable thoughts aside and tugged the bellpull.

The small, thin maid appeared and bobbed a curtsy. "Yes, sir?"

"Is Miss Simmons's bedchamber ready? She was caught in the rain and will need the warmth of a fire and a warm bed."

"Oh yes, sir. Her room is ready, and a fire has already been lit."

"Guid. I daresay the ladies could use a pot of hot tea, as well as a bath if that's possible."

"Indeed it is. It won't take long, as the

fire was already stoked for supper."

"Thank you. That will be all, then."

The maid hurried off and Conner turned back to the small group, well rewarded when Thea smiled at him. It was a sweet smile, a mixture of gratitude and appreciation.

He felt a surprising rush of — happiness? Pleasure at being useful? He didn't know, but the strength of his reaction shocked him.

Lance rubbed his hands together, looking eager, obviously wishful of being of some use. "We must get Jane into some dry clothes. She'll catch an ague if she stays as she is."

Thea looked surprised. "An ague? Please don't even suggest it! She's not shivering now, for the fire is warm and my pelisse is quite thick."

"You never know when an ague might come upon someone, especially if they have weak lungs. My younger sister Lucy has weak lungs, and being wet is a sure path to a dangerous infection."

Conner noted the frustrated look Thea sent the squire before she said in a bracing tone, "I'm sure Jane is in no danger of infection. It's merely a little rain."

Jane, her hair slicked back from her heart-shaped face, her lashes spiked about her wide eyes, looked more like a kitten than ever. "I'm afraid the squire is right. I have weak lungs. This could well develop into something harsher."

Lance said in a bracing tone, "You need a mustard plaster. The smell is horrendous, but they do wonders at holding illness at bay."

Jane looked hopeful. "Do you think one could be made?"

"I will see to it," he said. "I have a recipe for a most excellent one."

To Conner's amusement, Thea was looking from Lance to Jane and back as if they'd suddenly sprouted extra heads. "Jane, surely a mustard plaster won't be necessary. You'll feel much better after a hot bath."

"Oh, you don't know. I catch every sniffle that comes by. It's one reason my sister-in-law wished me gone. She felt I'd brought a number of infections into the household which threatened my nephew's health."

Footsteps sounded and everyone turned toward the door just as Spencer appeared carrying a small, worn trunk.

"Jane, there are your clothes." No one looked happier about the arrival of Jane's trunk than Thea. "Spencer, carry that to Miss Simmons's bedchamber. The maid knows which one it is."

"Aye, miss." Spencer disappeared from sight.

"I'm being such a bother," Jane said, obviously miserable. "I wish I could just change into fresh clothes and dry my hair, and all would be right. But I know how things are with me; if I get even the slightest bit wet I start to sneeze, and nine times out of ten it goes straight into an earache, and nothing will help but sleeping with a roasted onion tied to my head."

Thea blinked. "Did you say a roasted onion?"

Lance looked at her with true astonishment. "Surely you've heard of that remedy."

"No. Never."

"Everyone knows that if you've an earache, a roasted onion will draw out the illness." When Jane sent him a thankful look, he added in a gentle tone, "My youngest sister has the same issue — if the air's the slightest bit damp she takes ill, and often has an earache. A roasted onion tied to her ear clears it each and every time."

"It's an old cure and quite dependable," Jane agreed. "I did not believe it would work myself, until I'd tried it." She sent Thea an envious look. "I daresay you rarely take ill."

It was true; Conner could count on one hand the number of times he could recall

Thea's being ill. She was an amazingly strong woman, in body as well as spirit. *She'd take well to the sea, or she would if she didnae have her heart set on establishing herself in a home and never traveling again.* For some reason, the thought depressed him. He'd never thought about Thea's being at sea, but he could easily imagine it now that they'd traveled together.

"I'm sadly robust," Thea told Jane. "My father says I have a stronger constitution than anyone in my whole family, as I ride so often, and in all weather."

"For once, I find myself in agreement with your father," Conner said.

"A momentous day indeed." Thea sent him a humorous look as she rose and assisted Jane to her feet. "Since your bedchamber is warm, we will get you out of those wet clothes. Hopefully the hot bath Mr. Douglas kindly requested will arrive soon."

"That would be lovely." Jane pulled the pelisse tighter. "Do you think we might see if there's an onion to be had in the kitchen? Just in case. I fear if we do not bespeak it tonight, it might be made into soup or something not as helpful."

"Of course. I'll ask the maid when she brings the bath." Thea slipped her arm around Jane's shoulders.

As she reached the door, Conner said, "I'll bespeak dinner."

She smiled. "Thank you." The warmth of her look made his chest tighten in the oddest way.

Conner had captained ships over wild seas, fought in blood-soaked wars, and captured numerous enemy ships after deadly battles. He'd been rewarded for those efforts with awards, gold, decrees, and even a bit of fame. Yet he would trade them all for just one warm look from Thea.

Bloody hell, what's happening to me? He rubbed his neck, wondering at the power of Thea's glance as Lance followed her and Jane to the door, offering a steady stream of advice that included vinegar-soaked handkerchiefs to calm a cough, extra blankets to induce a sweat, and laudanum in warmed milk to encourage sleep.

Conner had a moment's satisfaction when he noted the irritated set to Thea's mouth. *Och, lass, if the man irritates you now, he'll infuriate you after you're married.*

Lance hovered in the doorway, watching the women until they disappeared up the stairs. Then he sighed, leaning heavily against the doorframe. "I hope Miss Simmons will recover."

"She's nae yet ill," Conner pointed out in a dry tone. "She'll be better after she's warmed up and had a hot meal."

Lance frowned. "You do not understand the effect of cold on someone with naturally weak lungs."

That was probably true. "Still, Thea has the situation well in hand. You know how she is — once she sets her mind to something, nothing will stand in the way, nae even weak lungs. She's a force of nature, that one."

Lance stiffened. "I beg your pardon, but Miss Cumberbatch-Snowe is a wonderful woman."

"I meant what I said as the highest compliment."

"It sounded like a critique. Women were not designed to be 'a force of nature.' "

"Mayhap nae the women in your life, but in mine they havenae been so weak."

"They are the weaker vessel. And while I don't know about women who sail, I know without hesitation that Theodora is a lady first and foremost, and would never wish to be described in such a way."

Conner didn't believe that for a second and it took every ounce of self-control he had not to say so. He had to settle for a terse, "Only Thea knows how she wishes to be described."

Lance nodded stiffly, but after a moment, he sighed. "I'm sorry if I'm overly protective. I've never been engaged before and I'm not sure what's — how I'm supposed to — Not that Thea would like it if —" He caught Conner's amused gaze and slumped, a sail suddenly without wind. "She can be prickly at times."

Well. That was something. "We all are."

"True. Theodora is sometimes a little lacking in empathy. And she can be out of sorts at times, although that's to be expected, considering the stress our elopement has put upon her tender sensibilities."

Tender sensibilities? Bloody hell, had the man carried on even one real discussion with his intended?

Lance waved a hand. "But that's what a husband is for. Females tend to be emotional, and it is up to us to calm their many fears and protect them from the harshness of life."

Conner chuckled. "Laddie, I fear you're in for a sad surprise. Thea will nae welcome someone protecting her, nae withoot her say-so. Hell, she barely allows me to offer oop advice, and those are just words."

Lance's smile never wavered. "Things are different between Theodora and I, aren't they, seeing as we're to be married."

"There's that." The words burned Conner's throat, and he wished he had whisky to wash the hurt away.

"Douglas, forgive me for saying this, but I still find it odd that you stopped at the same inn as we did."

"Mere coincidence," Conner lied without a pause.

"Perhaps, although . . ." Lance's eyes narrowed. "Are you following us?"

"I was here first," Conner pointed out. "Which means the real question is: are *you* following *me*?"

Lance flushed. "Of course not! I didn't know you'd be here."

"Ah. Then I was right to begin with; mere coincidence."

The squire nodded and then frowned, realizing the conversation somehow wasn't going the way he wished, but was unable to see his way clear.

Conner sighed. The squire's reasoning was lacking, a major weakness for a man hoping to be a life mate for a lively lass. *Och, Thea, when will you see this man is nae right for you?*

That thought was followed by a more chilling one: *What if you dinnae realize it until it's too late?*

His first impulse was to tell Thea every ridiculous thing the squire had said so far, but he immediately realized the error of that. There was no telling Thea anything; she'd regard anything Conner told her with suspicion.

I must make certain she sees and hears Lance's foolishness for herself. Conner thought of the week of travel they faced, and swallowed a scowl. A week might not be enough. He wished he could lengthen the trip two entire weeks, or even three, but if he drew it out too much, Thea's irritation with him would overshadow her calm reason.

The most Conner could do was add three, perhaps four, more days to the journey. And to make certain that Thea got the true measure of her intended, from now on, Conner would be there every damned step of the way to subtly highlight the man's flaws.

But that presented another problem. He now had less than two months left to marry, and he couldn't do both — continue on this journey to prevent Thea from making the biggest mistake of her life, *and* secure a bride of his own.

To be honest, he was quickly coming to the dismaying conclusion that there was only one lady of any quality he was *willing* to marry — Thea. He thought of the reasons she'd said she wished to marry, the desire for commitment, and sameness, of hearth and home and a husband who valued those things as well. Conner wanted none of it. He'd been looking for a marriage that would allow him the freedom to continue his life upon the sea, not banish it.

There was no bridge between their two visions of the future.

So that is that. She will never be mine. Never. It was a startling, depressing thought.

And neither would his inheritance. *So be it, then. The bloody Campbells can have it.* Odd as it was, he regretted losing Thea more than the inheritance. *Och, Anna, you would be surprised to know that, wouldn't you?*

"Mr. Douglas?"

Conner realized he'd sunk into a brown study, and the squire was now looking at him in concern. "You look distressed. Are you worried about Miss Simmons, too?"

Conner forced a smile. "Nae. I'm sure Thea has the sickroom well in hand. I was just feeling the weight of my thoughts. It's been a long day, has nae it?"

"It has." Lance raked his wet hair from his face. "I should probably call for a bath as well. I don't wish to take ill during my own elopement and I definitely feel as if I might be catching a chill."

"Och, you need a wee dram, that's all."

The squire brightened. "That could be just the thing."

It certainly could. Conner retrieved his glass and carried it to the sideboard. He splashed whisky into his glass and a clean one. Then he brought them to the fireplace and handed one to the other man. One could never know too much about one's enemy. "It's Meldrum's, the best there is." Conner held up his glass, admiring the amber liquid. *Slainte.*"

Slainte." Lance took an experimental sip. "That's quite good."

"So 'tis." Conner sat in a chair and nodded to the one across from him. "Have a seat. You're in nae hurry, are you? It will be some time before you can call for a bath, as the kitchen maids will be busy filling one for Miss Simmons."

"True." Lance took the chair, looking about the parlor as if seeing it for the first time. "MacLeish was right; this is an excellent inn."

"One of the best. So, squire. Tell me aboot this farm of yours."

13

At a quarter after six, Theodora and Jane made their way to the dining room. Warmed by a bath, clothed in a dry gown, and snuggly wrapped in Theodora's best shawl, Jane seemed much more like herself, both chatty and breathless.

"I do hope there's some fish to be had," she said as they reached the top of the stairs. "That's good for the digestion, and I always take a little stomach complaint when I get a cold."

"In addition to an ear infection?"

"Oh yes." Jane nodded vigorously. "People with weak lungs are very susceptible to other complaints, especially when there's a full moon."

Theodora decided not to point out that there wouldn't be a full moon for another week. Ever since her teeth had stopped chattering, Jane had been an unending litany of specious cures. "Perhaps it's the damp air,"

Theodora said. "We've been traveling along a river all day."

"We must be close to the ocean, too." Jane reached the bottom step. "I could smell the salt water all afternoon."

Theodora joined her. "I'm afraid you're mistaken; the road north curves inland."

"Does it? Then I must have been imagining it." She cast a shy glance at Theodora and said in a far-too-casual voice, "It was quite thoughtful of Mr. Douglas to make certain I had a fire and a hot bath."

"So it was." Theodora adjusted her lace shawl.

"He's quite handsome, too. *Very.*"

The way Jane said those few words made Theodora look at her sharply. "I suppose he is handsome."

"Suppose? Oh, he is *definitely* handsome. Why, he's one of the handsomest men I've ever met!"

Thea just looked at Jane.

"Those eyes!" Jane sighed.

Here we go. Would she ever have an acquaintance who didn't fall in love with Conner? "He can be very useful when the situation demands it."

"I vow, but I shiver every time he looks my way. Surely you feel the same."

"No." She winced — she hadn't intended

243

the waspish note in her voice.

Jane looked disappointed. "I thought him thoughtful and charming."

"He can be. He's also exceptionally good at ordering people around. Perhaps too good."

Still, Theodora had to admit Jane was right — it *had* been thoughtful of him to see to Jane's comfort in ordering the bath, and she'd been very grateful for his assistance, especially as Lance had fallen into hovering do-nothing-ness. Conner never hesitated; he decided on the best course of action and efficiently saw to it that it was done. "He's a ship's captain, which is why he is often so commanding."

"I find that very reassuring in a man."

Theodora sent the younger woman a sour look. "Yes, well, I find it annoying. Since he captains a privateer ship, he is far too used to getting his own way."

Jane's eyes widened. "A privateer? That's just like a pirate, isn't it?"

"In more ways than one," Theodora said drily. They reached the parlor and Theodora opened the door and gestured for Jane to continue in.

The innkeeper's wife and her maid had just placed the last dish on the table, and they curtsied and left. The men stood by the fire, both dressed for dinner. Though soberly dressed, Conner's dark hair, pale blue eyes, and sharp expression gave him a decidedly rakish look, and Theodora's heart gave an odd leap when their gazes met.

As if they were in private, his gaze raked over her with warm appreciation and she had to fight the urge to cover herself. How did his mere gaze always make her think of the most inappropriate things?

He bowed. "Good evening." His deep voice, warmed by his Scottish lilt, made Theodora shiver. "You both look as lovely as a fresh moon upon a glassy sea."

Jane was instantly cast into a flutter of stutters and blushes, which irritated Theodora for no reason she could think of.

Lance, looking quite handsome in his blue coat and buff breeches, stepped forward. "I hope you're ready to eat despite the early hour, for we've enough food for five or six more people."

"We are quite ready for dinner," Theodora assured him, glad to have something to focus on other than Conner.

Jane smiled at him now. "I'm sorry we're late, but Theodora insisted I should have a shawl, one to match my gown, and it took a while to find it. She has been so, so kind. No one could be kinder."

Lance turned an admiring gaze on Theodora. "She is an angel, isn't she?"

Jane nodded with such enthusiasm that her curls bounced. "Oh, she truly is."

Irked at the wry, amused curve of Conner's mouth, Theodora said in a cool voice, "It was nothing." She looked at the table. "I'm suddenly famished. Do I smell roasted beef?"

Lance brightened. "The cook has outdone herself. There's beef, fish, an oyster sauce, a goodly duck, turnips, two pastries, a ragout — come and see for yourself."

They were all soon seated, Lance gallantly filling their plates. Outside, dusk rode heavy on the light coming through the window. The room felt cozy, with lamps and candles that spilled a golden glow over the table and set the glassware and crockery agleam.

They ate, and talked, awkward moments smoothed by Jane's breathless chatter. During a pause, while Lance extolled the virtues of the oyster sauce, Conner leaned back in his chair, his gaze resting on Theodora's face, his expression oddly somber.

She'd never seen him so serious or quiet, and she couldn't help sending him a concerned glance. She was wondering if she dared ask him what was amiss in front of the others when Jane, picking up her spoon to taste her plum pudding, shot Conner a curious glance. "Mr. Douglas, may I ask you a question?"

Conner, who'd rejected the pudding in favor of another glass of whisky, sent her a measuring look. "Please. Call me Conner."

"Oh, I could not."

"Och, but you could." He smiled at Jane over his whisky glass, his warm accent caressing each word. "And you must."

Theodora had to fight to keep from rolling her eyes.

Jane flushed and couldn't have looked more pleased. "I suppose I will, if you insist."

"I do. You said you have a question?" Conner reminded her gently.

"Oh yes! As we were entering the parlor, Theodora said you were a privateer."

"Did she?" Conner's dark gaze rested on Thea's face once more, and he noted with pleasure the way her cheeks pinkened as if he'd touched her. After admiring the delicate hue of her blush, he reluctantly turned his attention back to Jane. "Aye, I am a privateer."

Jane leaned forward, her shawl slipping from one shoulder. "What exactly *is* a privateer?"

Over the years, numerous women had

asked Conner this same question, and he usually used it as a way to open a dalliance. But tonight he had other goals in mind, so he merely said, "We protect our country by waylaying our enemy's vessels and keeping them from attacking our merchant ships."

Jane's mouth formed an impressed "O," while across from him, Thea raised an eyebrow, and he knew she was holding back a tart comment. Their thoughts were uniquely aligned, which was why he'd always felt such peace in her company. Or used to. Now, he felt an oddly restless longing, and a wistful sadness as if he regretted . . . well, everything. He hid a grimace. *Bloody hell, I'm maudlin.*

"Ever since I was a child, I've been enamored of pirates," Jane confessed blithely. "I still am. I read about them every chance I get."

Lance smiled kindly at her. "Mr. Douglas is not a pirate. Privateers are quite a different matter."

"I'm sure they are," Jane said, looking chastised. "But they capture ships like pirates. And life at sea must be so romantic — the wind taking you to distant lands, the waves bearing you across the seas, the fellowship of the other sailors."

Thea, who'd been toying with her plum

pudding, grimaced. "I think living on a ship would be wretched. It's such a small space, and there'd be no privacy."

Jane blinked. "Oh. I hadn't thought of that."

"I daresay the ship smells, too — all those unwashed bodies, since fresh water is very precious on a ship."

Jane's rapturous expression fell. "Well, there's that."

"And the ship would be constantly sailing through great expanses of the ocean, through heat and cold and storms."

Jane paled a bit. "I hadn't thought about storms. I daresay they are very unpleasant."

"*Especially* at sea," Thea said in a flat, heartless tone.

"Thea, enough!" Conner protested with a laugh. "Next you'll say there's an outbreak of the plague at least once a week, too. 'Tis nae as bad as that."

Her lips twitched into a reluctant smile. "I was going to mention cholera, rather than the plague."

Conner chuckled and told Jane, "Dinnae listen to her. While the sailing life is nae withoot hardships, it can be verrah exciting, too. And as we hover near shores while waiting on our prey, we've water and food aplenty for washing and such. 'Tis the long-haulers who face more rigorous conditions."

"But the storms —" Jane shivered.

"— are nae a worry. A guid captain can read the weather and will find a safe harbor when storms come."

"You can read the weather?"

"Aye." His gaze found Thea again, enjoying the play of the candlelight over her expressive face. Her gaze was on her pudding again, her thick lashes casting crescent shadows over her cheeks. "Nature is as unpredictable as a woman, but if you know the signs, you will recognize trouble before it arrives." And oh, did he see trouble on his horizon.

"Have you been in many battles?" Jane asked.

Conner shrugged. "A few."

Thea gave an inelegant snort, looking up from her plate. "Which means not as many as he'd like."

Conner winked. "I enjoy a brangle now and then. Who does nae?"

Thea told Jane, "My brother believes Mr. Douglas is addicted to the excitement of those sea battles, and it is that which has kept him from staying on land and accepting his familial responsibilities."

Lance cast a concerned look at Conner. "Privateering is not the most secure profession, if one has family."

"I've brothers, both capable of living withoot my assistance. I'm nae sure what Thea is referring to." Conner rocked back in his chair and crossed his arms over his chest. She was at least looking at him now. "Well, lass? What responsibilities have I been so remiss toward?"

A shadow passed over her face, then she shrugged. "We all have responsibilities to our family name. For one, you haven't yet settled down and married."

Conner considered announcing he'd decided to forgo his inheritance. But if he admitted that to Thea, he lost his reason to accompany them on their way north. So it was with a shrug that he said, "I'm on my way to find a wife now."

"Only because your sister's will has forced you to do so — not because you wished to do your duty."

Lance said to Jane in an aside, "Mr. Douglas is compelled to marry in order to obtain his inheritance."

"Ohhhh!" Jane eyed Conner with even more interest. "Really?"

"Aye. A condition of my sister's will is that if I dinnae marry, the family funds will be dispensed to our biggest enemy."

"Oh no! What will you do?"

251

"He's decided to marry a woman he barely knows." Thea sent Conner a black glare.

Jane nodded. "No one will have you because of your dangerous profession."

Conner frowned. "I could marry today, did I wish it. I just decided to wed someone I've met before."

"So you know her. How many times have you met her?"

"Two or three times. Perhaps more. I'm a bit fuzzy on the details."

Thea's brows rose. "Fuzzy? What's her nam—"

"But that is what the engagement is for, nae?" Conner interrupted ruthlessly. "To get to know one's intended and make certain 'tis nae a mistake."

"I suppose that's true," Jane said, although she didn't look certain. "But . . . if you don't know her well, don't you worry that this lady might reject your proposal?"

"That's what I've been telling him," Thea confided.

"It's the obvious question," the younger girl agreed. "Such a marriage would be very difficult, what with Mr. Douglas's risky career. Why, he'd be gone all the time."

"Exactly," Thea said smoothly.

Conner scowled. "I suppose 'tis true that

my being gone could pose an issue. But I've heard of couples who've only known one another a few weeks who've decided to marry. People who've spoken only a few times, perhaps visited one another for two or three weeks —"

"If you're talking about Lance and me," Thea replied in a chilly voice, "we spoke quite a bit over two entire months."

"Well . . ." Lance rubbed his chin. "All together, we only spoke over the course of three weeks."

Thea looked astounded. "It was more than that. We began speaking in September, and it's now the beginning of November."

"We first spoke during the *final* week of September, but then I returned home and didn't return until the second week of October, as my sister was ill and I couldn't leave my mother to care for her and keep an eye on the farm."

"Oh."

"Of course I visited when I could for the next two weeks, but then it was time for shearing, and I had to be gone for that."

"But we wrote," she said valiantly.

"True. Long letters, too. Still, all told, we only *spoke* over the course of three weeks."

Thea blinked, and appeared so uneasy that Conner had to fight the desire to exclaim, *"Finally!"*

"Oh my, but that was a very fast court-ship," Jane said. When Thea flashed a look at the younger woman, she flushed and hurried to say, "But sometimes it doesn't take long for people to realize they're in love."

"Very true." Lance smiled at Theodora and reached over to take her hand between his. "You cannot always predict love."

Thea's eyes widened and she looked every type of uncomfortable there was. Conner wondered if this was the first time the squire had used the term "love." Satisfied to see a chink in her armor, whatever the cause, Conner said in a cool tone, "A few weeks is hardly time for true love to grow roots."

"It could happen!" Jane said stoutly.

"In books, perhaps. Or on a stage. But in real life? Never."

Thea sent Conner a hard look as she tugged her hand free from Lance's grip. "Not that it's anyone else's business, but I'm quite satisfied with my engagement."

"Of course you are!" Jane looked shocked anyone could think otherwise. "You and the squire are perfect for one another. Anyone can see it."

"Thank you, Jane," Lance said in a solemn tone. "You are most kind."

The younger girl flushed. "Squire, I'm

only —"

"Please, it's Lance. We are all friends here."

Her flush deepened and she cast him a shy look. "Yes, of course. You have an interesting name. Does . . . if you don't mind me asking, does 'Lance' stand for Lancelot, perhaps?"

Lance grimaced. "Yes. For all her stern ways, my mother is a bit of a romantic at heart."

"My mother was stern, too, although I don't believe she was much of a romantic."

"Ah, yes, your esteemed mother," Conner said. "You mentioned her last night and that she lives with you. I suppose she'll be moving oot after the wedding."

"Move? Oh no. She will live with me for as long as she wishes."

Thea's brows snapped down. "She will?"

"Of course. My father died four years ago, and Mother was quite distraught. She leans on me to take care of things, you know. She could not do without me."

"So we'll be living with her," Thea said in a hollow tone. "Forever."

He looked surprised. "I thought you knew that."

"You mentioned you had another house in the village, and I assumed that once we wed, your mother would be using it as a dower house."

Lance chuckled indulgently. "It's rented to the local vicar. He's lived there for over twenty years and I could never ask him to move. Besides, my mother will need our assistance with my sisters."

Thea's smile was rigid. "Of course. If your mother is living with us, then your sisters will, too."

"They are coming of age, and you will be quite busy escorting them about when you're not working on the house and the farm."

"I see." Thea's knuckles were now white around her spoon.

As if totally unaware of the turbulent waters through which they sailed, Jane gazed at Lance with true admiration. "You are so kind to take care of your mother and sisters."

"What else could I do?" Lance asked, looking surprised.

"You are a paragon, my friend!" Conner exclaimed, deeply amused. "You are indeed like your name, then — Lancelot. A true hero!"

Lance flushed, but looked pleased. "I cannot take such credit; it is a family name."

"So you mentioned last night." Conner

slipped a glance at Thea and waited.

"I'm the fourth," Lance announced. "The whole name is quite a mouthful. It's Archibald Montague Lancelot Fox."

Conner tried not to laugh, but was only marginally successful.

Lance chuckled as well, "I know. It's a bit much."

"*I* like it," Jane said, clasping her hands together. "It's like a name from a *novel.*"

Thea shot Conner a hard look. *Don't say another word,* her expression warned.

Oh, there were so many things he wished to say, but he could not ignore that look. Though it cost him dearly, Conner swallowed his thoughts.

Lance waved a hand. "It's a ridiculous name, and so I've told my mother countless times. To be honest, I've hated it since I could first write."

"Why, you'd use every letter of the alphabet!" Jane exclaimed.

Which won a laugh from Lance. "It felt like it," he confessed. "But now you know why I chose to go by the name Lance."

"I like the name Lancelot," Thea said. "It's quite romantic."

The squire brightened. "Do you think so?"

"I do," she said in a stout tone intended, Conner decided, to show him the error of his thinking. "In fact," she added, "I like *all* of your names."

The squire couldn't have looked more relieved. "And here I was afraid to mention it, as many people laugh when I tell them."

"One must bear the family banner." Conner leaned back in his chair. "Since it's a family name, I suppose you'll pass that name on to your own son, when you have one."

Thea's gaze jerked back to Lance.

Lance nodded. "I must."

"You must?" Thea repeated blankly.

Lance's expression grew grave. "My mother would be devastated if we named our firstborn son anything else."

"I see." Thea stabbed her spoon into her pudding. "And naturally, we must do as your mother wishes."

"It would break her heart if we did not. She is very tenderhearted, which she cannot help. My oldest sister Sally says the whole family dances a tune to Mother's tears."

"That's —" Thea bit back her own words, finally saying, "That's a colorful way of putting it."

"Indeed it is. I hope you don't mind naming our son in the family tradition." Lance brightened. "But never fear! I'll give you leave to name the other five or six children whatever you think is appropriate."

Thea had lifted a spoonful of pudding, but at his words, she almost dropped her full spoon onto the table. "The *other five* children?"

"Or six," Conner added helpfully.

Thea shot him a dagger glance.

Lance didn't seem to notice, adding in a thoughtful tone, "I would like at least six children. More hands for the farm, you know. And, Theodora, if you wish, we could name one for your father, as well as your brother. And any girls could —"

"Lance!" Thea snapped out the word as if it were a firecracker.

He blinked. "Yes?"

"This is a conversation for another time."

He looked at the others in the room before flushing. "Of course. Forgive me. I'm just excited about our future."

"With guid reason." Conner leaned over to slap the other man on the back. "You've a bright future ahead of you, my friend. You and your lovely wife, and all six of your children, *and* your sisters, *and* your mother. That'll be quite a house full."

"It's a large house. We've seven bed-chambers."

"Seven? But with so many people —" Thea caught Lance's hopeful look and clamped her lips over the rest of her sentence. After a stifled moment, she said, "We will discuss that later, too."

"Of course. I look forward to introducing you to Mother. You will love her, and she will love you."

"Aye," Conner said. " 'Tis a pity she dinnae know aboot the marriage and will be — How did you put it last night, Lance? 'Livid,' was the term you used, I believe."

Thea's gaze flew to Lance. "You said you thought your mother would welcome me into the family."

"And she will," Lance said stiffly. "Eventually."

Thea closed her eyes and pressed her fingers to her temples.

Jane's face grew shadowed. "I don't remember my mother. I was six when she died."

"It is a loss one never forgets," Conner agreed. "But Lance, your mother seems quite strong in character."

Lance beamed. "She is wonderful. Though she is stricken with ailments, as many women are, she is forever finding the strength to involve herself in all of our lives."

"That is so kind of her." Jane sighed with obvious envy. "I often wish my mother were still alive, so that I might benefit from her advice."

"Mother never hesitates in that area, I assure you." He began a long litany of enthusiastic praise for his surviving parent that included so many instances of intrusive actions into his and his sisters' private lives that even mild-mannered Jane was made to wince a time or two.

Listening with growing horror, Theodora fought a very real desire to run away.

Lance was good-hearted; he was pure of intentions, loved his sisters and his mother — weren't those important traits for a husband? Listening to him now, she found herself wishing she could silence him and spend a day or ten away from his presence, which seemed to grow more stifling each day. Worse, she felt no passion for him, no . . . anything.

Meanwhile, Conner had but to look her way and her skin grew warm, her heart raced, and she yearned to touch him and be touched by him.

It was so wrong. *Lance* should make her heart race and her mouth go dry and her palms grow damp with excitement. *It must be because he's never kissed me. Why* hasn't *he*?

Was he too predictable? Too safe? Lance

was calm, and pragmatic, and she'd wanted a comfortable, trusting marriage. She'd believed passion would eventually grow, based on mutual respect and compatible goals. But now she wondered if she'd been naïve.

Was she wrong to believe passion something one could cultivate like a rose garden? She had no idea, but the thought of being in a passionless marriage made her ache with loneliness.

There was only one thing to be done. *I must kiss Lance. That will stir the passion between us, and I'll know for certain that our marriage will be all it should be.*

Jane asked a question about Lance's farm, and he answered, looking animated and handsome, his dark hair framing his strong jaw. Yes — a kiss should prove she wasn't making a mistake.

But even as she had the thought, her attention slid to Conner, and their gazes locked. Her throat tightened, her skin prickled awake, and her breath came faster as she imagined feeling his arms about her, pulling her toward him as his mouth lowered to —

No! I cannot think this. I cannot feel *this.*

She jerked her gaze away from him, her mind reeling, her body aching as she turned back to Lance. *That will change — starting tomorrow.* She could do nothing more tonight, not with Conner watching her with that blazing hot gaze.

As soon as Lance paused, she stood.

Lance hurried to do the same. Conner stood as well, pausing to assist Jane from her chair even though his heated gaze followed Theodora in the most unsettling way.

"I'm sorry to retire so early," Theodora said. "I'm just so tired. Jane, you should come, too. You need your rest." And *she* needed time alone to think.

With almost indecent haste she made her good-byes and led the younger woman out of the parlor, leaving behind a solicitous Lance, a simmering Conner, and a welter of unanswered questions.

14

That night, Theodora dreamed she was locked in a huge house and every door she opened revealed a bare-chested Conner, who grinned as if he knew she couldn't resist him. She awoke from that disturbing image only to fall back into a fitful slumber, where she dreamed she and Lance were sitting at their dining room table that stretched on and on as far as the eye could see, every seat taken by identically dressed, noisy children. Dishes were passed, each progressively emptier. As the dishes emptied, the children's voices became more shrill and demanding until she awoke in a panic, panting as if she'd been running up and down stairs.

There hadn't been much sleep after that, and she was glad to see the sun peek through the cracks in her curtain. Quietly, so as not to awaken the other guests, Theodora dressed and went downstairs.

Glancing inside the breakfast room, she was relieved to see Lance alone there. She paused in the hallway to smooth the skirt of her green silk traveling gown, which she'd chosen with great care, and to place her cool hands over her heated cheeks. She'd never asked someone to kiss her, and had no idea where to begin. *This is not an undertaking for the weak,* she told herself firmly. *But it must be done.*

With a final, deep breath, she plastered on a smile and entered the breakfast room.

Lance sat at the table, buried behind a newspaper, a half empty cup of tea before him. Dressed in a blue coat and buff breeches, his boots clean and shining, he looked exactly like what he was: a handsome, good-hearted country squire.

She approached the table, noting he hadn't heard her enter. Smiling, she leaned across the table and tapped on the back of his newspaper.

He lowered the paper, his expression brightening. "Theodora!" He put down the paper and stood, looking absurdly pleased to see her. "Good morning!"

That was a good start, she decided. "Good morning." Her uneasy dreams and concerns still filled her mind, but she resolutely pushed them aside. *But when I kiss him, will he kiss me back?*

There was only one way to find out. She stepped forward, her skirts swinging to brush his legs, her toes just touching his boots.

Lance's eyes widened. "Th-Theodora?"

She placed her hand on his arm. It was firm, although not as hard-muscled as Con — *No, don't think about anyone but Lance.* Steeling herself, she slid her hand up his arm.

"Theodora!" Lance's voice sounded strangled. "I — This isn't — What are —"

The door opened, and a maid with a covered serving dish appeared.

Lance's hands dropped to his sides and he instantly stepped back. "Ah! The eggs!" No man had ever sounded more relieved to see his breakfast.

And just like that, the moment was gone, leaving Theodora with a desire to curse.

"Aye. I've brought your eggs. Hot, they are, too." This maid was different from the one they'd seen last night. She was large-boned, with a broad freckled face topped by thick, curly blond hair. Seeing Theodora, she dropped into an awkward curtsy, the platter wavering in her hands. "Good morning, miss!"

"Good morning." Theodora took a seat,

Lance doing the same.

The maid popped back to her feet and set the dish on the table. "Here you are; fresh from the chicken. I stole these from beneath the hen just this morning."

"Fresh eggs are always best," Lance said politely.

"Aye, although the hen was nae happy to give them up. But that could have been due to my cold hands. I'd be clucking up a storm if someone put their icy hands on my bare behind, too."

Theodora had to stifle a laugh, while Lance made a strangling sound.

The maid lifted the serving cover. "Nice and hot! I daresay the chicken wouldn't wish to sit on them now, eh? They would burn her bum if she tried."

Theodora choked back another laugh, hiding it behind a cough. She looked at Lance to share her amusement, but he was watching the girl with a confounded look on his face.

Theodora cleared her throat. "Thank you."

"You're quite welcome," the maid said, grinning cheerfully, but making no move to leave.

This maid wasn't as well trained as the last, and Lance cast an almost desperate look at Theodora. "If you don't mind, I think I'll finish the newspaper before I eat." With that, he hid behind the paper, leaving Theodora to handle the wayward servant.

"Ye'd best eat the eggs quickly," the girl said, sliding the dish forward. "There's nothing less tasty than cold eggs — unless it's greasy, uncooked pig head or —"

"I beg your pardon," Theodora said hastily. "Have we met?"

"Oh no. Polly Shoales usually helps Mrs. Landry, the innkeeper's wife, but late last night Polly went and hurt her ankle, perhaps even broke it. This morning, Ma — she's the laundress here — says to me, she says, 'Alice, you're going to have to help.' So here I am. Normally Ma don't like me and my sisters to help. She says we're clumsy, the lot of us, and I cannot disagree, but this was an emergency."

"Ah. I'm sorry to hear about Polly."

"I'm not. Polly isn't very nice to me — not since the Trivet boy started saying he thought I was prettier than her." Alice sniffed proudly. "She didn't take to that kindly."

Theodora ignored Lance's irritated shake of the newspaper. "She didn't?"

"No. So I'm not the least bit sorry Polly's hurt herself — though I suspect she has naught but a tiny sprain, *if* that, and she just wanted the time off to snuggle up to Tom the butcher's son."

Fascinated, Theodora asked, "I thought she liked the Trivet boy?"

"She likes them all, and too much, if you ask me." Alice tugged at her lace collar. "So now I'm left to be the maid, and Polly will choke her goat when she finds out how uncommon busy we've been, what with you and the squire, and your chaperone, and that handsome gent as looks as if he were tossed from heaven."

Choke her goat. I must remember that one. With a quiver of humor in her voice, Theodora said, "I daresay Polly will indeed regret treating you so poorly. Thank you for bringing the eggs. As you said, we'd best eat them now, before they grow cold."

"Indeed, miss. Ring if you want more." The maid gave a quick curtsy and left.

The second the door closed, Lance lowered his newspaper. "Good God, what was that?"

Theodora laughed. "That was Alice."

He folded the newspaper and placed it on the table before he eyed the plate of eggs with great interest. "She was quite loquacious."

"She was. Lance, may we . . . may we talk?"

He looked uneasy, but offered a quick smile. "Of course. What is it?"

"It's —" She struggled to find the words, wetting her suddenly dry lips. "I'm glad we are finally alone."

He flushed, and cast a quick look at the partially open door. "Yes, well, we haven't had much time together over the last few days. I have missed our conversations."

But conversation wasn't what Theodora wanted. She tried to imagine Conner saying such a thing, and couldn't. Now was the time to kill her fascination with him.

She pushed herself from the table. "Would you . . . would you mind standing?"

Lance flushed an even deeper red, but after a stilted moment, he pushed himself from the table and joined her. "Theodora, I'm not sure what —"

She rose up on her tiptoes, and pressed her mouth to his.

He froze, his eyes wide, looking so startled that she broke the kiss almost the second she'd started it, blazing with embarrassment as she stepped away. "I'm sorry! I shouldn't have — I don't know what I was thinking." She started to turn, but Lance caught her arm.

"No!"

She looked up at him, hoping for . . . she didn't know what.

Lance captured her hands and held them to his chest, pulling her closer. "Please don't think I am not — Or that you —" He took a breath and gave a shaky laugh. "You surprised me, that's all."

She bit her lip. "I shouldn't have done it. I was just —"

It had been a desperate attempt to smother the passion stirred by Conner's kisses. But when her lips had met Lance's, she'd felt nothing. Not a single thing.

Our marriage will not be passionate. She now knew that without a single doubt. *But that is fine, isn't it? Many marriages survive without passion.* Wasn't it more important to share common interests, enjoy easy conversations, and savor the joint enjoyment of a quiet, well-organized life, than to recklessly pursue a man who made one's knees weaken when he flashed a wicked grin, and who had the power to send one's spirits soaring or plummeting to the ground?

Common sense instantly answered that question. Sadly, her heart answered it in the opposite direction. Life with Conner would be wildly passionate and undeniably bliss- ful . . . or it would until he tired of being with her and at home, and sailed away, leaving her alone and forgotten.

Perhaps the truth was that neither of these men were right for her. The thought was lowering indeed.

Red faced, Lance smiled and gently squeezed her hand. "I didn't respond in a satisfactory way, did I? No, don't answer that." He took a steadying breath. "Perhaps . . . perhaps we should try that again. This time, I will try to —"

"Lance, I can't marry you." The words tumbled from her, propelled by her wretched thoughts, horrid dreams, and exhausted mind. She blinked, shocked that she'd said the words aloud.

"Well," he said, looking stunned.

That was it. Just "well."

She wetted her lips. *I hope I haven't broken his heart.* "Please. I-I'm sorry if —"

"Thank *God.*"

She stared at him.

Lance went back to the table and sank into his chair limply. "I'm — This is so — Theodora, *thank you.*"

She didn't know what to say. "You're glad."

"Ecstatic!" He flushed. "No, no. Not that I don't think you're — Theodora, you're an exceptional, beautiful, capable —"

"We would not suit."

"At *all*."

They exchanged surprised looks and then burst out laughing, both of them punch drunk with sweet relief.

Theodora sat back in her chair, gasping for breath. "Oh Lance! I've been questioning our relationship since we first eloped, but I couldn't find the words to say it."

"And I couldn't say it to you. Men cannot cry off."

"No, they can't. Society is brutally strict about that. How wretched for you. How long have you known this elopement to be an error?"

"To be honest, I suspected it the night before we left, and I knew it for certain once we were under way and you kept demanding I let you take the reins."

"I'm a good driver."

"And I'm not," he said frankly. "But I wished you'd *pretended* that I was."

"Oh. I'm not very good at pretending."

"No. And I fear my vanity rather wishes you were." He laughed. "I know, it's absurd."

She shrugged. "We all have expectations."

"I suppose so. I haven't slept a wink since we left, worrying . . ." He looked at her and said in a cautious tone, "To be honest, some of my concern was about Mother."

"I'm not surprised. She seems rather forceful."

"She is. I fear she might take umbrage at your spirit, which I like, of course. But Mother —" He spread his hands. "She is what she is."

"I was a bit worried about that, too. And your sisters . . . I had no idea I would be expected to launch them for their seasons."

"I suppose I should have mentioned that."

"*And* that you wished for six children —"

"Or more."

She shuddered. "One, perhaps. Two, maybe. I was also unaware that your mother would wish to name our first son, and that she'd live with us, and —" Theodora threw up her hands. "So many things! Didn't we talk *at all* before we eloped? What were we thinking?"

He chuckled and leaned back in his chair, looking younger and more carefree than she'd ever seen him. "Apparently we weren't thinking at all. We just met at a fortuitous time. I was looking for a wife. Mother has suggested repeatedly during the last year that it was time I married."

"But she hasn't liked your choices."

"Not yet. But it's made me realize how much I'd like to be married and have children and all that comes with it. So when I met you, and you are a beautiful, accomplished woman —" He smiled. "It seemed meant to be."

"Until you realized I am not what either you or your mother was hoping for."

"You're much too spirited for life on a farm." He hesitated. "I hope you will not think badly of either me or my mother. I truly respect and admire you. And Mother means well, but she's been different since Father died and —"

"Please, don't say another word. I honor you for caring so much for her. Was she the only reason you decided to marry?"

"No. There was more."

"Yes?"

He bit his lip and then said in a rush, "The honeymoon."

"The . . . *honeymoon*?"

"I never had the chance to take my grand tour — Father was ill, so I stayed home. Last year I decided that perhaps now was the time, so I began to plan a trip. That's when Mother suggested it was time I look for a wife."

"Ah! She thought getting married would keep you home."

"Foolish of her, I know, but I thought that I could do both if I planned a lengthy honeymoon." He looked around the cozy breakfast room and gave a regretful sigh. "I must admit, I was enjoying our trip. That was one of the things I liked about you — that you've traveled so much."

She smiled. "Too much. Meanwhile, I found your fondness for home life quite attractive; I'm worn-out from traveling so often."

"How ironic!" He shook his head at their foolishness. After a moment, he said simply, "So. What do we do now?"

What *did* they do now? "I suppose we will return to our homes and try to explain things."

"Oh." Lance's shoulders slumped. "Yes. I suppose we must." He absently folded one corner of the newspaper. "I wish we'd at least reached Scotland. I've always wanted to visit, but —" He sighed. "It's not to be."

"Apparently not."

"It's a pity, for I hear it's beautiful. I must admit, I wasn't looking forward to marrying over an anvil. I only suggested fleeing to Gretna Green because I didn't wish Mother to sabotage our engagement, which she would have done."

"I thought it would be romantic, but . . . no."

"We are both of a commonsensical nature.

I'm not sure romantic love is for us."

That might be true for Lance, but Theodora was perfectly capable of falling wildly, madly in love. It was annoying that life wasn't planned like the craft patterns in women's magazines — each step carefully explained, and accompanied by a clear, simple drawing showing the desired outcome. Real life was like trying to make one of those projects in the inky dark of night, without any instructions or the final picture, and sometimes, without either glue or scissors.

She sighed. "I don't look forward to returning home and telling my family we've changed our minds." And Conner . . . oh God, what would she tell him? He'd be so pleased, and would woo her with even more fervor than before. *How will I resist him?*

"Neither do I," Lance admitted. "I shall have to return home and this adventure will be over." He sighed, looking sad. "I suppose all good things must end." He reached into his pocket to pull out a small book and looked at it with a wistful smile. "I'll tell you something, if you promise not to laugh."

She smiled. "I promise."

He opened the book to the first page and handed it to her. "Before I left, I listed all of the places of interest near Gretna Green.

After we married, I was going to suggest we take some time and visit the area."

She looked at the list. "Carlisle Castle, the Cathedral —"

"Beautiful structures, both. I saw pictures."

"The gardens at Wordsworth House. I've heard of those."

"The roses are renowned. There are five more places that I thought we might enjoy seeing." He laughed ruefully. "Silly of me, wasn't it?"

"Not at all. I would have enjoyed them all."

"Really?"

"Absolutely. In fact . . ." She looked at the journal, a thought growing with each passing second. "Lance, what if we go anyway?"

"What?"

"You want to see the sights, and I'm not averse to that. We have a chaperone, and neither of us are eager to return home. Heaven knows I don't look forward to explaining the situation to my family, or Conner . . ."

"Ah yes, your family friend."

Something about the way Lance said it made Theodora look at him sharply. "He *is* just a family friend."

"Of course. He also needs to wed, and soon. Added to that, he knows you quite well, and . . ." Lance spread his hands wide. "I'm not a fool, Theodora. I can see, you know."

"Then you can see how red my face is right now."

"No, no! Don't be embarrassed." Lance's eyes softened with humor. "I don't blame Douglas for wishing to marry you; I rather wanted to myself."

"That was different. You were being noble, while he's being a pain in the —" She caught Lance's shocked expression and hastily said, "Either way, if you don't mind, I'd rather he didn't know our engagement was off."

"You don't wish to marry him."

"No."

"He won't just go away if you tell him to?"

"Lance, he was planning on following us all the way to Gretna; he's a stubborn, difficult man. Once we reach Scotland and he thinks the marriage imminent, he'll realize there's nothing more to be done and leave us be. Then we can explore the area at our leisure before we return home to face the music."

She handed him back the small journal and he slipped it into his pocket. "It's tempting," he said. "As you say, we have Miss Simmons to answer the concerns of propriety. I think she'd enjoy seeing some of the sights, too."

"I'm certain she would. She doesn't seem to have had a very exciting life so far."

Lance leaned back in his seat, and stared for a moment at his hands where they rested on his knees. Finally, he slapped the table with a decisive whack and stood. "Let's do this!"

She stood, too, relief making her dizzy. "Now I wish I'd said something several days ago!"

Laughing, he gave her a swift, brotherly hug. "Me, too. But this is going to be great fun —"

"Bloody hell!" The words cut through the room like a brutal swing of a sword.

Lance dropped his arms from Theodora's shoulders and stepped away like a thief caught in the act. "Douglas! You startled us!"

"Obviously." Conner's tone was ice-cold and deadly.

"We were just having breakfast. Care to join us?" Lance resumed his seat at the table, although his color was high.

Her heart sinking, Theodora was unable

to meet Conner's gaze. "It's a lovely morning."

"Is it?" he snarled.

She risked a peek and found his eyes blazing with fury.

Although Conner was dressed much the same as Lance, he managed to look more masculine, more sensual, more dangerous, more everything. His blue coat stretched over his powerful arms and shoulders, while his breeches clung to his muscular thighs in a way that made her knees go weak.

Her gaze locked on his sensual mouth, now pressed into a furious line.

She collected herself and said, "You're just in time for breakfast." She took a seat at the table, then pulled the forgotten dish of eggs to her plate. "I must say, this inn has an amazing cook." She smiled stiffly at Lance. "We should remember that, should we travel this way again."

He nodded. "So we should. Come, Douglas, the ham is exceptional." Despite his bold words, she was disappointed when Lance picked up his newspaper and disappeared behind it.

Conner fought the desire to rip the paper aside and punch the squire's face. How could the fool — and Thea — expect him to act as if nothing unusual had happened after he'd seen Thea in that man's bloody arms? How could he do *anything* after witnessing that?

His chest had tightened until he felt he couldn't breathe, and his head rang in the oddest way. But as they were not reacting, neither could he. They were engaged to be wed, and an embrace was perfectly normal.

But it didn't help him fight the fury that turned his vision red, and made his hands ache to throttle the squire, and it did nothing to cool the passion that burned through his veins at being so close to Thea.

He knew he should leave until his blood had cooled, but he'd be damned if he left them alone again. *Ever.*

Scowling, Conner sat down across from Thea.

Ignoring him, she filled her plate, the scent of thyme eggs and bacon making Conner's stomach growl to match his mood. She returned the serving spoon to the dish, and then poured herself some tea. The morning sun slanted over her creamy skin and light brown hair, lighting strands to gold and caramel. Her thick lashes crested her cheeks as she added a lump of sugar to her tea.

She doesn't look like a woman who's just been kissed. After *he'd* kissed her, she'd been breathless, flushed with passion, and panting with desire. But she wasn't the least bit breathless after Lance's embrace — and though her color was high, her gaze was locked upon her tea. *As if she were simply embarrassed.*

Some of Conner's fury abated and he leaned back in his chair. *Perhaps this is not a disaster after all.*

He couldn't stop looking at her. God, but she was lovely. Every move she made was graceful, and though she was doing the most mundane of tasks — stirring her tea, taking a sip, blowing on the hot liquid to cool it — every gesture was fraught with sensuality. He found himself imagining her in his bed, naked except for her unbound hair, her lips pursed in just such a way, only instead of tea she was blowing on his —

"I vow, but the Regent is a disgrace!" Lance said from behind the paper, rattling it in irritation.

Startled, Thea looked up from her cup, and her gaze met Conner's.

It was as if the world around them stilled, and disappeared. Her eyes, a deep melty brown, her lips — damp from her tea — parted as her breath rushed across them.

God, what he'd give to kiss that plump mouth. His body raged with fire, his cock so hard he wondered how it didn't hit the bottom of the table.

He could see she was affected by him, too. Yet she'd just kissed that buffoon.

Or had she? All he'd witnessed was a hug, and not a very passionate one, now that he thought about it. *Not yet, anyway.* Conner frowned, and Thea dropped her gaze back to her teacup, a wistful expression crossing her flushed face.

And then it hit him. He was responsible for what had happened. *I've been placing doubts in her head about this marriage, and it's sent her into Lance's arms, looking for assurance.*

Conner could have kicked himself. He'd been trying to push them apart, and all he'd done was — He frowned. "Where's your chaperone?"

Lance lowered his paper. "I hope she's still sleeping. It would be good for her, considering the shock her system took from the icy rain. It wouldn't surprise me if she took an ague —"

"Pardon me!" A voice from the door caused them all to turn toward a plump, yellow-haired maid ducking a curtsy.

"Alice." Thea looked relieved. "We will need more eggs now that Mr. Douglas has joined us."

The maid smiled at Conner, revealing a

missing tooth. "Good morning, sir."

He nodded.

It wasn't encouraging, but she simpered nonetheless.

"Alice?" Thea asked gently. "The eggs?"

"What? Oh. Of course. But I came for a different reason. Mrs. Landry says the squire here asked about the turnips we served at dinner last night." Alice cocked a disbelieving eye at Lance. "I told her she was suffering from deluges, but she swore you'd said it."

"I believe it's *delusions*," Lance said.

"I knew it! I'll tell her you said so." Alice spun and began to tromp out of the room.

"No, wait!" Lance stood, tossing the paper aside. "I did indeed ask her about the turnips, and she said she'd let me know when the farmer who'd supplied them returned."

"Gor', I'd have never thought it. You like turnips that much, do you?"

"I have a farm and they were excellent. I'd like to see if I can buy some."

"Oh! Well, he's here now, he is. I'll have him come see you."

"That's quite all right; I will speak with him in the kitchen. I daresay his boots are muddy. I assume he brought some other items with him?"

"He's delivering potatoes today."

"I'd like to see those, as well." Lance bowed to Thea. "Pardon me, if you will. I want to see if I can get some turnips for my own — *our* — farm."

"Of course," she said.

Conner watched with satisfaction as Lance left.

The second the squire's footsteps faded, Thea stood, dropping her napkin on the table. "I should go."

"Why?" Conner spooned eggs onto his plate and then picked up his fork. "In a rush to find another mon to kiss?"

"You cannot be upset I kissed my own fiancé."

He could, and he was. It was as if acid had been poured on his soul, and he couldn't keep the bitterness from his voice. "You're taking great chances with that mon."

"Nonsense. I'm quite safe with him."

"You're nae safe with any mon — nae alone." *Not even me.* Especially *not me.*

Her brows lifted, and she blew out her breath in disbelief. "I can't believe you, of all people, are warning me about the dangers of being alone with a man!"

She had a point. "Aye, 'tis strange. But I worry aboot you and this —" He bit off his words, worried they'd pour out like molten lava.

"You've nothing to worry about when it comes to Lance. He's a gentleman."

She sounded . . . disappointed.

Had the kiss been unsatisfactory? Conner's spirits rose a bit. Still, sometimes first kisses were awkward, but future ones — He frowned. He had to stop any future kisses. "Your chaperone should be here," he said bluntly. "What guid is she if she's sleeping while you're being ravished over breakfast?"

"For the last time, it was just a — Blast it, I don't have to answer to you, Conner Douglas." Thea's eyes flashed fire as she whirled on her heel and swept toward the door.

He threw his fork onto his plate, the sound making her steps quicken yet more. *Like hell you'll run from me!* He leapt up from the table and was after her, catching her just as she grasped the doorknob.

He slapped his hand on the door above her head and held it closed. "We're nae done talking."

She spun to face him. "I have nothing to say to you."

She was so close, he could see the golden streaks in her deep brown eyes.

"Thea, I'm worried aboot you —"

"I'm not a child."

"But I —"

"No. No. And no."

He opened his mouth.

"No!"

Dammit, I'm doing what I said I wouldn't — *challenging her until she's forced into that* *man's arms.* Conner ground his teeth and then took a steadying breath. "I dinnae mean to anger you, lass."

She crossed her arms. "Just move. I wish to see how Jane is faring."

Conner scowled. He had no reason to keep her here, but he couldn't make himself let her go.

She plopped her hands on her hips. "Move!"

"Not until you explain that embrace."

"It's none of your business."

"Everything aboot you is my business."

Her eyes narrowed. "No. Everything about me is *Lance's* business. *He* is my fiancé, not you. I don't answer to you, so it's my concern and no one else's."

"That's — I'm nae — I should bundle you oop and take you back home, where you'll be safe from your own foolishness!"

"I'm not going home. I'm moving forward with my life — or I am once you move out of my way."

Conner didn't budge.

She stepped forward, stubborn and furious, her chest a mere hairsbreadth from his. *"Move. Now."*

He moved, his fury pushing him forward. He wrapped his arms around her and pulled her to him, smothering her protest with a kiss. He kissed her with every bit of the hurt he felt, every bit of the anger that simmered through him, every bit of the deep longing he felt every time he remembered that she'd chosen another man over him. *I want her with every ounce of my soul.*

For a second, she stayed frozen. But when he deepened the kiss, she melted against him with a suddenness that sent his senses reeling. Her arms slipped about his neck and she pressed herself to him, moaning softly as she opened her mouth to him.

The kiss deepened further, their breaths mingling, their bodies straining against one another. Her perfume filled his senses until he was drunk with it. The room disappeared, their anger burned away by the fury of passion. His hands slid up her back, and then down, cupping her perfect bottom, wanting her so badly he burned with it.

Her hands tangled in his lapels to hold him closer as her tongue brushed his, sending a wild flame through him, driving him into a wave of lust so strong he thought he would drown.

God, he wanted this woman. Desired her. *Needed* her. He lifted her off her feet and Thea shivered, her hands twining about his neck. Her full breasts were pressed to his chest, stirring —

Footsteps sounded on the stairs, accompanied by a feminine cough.

Jane.

Thea broke the kiss, blinking as if she'd just come awake, her breath as ragged as his own. Her gaze locked with his.

And he saw passion, regret, and a flash of deep sadness.

The intensity of her feelings stole his thoughts and chilled his roaring passion like ice on a fire.

He'd never meant to make her sad. Never.

His heart ached, and he leaned his forehead against hers. "Thea, my love. We —"

She pushed free, her eyes shiny with tears. "That wasn't supposed to happen. Not again. I — I can't have it." She spoke quietly but with certainty, her voice husky.

"There's something powerful between us," he protested.

"Oh? Then what is it?" She waited, her gaze so direct that it burned.

He raked a hand through his hair, his

thoughts still muddled by passion. "We're . . . attracted to one another."

"Attracted." Her voice was dull, as if her feelings had been severed by his statement. "That's all."

Damn, he didn't know what was what, not after that kiss. All he knew was that she burned him to the soul. "Dammit, I wish to God I'd seen this before now. Seen *you.* Somehow I missed this passion. You were always there, right in front of me, but I didn't recognize you."

"Why? What would you have done?"

He rubbed his jaw, his mouth still warm from her kisses. He tried to think, but his gaze fell on her lips and all thought disappeared. "Hell, lass, I dinnae know."

She gave a pained laugh. "And *that* is why that kiss should have never happened. Now, if you'll excuse me, I'm going to meet Jane."

"Thea, wait." Conner took a step toward her, but he was too late.

She'd already yanked open the door and whisked from the room, her skirts swirling as she disappeared.

He was left with empty arms, his body still afire.

Blast it to hell! Conner scowled, the coolness of Thea's expression as she'd left sinking the small amount of hope he'd managed to find. He'd made things worse. He should never have kissed her. Every time they were alone, he found himself pulling her into his arms, which only made her more determined to avoid him.

Bloody hell, I sailed my ship directly into the eye of a hurricane. He'd have to change course quickly, or there would be no recovering.

So what the hell was he supposed to do now? Thea needed to spend time with the squire in order to see his unsuitability, but Conner would never again trust that man to be alone with her. Sadly, Jane wasn't a fit chaperone. The girl could barely take care of herself.

Out in the hallway he could hear Jane telling Thea of the restless night she'd faced and all of her new complaints, every tenth word or so accompanied by an annoying sniff.

Conner couldn't handle more people right now. Cursing to himself, he headed for the servants' door, leaving the breakfast room empty.

15

Muttering to himself, Conner stalked down the dark hallway and into the kitchen.

The innkeeper's wife gasped on seeing him, while the yellow-haired maid eyed him as if he were a rasher of bacon and she a starving wolf.

"Law!" Mrs. Landry dipped a curtsy. "Are you lost, perchance?"

"Nae. I merely wished to go to the stables, and it seemed shorter to travel through here."

"It is shorter," the apple-cheeked maid agreed, her lashes fluttering in an odd fashion.

He wondered if she had something in her eye, but decided it would be rude to mention it.

Mrs. Landry pointed to a large wooden door. "Go through that door and down the garden path, then to the left."

"I'll take you, if you'd like," the maid offered, smoothing her hands over her skirt in a suggestive way.

"Alice!" Mrs. Landry hissed, her face red.

"What? I can't be kind to the gentleman? He doesn't mind, do you, sir?"

Conner wondered if the poor lass was having a fit of some type, the way her lashes quivered. "Thank you, but I'll find my own way." He strode to the door.

The scent of dried leaves and winter dampness met Conner as he entered the garden, the gravel pathway crunching under his boots. As he turned the corner, he caught sight of Lance down the lane that curled around the back of the house, speaking earnestly to a rough-dressed farmer.

Neither of them noticed Conner as he reached the end of the path and made his way to the stables. Inside, Ferguson and Spencer polished the trace links, arguing about the coming weather.

"Cap'n!" Spencer tossed his rag over the edge of a nearby bucket and wiped his hands on his breeches. "You're oop early."

"So I am," Conner bit out.

The men exchanged glances and Ferguson hung the traces on a hook before saying in a cautious voice, "Did you have breakfast? Should I fetch you a bite from the kitchen?"

"I've nae wish to eat. Nae now." He

scowled. "Our plan to rescue Miss Cumberbatch-Snowe has hit some shoals. This morning I found the squire making improper advances to her."

"That lout!" Ferguson lifted his fists. "I should give him a lesson in how to treat a lady."

"Miss Cumberbatch-Snowe must be furious," Spencer added.

Conner scowled, remembering how Thea had leaned into that damned idiot's embrace, a smile on her face. His chest tightened until he couldn't breathe.

The silence grew.

Spencer's fists lowered. "That improper advance . . . it dinnae make her furious?"

"Bloody hell, nae," Conner snapped. "Which is why 'tis a problem." He paced up and down the straw-covered floor, raking his hand through his hair. "I may have made an error in thinking that the squire and Miss Cumberbatch-Snowe should spend more time together. I'd hoped she would come to see it isn't a guid match, but that has nae happened." Scowling, he turned and tromped back the way he'd come. "My rigging is in a right knot over this."

"Women!" Ferguson blew out a sigh. "They're hurricanes in the making, the lot of them. You cannae predict them, and when they come your way they're bound to flounder you, if nae worse."

"Aye," Conner said glumly.

Spencer said, "What do you suggest, Cap'n? If the miss has taken a liking to the squire, it dinnae seem as if there's aught as can be done."

"She has nae taken a liking to him." Conner spat the words. "She likes him, aye, but she's nae in love. She needs to get to know him better, but withoot the bloody kissing. She needs a better chaperone."

"Nae to be disrespecting Miss Simmons," Ferguson said, "but she's a wee bit young to be a chaperone."

"At her best, she's but half a chaperone," Conner agreed. "And when she's indisposed or just late coming doon to breakfast, she's nae a chaperone at all."

Spencer rubbed his chin. " 'Tis a pity Miss Cumberbatch-Snowe dinnae have a lady's maid."

Ferguson snorted. "What guid would a lady's maid do?"

"Think on it: if Miss Simmons is half of a chaperone, then a lady's maid might be the other half."

Conner considered this. "That's nae a bad thought." Two chaperones might keep Thea free of the squire. But would it be enough to curb his own ever-growing desires? It would have to. "Ferguson, bring me the itinerary. I've a mind to set a new course that slips to the west before heading north. That will add a few more days."

"Ah! Setting a kedge, are you, Cap'n? Verrah guid. I'll fetch the maps." Ferguson hurried out of the stables to the coach, and soon returned with a small leather packet.

"Excellent." Conner tucked the packet under his arm. "Get the coach and horses ready. The squire cannae continue his seduction crammed between a sneezing Miss Simmons and a lady's maid. Now, to find a maid willing to —" He blinked. "Bloody hell, I think I've an answer. Thank you, men. You've been a great help."

Deep in thought, Conner retraced his steps through the garden, stopping short when he saw the squire walking back to the inn. Perhaps . . . just perhaps . . . this was the answer to his problem.

He strode swiftly forward and called out, "Lance! So tell me, what did you find oot aboot your amazing turnips?"

16

Theodora watched as the final pieces of luggage were strapped to the coach. It was barely nine and they were already preparing to get under way. Now that Lance was sightseeing rather than eloping, he was much more prompt.

"Ah! Theodora!" Jane came out of the inn, holding her knitting basket and a handkerchief. "I was just looking for —" She sneezed into her kerchief.

"I wish we had medicine for that sneeze." Poor Jane's face was flushed and her eyes shiny as if they were watering. "Perhaps you should see a doctor before we leave."

"I'm fine, truly." Jane tugged her coat closer about her, her gaze drifting to where Conner spoke with Lance near the horses. "Is Mr. Douglas riding in the coach with us?"

Theodora tried to ignore the hopeful note in Jane's voice. "No, he's not." *Because I won't let him.* "Conner will ride his horse and will likely meet us at the next inn."

Jane watched Conner as she absently sneezed again into her kerchief. "It's a pity he's not riding with us. He's a very interesting man."

He was a thorn in Theodora's side, was what he was, and their journey would be much better off without him. Life would be less complicated, and right now that was all she wanted.

She tried not to watch Conner, but it was difficult. Even though he was dressed with unusual propriety today in a typical blue coat and buff britches, he'd managed to make the outfit seem rakish. In addition to the sensual slant of his smile, he wore a wide leather belt that held a brace of pistols. The silver handles, heavily engraved and shiny, peeped out when he lifted his arm, as he was doing now.

It was just like him to appear in some ways so very normal and perhaps even marriageable. But then he lifted his arm and reminded one that he was neither, but was instead a dashing privateer with a deep desire to sail away from everyone and everything he knew.

"His horse is lovely." Jane patted her pink nose with her kerchief. "But so spirited! It keeps prancing about — I don't know how Mr. Douglas will stay astride."

"He's an accomplished rider," Theodora said grudgingly. She envied Conner his ride, for the unexpectedly mild weather combined with the rolling green hills beckoned to her. She wished she'd thought to bring her favorite mare.

Jane tucked her handkerchief into her knitting basket, her gaze still on Conner. "Perhaps I'll knit a man's scarf. I have some pale blue yarn left over from another project."

Pale blue, like Conner's eyes. Theodora stifled the urge to say something cutting for no good reason whatsoever. "Come, let's get in the coach. Perhaps that will encourage the men to be on our way."

"Gor', I get to ride in *that*?"

Theodora turned.

The maid Alice stood in the doorway, a limp bonnet mashed over her curls, a serviceable coat hanging from her shoulders, and a bruised hatbox clutched in one hand. "It looks like a fairy-tale coach, it does!"

Theodora blinked. "I'm sorry, but what —" She spoke to air, for Alice had already stomped past and was now peering into the coach's open door.

The maid dropped her hatbox and then

reached in and pressed a fist against a velvet-covered seat. "Why, my bottom will be as comfortable as that of a fat angel sitting on a cloud!"

Theodora looked at Jane, who appeared equally shocked. Collecting herself, Theodora forced a smile. "Alice, there seems to have been a mistake. You aren't coming with us."

Alice kept punching the seat. "Oh, but I am."

Theodora narrowed her gaze. "By whose request?" *Conner Douglas, if you are up to more trickery* —

"The squire asked me to come."

That brought Theodora up short. "The squire?"

"Oh yes. He's unhappy you don't have no lady's maid."

"A lady's maid? But I never asked him to —"

"He said it were to be a surprise, miss. But a *necessary* one."

Though Conner's name hadn't come up, Theodora couldn't help sliding an accusing glance his way. He was still laughing and talking with Lance, which suddenly seemed suspicious indeed. "He did, did he?"

"Aye. I'm to go with you all the way to wherever you're going, which I hope will be

Lunnon, as I've never been."

"We are not going to London," Theodora said with finality.

Alice's face fell, but she recovered instantly. "Oh well, wherever you go, I'm sure it will be better than here." She reclaimed her hatbox and beamed at them both. "So? Do we leave soon?"

"No," Theodora said grimly. "Excuse me for a moment, I must have a word with the squire." She gathered her skirts and marched across the inn yard.

Conner's gaze met hers the instant she moved in his direction, and she detected a hint of laughter there. He nudged Lance, whose back was to her, and the squire turned.

On seeing her expression, Lance's smile faltered, but by the time she reached him it was back in place. "Theodora! There you are. We should be leaving soon, so —"

"Did you hire that girl to be my lady's maid?"

Lance's smile faded a bit. "Alice? Why, yes. I thought it would be a nice surprise and —"

"I do not need a lady's maid. I've been using Spencer's services."

"I know, but he won't be with us forever." Lance gave her a significant look as he spoke that made her pause.

"Oh." Lance was right. Once they reached Gretna, and rid themselves of Conner and his servants, she would be without any help with her clothes. "Does Alice know anything about being a lady's maid?"

"She'll learn. Besides, it's only for a few days and then we'll be home, and you can hire someone more to your liking." Smiling, Lance took her hand and pressed a kiss to her fingers. "The least I can do is provide you with the proper servants, seeing as how our trip has become so convoluted."

There was a hint of the theatric to Lance's gesture, and she knew it was for Conner's benefit. Well, two could play that game. Aware of Conner's gaze, she smiled up at Lance. "You were being thoughtful, as usual."

"I was trying to be. But if you don't wish her to join us —"

"No, no. You're right; Spencer won't be with us forever," she said sweetly, slipping a glance at Conner. She was rewarded to see a black scowl flicker over his face, and she fought the urge to laugh. *Your machinations are not working, are they?*

What had he hoped to accomplish by encouraging Lance to hire Alice as a maid? The girl couldn't have the skills to perform the work. All she would do was take up another seat in the coach and — *Ah ha. Jane isn't enough of a chaperone now that she's ill — so now I've two.*

Theodora looked back at Alice, who was now patting the coach's glazed window as if it were a puppy, her expression blissful.

The girl would enjoy the trip, at least. Frustrated, but unable to do more, Theodora slipped her hand into the crook of Lance's arm and smiled in what she hoped was a lovestruck way. "Shall we go, then?"

"Of course." Lance tipped his hat to Conner. "Enjoy your ride."

"Thank you." Still scowling, Conner turned to his horse and climbed into the saddle, looking like the dashing hero of some novel, rather than the annoying man she knew him to be.

The animal stamped its feet and shook its mane, anxious to be off.

Conner touched his hat to Theodora. "Until dinner." Still looking vaguely put out, he lightly touched his heels to his steed and cantered off, leaving Theodora glaring at him hard enough to drill a hole between his shoulders.

17

Theodora leaned her forehead against the window, hoping the cool glass might ease the headache that had grown throughout the day. Across from her, Alice was blithely chatting about all the things she hoped to see on their trip north — other inns, lakes, military men (who seemed to be great favorites with her), large pigs (really large ones, not the smallish ones she always saw in her village), fine ladies, and (inexplicably) bears. Lance hid behind a book on crop rotation, while Jane alternated between sneezing, knitting, and dozing.

The coach, which had seemed luxuriously large before, now felt stiflingly small. Between Jane's knitting basket, Alice's large hatbox, Lance's satchel of books, Theodora's reticule, three foot warmers, and a number of coach blankets, there was little room to do more than lean against one's assigned corner, while every bump knocked someone's knee against someone else's.

Pressing her fingertips to her temples, Theodora wished she could throw open the door and jump to freedom.

Jane sneezed again, this time followed by a long cough.

Alice tsked. "Law, miss! You sound like the devil's crawled into your lungs and died."

Jane flushed and looked miserable. "I'm sorry!"

"Alice!" Lance said in a reproving voice. "Jane does no such thing!"

Jane gave a wobbly smile. "It's quite all right. I sound worse than I feel."

Theodora didn't believe that for a moment, but wisely made no comment, and returned to gazing out the window. Outside the day grew darker, clouds gathering. A soft rain pattered on the coach roof, streaks of water racing down the glass. The minutes passed and Alice, her observations apparently exhausted, fell asleep in her corner, her head tilted back, her mouth wide open as she snored.

Eyes watering, Jane tucked her kerchief into her pocket and then tugged more yarn from her basket. "It's so dreary this afternoon. I —" Her gaze moved past Theodora and caught on something. She blinked once.

Then twice. Her mouth dropped open.

Theodora turned and there, riding outside the window, was Conner. She looked away. *I will not look. I will not look. I will not —*

But she couldn't resist. She not only looked, but she stared. The light rain beaded on Conner's shoulders, pooled in the brim of his hat, and then splashed onto his broad shoulders, his handsome face wet, his hair clinging to his neck in a beguiling fashion.

She scowled. Why was it that when women were drenched by rain, they merely looked soggy, while men mysteriously appeared even more attractive and powerful? *The whole thing is bloody unfair.* Conner tugged his hat low, the brim funneling water down the sweep of his cape, his boots shiny and wet in the stirrups. As if he could feel her gaze he turned his head, and their eyes met.

For a breathless moment they looked at one another, and the feel of their last kiss burned Theodora's lips anew.

It was hard enough to travel with a man she'd once been in love with, without his looking so damnably romantic, riding in the rain, his clothes clinging to him, his blue eyes warm with — lust?

What else could it be? He knows no other feeling where women are concerned.

Yet her heart thudded wildly, and she

found herself leaning toward the glass. Conner smiled, his intriguing eyes crinkling. The ice-blue color set in those thick, dark brown lashes was a surprise, and they burned with an intensity that made her wish for all the things that would never be.

Conner's teeth flashed in a grin and he winked, and she felt a tremor from her heart all the way to the bottom of her feet. She pulled away from the window. It took all of her self-control not to look outside again, but she managed. When she finally peeked sideways, he was gone.

She leaned to the side and saw him ahead, trotting farther and farther away.

The sight invoked a memory she'd almost forgotten. When she'd been sixteen, her horse had thrown a shoe while she'd been out riding. Leading him home, she'd been caught in a rainstorm and had sought shelter in the folly across the lake near Cumberbatch House. A "ruined" Greek temple with toppled columns, ivy-covered statues, and a raised pagoda, it had been designed for romantic summer picnics.

Since she was so late returning, her parents had organized a search party that Conner, visiting with Derrick on a school break, had joined.

And he'd been the one who'd thought to

look in the pagoda.

Theodora had already been half in love with him, and when she'd seen him ride up, rain-wet as he was now, her imagination had turned his shiny, wet cape into a suit of armor, and his gelding into a magnificent steed worthy of carrying a knight into battle.

Naturally he'd had no idea of the romantic thoughts racing through her head, and had treated her like a younger sister, teasing her about hiding from dinner because she'd heard Cook was to serve parsnips, and laughingly demanding a shilling for giving her a ride home.

For her, though, he was already the focus of all of her youthful dreams and desires. So when he'd climbed into the saddle and swept her up in front of him, covered her with his cape and taken her back to the house with his arms around her, it had been a golden moment stolen from her own romantic imagination.

Getting ready for dinner that night, she'd floated about her room, remembering the strength of his arms, the warmth of his smile when he'd found her, as if she were the only woman for him; had pictured his declaration — oh, she'd imagined all sorts of things. And her imagination added details to the events that had happened — that his gaze had lingered on her for an unusually long time after one of the grooms had lifted her down, that he'd walked his horse very slowly on the way home as if prolonging their moment, and that he'd seemed *especially* happy to have been the one to find her.

When she'd gone down to dinner, she'd breathlessly waited to see him again, thinking things would be different now — that *they* would be different. But he'd merely chucked her under the chin as if she were a child and said in a teasing voice, "I hope you've learned to take an umbrella when you ride!" He'd laughed as if he'd made a great joke and, called away by her brother to see something, made no effort to speak to her again.

Devastated, she'd fought tears throughout dinner, her heart torn in two. As soon as she could, she'd escaped to her bedchamber where, cheeks hot and spirits low, she'd wept and paced the floor, cursing her stupidity for so childishly *hoping*.

It was a lesson she needed to remember now. She was through imagining her happiness; she wanted *real* happiness. The kind that climbed into bed with one each and every night. The kind that stayed during the good times, the bad times, and the slow times in between. She hadn't given up the belief that somewhere there was a man willing to be just that for her, someone she could respect and admire, someone capable of loving her as fiercely as she would love them.

Conner disappeared from sight, and a hollowness settled into her heart as she leaned back against the squabs.

Why must he follow us? But Thea knew why, and part of her trembled with excitement, the other in fear.

Jane tsked. "It's too cold and wet to be outside like that. We could have offered him a seat in the coach."

Theodora made a vague noise in response.

"He will take cold in that rain," Jane fretted. "The poor man must be drenched."

Good. Maybe he'll stop early at a different inn than ours.

Jane sighed. "I do hope Mr. Douglas doesn't take ill —"

"He'll be fine!" Theodora burst out.

Jane's eyes widened while Lance lowered his book, surprise in both their gazes.

Her face hot, Theodora said in a defiant tone, "Conner is forever outside in all sorts of weather — he loves it. You should hear him talking of the storms he's faced aboard ship."

"That's true," Lance mused. "The life-style of a privateer is indeed for the hearty — and usually the undisciplined, although Douglas does not strike me as the latter."

Which showed how little he knew Conner, Theodora decided, although she held her tongue on the tempting topic.

Jane and Lance embarked upon a discussion of the effects of being outside in the weather constantly, which led them to share seemingly every illness they and their families had suffered.

Bored, Theodora leaned back in her seat. Alice snorted in her sleep, muttering something about gooble-gooks and the need for a sharp knife, a comment so disturbing to Lance that he pulled himself farther into his corner of the coach, and tucked his coat about his legs.

Soon the coach slowed, and Theodora was relieved to see they were turning into an inn yard. "Here we are," she said with relief, peering out the window through the heavy streaks of rain at the inn. Two stories tall, with a rambling rock façade where a pink rosebush climbed, the thatched roof was golden in color. The building sat by the road surrounded by green fields and a stand of trees.

It was odd to see such a large establishment in the middle of a farming district, but perhaps they were close to the North Road, which was always busy this time of year.

Pulling her knitting basket together, Jane peered out the window, too. "It looks like a large fairy cottage!"

"Except for that cart blocking the entry-way," Lance said.

"Oh dear," Jane said. "It looks as if one wheel has sunk into the mud."

Lance tugged on his coat. "Stay here and I'll see what's to be done about the cart." He opened the door and jumped out into the rain, slamming the door closed.

Theodora frowned. "Moving the cart will only save us a few steps. There's no reason for Lance or anyone else to get soaked for that. We should jump out and run for the door."

Alice rubbed her eyes and yawned. "We'll get wet."

"Only for a moment if we hurry."

Jane didn't look so decided. "The mud looks treacherous. Just look at how deep that wheel is sunk."

"Gor', you're right," Alice exclaimed. "We would sink in up to our —"

"That's highly unlikely." Theodora shook out the cloak she'd rolled into a pillow for

Jane earlier, and slung it over her shoulders. She could just make out Lance under the overhang speaking to Spencer and a familiar figure in a black overcoat, his broad shoulder blocking the door from view. *Of course Conner's already here.* He *got to ride.*

She bit back a mutter. "I'm going to see what's happening."

"Aye, you go and find out," Alice said cheerfully. "We'll wait here."

Jane frowned. "Theodora, just wait until —"

Theodora threw open the coach door and hopped out, water splashing around her boots. The rain was harder than she'd expected as she shut the door and made a dash toward the overhang. Her shoulders became instantly damp under her cloak, and rain soaked through her hood into her bonnet.

She ducked her head against the rain, lifted her skirts, and ran. She'd only gone a few steps when she came to a puddle so deep, she knew that the water would go over the top of her boots.

Blast it!

She looked for a way around, but the puddle seemed to go on forever. The rain sluiced unrelentingly, water now trickling from her neck and shoulders down her back.

There was a slightly narrower section to her right, so she gritted her teeth and hurried over, splashing with each step. Once there, she jumped as far as she could, the rain pelting her face. To her relief, she cleared the puddle.

Then one foot began to sink into the mud.

She quickly lifted it free, which put all of her weight on her other foot, and *it* sank into the mire, soaking up the wet and cold.

"Blast it!" She put the first foot back down, but the other foot was now ankle deep in the mud and she couldn't tug it free. She was thoroughly drenched now, the rain soaking through to her skin. There was only one answer.

She bent down and unlaced her boots, her fingers fumbling on the wet laces. Finished, she stood and was taking a deep breath before plunging on, when a deep voice said, "Stubborn woman!"

Then she was summarily swung up into Conner's arms and carried away, her boots left behind in the mud.

18

"What are you doing!"

Conner looked down at the indignant woman in his arms. "Pulling your stubborn arse oot of the mud."

"I don't need your help!"

"Aye, you do, and you know it. You'd have ended oop face-doon in the mud if nae for me."

She glared up at him, despite the rain that fell on her face. "Put me down! I'll be fine on my own."

"You want me to put you doon right now? Into a puddle? I'm nae so ungentlemanly." His eyes glinted at her. "If I were, I'd make you pay a toll before setting you free." They reached the overhang, and he was glad to see that Spencer and Lance had gone to the stables to look for shovels and an oil canvas hay cover, if one could be found. He bent closer, his lips at her temple. " 'Twas a sweet toll to pay, too."

There was a moment of silence. "What was the toll?"

"A kiss," he murmured against her rain-sweet skin, his lips tingling at the brief touch.

Her gaze locked with his and she bit her lip, which caused him untold agony. "You shouldn't say such things," she said. "Some-one will hear."

"Everyone who could hear is in the stables or in the coach."

And if ever a woman looked as if she needed a kiss, it was she. Her hair clung to her cheeks in wet curls, her skin glowed pink from his teasing, her moist lips were slightly parted — he yearned to devour her.

Conner reluctantly set Theodora on her feet, sliding her body down his. Their wet clothes were warm where they pressed together, and he was glad she didn't move away.

A quick look told him Lance was still gone —

And then Thea sighed and stepped back. "We must fetch the others. Jane's cold is growing worse."

"Lance is looking for a canvas cover to shield them from the rain, so he may lead them around the edge of the inn yard, away from this mud. Had you waited, you'd have benefitted from that and might still have your boots."

She flashed him a *don't start with me* look, untied her bonnet, and dragged it from her head, her wet curls framing her beautiful eyes.

She's like a rain-drenched flower, she is.

She looked down at her muddied, stockinged feet. "My poor boots," she said mournfully.

"After this rain lets up, I'll send Spencer to fetch and clean them. They'll be as guid as new." Or so Conner hoped.

"You mean Alice, my lady's maid, will clean my boots."

"I doubt she'd know how to clean leather."

"Or anything else." Thea poked him in the chest. "*You* are the reason I've been saddled with that poor girl. You convinced Lance I needed a maid; that I would feel ill-used if I did not have one."

Conner was fascinated by the way her bottom lip pressed outward when she was angry. It was damned tantalizing, and made him yearn to kiss it back into a smile.

He realized she was waiting for his answer and said, " 'Tis possible I said something to that effect."

"And you did it because you wanted to keep me from being alone with Lance."

"Nae."

"No? Then why did you do it?"

"Stop, Thea. Just accept 'tis for the best."

"Because you say so?" Her chin went up, her eyes flashing fire. "I will *not*. I want to know why you —"

"Bloody hell!" he burst out. "Dinnae you see? 'Twasnae just the squire. I could nae trust *myself*!"

The words hung between them like ice on a ship's rail, hard and brilliant.

She looked at him, wide-eyed and shocked. *"You?"*

God, why had he admitted that? "Aye, me," he snapped. "Every time we're alone, I end oop kissing you. At this very moment, you're fortunate we're in full view of those blasted women and my servants, or I'd have you in my arms right now. For *much* more than a kiss too."

Her lips parted and something glistened in her eyes — Fear? Desire? He had no way of knowing.

She swallowed hard. "And . . . that would be . . . bad."

The hesitation in her voice sent hot blood rushing through him, and he fought a deep moan. God, he wanted her so badly — his body yearned for her with a depth he couldn't quell. "With you, Thea, I want more than kisses. I want everything."

She knew what he meant; her cheeks warmed to a delicious shade of rose. But he also saw a hint of longing, as if she wondered what that "more" *could be.*

His cock grew rock hard, and it took all of his determination not to drag her into the inn and kiss her breathless, touch her in ways he'd dreamed of, make her cry out his name with —

"So you hired Alice to keep that from happening."

He had to take a deep breath before he could talk, and even then his voice was harsh. "Aye. Between the chaperone and a lady's maid, I hoped to make you safe."

A movement caught his gaze, and with relief, he saw Lance and Spencer approaching the coach. "Jane is aboot to be liberated."

Thea's lashes dropped to hide her expression as she turned toward the coach, and Conner wondered whether she was disappointed or happy at the interruption.

Spencer opened the coach door. Holding a large canvas cover, Lance leaned inside. Conner could see Jane's dark head through the opening. Lance spoke earnestly, but Jane, pink-faced, kept shaking her head.

Lance argued, but still Jane shook her

head. Obviously frustrated, he finally reached through the door, threw the cover over Jane, and pulled her into his arms.

Then he strode around the edge of the muddy yard to where Conner and Thea stood, and set down his wriggling burden.

"Oof, you — you —" Jane pushed the cover from her head, her bonnet askew as she glared at Lance. "That's — I never — What —" She coughed and scrambled for her handkerchief.

"Here." Conner tugged out his own handkerchief and pressed it into her hand.

She covered her mouth until her coughing had subsided, her cheeks sporting blooms of color. Her gaze never left Lance. "That was uncalled for!"

"It was for your own good," Lance said apologetically.

"Jane, we must get you inside," Thea announced.

Jane's hurt gaze remained on Lance. "I told you I'd wait until the rain had subsided."

"It's too cold."

"But I —" She coughed again, this one deeper.

"Get inside," Theodora ordered.

Conner added, "Our bedchambers will nae be ready yet, but I've hired a private parlor and there's a fire."

Jane's cough subsided. "I'm not —"

"Either you get inside where it's dry and warm," Lance announced, "or I'll carry you."

Jane's eyes widened, and Thea slipped her arm into Jane's. "Come. You may not need that fire, but I do."

Jane's lips pressed into a straight line, but then she said, "Fine. But only because you need the —"

"Helllllllooooo! Mr. Douglas! I'm still here!"

Everyone turned back to the coach, where Alice was standing in the open doorway, waving frantically.

Thea unwrapped the cover from Jane's shoulders and handed it to Conner.

"Me?" Conner looked through the pouring rain to where strapping Alice waved enthusiastically. "But I —"

"You." Then she turned back to Lance. "Lead the way to this fire."

"Of course." Pulling off his wet hat, Lance held the door open.

As Jane went inside, Thea looked back at Conner with a smile and a twinkle in her eyes that made the gloomy afternoon seem much brighter.

He found himself returning her smile. At

least he could make her laugh. That was something.

He watched her until she disappeared inside. Perhaps he'd been going about this all wrong. Seduction was only one weapon. He could also —

"Helllllooooo! Whot about me?" Alice jumped up and down, the coach bouncing.

Sighing, Conner held the cover over his head and headed back into the rain.

19

Theodora sighed, her breath wafting in the steam rising from the copper tub.

Once Alice had alighted from the coach, she'd changed into dry clothing and then arrived in Theodora's room with a dry gown and a robe. Without being asked, Alice had ordered tea to be brought to the room and a hot bath. She'd been quite picky, twice sending back water she deemed not hot enough, ordering a gawking footman to "stop lollygagging like a lump" and fetch soap and towels, and in general taking over with such aplomb that Theodora's opinion of the girl increased significantly.

For someone who'd never served as a lady's maid, Alice had done remarkably well, her fingers nimble, her manner sure if a little outspoken. Plus her forthright attitude was quite effective with the servants at the inn, so even that couldn't be found wanting.

Now Theodora looked at her pruning fingers, sighed, and rose from the tub. She dried off with the towel Alice had left to warm over a chair before the crackling fire. Sighing with the luxury of it, Theodora finished drying and wrapped herself in her robe.

It was late afternoon now, the rain a mere drizzle. Jane must be asleep, for silence came from her room, which was connected to Theodora's by a narrow door. Somewhere downstairs, she could hear masculine voices and the clink of cutlery.

No doubt Conner was busy manipulating Lance into acquiring more staff. It wouldn't surprise her if she climbed into the coach tomorrow morning and found it stuffed with a housekeeper, a chef, and a squadron of kitchen maids, as well.

And all to protect me from him — not Lance. That had been an astounding discovery. She couldn't help being relieved that she wasn't the only one fighting this blinding attraction. But the fact that he'd gone to such an extent to keep from being alone with her made her feel cheated in some way, as if he was stopping the natural progression of things.

But he's right to stop this now. I know the dangers all too well.

Theodora pulled a chair near the crackling fire and sat down, the heat soaking through her silk robe and heating her to toasty warmness. She glanced up at the clock — good, she still had an hour before dinner.

Alice had ironed a gown and left it on the bed. It was one of Theodora's favorites, pale blue with long sleeves and delicate cream lace trim. She slipped into her chemise and petticoat, then the gown, but she couldn't reach the laces. She sighed, and went toward Jane's room to see if she was awake. Theodora had just taken a few steps when she heard a scuffling sound in the hallway outside her door. *Ah! Spencer has finished cleaning my boots.* The footman had kindly retrieved them from the mud and promised to deliver them once he was done.

She hurried to her door and swung it open, her gaze on the floor. There, still wet but brushed into submission, were her favorite boots, every vestige of mud gone. And beside them was another pair of boots, masculine and shining, the toes facing her direction.

Her heart pounding, she allowed her gaze to move up those boots to the breeches that caressed familiar muscular legs, to a deep green waistcoat over a powerful chest, a beautifully fitted blue coat resting on wide shoulders, his hair still damp from the rain.

"Conner." Who else would be so bold as to stand outside the room of a woman betrothed to another? She lifted her gaze to his, which was ablaze with illicit desire and barely controlled passion. Her body instantly leapt in response, her stomach heating, her nipples tightening in need. *Oh my God. I* like *that he is unbridled and wild. I* enjoy *that about him, and crave it.*

She wanted — lusted for — a man who was fiery, untamed, and uncontrolled, someone who pushed her to feel and be the same. It was disquieting to think she might like such a dangerous sort of man, she who craved hearth and home. *The two will never fit.*

She backed up a step, the cool air reminding her that her gown was still open at the back. Her face hot, she whipped to the side so her back was against the doorframe. "Wh-what are you doing here?"

"I brought your boots. I was just going to leave them here, but then you opened the door."

God, but she loved his voice. Rich, and deep, with that delicious Scottish lilt. How could she ever live with a flat English accent after hearing such?

She realized Conner waited for her reply.

"I didn't know you were in the hallway." It was a stupid thing to say, but right now, she couldn't think of anything better.

"You surprised me, as weel." Conner placed a hand on the wall by her head, his gaze moving over her damp, tumbled hair, then over her face and finally coming to rest on her lips. "Spencer did a fine job cleaning your boots. He'd have brought them himself, but he's under Lance's direction in the kitchen. They're making a posset for puir Jane."

Theodora looked at the door next to hers. "Is she worse?"

"She's nae in that room, lass. Her bedchamber is doon the hall now. The fireplace in that room smokes, and Lance feared it would worsen her cough, so he had Alice move her."

"That was kind of him."

Conner's gaze met hers and after a hesitation, he sighed. "He's a guid mon, as much as I wish I could say otherwise. He says this posset is something his mother makes for one of his sisters when she has a cough. 'Twill make Jane sleep easy."

"Poor thing. I should go to her." Theodora started forward, but her sleeve slipped, which reminded her yet again that her gown was not laced. "Oh."

Conner raised his brows. "Aye?"

"I'll see her after —" She clamped her lips closed.

His eyes lit with curiosity. "After what?"

"Nothing. Thank you for my boots." Her face hot, she stepped back and pulled the door closed behind her.

But it wouldn't close all the way. Startled, she looked down to see Conner's foot blocking the door. "Remove your foot."

Conner looked down at his boot. He should move it. Any gentleman would do so. But when it came to Thea, he wasn't always able to do what he knew he should.

Why had he lingered after he'd delivered her boots? He'd started to leave, but those saucy boots had reminded him of Thea, of the way her light brown hair had been soaked from the rain, her lashes spiked with wetness, her lips pursed with irritation. And like a fool he'd stood there staring at her boots, mesmerized like a green boy after his first kiss, bemused, bewildered, and aroused.

Bloody hell — Thea was gaining a hold over him that frightened him as much as it excited him. And now seeing her here, her damp hair unbound and curling around her shoulders, her skin flushed from her bath, her gown loose at the shoulders — He froze in place. *Her gown is undone.* Somehow that had escaped his notice, and his desire flared anew at the thought of her creamy skin bared to his touch.

Some of his thoughts must have shown, for she took a shaky breath and said in a low, trembling voice, "Conner, no." Her lashes dropped to her cheeks, as if she were afraid to look at him.

She was so close that he could smell the lavender of her freshly washed hair. He wanted to slip his hand underneath and feel the weight of those silken strands. He wanted to slide his fingers along the satin of her skin, taste the heat of her cheeks, and —

"Conner, we can't," she whispered, so urgent, so pleading. Her velvet brown eyes shone as if she held back tears.

He winced and moved back. "Och, lass, I'm wild for you, but I would never hurt you."

"I know." She wetted her lips, and the sight almost made him groan.

Jaw set, he picked up the boots and handed them to her, their fingers brushing. "They're still damp, but Spencer did his job well."

Although he no longer blocked the door, she didn't move, and the naked longing in her eyes nearly undid him. He captured a strand of her hair and slid the silken length through his fingers. "Och, Thea," he whispered. "What are we to do? I cannae think aboot anything but you."

"That's — You shouldn't — I can't —"

His laugh was more a groan. "Bloody hell, lass — I know what we should nae and cannae do, but it dinnae matter."

She closed her eyes and rested her temple against the doorframe. "I know," she whispered, her voice smoky with desire. "We —"

A door down the hallway opened, and Conner stepped back.

Jane appeared wrapped in a blanket, her eyes watery, her nose red, a handkerchief clutched in her hand. Dressed in a day gown of wrinkled white muslin, her hair half undone, she looked pale and even younger than usual.

Seeing them, she mustered a sniffly smile. "The fire in my room keeps sputtering out, and it's gotten so cold." She coughed long and deep, leaning weakly against her doorframe.

Thea peered past Conner. "Jane, come to my room. The fire is blazing and you'll be warm here."

Jane shook her head. "I'd bother you with my coughing."

"Pah! As if you could bother anyone."

Thea set her boots to one side and then held the door open. "Come and get out of the drafty corridor."

Still looking uncertain, the younger woman came down the hallway and, pausing to murmur a greeting to Conner, disappeared into Thea's room.

Thea's gaze met Conner's. Forcing a smile, he reached out and tugged a lock of her long hair. "Go help the lass. She needs you."

Thea nodded and with one last heated look stepped back, her hair slipping from his fingers as she quietly closed the door.

The light seemed to have fled the hallway.

But this was what he'd wanted, he reminded himself grimly. He'd wanted her to have a chaperone at all times, someone to remind him not to cross the line his body ached to leap over.

Yet no matter how many chaperones Thea had, how many fiancés, how many obstacles stood between them, none of it relieved his desire to have her.

But he'd just have to live with that painful fact — for what she wanted in a man was the opposite of who and what he was, and try as he would, he could find no answer.

20

The next morning Theodora went to breakfast and found herself the only one present, Lance having already eaten, Jane still asleep, and Conner nowhere to be seen.

Trying not to feel disappointed, she ate and then called for Alice before returning to her bedchamber to oversee the packing of her trunks and valise. Except for chattering the entire time about one of the postboys who'd been "as forward as a Christmas goose," Alice seemed to have enjoyed her stay, admitting she had much more standing as a lady's maid than she'd ever had as a mere kitchen maid. "Why, all the other servants practically bow to me whenever I step into a room. I could get used to that, I could."

Theodora couldn't disagree. "Have you seen Miss Simmons this morning?"

"She's still fast asleep. One of the other maids looked in on her not an hour ago."

"That concoction Lance made for her must have worked. I warned her not to drink all of it, for heaven knows what was in it, but she said since he was so kind as to make it, she didn't want to disappoint him."

"She's a very kind lady if a bit soft, if you know whot I mean."

"I don't know, and I'll appreciate it if you don't say such things." Jane's innate goodness made Theodora wish to do more for the girl. "She is kinder than I'll ever be."

"Gor', miss! I wouldn't say that."

Theodora shook her head ruefully. "She's gentle and forever sweet, while I can be prickly at the drop of a hat."

"Pah, it's just a different sort of kindness, is all. One is milk and toast, the other is cinnamon and spice."

Theodora had to laugh. She picked up her cape and gloves. "You are buttering me up for something; I quake to think what it might be."

Alice snorted. "I doubt you've noticed, miss, but I'm not one for hints."

"I'll remember that. When you finish here, would you see that some breakfast is taken to Miss Jane? I hate to awaken her, but the squire wishes to get on the road by ten, and it's almost nine."

"He does like to tell people what to do,

that one."

"He's been in charge of his family since he was quite young; I fear it's made him a bit bossy."

"So he is. And while Miss Simmons doesn't seem to mind, I do. Just this morning, he stopped me on the stairs to say he was sure I could carry the tray better if I didn't hold it so high." Alice puffed out her cheeks. "As if he'd ever carried a heavy tray up a flight of stairs! I had it high because otherwise, my knees would have hit the bottom as I climbed. I showed him that, too, which made some of his tea spill. But he's the one who said whot he said, so I can't help but feel he deserved it." The clock on the mantel chimed nine. "I'd best get to Miss Jane. Do you need anything else, miss?"

"No, thank you."

"Very good. I'll send Spencer to fetch your bags." The maid dipped a curtsy and left.

Theodora went to the window and pushed back the velvet curtain. MacLeish was climbing down from the coach, which he'd just brought to the door. Ferguson stood near a pile of luggage, and she recognized Conner's leather valise and small gray trunk.

She wondered how many miles that trunk had traveled, how many storms it had weathered.

She sighed. While this elopement had cured her desire to wed Lance, it had done nothing to cure her fascination with Conner. If anything, it was worse. Before, he'd never reciprocated. Now he not only responded to her, but was stirred by passion himself. She'd seen it in his eyes, felt it in his hands —

She shivered. *It's just physical attraction. Don't allow yourself to imagine it's anything more.* He would never change; she knew that. She had no control over him — only over herself.

She frowned as a new thought suddenly struck her. Perhaps . . . just perhaps . . . the person who needed to change was her. Perhaps she needed to be more reasonable, more honest in her expectations. And far more cautious about being alone with Conner.

A knock came at the door, and sighing, she went to let Spencer in. There would be plenty of time to think things through as she traveled. She could only hope she might finally find an answer.

Half an hour later, Theodora found Lance and Conner bent over a stack of papers in the common room. From their conversation, this seemed to be the infamous itinerary.

Amused by Lance's enthusiasm for the small towns they would be traveling through, she cleared her throat.

"My dear! I didn't see you there." Lance looked approvingly at her bonnet, which she carried. "You're ready. And early, too."

While Lance's expression had opened on seeing her, Conner's had closed, his gaze on her face as if to read her expression.

Lance folded the list and slid it into his pocket. "Where's Jane?"

"Alice took up her breakfast a while ago, and was to help her dress. I think I hear them now."

Indeed, Alice could be heard telling Jane that there was no need to hurry, and perhaps she should return to bed.

Lance frowned. "Why is that maid telling Jane to return to bed? We're to leave soon."

Jane appeared in the doorway, swaying slightly. She was even paler than before, but fever-bright spots burned in her cheeks. She carried her coat, her bonnet hanging from her limp fingers.

Theodora took a step forward. "Oh dear! You do not look well."

The younger woman managed a smile. "I'm fine. Just a headache is all, and —"

She was taken by a fit of deep, heavy coughing.

"You're far too ill to travel," Theodora said worriedly.

"I'm fine, really. I'll sleep once we're on the road." Jane's voice faded and she looked down at her coat with a flicker of surprise. "I should put this on." She swallowed as if it pained her, and then shivered and rubbed her arms. "It's so cold in here. Is there no fire?"

"There's fire aplenty." Conner moved forward, his brows lowered. "Thea is right. You should be abed."

"Nonsense. We must go." Jane forced a smile, though she shivered as she tugged on her pelisse. "In case you didn't know, there's a very important elopement going on." She coughed again, leaning against the doorframe, weakened by her effort.

"Back to bed with you," Lance said bluntly. "I will send for a doctor."

"I wouldn't suggest she take the stairs again," Alice said. "She near fainted on them whilst we were coming down."

"Then she will wait for the doctor here." Theodora went to the settee and plumped the pillows. "Come and sit. You should not be standing in that drafty doorway."

Jane cast an anguished look at Theodora.

"I must . . . I can't . . ." She put her hand to her head, frowning as if the words were swimming before her eyes. ". . . there's no . . . I'm . . ." Her eyes fluttered. She took a step, and began to sag.

With a muffled exclamation Conner stepped forward, trying to catch the poor woman before she fell, but Lance was faster, scooping Jane into his arms and carrying her to the settee.

He carefully placed her on the cushions. "I had no idea she was so ill. She keeps saying she's better."

Theodora placed her hand on Jane's forehead. The heat took her by surprise and she looked up, past Lance, to Conner.

Their eyes met and though she never said a word, he moved toward the door. "I'll ask the innkeeper to send for the doctor." Conner was gone before she could thank him.

Lance hovered over the settee, his face dark with worry. "Poor Jane!"

Theodora looked at Alice, who stood watching from the doorway. "We need cold water and a cloth."

"Yes, miss! I'll bring the coldest water as can be had." Her jaw set in determination, Alice marched off toward the kitchens.

Theodora took Jane's hand between her own, the thin fingers seeming far too thin and delicate. "She should have sent word she was too ill to travel. She tries far too hard not to be a bother."

"She's not a bother at all." Lance stood at the foot of the settee. "What can I do?"

"Can you find a blanket or a cover of some sort?"

"My coat is in the hall. I'll fetch it." He left just as Conner returned.

He looked grim. "I'm sorry, lass. The closest doctor is almost twenty-five miles from here. And worse, the innkeeper thinks the road impassable because of yesterday's rain."

Lance, who'd just returned with his coat, cursed under his breath, drawing a surprised look from both Conner and Theodora. He flushed as he handed his coat to Theodora. "I'm sorry. I just — We must find a doctor."

Alice returned with a bowl of water, a clean cloth hanging over her arm. She placed the bowl on a table near the settee.

"Thank you." Theodora spread Lance's coat over Jane and then dipped the cloth into the water and wrung it out. She laid it on Jane's forehead.

Jane's lashes fluttered, and she opened her eyes. "What . . . where am I?"

"The parlor of our inn."

"But —" She pressed a hand to her head,

her brows knitting, and clenched her eyes closed. "Oh, my head."

"You're ill." Theodora dipped the warm cloth into the cool water and pressed it again to Jane's forehead. "You've a fever. You need to see a doctor."

"No. We must leave." Jane tried to get up.

Lance protested as Theodora pressed Jane back onto the settee.

"Stay where you are," Lance said firmly.

Jane coughed violently, her small body shaking. Afterward, she lay panting, as white as a sheet.

Her own heart tight with worry, Theodora looked at Conner and said in a low tone, "Without a doctor . . ." She didn't dare finish the sentence.

Lance closed his eyes and turned away.

Conner's gaze rested on Jane's thin face. "I know a doctor who's much closer than the one the innkeeper spoke of."

"Where —" Theodora started to ask.

Spencer appeared at the doorway, holding his hat. "The luggage is loaded, Cap'n."

"A change of plans: we're headed to Portpatrick," Conner told him.

Alice frowned. "Portpatrick? Isn't that on the coast? One of the footmen from the inn came from there."

Theodora frowned. Conner's house sat

high on a cliff overlooking Portpatrick. "That's too far away. We're going north and —" The expression on Conner's face stopped her. "We weren't going north, were we?"

He merely told Spencer in a short tone, "We'll travel to Dunskey House. Miss Simmons has taken ill."

Spencer grimaced. "Och, Murray."

Conner frowned. "There's nae better doctor in all the world, and you know it."

"Aye, but —"

"She's verrah ill, Spencer. She needs help now."

The sight of the girl's pale face made the man nod. "Then Murray 'tis."

"Send Ferguson to Dunskey by horse to let them know we're on the way. Have we blankets and pillows in the coach?"

"We've blankets aplenty, but nae pillows," Spencer replied.

"I'll fetch pillows," Alice offered.

"Guid." Conner turned back to Spencer. "Tell the others we're nae to dawdle."

Somber, Spencer bowed and disappeared, his footsteps hurrying down the hallway and out the door. A second later, he could be heard shouting orders.

"Who is this Murray?" Lance asked.

"My ship's doctor. We'll stop and fetch

him on our way to Dunskey."

"Dunskey? That's your seat. I thought it was on the western shore of Scotland." Lance looked perplexed.

"It is." Theodora dipped the cloth back into the cool water and wrung it out, wishing she were wringing Conner's neck instead. "I fear we've been led astray by the blasted itinerary — west, instead of north."

"It was taking us that far away from the main road?"

"It would have taken you to Gretna Green eventually," Conner replied. "I thought it best the two of you had more time together to get to know one another, before you made your relationship permanent."

Lance's mouth thinned. "That was not your concern. *None* of this has been your concern."

Conner's jaw set to a mulish angle. "Thea's family is like my own —"

"But they are *not* your own. And to say our journey would have gotten us to our destination 'eventually' is the grossest impertinence —"

"Stop!" Theodora glared at both of them. "We've more important things to think about right now."

"Law, don't stop them, miss!" Alice rubbed her hands together. "I'd like to see a proper mill, I would."

Lance flushed, while Conner, looking sheepish, bent to tug Lance's coat over Jane's exposed feet.

Jane had been lying still, her eyes closed, the tightness of her mouth telling of her pain. At Conner's gesture, she cracked her eyes open and gave him a grateful, trembling smile.

His expression softened and Theodora's throat tightened, surprised at his tenderness toward the young girl.

Lance cut a hard look at Conner. "How long before we reach Dunskey?"

"An hour and a half. The *Emerald* is docked in Portpatrick, which is less than a mile from the house. Murray will be waiting on us there."

Theodora sent him a flat look. "If we're that near to shore, we'd have guessed your perfidy soon."

"Most likely. But 'tis a guid thing now, for we're close to help. I'll ride with the coach to town, and then leave you to continue to Dunskey House while I fetch Dr. Murray from the ship."

"I wish to help," Lance said. "Your staff will be more efficient with you giving the orders, so you can lead the coach there. I will ride to fetch the doctor."

Conner gave a reluctant nod. "You'll need a horse. There's a neat mare in the barn that's for hire."

"Perfect. It will be best to lessen the number of people in the coach anyway; Jane will need room to lie down."

"Please don't," Jane said weakly. "It would be —"

"Pssht," Theodora said soothingly. "Lance is right; you'll be far more comfortable lying down." She brushed Jane's hair from her forehead, which felt even hotter than before. Worried, Theodora cast a look at Conner.

He turned to Lance. "Hire that horse. We leave in five minutes."

Lance spun on his heel and left, his boot steps ringing as he hurried in search of the innkeeper.

Theodora took Jane's hand. "Do you think you can stand? We must leave, so we can get you to a doctor."

Jane nodded and started to sit up, but she instantly went pale and sank back onto the pillows.

Conner tucked Lance's coat more securely about Jane and then scooped her into his arms.

Her eyes widened. "No, you can't —"

"Just rest and let me get you to the coach."

Conner's firm tone seemed to calm the girl. She sighed and rested her head against his shoulder, murmuring a soft "thank you." As she spoke, she looked at him through her lashes.

Perhaps it was the flush caused by her fever, or the way the light hit her at that moment, but for a second, Theodora thought Jane's face was suffused with something far more than girlish admiration.

Good Lord, does Jane think herself in love *with Conner?* Her stomach sank at the thought. How could an innocent like Jane withstand his careless charm, when Theodora couldn't do so herself?

As he carried Jane out of the room, Theodora followed, hurrying past them to open the door.

"That's my lass," Conner murmured to Theodora as he walked past her. "You're always thinking ahead."

"I try," she said, her heart warming in a ridiculous fashion.

She followed Conner into the yard, the wind tugging her skirts. "Spencer!" she called to the footman. "Open the door for Miss Simmons!"

Spencer did so and Conner slid Jane onto the seat. Theodora climbed in after the poor girl and piled several blankets over her.

Conner stepped back from the coach and glanced at Spencer. "Foot warmers?"

"Ferguson is filling them with guid hot coals even now."

"Thank you." Theodora rubbed her cold arms.

Conner's brows snapped together. "Bloody hell, lass, where's your pelisse?"

"It's inside. I —"

He cursed. "I'll fetch it. Wait here." He stalked off before she could say another word.

Jane, who'd been watching him with obvious longing, appeared disappointed he'd left without a single look in her direction.

Of course, the girl didn't really know Conner. Perhaps Theodora needed to drop a hint into Jane's ear about the futility of falling in love with a man like Conner Douglas. Once the girl felt better, Theodora would do just that.

She'd just tucked Jane in more securely when Conner reappeared in the doorway carrying her pelisse. "Put this on. There's a nor'east wind today and 'tis nae forgiving. I can feel it, and I'm wearing far more than you."

As she reached for her pelisse her hand touched his, and warmth flooded through her, her gaze jerking to his.

They stayed with their fingertips touching, the pelisse held between them, silence weighting the air around them. It was only a second, but it felt like centuries.

Then Conner stepped away.

"Where's Alice?" Theodora managed to keep her tone cool, though her face was hot.

"She's coming out of the inn right now. Good God — what's happened to her?"

The maid was indeed coming toward them, encased in the large coat that had probably belonged to her father. It wasn't the coat that gave anyone pause, but how much Alice now filled it out. She looked as if she were with child.

"We should leave now." Alice pushed past Conner and climbed into the coach. "Right now."

Theodora looked at Alice's midsection. "What on earth?"

"Whot? This?" Alice slapped her stomach, leaving an indentation. "Mr. Douglas said we need pillows, so . . ." She reached inside her coat and produced a pillow, and then another, and another. Five pillows in all were placed upon the seat beside Jane. "There you go, miss."

"Where did you get those?" Theodora asked.

"Miss Simmons's room, and yours."

"Did you ask the innkeeper?"

"Lud, no! Why do you think I had them under my coat?"

Conner snapped, "Just go. I'll pay him."

Alice's smirk vanished. "Gor'! Why would you do that? He don't even know they're gone! Besides, had he proper pillows I would have only taken one, but these are so thin —"

Conner closed the coach door and shouted to MacLeish.

Alice sniffed. "That was rude."

"What was rude was stealing pillows!" Theodora tucked some pillows under Jane's head and made the girl as comfortable as possible as the coach rolled out of the inn yard. She spared a glance out the window and saw Conner on his horse, Lance nearby on a neatish mare.

And then they were all headed to Dunskey House.

21

An hour and a half later, the coach rumbled through the cobblestoned streets of Portpatrick, the damp salt air announcing their proximity to the sea. The small, picturesque town rested at the edge of a harbor that had been partially enclosed fifty years earlier to provide protection from the strong North Channel gales.

Many said the man-made breakwaters, which had been put in place with neither the advice nor the consent of the locals, were already on the verge of collapse. But for now they held, the ocean beating at them with each storm, every tide digging at their foundations beneath the deep water.

Jane slept restlessly but did not awaken, which Theodora was glad for. She suspected from the way Jane's mouth had grown so tight at the start of their trip that the rocking of the coach had made her headache even worse.

Theodora pushed back the curtain, glad they were so close to Dunskey House.

Outside were simple seaside buildings — an inn, a tavern, and several small white-washed, thatched-roof houses inhabited by the fishermen who manned the boats moored along the quay. The fresh scent of the ocean mingled with that of peat fires and the sea.

They turned down the main street and there, at the dock, sat the *Emerald*. Theodora had seen Conner's flagship before, but it had been several years. The ship appeared so noble, polished and cleaned, more like a painting than a ship. Derrick had said time and again that no one kept a neater ship than Conner Douglas. *Which shows where his heart truly is.*

She leaned out the window to see Lance and Conner close behind. As they passed the street that led to the dock, Lance said something to Conner, then turned his horse down the lane and rode toward the ship.

"What's happening?" Alice asked, crowding forward.

Theodora returned to her seat. "The squire is on his way to fetch the doctor from Mr. Douglas's ship. They'll join us at the house as soon as they can."

"Oh. Have you seen Dunskey House? Is it

very grand?" Alice asked.

"Mr. Douglas's house is not grand, but with some work, it could be."

Alice leaned past Theodora to the window. "Lor'! Mr. Douglas is riding right outside!" The maid waved wildly.

Sure enough, Conner was now riding alongside the coach, and Alice gazed at him greedily, her nose pressed to the glass. "He looks good enough to lick, don't he?"

"Alice!" Her face hot, Theodora pulled the maid from the window.

As she did so she met Conner's gaze. He winked and touched the brim of his hat.

It was a polite gesture any gentleman might make to a lady. But Conner did it with such rakish impudence that he stole her smile before she could stop it.

Embarrassed, she slid back in her seat, checking Jane, who was muttering in her sleep. With Theodora's cool hand on her forehead, the girl rested more comfortably.

The road began to climb, and the coach swayed as the road became more deeply rutted. Theodora was glad for MacLeish's cautious driving, which kept the movement to a minimum, for every jarring swing stirred poor Jane. After a few miles the road began to turn inland and the coach slowed before turning into a long, curving drive.

Theodora held back the curtain as Dunskey House came into view. The manor house sat on a bluff near a cliff on the North Channel, where majestic oaks cast shade over a long, grassy field that separated the house from the treacherous drop into the crashing water below. The crushed sandstone drive had aged over the centuries from gray to a creamy white and led the eye to the imposing house.

With red shutters and a gray slate tile roof, Dunskey was a large, square, three-story structure, with tall windows and a huge oaken door set within a simple pilaster. Thick vines climbed one wall, framing the windows and reaching for the roofline, while a huge oak — bigger than any tree Theodora had ever seen — sat to the east of the house, sheltering it from the heat of summer.

The overall impression was antiquity, simplicity, strength, and elegance. Or it would have except three of the shutters hung askew, having been broken in some storm and never repaired. Two windows were broken, as well, and several panes were missing in other windows, while several large tree limbs had fallen among the uncut shrubbery that had once been an imposing garden.

"Good lord, you've brought us to a hainted mansion!" Alice exclaimed.

"It's not haunted," Theodora said hotly. "It needs some care, but that's the fate of houses where the owner is often gone. I — Oh, Jane's awake."

Jane, her eyes glassy, pushed herself upright, the blankets falling away.

Theodora smiled. "We are just now arriving at Mr. Douglas's house."

"Mr. Douglas? Is he —" The poor girl's cough raked her body relentlessly.

Theodora waited anxiously until Jane's coughing had subsided. "The doctor will be here soon; the squire went to fetch him."

Jane's lips quivered and tears filled her eyes. "I feel dreadful."

The words were as plaintive as a child's, and Theodora brushed Jane's hair from her hot forehead. "You will feel better once we have you tucked up in a proper bed."

The coach rolled to a stop, and Conner opened the door. His gaze went immediately to Jane. "Miss Simmons, I hope the journey was nae too difficult."

Jane swallowed, grimacing at the pain. "I slept most of the way."

"We need to get you some tea and honey." He looked at Theodora.

"Of course," she said. "And some laudanum, if there's any in the house."

"I daresay the housekeeper has some. If nae, Murray always carries it in his case. Jane, allow me to sweep you off your feet for a few moments." Without giving her time to protest, he reached into the coach and lifted her into his arms.

The girl slipped her arms about his neck, resting her cheek against his shoulder trustingly.

Conner carried her to the house as Spencer came to pull out the steps for Alice and Theodora.

"Well!" Alice sniffed. "He didn't offer to carry *you* to the house, did he?"

"Don't be silly. I'm perfectly able to walk." Theodora allowed Spencer to hand her down from the coach, and Alice followed.

Ahead of them, Theodora could hear Conner telling Jane how he'd purchased Dunskey House with the proceeds of his first effort as a privateer.

Jane listened, rapt, her eyes wide as she gazed up at him, her arms tight about his neck.

Conner's expression was that of a brother with a sister, or perhaps even that of a parent with a child. Was this how Conner would be if he had a daughter? Theodora could almost imagine it — how tender he was, how careful he seemed to be of her feelings —

Good God. How could she imagine him as a father, when she couldn't imagine him being responsible enough to be a husband? She frowned, thinking about this. Conner wasn't lacking in the area of responsibility when it came to his ship and his position as a privateer. Then he took great pains to do whatever he could for the betterment of his fleet, ships, and crew. It was his damnable wanderlust that kept him from carrying that responsibility over into other areas.

The heavy oak door swung open as Conner reached it, and his housekeeper appeared. Mrs. MacAuley was an older woman with a mass of iron gray curls that peeked from under a lacy mobcap. She had a round face, a number of chins, and was so short that she seemed wider than she was tall.

As Conner strode past her the housekeeper started to curtsy, but the sight of her master carrying a young lady froze the curtsy in mid-dip. "Ah! This must be the ill young lady Ferguson was telling us aboot."

"Where should I take her?" Conner asked as he went into the house.

"We've two bedchambers ready, with more to come. You may put her in either the green or the blue bedchamber."

Conner walked straight for the stairs, Jane's skirts trailing against his legs. "Which is the warmest?"

"The Green Room, sir. Top of the stairs and to the left."

"Thank you." He hurried up the flowing staircase. Spencer appeared with Jane's small trunk and followed.

Theodora started to join them, Alice behind her, when the housekeeper exclaimed, "Miss Cumberbatch-Snowe! How nice to see you again!"

Theodora unbuttoned her pelisse and cast a hurried glance at Conner, but he was already at the top of the stairs and showed no sign of having heard the housekeeper's greeting. Relieved, she sent Alice after him, only waiting for the maid to disappear from sight before turning back to Mrs. MacAuley. "It's good to see you again. I didn't expect to be back so soon, but we had a bit of an emergency." She moved away from the staircase and added in a low voice, "I hope you don't find this uncomfortable, but would you mind keeping my visit here a few months ago just between us?"

Mrs. MacAuley's brows rose. "Och, 'tis a secret then, is it?"

"No, I just haven't mentioned it yet to Mr. Douglas and don't wish him to think I had nefarious plans in coming without him being aware of it."

The housekeeper chuckled. "Nefarious? You?"

Theodora smiled. "We've been too busy to discuss such things, what with Miss Simmons being ill. After I tell him, of course you may say anything you wish. It would just be awkward if he found out from someone other than me."

"Of course, miss."

"Thank you. I hope our sudden arrival hasn't put you out too much."

"We've done what we could. As soon as Ferguson brought word the master was on his way, I hired some girls from town to help set the rooms to order. They're working on the west bedchamber now, and should have it ready for occupancy soon."

"Excellent. I should join Mr. Douglas in settling Miss Simmons in her room."

"Shall I bring a tea tray? I've honey and whisky for the young lady, too. It might be of some help."

"Thank you. And some laudanum, if you have it."

"Aye, I've a wee drop or two. I'll also bring a basin and some rose water to bathe her forehead. If you think of anything else, let me know."

"Thank you." Theodora went up the stairs, stopping on the landing to smile down at the housekeeper. "Thank you again. I know it's a lot, being descended upon without warning."

The housekeeper looked pleased, but waved a hand. "Pssht. I'm used to such; Mr. Douglas never says when he's to come." She looked about wistfully. "I just wish we were able to keep this house to the standard she deserves."

"Perhaps one day," Theodora agreed. It *was* a lovely house, and she'd been appalled when she'd seen it the first time months ago. Appalled and awakened. *And launched upon this very journey, in fact.*

And now, she'd come full circle. Sighing, she hurried to Jane's room.

22

The green bedchamber was large, and although a fire smoked and crackled in the fireplace, the room was still chilly. Theodora was glad to note none of the windows were missing glass panes, and there didn't seem to be any strong drafts. Still, the bed was ancient, as were the threadbare velvet canopy and curtains, but at least an adequate amount of blankets were piled upon the bed.

A hand pressed to her temple, Jane sat on the edge of the mattress, looking up at Conner as if he could move heaven and earth.

"You should sleep," he was saying in a tone one usually reserved for cantankerous children.

"I cannot. I'm in my traveling gown and —" A cough cut Jane short, wracking her with spasms.

Conner handed his handkerchief to the poor girl, who clutched it like a lifeline and then shot a pleading look at Theodora.

"So we need a night rail, do we?" she said briskly as she went to Jane's trunk at the foot of the bed. "Some good news, Jane! Mrs. MacAuley has both honey and whisky, so your sore throat will soon be eased."

"I cannot drink whisky," Jane croaked. "I'm just cold, is all. Perhaps if I put my coat back on?"

Conner frowned at the fireplace. "It's smoking like a ship afire. I'll check the damper."

Theodora found the night rail and a matching robe and carried them to the bed. "The whisky will warm you up and open up your lungs."

"I had a sip of my brother's once, and it burned most unpleasantly." Jane pressed a hand to her throat and winced. "I'm coughing enough without it."

Having adjusted the damper, Conner added a log to the fire. "Whisky often does the same to me, although I find that quickly taking another drink helps."

Theodora lifted an eyebrow. "And then, after that, you'll need another —"

"— and another, and another." Conner grinned at her. "I cannae hide my secrets from you, lass. I never could."

Her gaze locked with his, and she knew

what he was thinking. He was worried for Jane, amused at Theodora's instant understanding, irritated at the path this trip was taking, and mixed with all of this was his desire for her.

She could sense it from across the room, taste it on her tongue, feel it in the sudden weight of her breasts against her lace chemise. Her throat tightened and she wished with all her soul that she could partake of his passion.

She forced her attention back to Jane. "Let's get you into that night rail. You need rest."

"If you've nae need of me, I'll take my leave," Conner said.

"Thank you." Theodora unlaced one of Jane's boots, saying over her shoulder to Conner, "Could you let Mrs. MacAuley know we need a bed warmer?"

"Of course. If you need anything else, ring the bellpull. I'll nae be far." His boot steps echoed on the marble floor as he left.

Theodora fought the urge to watch him. "There. Both boots off. The doctor should be here soon."

"I don't need a doctor." Jane's rusty voice carried a hint of petulant tears.

"Of course you do." Thea placed the girl's boots beside the bed. "And while I know 'twill be a bother to see a doctor —"

"One I don't even know."

"He is sure to be the best to be had, or he wouldn't be on Conner's ship."

Jane looked mournfully at the empty doorway. "That's true. If Conner trusts him, then I do, too."

"Quite so," Theodora said drily as she helped Jane out of her gown and into her night rail. Jane shivered piteously and it was a relief to them both when she was done and could huddle under a blanket on the edge of the bed while they waited for the bed warmer.

A few moments later, Alice appeared with the needed implement, fussing under her breath as she stopped by the fire and used the tongs to place hot coals into the metal pan. " 'Tis a sad day when a lady's maid cannot perform her duties. I had to wrest this blasted thing from Mrs. MacAuley, I did. I'm the one as should be waiting on Miss Simmons, not that pasty-faced house-keeper."

"Alice!" Theodora said reprovingly.

"Humph. Well, she *is* pasty-faced. And she don't like having help, even when I know better than her how to do things."

"You told her how to do something? In her own house?"

Alice sniffed. "It isn't my fault if she don't know the right way to cut candle tapers. And there I was, being nice and all!" The maid brought the bed warmer and slid it between the sheets, moving it in slow circles.

Soon the sheets were toasty warm, and Alice set the bed warmer on the hearth to cool while Theodora helped Jane into the bed. The warmed sheets did the trick and the girl was asleep almost before her head hit the pillow.

Alice unpacked Jane's trunk, and was just hanging up the final gown when Mrs. MacAuley appeared carrying a tray laden with a decanter, a small pot, and several glasses. She was followed by a young, awkward-looking girl who carried a pitcher of water and several washing cloths. The girl filled the bowl on the washstand from the pitcher, placing the cloths nearby, the sound of the water splashing into the bowl stirring Jane enough that she awoke.

"I've brought the whisky and honey as you asked, miss. There's also a small vial of laudanum." Mrs. MacAuley waddled to the bed and, after sending a frigid look at Alice, peered down at Jane. The housekeeper's face softened. "Law, you're but a child!"

Jane started to talk, although it quickly turned into a deep cough.

Mrs. MacAuley patted her shoulder. "There, lass, dinnae get excited. It cannae be guid for you."

Thea poured a splash of whisky into a glass, added a large dollop of honey from the small pot and a few drops of the laudanum, and stirred it. She carried the glass to the bed. "Take a sip. It will calm that cough."

Jane eyed the drink with misgiving, but she took a swallow and grimaced, her hand moving to her throat as she choked it down.

Alice chuckled. "We need to toughen you up a bit. I could drink more whisky out a teaspoon than you've got in that cup."

Mrs. MacAuley frowned. "What a pert lass you are, to be telling a delicate miss like this that she needs to 'toughen oop.' "

Alice puffed up like a threatened badger. " 'Tis the truth, and Miss Jane will be a sight better does she know it!"

The housekeeper's face turned bright red. "You are rude!"

"And you are a bossy old woman!"

Mrs. MacAuley planted her hands on her hips. "Why, I've never —"

"That's enough! Out, the both of you." Theodora pointed to the doorway. "Jane needs peace and quiet."

With a final glare at Alice, Mrs. MacAuley

gave Theodora a stiff curtsy, collected her things, and left, her maid following closely.

Alice snorted. "Good riddance, I say."

"Out."

"But I'm here to help —"

"Out! And while you're gone, find Mrs. MacAuley and apologize. We'll be here for two or three days, perhaps more, and I'll not have you two warring the entire time."

Alice sniffed, but after a moment, she grumbled, "I suppose you're right; it won't do to be on the wrong side of the house-keeper. She'll assign me to a hard bed if I'm not careful."

"I wouldn't blame her if she did. She has her hands full, trying to care for this house without the proper assistance. She's very shorthanded, and the house's owner is never here and never leaves her enough funds to run it properly, and flatly refuses to take care of the place. Mrs. MacAuley has been placed in a dreadful situation."

Alice pursed her lips and looked about her. " 'Tis a shabby house. Some of the inns we stayed at were better kept."

"Exactly. Mrs. MacAuley does the best she can, but there are limits."

"Very well. I'll apologize," Alice said grudgingly, and then left.

Relieved, Theodora held up the glass of

honeyed whisky and smiled at Jane. "A few more sips."

"Oh, please. No more."

"A few more, and I promise I'll let you alone for at least two hours, if not more." Theodora waited until Jane had choked down most of the whisky, then returned the glass to the tray. "There. Close your eyes and sleep."

"I hate being ill!" Jane's voice quavered.

"I know." Theodora plumped a pillow and slid it behind Jane. "As my old nanny used to say, what's for you will not go past you."

"What does that mean?"

Theodora sat on the edge of the bed. "It means that what's supposed to happen, will happen."

"That seems dreadfully fatalistic," Jane murmured. Her eyelids drooped as if weighted, but she moved restlessly, kicking at the covers and tugging at the sheets.

The girl clearly ached from her fever, but the whisky and laudanum would soon do their work. "Did you get to see much of Dunskey when we drove up?"

"No, not much." Jane's glassy gaze flickered around the room. "Mr. Douglas must be very proud of his house."

"I wish that were so."

Jane's gaze returned to Theodora. "Why

367

wouldn't he be? It seems lovely."

"It *could* be. But it's neglected, a fact Mr. Douglas refuses to address. He is a man of the sea, and has no desire to settle down. So he leaves his house to rot while he sails the seas."

Jane's brow furrowed and she stifled a yawn. "Men never think of houses and homes the way women do. For us, it's about comfort and restfulness, but men are taught from childhood that homes are buildings to be owned and even collected as if they were dollhouses. Why, look at all of the homes the king owns — castles, manor houses, lands — it's absurd, for he cannot live in a hundredth of them."

"This is Conner's only home."

"It's his only *house*," Jane gently corrected, her eyes fluttering as she fought sleep.

Theodora looked around the bedchamber, admiring the cornice work and trim. "This could be a lovely home. It was built in the Scottish style in the early 1700s. I don't know if you noticed when we drove up, but the house has a hipped roof, decorative moldings on the cornices, and — I should save this lecture for when you're strong enough to tell me you don't wish to hear it."

Jane managed a sleepy murmur: "Go on. I love old houses."

"So do I." Theodora arose and rinsed out a cloth and placed it on Jane's forehead. "You'll love this one once you've seen it; I do." She softened her voice and continued, almost sing-songing as she spoke. "There are gabled windows on the top floor, where the nursery and servants' quarters are, and there are six chimneys. The house is remarkably snug, even though it hasn't been taken care of properly."

Jane's eyes closed, although her eyebrows were slightly drawn.

"The ceiling in the ballroom is especially fine, and the plasterwork is so masterful it will steal your breath. It's of wreaths and small flowers, and is exquisite, although it could stand being cleaned, for you know how dust collects in crevices. There are also two especially fine mantelpieces in the ballroom, one of marble and the other of . . ." Theodora let her voice trail off as Jane's expression relaxed, and her breathing deepened into sleep.

Poor girl. Theodora smoothed the covers over her, then turned to tiptoe out of the room — and came to a halt.

Conner stood just inside the doorway, his

arms crossed over his broad chest, his brows knit.

Theodora's heart skipped a beat. "I didn't see you there," she whispered.

He continued to look at her, his expression dark, as if he struggled with a weighty problem.

Theodora came a few steps closer. "What is it?"

"How do you know so much about this house? I know I never told you half of what you just shared with Jane."

Blast it. He'd heard. She nervously wet her lips. "I don't know. Perhaps . . . perhaps I read it somewhere." To Theodora's relief, Jane coughed in her sleep, the sound breaking the tension.

Conner's gaze moved to the bed. "How is she?"

Thank goodness. He'll forget he even heard what I said. "Not well. She's hotter, I think. The fever grows."

He looked at Jane a moment more before saying in a somber tone deep with emotion, "She reminds me of Anna."

Surprised, Theodora glanced back at the sleeping girl. It took only a moment, and she realized Conner was right — the heart-shaped face, the sweetness of her expression, the paleness of her skin. "I don't know why I didn't notice that before."

"Anna's expressions were more determined, but she —"

Downstairs a door opened and then closed, and voices could be heard, footsteps climbing the stairs.

"That will be Murray. I will escort him here." Conner's gaze found hers, and she knew then that he hadn't forgotten his questions. "We need to talk, lass. And soon." He turned and left.

23

Lance paced the length of the parlor, his face folded in a deep scowl. After several passes, he came to an abrupt halt and announced in a furious voice, "We should be in there with that blasted doctor!"

Conner sat by the fire, his feet stretched to the flames. "Dr. Murray knows what he's aboot. He dinnae like interference, is all."

"One question is not interference!"

" 'Twas more like a dozen, and all of them shot oot like bullets from a pistol."

Lance flushed. "I was just trying to understand Jane's condition. She looks so —" He sucked in his breath and resumed pacing. "He had no right to send us from the room in such a manner."

"I tried to warn you. Set your mind at ease; Murray knows his business."

"How can you be sure, if he won't even let you ask questions?"

"He said he'd allow you all the questions

you wished, *after* he'd examined Miss Simmons. To be honest, you dinnae give the mon a chance."

Lance's shoulders sagged. "I didn't, did I? I — I am just worried."

"So I noticed." Conner regarded Lance curiously. "You seem to care a great deal for Miss Simmons."

Lance's expression grew guarded. "She's my responsibility. I hired her to come with us, and I promised her brother I'd look after her."

Conner wondered if that was all. *In a perfect world, the squire would find himself in love with someone else, and Thea would be free to marry me. If I could convince her to do so.* At one time, Conner had believed his only obstacle was the squire. But that was long ago.

The squire sighed. "The doctor seemed so callous, as if he didn't care."

"He's hired to take care of the men on my ships, and nae one else. He came oot of the goodness of his heart. Besides, Thea is there. She'll nae allow Murray to leave withoot knowing exactly what's what. You can trust her for that; she's nae easy to browbeat." Conner couldn't keep the admiration from his voice.

Lance brightened. "That's true. Theodora's a marvel, isn't she?"

Conner's hopes that the squire's affections had found a new focus died as quickly as they'd been born. And no wonder; who would take a faint spirit like Jane over a woman like Thea?

The sound of footsteps coming down the stairs made Lance hurry to the door. "It's Alice. Come here, please!"

Alice joined them, bearing a heavy tray and looking every bit as annoyed as Conner expected. The tray rattled as she moved, overfilled with empty glasses, two large pitchers, and other crockery.

She rested the edge of the tray on her hip and looked at Lance. "Aye?"

"You were in Miss Simmons's room just now. What is the doctor saying?"

Alice's jaw set. "He's not yet finished his examination. Now, if you'll excuse me, I need to return this tray to the kitchen."

"Not until you've told us everything the doctor has said."

She shook her head, the crockery rattling ominously.

Fire flashed in Lance's eyes. "You must —"

"Lance!" Conner interrupted. "We'll get the news when the doctor's ready. And that tray looks verrah heavy."

Lance's gaze focused on the tray and he blinked, instantly contrite. "I'm sorry. I should have noticed — There's no excuse. I'm just worried about Miss Simmons."

The maid sniffed, but said in a more charitable tone, "We all are. But you needn't fear. She's in good hands, she is."

He brightened. "Has the doctor said anything positive? Anything that lets us know Jane will not grow worse?"

"He's said nary a word to any of us, once he threw you from the room." Alice headed for the door, saying over her shoulder, "And when I said 'good hands,' I meant Miss Cumberbatch-Snowe's. That doctor may know medicine, but 'tis obvious he's a chucklehead." With those mysterious words, she disappeared from sight.

Lance looked confounded. "Chucklehead? What does that mean?"

A measured tread sounded on the staircase and a rough, masculine voice barked orders. Thea's softer voice answered.

"There's the doctor now," Conner said.

Lance started toward the door, but Conner called, "I would nae, if I were you. It sounds as though Thea's herding him to the door and if you go oot now, you'll just delay her report. Give her a moment to send Murray on his way."

"I'd like to speak to him directly."

"He never speaks when he's told to do so. Let Thea handle him. She's more than a match for a crotchety auld doctor."

Although it was obvious Lance didn't agree, he stayed put, and they soon heard the front door close.

Thea joined them, her face worried. She looked pale, her hair mussed at the temples from where she'd pressed her fingers. "Jane has an infection of the lungs."

Lance paled. "Good God!"

"Murray says it's treatable, but —" Thea's voice caught and it took her a moment to regain her composure. "The next few days are crucial. If her fever doesn't break . . ." Thea shook her head.

Conner had to fight the burning desire to go to her and hold her. Like many strong people, she didn't like to be coddled while she fought her own emotions. When she felt more stable, then would be the time to give her the hug she so obviously needed. Still, his heart ached on seeing her pain, and in thinking of the patient resting upstairs.

Lance cursed and took a rapid, jerky turn about the room before coming to a stop in front of Thea. "This Murray! If she's in such ill condition, why did he leave? Surely he should stay here and —"

"I sent him away. It's best that he's gone."

"Agitates the patient, dinnae he?" Conner said quietly.

"Very much. He doesn't mean to, but he's gruff and Jane is overly sensitive right now. But he left specific instructions about how to nurse her, and left the appropriate medicines. He was very thorough and quite knowledgeable. We're to call him should anything change."

Conner arose from his chair. "What do you need from us?"

She sent him a deeply grateful look. "There's not much we can do now but wait. I'll sit with Jane and make certain Dr. Murray's orders are followed to the letter."

Mrs. MacAuley appeared in the doorway, her brow creased. "Miss Simmons is calling for you, Miss Thea, and she will nae stay in bed, no matter how much we try."

"You must go at once," Lance ordered.

Thea didn't even blink. "Of course. Mrs. MacAuley, would you send a tray to the room with toast and weak tea? Perhaps I can convince her to eat something."

"Yes, miss. I'll bring it myself." The housekeeper hurried away.

Thea sighed and rubbed her neck tiredly. "We must keep Jane quiet. That's crucial and, to be honest, difficult. She's high-strung as well as being ill, and the toll of her coughing has made her ache from head to toe. She's frightened, too. She knows it's serious."

"If I could take her illness myself, I would," Lance said fervently.

"I know you would," Thea said, her expression softening slightly.

"I'm sorry I snapped at you. You're too good." He took Thea's hands in his, and pressed a fervent kiss to her fingers. "Thank you for taking care of poor Jane. You've been so kind."

Conner's jaw tightened. Bloody hell, he was in no mood for such displays, not now. *Not ever.* Scowling, he shoved the footstool out of his way, drawing the startled gazes of Thea and Lance. "You two may exchange romantic pleasantries later. There's a lass oopstairs who needs our attention now."

Thea flushed, her gaze blazing at Conner, although she pulled her hands free. "We were not being romantic, and you know it. But you're right; I'm needed elsewhere. And thank goodness for that!"

With her chin high, Thea sailed from the room, leaving Conner scowling, and somehow wounded in her wake.

24

A log dropped in the fireplace, sending a shower of sparks onto the hearth. The noise jerked Theodora awake.

She blinked hazily, uncertain where she was, or why. She was still dressed, with a shawl draped over her shoulders; curled on her side in a deep wingback chair, her cheek numb from resting on the thinly padded arm.

She slowly sat up and rubbed her cheek, grabbing at the book that tried to slide off her lap to the floor. A treatise on crop rotation? *Ah, yes. I was reading to Jane.* The plan had been to read a boring tome to put the girl to sleep. It had clearly put the reader to sleep, as well.

Yawning, she set the book aside and stretched, looking wearily at the clock. It would be dawn within the hour. It was a good thing she'd awakened now; Jane's medicine was due soon.

Theodora arose and went to her patient's side. Jane slept deeply, her cheeks flushed, her lips cracked and dry. It had been two days since Jane had taken ill. Two long, endless days and nights.

Theodora smoothed her hand over the girl's forehead. She still had a fever, but Theodora thought Jane's labored breathing was a trifle easier now. *Thank heaven for Dr. Murray's medicine. It seems to be working.*

But poor Jane was still restless, kicking off the covers one minute, shivering beneath them the next. She'd become very emotional, too, growing tearful whenever Theodora wasn't nearby.

Theodora rubbed her aching neck. Since they'd arrived at Dunskey, she hadn't gotten more than three or four hours of sleep in a row. And considering the lack of sleep she'd gotten the night before Jane had fallen so ill, it was a wonder Theodora could stand upright. She put her hands on the small of her aching back and stretched, fighting a yawn. She'd never been so tired.

A log fell in the dying fire and drew her gaze. Sighing, she went to add a log and stir the embers back to flames before she returned to the winged chair, looking longingly at the settee as she walked past it. She'd lie down and sleep, if she thought she would awaken in time to give Jane her medicine.

Determined to stay awake, she sat in the wing-backed chair and waited for the clock to chime seven. Her head heavy with tiredness, she leaned back against the cushions and closed her eyes to rest them from the light. Even the warm glow of the fire seemed too bright just now.

It seemed as if she'd just closed her eyes when Conner crept into her dreams, his deep, lilting voice tickling her ear. She frowned and shifted.

"Thea, lass."

His voice was as seductive as hot chocolate on a snowy winter day.

"Lass, wake oop."

Why would I want to do that? She frowned and shifted, curling deeper into the chair.

"Lass," Conner persisted.

He's demanding even in my dreams. Eyes tightly closed, she muttered, "Go away."

A warm hand cupped her cheek. "I will nae."

Her eyes flew open, and her blurry gaze locked on his face. It wasn't a dream.

He was stooped before her, one hand on the arm of the chair, the other on her knee. "You're aboot to fall oot of your chair."

Chair? She blinked and looked around.

Jane. Oh no, her medicine! She immediately pushed herself upright, her stiff neck protesting. "Good God, I feel like I've been kicked by a horse. What time is it?"

"Almost seven."

"Thank you for waking me. Jane's medicine is due." Theodora stood, but due to her cramped position in the chair, her left leg had gone to sleep, and it gave way.

Conner caught her, sweeping her to him easily. Her chest was pressed to his, the scent of his cologne tickling her nose.

Her senses, sound asleep a moment ago, roared awake, and she stifled a moan.

He chuckled and his breath, warm against her ear, sent another shiver through her. "Lass, if you wished for a hug, you'd but to ask." He rubbed his cheek to hers.

She *loved* being in his arms. He stroked her back, easing the tension in her tired muscles, and it was tempting to let him continue. If she just stayed still . . .

But Jane needed her medicine, and the doctor would arrive soon.

Disappointed, Theodora pushed free of his arms, her gaze finding the mirror over the fireplace. "Good God!" She patted her disheveled hair, strands sticking out because so many of her hairpins had fallen out while she'd slept. "I look like a pincushion!"

He captured her hands, and brushed each with a kiss. "You'd look beautiful had you nae hair, lass. You're all big brown eyes, lashes that curl to the moon, and a mouth —" His gaze dropped to it and he groaned. "God, lass, that mouth. I wish —"

"Theodora?"

Jane! Theodora pulled free from Conner's mesmerizing hold and hurried to the bed, pausing at the washstand to wring out a fresh cooling cloth. "Good morning! How are you feeling?"

The furrow between Jane's eyes said it all, and Theodora placed the cloth on the girl's brow. "That bad, is it? Fortunately, it's time for your medicine."

"No," Jane croaked, making a face. "It's so bitter!"

"Yes, but it calms your cough. Perhaps I can convince Mrs. MacAuley to make some of her famous scones. She hasn't made any since we've been here, and they'd be just the thing to chase away the taste of that horrible medicine."

Jane turned her face away. "I'm not hungry."

"You haven't tried these scones. They're the best I've ever had." When Jane didn't respond, Theodora leaned down to the younger girl and whispered, "You have a guest."

Jane turned back to Theodora. "Who?"

"A gentleman."

Jane's gaze moved past Theodora to where Conner stood by the chair. "Mr. Douglas!"

"That's Conner to you, lass." Smiling, he came over to stand beside the bed. "I will nae keep you long; you'll wish to get ready for the doctor's visit. But I wanted to see how you are doing."

A pleased smile flickered over Jane's thin face. "That's very kind of you."

"Did you hear that, Thea? I'm kind," he teased.

"I heard, but since Jane has a fever, we cannot hold her accountable for everything she says right now."

Jane blinked. "I meant it!"

Theodora smiled. "Of course you did. Lie back and let me tuck these blankets in. I just heard a coach, which must be the doctor."

Jane clutched at her blankets, tears instantly appearing in her blue eyes. "Tell him to go away. I don't like him."

"None of us do," Conner said in a soothing tone. "But he knows what he's aboot. Be guid for the worthy doctor, and dinnae take his manners to heart, and maybe —

just maybe, mind you — once he's gone, someone will come and read to you."

"Someone?"

"He means himself," Theodora said. "He's just being mysterious."

"Och, I'd be failing miserably at being mysterious were I that obvious."

Theodora waved him away. "Go fetch the doctor."

He winked at Jane, who went pink with pleasure, and then he headed to the door. Theodora followed, saying in a low voice once they reached the hallway, "That was well done. Hopefully she won't take the doctor's harshness so to heart today."

Conner's gaze moved over Theodora's face. "You look tired, lass. You need to have a care. You'll be ill, too, do you nae get some proper rest."

It was hard not to read the softening of his expression as having more meaning than it did, but she managed. "Once Jane's better, Alice can sit with her for a few hours at a time. But for now, she's more comfortable with me than anyone else."

"Bloody hell, you're a stubborn wench." Conner didn't like the faint circles under Thea's eyes, or the way she kept rubbing her neck as if it ached. It was plain to see she was exhausted. Dammit, why would she not listen to reason?

He looked past Thea to where Jane rested, her eyes closed, although her frown belied any idea she might be sleeping. "She dinnae seem to mind my visit."

"All women enjoy a dose of flirtation."

"You think that's what brought Jane around?" At Thea's nod, he said in a firm tone, "I'll be back to watch over the lass as soon as Murray has left."

Thea's eyes widened. *You?*

He frowned. "Why nae me?"

"Because . . . well, you're —" She waved her hand.

He crossed his arms over his chest. "I'm what?"

She bit her lip. "Nothing."

He snorted his disbelief. "I'll be back. If 'tis propriety as worries you, I'll leave the door open and have Alice sit ootside." "It's not that. It's a lot of work. Jane sleeps a good bit, but when she's awake she's quite peevish, like a small child."

"It'll be guid practice for when I visit my nephew."

Thea opened her mouth to voice another objection, but he placed his finger over her lips. "As much as I like to hear you speak, you're wasting time. Just agree and I'll fetch the doctor."

She captured his hand and lowered it from her lips, though she clung to his fingers for reasons she dared not explore. "Conner, I don't mean to be ungracious. I just didn't expect you to offer to help, that's all."

"Bloody hell, lass! How can you say such a thing? Have I nae been helping all along?"

"No. Most of the time, you've been doing the opposite — trying to stop my elopement, trying to show Lance in the worst light possible, trying to complicate matters by adding numerous chaperones, and —"

"All right, that's true aboot your elopement, but nae this." He took a deep breath and gently untangled his hand. "As far as your elopement goes, I'm done."

Her eyes widened, her expression cautious. "Done?"

"Aye. I've given oop on winning your hand. Now I just want to make certain you dinnae ruin your life by marrying Lance. He's a nice mon, but is nae the one for you."

Her gaze locked on his face. "You've given up? Then . . . you no longer wish to mar —"

The doorbell chimed, deep and melodious, and Mrs. MacAuley's voice could be heard raised in greeting.

Theodora's expression closed. "The doctor."

And just like that, the moment was gone. *For now, anyway.* "I'll be back later." With a final, lingering look, he left, but his mind raced. *Is there hope?* If only he could be certain.

"Ah! Just the mon I was looking for."

Lance, who'd been standing in the library in front of a shelf of likely books, took an eager step forward, a slender tome in one hand. "I heard you come downstairs. Has the doctor left? Is there any news on Jane?"

"Jane's with the doctor now. I just saw her though, and she seems more alert."

"That's something." Lance bit his lip, his brow furrowed. "It's been a long two days."

"So it has." Conner came farther into the room and cast a swift glace around. "I dinnae think I've been in this room since we arrived."

"Really? This is an excellent collection of books. What do you read?"

"Mainly books of a nautical bent, which I keep on ship. Most of these" — Conner put his hand on the closest shelf — "came with the house. I've meant to inventory them, but haven't had time."

Lance patted the book he held in his hand. "This one is on Italy. I've always wanted to go."

"You should do so. It's beautiful. But for now, I'd settle for some breakfast. Come." Conner threw his arm around the other man and turned him toward the door. "Have you eaten yet?"

"No, but I'm not hungry. I keep thinking about poor Jane."

Conner raised his brows. "And Thea, too."

"Oh. Yes, of course." Lance sent Conner a guilty look as they walked into the hallway. "How is Theodora?"

"Tired. She's been oop two nights and has had verrah little sleep."

"That's not healthy." Lance sighed and fell into pace beside Conner. "I wish there was something I could do."

"Sadly, there is nae —" Conner stopped. "Wait. There is one thing — but it may be too much to ask."

"No, no," Lance said eagerly. "What is it?"

"Do you think you could spend some time each day with our patient? Perhaps read to her? 'Twould give Thea time to rest."

"I would love to!" As if aware his enthusiasm was a bit excessive, he slanted a self-conscious look at Conner and then added in a more measured tone, "I'll do anything to help Theodora."

"Of course."

"Do you think Jane would enjoy hearing

about Italy?"

"Naturally." Conner led the way to the breakfast room, keeping up a stream of small talk. Soon he was sitting before his plate, listening to Lance talk about his desire to see all of Italy, especially Venice.

Breakfast was usually Conner's favorite meal of the day, but while Mrs. MacAuley exceeded expectations in many areas, cooking was not one of them. Normally, Conner brought the cook from his ship to serve in Dunskey, but he hadn't done so this time, for they'd done no entertaining. He missed Cook's way with breakfast cakes and ham. Perhaps it was time to bring him to Dunskey.

Sighing, Conner absently took a bite of his buttered toast, and wondered if he should ask Mrs. MacAuley to make her infamous scones. Thea had mentioned them and, now that he thought about it, it was an excellent idea. *Jane might be more tempted to eat if —*

Wait. He stared at his toast, thoughts suddenly crowding his brain. *Scones? How had Thea known . . .*

He returned the toast to his plate and stood.

Lance stopped in midsentence, obviously surprised.

"I'm sorry," Conner said curtly. "But I must see Mrs. MacAuley."

"Is something wrong?"

"Nae yet." And with that, he left.

25

Lance stuck his head in the door. "Mind if I come in?"

Theodora looked up from the small stack of clean cloths she'd just placed on the nightstand and smiled. "Ah, there you are. I wondered if you'd changed your mind today."

It had been a week since Jane had fallen ill, and each day, under Dr. Murray's brusque but professional eye, she had improved. Theodora would have been exhausted caring for her, except for two things — Lance's surprising offer to spend hours each day reading to Jane, and Conner's deftness at running the household.

Both things had surprised her. Lance's assistance had allowed Theodora time to rest, especially now that Jane was on the mend and was easily bored. Meanwhile, Conner's oversight had helped the woefully short-handed Mrs. MacAuley bring the house up to livable standards. He'd pulled men from his ship and placed them into key positions in the household; Spencer often brought the lunch trays, and she'd seen MacLeish doing the laundry out behind the kitchen under Alice's watchful eye, while a small Gallic man called "Cook," who was much given to ranting about everything from the lack of fat chickens to the quality of the pepper gracing the larder, now made magic in the kitchen.

Other members of Conner's crew filled out the remaining gaps, and she knew from Mrs. MacAuley that Conner kept them under tight orders.

When Theodora had attempted to thank him, he'd cut her short. He'd been abrupt lately, watching her with a dark, brooding gaze that disturbed her. Something was amiss, but she couldn't fathom what it was. If she weren't so tired Theodora might have pressed him on it, but even with the improvements in the house, she only had the energy to see to Jane.

"How is she today?" Lance tucked the book he carried under one arm, his gaze instantly going to Jane as he crossed the room.

Late-afternoon sunlight streamed from the windows across the huge bed. Thin from her illness, Jane seemed even tinier than usual, and she lay without moving, her eyes closed.

"She is much better," Thea announced. "Or she will be if she will take the medicine Dr. Murray has left her."

Jane's brows lowered, a frown deepening on her face, which made Lance smile and say in a pretend-grave tone, "So she's being difficult today, is she?"

Jane opened her eyes, frowning. "I hate that medicine."

"I know." Theodora went to smooth the blankets. "But it's good for you, so you must take it."

"It is wretched," Jane said in a peevish tone. "The doctor will not listen when I say it makes me gag, and he just —" Her voice quavered as if she was about to burst into tears.

"This is unacceptable!" Lance announced. "Shall I find this doctor and throttle thim for you? Perhaps I should force him to take a dose of his own medicine, and see how he likes it."

Jane's lips stopped quivering, and a faint gleam of humor appeared in her eyes. "I would like that very much."

"I shall make him take two doses, then."

She finally smiled. "Five."

"Five it will be. But first, I've been dying to know what we will find in our travels today."

To Jane's growing delight, Lance had taken to pretending they were really traveling through Italy as he read from a book he'd found in Conner's vast library.

"Where are we going?" Jane asked, interest warming her thin voice.

He sat in the chair that waited by the bed, opened the book, and removed a slip of paper that marked a page. "I thought we would travel to ancient Milan. There's a beautiful church there, and some paintings by the esteemed Leonardo da Vinci." He smoothed the pages. "If you remember, yesterday saw us in the small but charming town of Pavia. Today, we have a few hours by carriage — on a fairly good road, we are told — and then we'll be in Milan, which is quite a metropolitan area compared with our rustic travel of yesterday. Shall we begin our journey?"

Jane said eagerly, "Please do. You've been so kind to read to me." Her gaze searched Lance's face. "Are you sure you're not bored?"

"Perish the thought! I've had to fight the urge to read ahead while you were sleeping. I've always wanted to travel."

She sighed. "Me, too. I doubt I'll ever see these places, but it's fun to pretend." She sent him a shy look under her lashes. "I can't thank you enough. It helps the time pass."

Lance smiled. "I wish I could take credit for the thought, but Conner suggested it."

Jane's flush had nothing to do with her fever. "He has been very thoughtful, too."

Theodora wondered why that made her heart ache. He'd been so different of late, and it made her feel incomplete in some way.

She forced a smile. "I shall leave the two of you to your trip. Pray don't get lost. I'd hate to have to send a search party into the pages of your book."

"We never get lost," Lance said with assurance.

Jane smiled at him shyly. "I'm not sure that would be such a bad thing. Getting lost can be an adventure, too."

"So it could be — with the right person."

Lance spoke in such a solemn tone that Theodora looked at him curiously. It was a pity Jane seemed to have a preference for Conner, for she was far more suited to a steadfast, cautious country squire than a devil-may-care privateer.

Sadly, Theodora wasn't suited to either. A

surprising wave of self-pity made her shake off her thoughts and say briskly, "If you two will excuse me, I must ask Mrs. MacAuley to have someone check the window latches in this bedchamber, for at times there is a decided breeze on that side of the room."

Lance nodded. "I had the same issue with my bedchamber and mentioned it to Conner. One of his men fixed it within the hour. He has quite talented woodworkers on his ship."

"Does he, indeed?" She wondered if this week had shown Conner the price of letting his house go to rack and ruin.

Not that such a realization portended anything.

As Lance started reading, Theodora left, keeping the door open.

Alice sat in a chair in the hallway with a clear view of the bed, performing her duties as chaperone. At her elbow sat a stack of linens. She brightened on seeing Theodora. "Good day, miss! Our patient seems stronger."

"She is, indeed. I see Mrs. MacAuley has you mending the linens."

Alice sniffed. "I'm mending because it needs doing, not because some sour-faced housekeeper ordered me to."

"I thought you two were getting along better."

"We have an understanding. She don't tell me what to do, and I do what needs doing."

Theodora laughed. "As long as everyone is happy, so am I." She went down the stairs, her skirts rustling with her brisk steps. It was sweet to be out of the sickroom even for a short while. Before she retired for a much-needed nap, she needed to tell Mrs. MacAuley about the draft in the bedchamber and see if someone could fix it before Jane drifted back asleep.

Theodora reached the bottom of the stairs, noticing the doors to the front sitting room were open. *Ah, Mrs. MacAuley must be dusting.* Theodora went in, the thick rug muffling her footsteps.

The housekeeper wasn't there — but Conner was. He stood in front of the window facing the cliffs over the sea, arms crossed over his chest, his feet planted wide as if he were on his ship.

She came to a halt, unable to look away. Gone was his polished demeanor, and in its stead was his true self. His coat was off, tossed over the back of a nearby chair. He held a half-finished glass of whisky, and the almost-empty decanter on the desk suggested he'd had far more than one glass.

His cravat hung undone, and his shirt was unlaced to reveal his powerful, tanned throat. With a faint shadow of a beard, he looked wild and untamed.

She drew in a breath at the shiver that passed through her, and he turned, his gaze raking over her with icy possessiveness.

"So! You've finally fled the safety of the sickroom, have you?"

He was obviously tipsy and angry — a dangerous combination. Had she any sense, she'd turn on her heel and run. But even though her instincts warned her that this Conner was a danger, she was tugged toward him instead of pushed away.

His gaze traveled over her, looking at her as if he were torn by a million thoughts. His gaze, haggard and tormented, lingered on her face, her lips. "Och, lassie. What we do to one another."

She waited, almost willing him to come to her.

But after a burning moment, he turned back to the window, watching a ship that had just come into view. Deep lines carved down his face, intense longing in his pale blue gaze.

Outside the sea roiled, the white-tipped waves beckoning, and she knew they called him. A pang of jealousy rippled through her and she had to swallow before she could speak. "The sea is very green today."

"She's restless. There will be a storm soon, and she knows it."

Theodora noted how he leaned forward the faintest bit, as he fought the desire to join the unruly waves. "You can tell that by the color of the water?"

"The color, the direction of the wind, the way the waves curl before they crash — if you know what to look for, she gives oop her secrets."

He loves the sea. He lit up whenever he spoke of it. It was as much a part of him as breathing.

She took a deep breath, trying not to let her shoulders sag. *He would be unhappy on land, an angry bear trapped in a cage.* A deep tiredness weighted her down, and she longed anew for her bed. She turned to leave.

"Thea."

She closed her eyes as his voice rippled over her, her skin prickling as if brushed by crushed velvet.

Conner watched her for a long minute, noting how her shoulders moved softly with each breath. "Did you need something?"

She straightened and, with her head held high, faced him, her gaze shadowed. "I was looking for Mrs. MacAuley, but found you instead." Her gaze moved over his face, and then to the window. "You miss the sea."

He shrugged. "It has been my home."

Her lashes dropped as she looked down at her clasped hands, and Conner had the impression that what he'd said bothered her. "You know that," he said impatiently.

"Yes." Her gaze flickered past him to the ocean beyond, and she came to stand beside him, looking out the window at the roiling waves.

Her arm brushed his, and the faint scent of her perfume tickled his nose. "Do you see where the *Emerald* is docked? If you follow the line from that pier oot to sea, you'll notice the waves roiling deeper."

"Ah. I do. They've more of a crest."

"Fairy flags, the white of a wave."

"Your crew calls them that?"

"Every seaman known to God calls them that." He moved behind her and cupped her arm. "There's more."

She sucked in her breath, but didn't move.

He slid his hand down to her hand and lifted it so she could sight down the length of her arm. "Do you see that point?"

She leaned back the faintest bit, her shoulders against his chest. "Yes."

"The cliffs there, see how the ocean curls

before it? The waves are the dancer you see onstage, but the real work is behind the curtain — when the currents come together."

"The water swirls at the foot of the cliff."

"Aye. Two currents come together, and dance aboot the shoals. 'Tis nae a happy love story, for they tear at one another, and those around them. Those currents carved that cliff from the rock."

"That's a tragedy." *And so are we.* Her throat tightened and she leaned back against him yet more.

He accepted her weight, wrapping his arms about her, lowering his mouth to her ear. "She's beautiful, nae?"

"Very." Thea took a breath, and he knew her body quivered with desire. After a breathless moment, she said, "But as lovely as the sea is, it's not a home. *This* is your home."

He tightened his arms about her, resting his chin against her cheek. "I dinnae buy this house for a home. I needed a base for the ships, and Portpatrick is an excellent port."

"That's the only reason you bought Dunskey House? Because of the port?"

"Aye. At the time, it was enough." He spoke against the silk of her cheek, inhaling her as if she were the air he breathed. "Och, look at that." A ship appeared at the horizon, tacking toward the port. The white sails danced over the waves, and he could almost feel the freedom of the moving deck beneath his feet. "My sister taught me to love the sea, you know."

She turned her head and looked at him. "Anna?"

"Aye. She would read to us after dinner, because it was what our father had done. She had such a way with it! Her voice would change, and she would breathe life into the words. It was as if the story happened before your eyes." Vivid memories flooded him, and he cleared his throat to continue. "As wild as we were, her stories were wilder yet, many of them filled with pirates and lost caves, treasures and ships with billowing sails." God, how he missed Anna. His chest ached with the memories.

Thea rested her hand on his cheek as if she knew, the warmth reassuring. "And so you and your brothers grew up to have those very adventures."

"Aye. I never feel more at home than when I'm at sea."

Thea's warm brown gaze moved over his face. "I know."

The words were simple, yet he felt the sadness in them, and his own heart ached in return.

It was as if, although they could see one another clearly, an endless ocean stood between them.

He raised his gaze back to the window, where the ship was now close enough for the flag to be visible. "That's one of mine."

Thea followed his gaze. "She's beautiful."

"She's *The Promise,* part of my secondary fleet." He looked past the ship out to sea. "I wonder where the other four are? They rarely come to port alone. But she's the fastest, and probably sprinted ahead, racing the others." Conner smiled indulgently. "The captain is young and nae known for his temperance."

"Your men are your family, in a way."

"They are guid men, Thea. If you got to know them, you'd see it, too." But that would never happen. After Jane was better, Thea would leave and he would be here, alone.

He released her and moved away, turning so that he could see her face more clearly. "I've shared a story with you. Now you can share a story with me."

She looked confused. "A story? About what?"

"Scones," he said succinctly.

She blinked. "Scones?"

"Last week, you said Mrs. MacAuley made excellent scones. At the time I did nae think aboot it — but how would you know what sort of scones Mrs. MacAuley makes?"

Theodora took a deep breath. *Oh no.*

"You've been to Dunskey before this."

She rubbed her arms, wishing she were back in his arms. "Once."

"When?"

"A few months ago."

"Why dinnae you tell me?"

"Because —" *Because that visit changed everything for me, and if I admitted that, you'd want to know why, and that is a secret I cannot share.* "I visited on an impulse. I was with Mother, who was visiting a friend down the coast. While they were napping one day, I took a ride and thought . . . why not?"

"You never said a word to me aboot it. Why did you hide your visit?"

"Because it wasn't important."

His gaze narrowed and he smiled, a cool, calculated one that didn't reach his eyes. "Come. You can do better than that."

He made it difficult to think, much less speak. He was just so *there.* He took up the whole space around him, warmed the air, and made every inch of whatever room he was in his.

And me, too.

Her heart leapt with a surge of raw passion that made her breath catch.

Unaware of her thundering heart, he moved closer, his gaze still locked with hers. His heady scent floated over her, making her skin tingle. "You have some explaining to do, lass."

"There is nothing to explain." She hated how breathless she sounded, but couldn't find enough air. "I just happened to be in the area and thought I'd stop and see the house. People do it all the time."

"I would believe that, had you told me of it sooner. But you came here for a reason — one you will nae admit to. I must know what that is."

She lifted her chin and didn't answer, her face heated under his gaze.

"Och, lass. You try my patience like no other." He captured one of her curls, his warm knuckles brushing her neck and making her breasts peak as if he'd touched them. "And yet I cannae stay angry with you."

The air around them grew thick, and she fought a wild impulse to step closer to him. "I should have told you."

"Aye." He lifted her curl and rubbed it against his cheek, and she shivered. "I can think of only one reason that would make you keep such a visit secret."

Good God — did he know she was in love with him and had been for years? Surely not. Her pride was all she had left, and she refused to surrender it. But it was hard to remember that when he was so close, and so devastatingly *Conner,* disheveled and forbidden. She couldn't keep herself from leaning forward the faintest bit to inhale the essence of this powerful, tormented man.

He released her curl and slid his fingers around her neck, cupping her face between his palms as he pulled her close. "You're nae leaving this room until you tell me everything."

26

She should have pulled away, run from the room, found safety somewhere — instead, she tilted her face to his and closed her eyes.

He bent down so close that his breath mingled with her.

But no tantalizing kiss touched her lips.

She moved closer, pressing her chest to his, her lips parting, aching with want as she waited. She burned for him, her body tight with desire.

He slipped an arm around her waist and held her against him, but still didn't kiss her.

She bit back a moan and opened her eyes, her hands tangling in the loose folds of his shirt.

"Why, Thea?" he whispered, his lips a hairsbreadth from hers. "Why did you visit Dunskey and then nae tell me?" His hands moved slowly up her back, then down, paths of torture and pleasure.

"Because . . ." She shouldn't say it. Yet as his hands moved over her, molding her to him, the final threads of her pride caught on fire and burned in a single whoosh of lost hope. The words tumbled over her lips, ripped from her like the currents that had formed the sea cliff. "I wanted to see the home of the man I loved."

She closed her eyes. *Oh. My. God. I told him. I shouldn't have, but I did.*

She took a steadying breath and opened her eyes. He stepped back, his arms dropping from her. Then he turned and walked away.

Pain laced through Theodora, shards so thin and wickedly sharp that she almost cried. *I told him the truth and now he's leaving. He'll never —*

The door closed, and she looked over to find Conner turning a key in the lock. *What does that mean?* She couldn't breathe or think or do anything but watch him.

He rejoined her. "Say it again."

Her throat dry, she shook her head.

He pulled her into his arms and held her tight. "Then I'll say it for you: you love me."

"No!"

"You said —"

"I said I *loved* you. But no more."

His brows drew down, and he couldn't

have looked more confused. "You're going to have to explain."

"Oh Conner. I loved you for so long." She couldn't keep the bitterness from her voice. "For *years*. And you never paid me the slightest heed."

"I did! I visited you every chance I got —"

"You visited my *brother* every chance you got. And although we've become friends over the years, you never noticed me the way a man notices a woman. At least, you didn't until I eloped with someone else."

"Och, Thea. I cannae pretend 'twas otherwise. You know me too well, but . . . lass, why dinnae you tell me? If you had, I'd have —"

"Felt sorry for me and sent me away."

"Nae! I've been a blind fool, but nae more. If what you say is true, that you've loved me for a long time, then there's nae reason we cannae be together now."

"I'll always care for you, Conner. But I cannot love you. You're married to the sea. I knew that the moment I stepped into this house. When I saw how you'd let this beautiful home rot away while you chased distant treasures, I realized I couldn't be a part of that. I couldn't be a part of your life. I was in love with something that never

existed — you, but you on land, as a husband and father, with a home and hearth,
happy and content." Tears burned her eyes.
"That's a beautiful dream, but that's all it
is."

"Thea, dinnae say —"

"No. It's time. It must be said. Love is
not enough for a happy marriage. And I will
not stay here and rot while you're off sailing
the seas. I cannot."

"I would never leave you to 'rot.' "

She met his gaze straight on. "If we married, would you stay here, at Dunskey?"

"Part of the time, of course!"

She shook her head. "I cannot accept a
part-time marriage. And that's why I decided I could no longer love you. That's why
I agreed to marry Lance."

The words flooded over Conner, drown-
ing him in a wave of painful yearning for —
God, he didn't know *what* he yearned for.
Her, of course, but more than that. He
wanted — *What?*

He didn't know. All he knew was that he
was losing her with every word she spoke,
and he'd only this second found her. His
eyes ached, his heart too heavy to be lifted.
"Thea, please . . ."

She shook her head, her eyes wet with
tears. "I cannot. And neither can you. We

are not meant to be, either of us."

For a long time, neither spoke. Yet their gazes stayed locked, their bodies still connected although neither of them touched. The air in the room grew as still as the final moments before a storm.

Desperately fighting to breathe, Conner reached out and drew her close, tracing his fingers from her cheek to the side of her neck, following the edge of her gown to the fascinating hollows in her neck. He wanted to devour her. He couldn't let her go. He couldn't. It would be easier to cut off his own arm than allow her to walk from this room.

Theodora's heart thundered wildly as Conner's fingertips brushed her bared skin, and she shivered wildly, pressing against him. His touch grew bolder and more desperate, and she clutched him tightly, torn and lost, unwilling to leave and unable to stay.

God, but he knew how to touch a woman — slow, deliberately, without hesitation. Yet he never moved without waiting for a sign of acceptance. She could stop him now if she wished.

But she didn't, wanting more. It wasn't love, but desire, she told herself. Surely true love would find a way over their obstacles?

"Och, lassie. You always surprise me." Conner trailed the back of his hand across her shoulder, tracing an invisible line to the bow at the edge of her gown, several inches below her chin. He hadn't touched her breasts, but they ached and swelled as if he had. "How long did you love me?"

"Too long." Her voice was a hot whisper.

"Tell me exactly how long, my lovely Thea."

"No. I cannot."

He bent down, his mouth close to her ear, his breath sending heated shivers through her, his fingers now hovering over the bow that rested between her breasts. "Swear on your life that you no longer love me — for I think otherwise."

She closed her eyes, struggling to think, when all she wanted to do was kiss him until neither of them could breath. To press her body to his and savor every forbidden part of him. "Too long," she whispered again.

His sigh moved the hair at her temple as he traced the neckline of her gown, his fingers warm against her skin. "And I lost you when you came here. I do nae understand that. 'Tis just a house."

"But it isn't; it's a *home,* too. Or it should be, but never will."

He brushed his hand over her breast and

she gasped with pleasure as he whispered fiercely in her ear, "You want me to give up the sea."

"It's who you are. But if you're gone all of the time, then Dunskey isn't a home. I *want* a home, Conner."

His frown deepened and he cupped her breast more firmly, his thumb finding her nipple.

She arched against him, her body aflame as she pressed into his willing hand.

He flicked her nipple through her gown and her traitorous breasts swelled with pleasure. She fought for breath, clutching the folds of his shirt. Why had she fallen in love with a man too wild to tame.

Yet she loved his wildness.

And she was so damned tired of being sensible.

She lifted up on her toes and kissed him, slipping her tongue between his lips in a wanton way.

Instantly, her troubled thoughts disappeared in a blaze of sensual heat so strong, she could only give in.

Conner fiercely tugged her into his arms, sliding his hands over her with a bold possessiveness that weakened her knees. Her heart thundered in her ears, her breath shortened until she could scarcely breathe, and she melted under his hot possession. God, she loved him. No matter how she tried, no matter how many times she told herself to stay away from him, she couldn't. She wanted him. *Needed* him.

He consumed her, his mouth plundering hers, forcing her lips to part, his tongue brushing hers in a wanton way that made her ache. Her breasts swelled as he touched her, her nipples tightened with need, her skin tingled in a million ways. He played her as if she were a piano and he a bold composer, his hands never still as he lifted her to higher and higher heights.

And then suddenly he picked her up, his rock-hard manhood pressed against her as he carried her to the settee. Shrugging out of his loose cravat and waistcoat, he covered her body with his. He kissed her, murmuring desperate words against her hair and ear as she pressed her lips to his rough cheek and neck, tasting and devouring him as if she were starving.

Somehow he'd untied her gown, and had pulled the neckline free. She gasped as his hands slipped under her chemise and cupped her breasts, his skin as hot as his kisses.

"God, but I've wanted to do this for weeks," he murmured, trailing kisses that burned like fire down her neck.

He rolled his palm over her bared nipple and she gasped and arched wildly, hot tremors jolting through her. "Yessss," she breathed through her clenched teeth.

"God, yes," he answered as he tugged her gown over her head and threw it aside, her chemise following. He stared greedily at her bared body.

She felt as wild as the sea, and she moved against him, parting her legs and pulling him to her. He bent to capture her nipple with his teeth, rolling it softly, laving it with his tongue. The hot wetness made her moan deeply, thrashing under the exquisite torture.

She lost all track of time and thought, and merely existed, the wildness of his caresses and the wantonness of his touch igniting her until she could only *feel.* She restlessly moved her hips against his, grasping handfuls of his shirt and tugging it loose from his breeches and pulling it over his head. She slid her hands up his naked back, exploring his muscled shoulders, holding him as she pressed her breasts into his hands, his mouth.

He blew softly on her wet nipple and she went wild with pleasure, hissing "Yesssssss" in desperate need.

He pulled away and undid his britches with one hand, and she helped him tug the material free. All too soon, nothing was between them but her silk stockings. She reached down to pull them off, but his hand closed over hers. "Leave them," he whispered against her ear.

His hands wandered over the silken expanse, sliding up and then down. The thin sheath of silk was all that separated them, and she gasped wildly when his hands slid over the tops and found her bared thighs.

She parted them instinctively. It felt so right, so natural, that she wished he'd never stop.

Conner found the damp juncture of her thighs, and he trailed his fingers over her womanhood, her wetness driving him wild with need, his cock leaping in response.

She was here, and willing, and wildly passionate, her thighs parted, her eyes closed as she tugged him closer. Had it been any other woman, he would have taken her now — but this was his Thea. And it felt as if he'd wanted this, wanted *her,* his whole life, but had refused to admit it.

Now he couldn't get enough of her, of her soft moans, of her full breasts and soft lips. He bent to capture again first one nipple and then the other with his teeth and tongue. She had beautiful breasts, rounded and high, pouting and pink. He laved them as his hand slid up and down her slick wetness, teasing and tormenting.

She moaned wildly and surged against his hand, and he pressed harder.

Theodora thought she would explode into flames. She threaded her hands through his thick hair, holding on as his hand took hot possession of her. He didn't hesitate or waste time talking; he just *did,* and did it well. She writhed under his touch, the sheer wrongness of it making her want it all the more.

He pressed kisses from her breasts to her shoulder, burrowing against her neck.

"We shouldn't," she panted.

"We must," he growled back, kissing her again and again.

And he was right. There was no going back now. She kissed him, thrusting her tongue into his mouth in the rhythm his hands had set. Her thighs were slick with her desire, his hands never still as with the suddenness of a lightning strike, passion overtook her, crashing over her with waves wild enough to stop her bruised heart. She clung to him, gasping his name, holding on to him as wave after wave shook her body.

He held her close, murmuring her name

as she clutched him, struggling to find her breath. Never had she experienced such raw wildness of feeling. Her entire body quivered over and over, clinging to the final passionate tremors.

Slowly, her breathing returned to normal, her skin cooled.

Conner shifted and she felt his manhood pressed against her hip, still hard and ready. She looked at him, an unspoken question in her eyes.

He rested his forehead against hers. "Nae, lass. I'll nae have your first time be wasted oopon a settee. We'll have a proper bed, and do it right."

His words sent a new wave of longing through her, but before she could pull him closer, he moved aside, sitting up. For the first time, she was aware of an extremely uncomfortable pillow under her shoulder, and that one of her legs threatened to develop a cramp. She sat up, and looked for her gown, which was crumpled on the floor near their feet.

Conner handed her the gown. She clutched it to her, unwilling to dress just yet.

He smiled and gently brushed a strand of her hair from her cheek. "You are magnificent."

She didn't know what to say.

A wicked light warmed his eyes. "I'm nae one who fishes for compliments, but I feel my talents deserve at least one happy sigh."

He looked so pleased with himself that laughter bubbled unexpectedly to her lips. "Certainly. You and your talented hands were quite . . . adequate."

His smile disappeared. "Adequate?"

She laughed. "You look so shocked."

"Ha! One partial lovemaking session and you're suddenly a bold tease." He bent to kiss his way along her jaw to her ear. "You." *Kiss.* "Are the most passionate." *Kiss.* "Woman." *Kiss.* "I've ever met." *Kiss.*

"That was —" She wet her dry lips. She had no idea what a woman should say after being so thoroughly pleasured. "Thank you" seemed oddly impersonal, and anything else seemed coarse and unnecessary, but to say nothing at all left the impression that one hadn't enjoyed —

"Thea, love. You're thinking too much." Conner captured her hand and pressed a kiss to her fingers. "There are some things we cannae reason our way through."

And just like that, she remembered why she couldn't marry Conner, why this — being with him and loving him — was a bad idea. Her heart sank, and her gaze moved past him to the peeling wallpaper near the windows, to the smoke-stained fireplace, and the threadbare carpet. *He doesn't want a home. He wants a woman who will keep his house and never ask for more.*

She remembered the longing in his eyes as he'd gazed out at his ship, and the last vestige of her euphoria seeped away.

He was happy to be with her now, passing the afternoon with a romp on the settee. Who wouldn't be? But where was his heart?

Reality was a cold, hard mistress who saw every imperfection. Theodora needed to stand up, dress, and leave. And she had to do it with what was left of her pride intact.

It wouldn't be easy, for more than anything, she wanted to pull him back down on the settee and repeat their tryst. She wanted to feel him, to touch him, to taste him —

But I cannot. Regret so deep it never ended coursed through her and she pretended to be absorbed in dressing as she fought to keep from weeping. Her arms already ached at the thought of walking away. When she was away from him, she died. When she was with him, she died. God save her from a sensual, forbidden man.

Her thoughts must have shown on her face, for he cursed low and deep, then reached for her.

She pulled free, murmuring "no" as she refastened her gown.

"Thea, dinnae . . . Please. We have to talk."

"There's nothing left to say. We didn't make it, Conner. We never had a chance." She was no empty house to be left behind. She was a woman with hopes and dreams, a woman who knew what she wanted and wasn't afraid of doing what she had to in order to be happy. Passion might fan the flames of love, but without respect, concern, and constant tending, it would leave nothing but charred ruins.

As for him, he loved his freedom, and she couldn't fault him for not wishing to give it up.

His brow lowered, a flash of irritation in his blue eyes, he dressed, his movements barely controlled fury. "You torment me, woman. You are making this harder than it needs to be. I want to get married, I *need* to marry — that works for us both."

"It's not that easy, and you know it. We're doomed, Conner. We want the opposite in life, and were we to marry today, we'd come to hate one another. Perhaps not right away, but eventually. I won't have that. Not if I have to cut off my own arm, would I agree to such a painful, prolonged death." The words tumbled from her lips like water from an overfilled cup, splashing them both with the bitter tones. "Just *look* at this place. The house is a wreck, the lands have been left to ruin, the fields have not been plowed in years, the stables are falling down, the drive is cut through with erosion, the ditches filled with debris —" She threw up her hands, clinging to her anger, hoping it would give her the strength she needed to leave him. "But you don't care. If it's not a ship, then it's not important or exciting enough for you."

His expression had grown increasingly grim as she spoke. "You test my patience!"

She returned his glare. "And you destroy mine! As soon as Miss Simmons is better, we will quit your moldering house and return to where people care about their lives and their families, and wish to do more than run away to the sea."

"Run away? Bloody hell, woman! If that's how you feel, then go, dammit. I'm nae keeping you here."

She fisted her hands so tightly that her fingernails cut into her palms. "We are done. But if it will set your mind at ease and give you some peace so you can sail away with the next sunrise, then I'll admit one thing: you are right — Lance. He isn't the man for me."

"There! Finally!"

Conner took an eager step toward her, but she threw up her hand. "But neither are you."

The front door banged open and footsteps ran through the marble entry. Through the door they could hear Spencer's breathless voice shout, *"Cap'n!"*

When no one answered, they heard his footsteps going up the stairs.

Conner swore under his breath. "Something's wrong. I must go. But I'm not finished with us yet, lass. We'll talk again."

They wouldn't; she would make certain of it. She turned away and set herself to rights.

Conner unlocked the door and opened it. *"Spencer!"* he shouted.

There was a second of silence and then Spencer came running back downstairs to meet him. "Cap'n, you have to come quick! *The Promise* just made dock."

Conner sent him an irritated look. "I saw her. I'll go once the other ships arrive."

"But that's just it — *The Promise* is the only one that returned. They had a run-in with the French."

Instantly, deep concern filled his eyes. "Are the others lost? What does Captain Reeves say?"

"Two of the other ships took hits, but nae one is certain what happened beyond that. The Cap'n lured the biggest frigate oot to sea to distract her from the fray. She'd been causing most of the damage, and he hoped she was nae stocked for the open waters. He must have been right, for she dinnae follow long. Once she turned away, he returned to the fight, but there was nae one to be seen."

"So there's hope. Are there injuries on *The Promise*?"

"Aye. The doctor is with them now. Cap'n Reeves came with me, sir. He's ootside, waiting to speak with you."

"Tell him I'll be right there."

"Aye, aye, Cap'n." Spencer hurried away.

Conner turned to Thea. "I must go."

"Of course. Your men need you." Despite her best efforts, she couldn't keep the faintest hint of regret from her voice.

His jaw hardened and he raked her with a final blazing look before he walked to the door.

He'd just reached it when he stopped and then spun back around and strode straight to her. Without a word, he swept her to him. Hot, demanding, and possessive, he kissed her as if he would devour her.

When he finally set her back on her feet,

she blindly reached for the back of a chair to hold herself upright.

"*That,* lass, is worth fighting for." With that, he left.

Theodora sank into the chair. Life was so unfair. She'd thought she'd loved Conner before, but that was nothing compared to how she felt about him now. During their journey she'd learned so much about him, and about herself, that her love was now deeper than ever, and the passion she felt for him had grown with that love.

Which only made things worse. Unable to sit still, she arose and went to the window. Conner was speaking with the other captain, who was obviously in great distress, for he gestured wildly as he spoke, his face pale with emotion.

Conner put his hand on the young man's shoulder and said something. The man calmed almost immediately, nodding as he regarded Conner with gratitude and admiration. *His men love him. They wouldn't be the same without him, and he wouldn't be the same without them.*

She stifled a painful sigh as Conner climbed onto his horse. He looked back and she quickly moved behind the curtain, holding her breath until she heard him and his men gallop away.

She came out from behind the curtain and rested her forehead against the cool glass, her heart heavy. *If only he wanted a home and didn't find leaving so infinitely satisfying.* Why, oh why, couldn't she love an easy man?

27

The next few days were a whirlwind for Conner. The missing ships limped into port a few hours after *The Promise.* The fleet was battered but sat low in the water, still filled with their prizes. Conner oversaw the unloading of each ship, made certain Dr. Murray had what was necessary to heal the injured, and sent Spencer and Ferguson to scour the local villages to find woodworkers to make repairs.

On top of that, there was cargo to declare, dockets to be filed, bills of lading to see to, and a dozen other mundane tasks that he usually performed with a deep sense of satisfaction, since they represented his successes. But even with so many tasks to see to, he found himself standing at the curved window of his cabin, important papers strewn forgotten on his desk as he gazed up at Dunskey, wondering what Thea might be doing.

She would be watching over Jane, of course, and seeing that Mrs. MacAuley had the house running well. She would make sure Alice wasn't being too much of a pest, that the men Conner had assigned to the house were doing as they were told, that dinner would be served at the same hour, and a million other things she did without being asked. She was efficient. And resourceful. And too bloody stubborn for her own good.

He raked a hand through his hair and scowled, overwhelmed by a deep hunger for her; the taste of her, the way her soft curves melted against him. But more than that, he couldn't stop thinking of the sadness in her eyes when he'd left the library.

He turned away from Dunskey and watched the sea roll gently. He needed to talk to Thea, to explain himself. But each evening when he returned home, she was either with Jane in the sickroom, dining with Lance, or had one or more servants with her.

She was avoiding him, and he knew it. He'd tried to catch her alone during the limited time he had on land, but she'd thwarted him every single time. It was maddening, and his patience was wearing thin.

He rubbed his neck and wished for the

thousandth time he could ask Anna what to do. His sister had been gifted in giving advice, asked for and not, something that used to irk him to no end. Now, he'd give his right arm to hear her calm, patient voice telling him how to handle this frustrating situation. Was Thea right? Was he lacking what it took to be a good husband? Could he settle down and live on land?

The sea rocked the boat, the waves beguiling. Conner sighed and wished again that he could talk to Anna.

"Cap'n?" Ferguson peered in the open doorway, clutching a small leather book. "Here's the captain's diary from the *Frolic*. Cap'n Jessup said you'd be expecting it."

"I am. Please put it on the desk." Conner clasped his hands behind him and turned back to the window. He was almost lost again in his own thoughts when Ferguson cleared his throat.

Stifling a sigh, Conner turned a wary eye on his first mate. "What is it?"

"The men and I . . . we was just —" The grizzled old man straightened his shoulders. "We've been noticing you seem a bit preoccupied. And we think we know why."

"Do you?" Conner said in a warning tone.

Ferguson ignored it. "Aye — Miss Cumberbatch-Snowe." Conner's irritation must have shown, for the old seaman threw up his hands. "Easy now, Cap'n. Dinnae fire on a mon merely for noticing how the tide was turnin'."

"I was nae going to fire on you," Conner said stiffly. "Miss Cumberbatch-Snowe and I are none of your concern. We're . . . talking."

Ferguson didn't look convinced. "Aboot what, might I ask?"

"You may nae!"

"If you dinnae talk, Cap'n, you'll explode with it. You've been pursuing the lass from one side of England to the other side of Scotland, and you dinnae seem to be making headway."

Which was irritatingly true, dammit.

"Fine. If you must know, I've asked her repeatedly to be my wife, and she refuses." God, it hurt to even say that aloud.

"Still?" At Conner's hot glare, Ferguson flushed, but continued. "And your inheritance?"

"Damn the inheritance; I dinnae care if I ever see a groat of it. This is aboot the lady and naught else. I want to marry her because —" *I can't live without her.* The words echoed in his head so loudly that for a horrified second, he thought he'd said them aloud. But a quick glance at Ferguson's face

431

consoled him — the old man didn't look the least shocked. Conner, on the other hand, was very much so.

He *loved* her. Loved her deeply and thoroughly and with every breath in his body. *Bloody hell, when did that happen?* It seemed like she'd always been in his life, reliably there on the edge of it, and he'd just taken her — and his own feelings — for granted.

Conner crossed his arms over his chest, feeling as if he'd made a priceless discovery of some sort. He wasn't sure how he felt about his new realization, but he certainly wasn't about to discuss it with Ferguson. "It's neither here nor there. She'll nae have me, but I've nae given oop." *By God, I will never give up.*

Ferguson scratched his chin. "Pardon me, Cap'n, but has she ever told you why she dinnae wish to marry you?"

"Aye, 'tis the usual nonsense. Because I'll always be away at sea whilst she's left at home alone, which is ridiculous. I would nae be gone all the time. I'd be home a week or two every couple of months."

"Hmm." Ferguson pursed his lips. "Our last venture had us oot to sea for five months."

"Aye, but we were in the Indies. And we

only went because we'd heard aboot that fleet of Portuguese merchant ships."

"A worthwhile prize, Cap'n. But it *was* five months."

Conner scowled. "The venture before that was only a month long."

"True. But the one right before that, where we visited Cairo and swung by Venice, was four months and three weeks. I remember because MacLeish's daughter was born whilst we were gone, and he'd nae thought we'd be oot to sea so long. He was counting doon the days by tying knots in a rope." Ferguson sent Conner a side look, then shook his head sadly. "Poor woman, his wife. I feel for her, I do. Nae woman should be alone at such a time."

Conner scowled. "MacLeish never mentioned that to me."

"He's a quiet sort. Does what you tell him, and dinnae offer any complaint. Or much of anything else, now that I think on it."

"Think elsewhere," Conner said shortly. "We've work to do."

"Aye, aye, Cap'n. I'm off to find lodgings for the men of the *Spirit.* Their ship has the most damage and they'll nae be able to stay aboard like the others."

"Send them to Dunskey House. They can

stay in the two crofters' cottages in the back field. The cottages will need to be cleared and beds found, so take enough men to make it happen."

"Very guid, Cap'n."

Ferguson left, and Conner turned back to the wide bay window. His gaze moved from Dunskey House, down the cliffs, to the deep blue sea below. Waves crashed and rolled, slicing themselves upon the rocky cliff wall, beckoning him. And he felt the longing and deep restlessness he always did when he was on land and the sea called. *Soon,* he told himself, and some of the tightness in his chest eased. He loved the sea. She was his home —

He frowned. *That's what Thea said.* He'd never thought about it before; it just was. He was home here on ship. He thrived in the excitement of chasing their quarry across the unpredictable sea, enjoyed the camaraderie of being part of a well-functioning crew, and was thrilled to bring home prizes. It was who he was.

Dunskey was merely a chest to hold his non-seaworthy things. Yet the idea of being at sea while Thea waited on shore — he already ached at the thought of never seeing her. Leaving her behind was no more palatable to him than it was to her.

He looked back at the house. Those four walls held Thea, and he was swept with the desire to go there now and be with her. *She won't be there for long. Once Jane has healed, Thea will leave and Dunskey will be empty once again.*

He cursed under his breath. There had to be a way around this, a way to — Suddenly he straightened. Could he . . .

Good God, did he dare?

He turned and looked out at his fleet. Maybe, just maybe . . . He spun from the window and stalked back to his desk, where he gathered his ledgers and the logbooks of every ship he owned. And then he sat down and pored over them long after the sky had darkened.

28

"Eight courses — very impressive!" Theodora handed the evening's dinner menu back to Mrs. MacAuley.

"As it's to be Miss Simmons's first foray oot of the sickroom, I thought we should celebrate a bit."

"Are you certain Cook can prepare all that? He normally runs the galley on one of Conner's ships. I wouldn't think he'd know how to make turtle soup."

"He knows, for he drew oop the menu himself. Mr. Douglas dinnae travel like other privateers. He's civilized."

In some ways, yes, while in others — Theodora hid a pleasurable shiver. "I'm glad you have Cook to help in the kitchens."

Mrs. MacAuley beamed. "I should nae say anything, but oh, miss! The day before yesterday, the master stopped me in the hall and gave me an extra two hundred and fifty pounds for the household budget."

"Excellent!" Theodora had known Conner had been in the house, and she'd kept herself tucked away with Jane so that she wouldn't have to see him alone. *Temptation, thy name is Conner.*

"But there's more." Mrs. MacAuley looked as if she might burst with pride. "He said he was going to put Dunskey to rights! He said that as soon as his fleet was back in good fettle, he'd send more workmen here to finish oop repairs on the house."

Theodora moistened her dry lips. "Did he say why he was doing that?"

"He just said it was time."

"Do you —" The words caught in Theodora's throat and she had to swallow before she could speak again. "Do you think he'll stay here, then? Live here?"

Mrs. MacAuley's expression dimmed a bit. "Nae. I heard Spencer and the others saying two of the ships are nigh ready to sail again, and the cap'n has been after them to finish the rest, for he's anxious to be off."

"So he's leaving again." And when he did, he'd take her heart with him. Theodora pretended to examine her cuff as she hid a sudden spate of tears.

"Aye. But at least Dunskey will be left in better fettle than before."

"Good. I'm glad he's taking his stewardship of the house more seriously." Sadder than she'd ever been before, Theodora glanced at the clock. "I must go see Miss Jane. Lance has been reading to her for almost two hours now. He will be hoarse, do I not return."

"Yes, miss." With a quick curtsy, Mrs. MacAuley left.

Theodora made her way to Jane's room, her slippers silent on the thick carpets. Outside the room she found Alice asleep at her post, a candelabra and a polishing rag resting in her lap. Theodora tiptoed past the sleeping maid. "Jane, I —"

Lance stood with his arms around Jane, his hands sunk in her hair, his mouth over hers. He immediately broke the embrace and stepped away, looking both flushed and pleased.

Theodora blinked. "Oops."

Jane hid her face in her hands, gasping "No!" over and over.

Stifling a laugh, Theodora closed the door and leaned against it. "You two!"

"Please!" Jane threw out a hand, keeping her eyes covered with the other. "Don't say it! We shouldn't have —"

"No, you *should* have. I'm just surprised it took you so long."

Jane dropped her hand from her eyes.

"Theodora! You're not angry?"

"Not even a little." She looked at Lance. "I take it you haven't told her?"

His face red, he gave an awkward laugh. "I was going to, but then she looked at me in such a way that I couldn't help but kiss her —" He looked at Jane, his face aglow with wonder. "I tried to resist you."

"But you didn't," Jane said mournfully. "And you're engaged to Theodora! Lance, we —"

"Actually, I'm not."

Jane's eyes widened. "But . . . Theodora, when — what —"

Theodora laughed. "It's true. Lance and I ended our engagement before we arrived at Dunskey."

"But you never said a word to anyone!"

"It's a complicated story, one I'm sure Lance will share with you." Theodora smiled, some of her own sadness dissolving in the happiness that shone from her friends' faces. "In the meantime, there's something I must do, so if you two don't mind, I'll leave you alone to discuss your future."

Without waiting for another word, she took her leave, trying not to feel too envious of the happiness that filled the room behind her.

■ ■ ■ ■

"She is an angel!" Lance, bright with love, strode across the sitting room after the celebration dinner. Jane had excused herself after the final course, saying she was tired, and had left Lance to Theodora's company.

He grinned at her now. "I've never felt so — She's just the most — I'm the most fortunate man in the world!"

Theodora found his enthusiasm charming. "Your mother and sisters will welcome Jane far quicker than they would have welcomed me."

"Oh yes." He flushed. "I'm sorry. I didn't mean they wouldn't have welcomed you. They would welcome any woman I took to wife, but you are —" He grimaced. "I should stop speaking, shouldn't I?"

Theodora laughed. "Yes, please do."

"You will come to the wedding, won't you? Jane says you must."

"Nothing could keep me away. I predict a very happy future for you both."

Lance beamed. "She is everything." His gaze moved to Theodora, and his smile faded. "But . . . what about you?"

"Me?" She paused. "I don't know."

Lance drew up a chair and took her hand

between his own. "We must talk about Conner Douglas."

She quickly stood. "No."

"We must. I'm responsible for you being here. And I've been watching you lately, which is why I must ask about Conner. You're avoiding him. Is there a reason?"

She sighed, but sat down again.

"You love him."

"Perhaps."

Lance raised his brows.

Theodora threw up a hand. "Fine. I do. I have for a long time. But it's useless; he will never settle down and marry. He's said as much, although he didn't need to, for I already knew it."

"I see." Lance sighed. "Then there's no hope? You're certain of it?"

"I am."

"Then that makes what I have to say all the easier. Jane and I are leaving in the morning, and we want you to go with us. In fact, we insist."

Theodora frowned. "You already discussed this?"

Lance flushed. "We consider you one of our dearest friends and . . . well, it's obvious something happened between you and Conner."

Theodora sighed. "We must ask the doc-

441

tor if Jane can travel."

"I did, this afternoon. So long as she avoids damp drafts, he thinks she will benefit from going home."

"To her home? You're not taking her to Poston?"

"After the wedding, which will be as soon as possible. But you can't stay here once we leave; it wouldn't be proper." When she started to speak, he threw up his hand. "And don't say your reputation is already ruined by our elopement, for Jane and I have a solution for that, as well. We'll tell people I was eloping with Jane, and that *you* came as *her* chaperone."

"But Jane —"

"Is getting married to me. No one will say a word, and if they do, we're fairly sure her sister-in-law would crush such rumors before they're even uttered. She's very protective of her own reputation and is quite a formidable woman."

Theodora paused. That would indeed work — not that it mattered. Since she wasn't going to marry Conner, she wouldn't marry anyone.

But Lance was right about one thing — it was time to leave. She managed a smile. Though her heart ached at the realization that she'd never see Conner again, it had to be so, for her own peace of mind if not his. "It's decided, then. I'll go with you."

Looking pleased, Lance stood. "Excellent! I wish to leave at eight sharp, as we'll need to stop several times along the way. Jane will need to rest frequently."

"Of course."

"We're settled, then. I'll go tell Jane." With a ridiculously pleased grin, he left.

Theodora sank back into her chair, the house quiet. Conner was still with his men on his ship and, as he'd done every night since his fleet had returned to port, would not return until late.

Although the fire crackled loudly, and the house was still filled with the delicate scent of their excellent dinner, Theodora shivered at the emptiness. This would be her last night here. Her last night with Conner, although he wouldn't know that. He'd come back late, and she'd leave early in the morning, and they would never see one another again.

Tears blurred her vision, and she picked up a decorative pillow and hugged it, resting her cheek on the silky surface. She had to at least say good-bye. Sighing heavily, she curled into the wide winged armchair and watched the fire.

29

Conner locked the front door, the bolt loud in the silent house. Sighing, he leaned against the door and tugged off his gloves, tossing them with his hat onto a side table. God, he was tired, but also quietly ebullient. His plans were coming together, and while he was anxious about the outcome, if he could pull it off, it would all be worthwhile.

The clock chimed midnight. *Thea will be asleep now.*

He sighed and walked toward the stairs. He'd almost reached them when a sound from the sitting room made him turn.

He went to the door, and walked inside. Curled in a chair, her cheek on a red silk pillow, Thea slept. He crossed to stand beside her, noting how young she appeared, her hand trustingly open on the arm of the chair, her thick lashes resting on the crescent of her cheeks, her lips parted.

God, but he loved her mouth. And her hair, which curled so beguilingly against her creamy skin. And her — *Damn, I love everything about her.*

He brushed a curl from her cheek, and she frowned, independent even in her sleep.

Smiling, he slid an arm under her knees and another behind her back, and lifted her, one of her slippers dropping to the rug.

Her eyes fluttered opened and she gasped, slipping an arm around his neck. "Conner?"

"You fell asleep in the sitting room, so I'm putting you to bed." He carried her from the room. "You lost your slipper, by the way."

"I know. My toes feel the cold." She rested her cheek against his shoulder and closed her eyes.

"They'll be warmer in your bed." *They'd be even warmer in mine.* He tamped the thought down and carried her up the stairs. "You're spending too much time watching over our patient."

"Lance has spent more time in the sickroom than I. And Jane is much improved. She joined us for dinner tonight."

He took the steps slowly; it was heaven holding her in his arms. "I'm glad she's doing well."

"Me, too." Thea placed her hand on his cheek.

He stopped and looked down at her. Her gaze locked with his, and desire flickered in the chocolate depths. Conner recognized it because he suffered from the same condition. Even now, his groin ached with the need to feel her, to join her and — *I cannot think like that.*

He reached her bedchamber and pushed open the door. The room was dark except for the light from the flickering fire. He'd taken only one step inside when she murmured, "Close the door."

He stopped and looked down at her. "Thea . . . are you sure?"

She met his gaze steadily. "Positive."

His heart leapt eagerly, and he closed the door with his hip. The latch slid into place with a click, and he carried her to her bed.

Unwilling to release her, he stood holding her. She was so warm in his arms, her curves soft and beckoning, while her silken hair smelled of lily and rose. He tightened his hold. "I dinnae wish to let you go."

"Then don't." She rubbed her cheek against his shoulder, "At least not tonight."

His heart thrummed madly as she slowly slid her hand from his heart to his neck, and then his chin, her eyes locking with his as she whispered, "We know one another so well. We should see where this" — she slid her fingers over his mouth, sending a throb of desire through him — "passion takes us."

And then she would be his in every way.

Within seconds, she was on the bed and he beside her as he tugged off her clothes, and she tugged his. With hands that trembled in eagerness, laces were untied, buttons undone, and clothing thrown from the bed like sea spray from a ship's bow.

Conner had to stop to undo his boots and toss his breeches to the floor. That done, all that remained was Thea's lacy chemise and stockings. He leaned at her side, resting on his elbow as he appreciated the sight of her naked except for that thin froth of lace that hinted at her dark areolas, and the tempting curl of hair at the juncture of her legs.

"God, but you're beautiful," he said hoarsely. He put his hand on her gently rounded stomach, sliding it lower.

She gasped and stiffened.

He smiled. "Easy, sweet." He leaned closer to whisper in her ear, "I've just begun." Over the silk of her chemise, he cupped her breast, resting his thumb on her nipple.

She arched into his hand with a suddenness that made his heart thunder anew. Knowing that she wanted this, he was free to pleasure her as he would. To show her that they belonged together. To make her admit *she* was *his.*

He tugged the tie that held her chemise and slid it from her shoulders, exposing the creamy slopes of her breasts, the dusky pink of her nipples, the tantalizing lines of her stomach as it disappeared behind the cloud of silk. "Take it off. All of it."

She shimmied from the garment while he watched in appreciation, pausing to roll the silk stockings from first one leg, and then the other, each inch revealing more of her creamy skin. "Och, lass, you're as delectable as a warm pasty on a frozen night."

He couldn't stop devouring her with his eyes. She was so beautiful, so lush and curved. The warm firelight flickered over her skin, turning it gold, reflecting in her brown eyes, and beckoning him onward.

He cupped her breast again, and this time, he bent to capture her nipple between his lips. He twirled and nipped at the tender bud, making Thea gasp and writhe with desire. He moved to the other breast, pausing to blow gently on her damp nipple. The bud tightened yet more, and she grasped his shoulder as she moaned softly.

God, he loved her moans, the way they started in her throat and slipped over her damp lips, so that he could capture them with his own. He wanted to hear more, feel more. He trailed his fingers over her stomach, trailing his fingertips across her warm skin and down, down until he found the top of her curls. He splayed his hand and slowly drew it through her lush patch, pausing only when he reached her womanhood.

He captured her mouth as he drew his hand over her mound. Her lips parted and she threw her arms about him, pressing against him, her legs spreading, drawing him forward.

He fought the urge to claim her then and there. "You drive me wild, *searc.*"

Theodora clutched at Conner, pressing against him in abandon. God, he knew every spot to touch and how to stir her in ways she couldn't even imagine. He made her entire body tingle with nothing more than a look.

Conner shifted slightly, his mouth close to her ear. "I want you so badly it hurts."

She lifted her leg over his hip, pulling him closer, her thighs slick from her excitement, her breath ragged and harsh.

The head of his manhood rested against her, and she quivered. Without thought, she planted her heel on the mattress and lifted herself, opening to him.

He slipped in, then drew a breath, closing his eyes as if in pain.

And there was pain — swift and fleeting, and then she was filled, her thoughts a jumble of mad pleasure.

"*Searc,* what you *do,*" he gasped against her neck, kissing and caressing as he slid his hands to her bottom and lifted her to him.

She threw back her head and gasped loudly as he began to move, thrusting into her, the movement sending waves of wildness up and down her, her skin prickled with a million tremors.

Never had she felt anything as delicious as this. She met him thrust for thrust, pulling him closer, grasping frantically at his muscled shoulders, his broad back, twining her fingers in his thick hair. A low hum of wanton excitement began to grow, and the ache between her legs was lost in a swelling tide. She moved faster and he matched her, repeating her name as he took her, thrusting harder and faster. "Mine," he breathed as he rocked his hips to hers. "All. *Mine.*"

She clasped her legs about his waist and opened wider to him, breathless and wild with desire. With a suddenness that shocked her, a wave of passion so furious that it stole her breath and raced through her, making her cry out as she arched against him. *"Conner!"*

He pressed into her as she writhed beneath him, her passion stoking his. As she gave a final gasp he roared her name, pulling free just as he spent his seed.

Breathing hard, Conner slid his hand to hers, tangling his fingers with hers. Their bodies damp, they clung to each other, lost in the moment.

Finally, Conner breathed out her name in a long sigh and then turned on his side and tucked her against him. "That was unforgettable, lass. Should I live to be two hundred, I'll remember this moment."

She would, too. She snuggled against him, rubbing her cheek against his chest, his hair crisp against her skin. When she left tomorrow, at least she'd have this to take with her.

Her throat tightened and she closed her eyes, savoring his arms about her, fighting the loneliness the thought of leaving him caused. She burrowed against him and he held her close, neither speaking as their breathing slowed.

Soon, the only sound was the crackle of the fire and Conner's deep breathing as he fell asleep holding her close, while she stared into the flames, dreading the coming morning.

30

Conner awoke slowly to sunlight streaming across the mussed bed, the light warm on his bared skin.

Memories of the night before flashed through him, and smiling, he reached for Thea . . . his searching hand finding nothing but cool, empty sheets.

He opened his eyes. The pillow beside his still held the imprint of her head. He scooped it to him and sat up, stretching. God, what a night of passion! He'd known Thea would be exciting in bed, but he hadn't anticipated her adventurous spirit. She was fearless, bold, and his.

He grinned, wanting to bellow like a happy bull. She'd laugh at him, and who would blame her? She was everything he'd ever wanted.

He rubbed his face, noticing that the house was quiet.

Abnormally so.

Usually when he awoke, there was the chatter and soft laughter of the maids, the sound of doors opening and closing. Over the last week he'd gotten used to those noises, and now the silence seemed deafening.

She is gone.

The words hung in his thoughts as solid as stone, and his heart ached as if struck by them. He swung his feet from the bed.

She couldn't have left.

Not after last night.

He'd pledged himself to her body and soul, and she'd accepted that pledge. For her to leave —

His chest tightened. He'd been pledging his love, but had she been saying good-bye? Telling him what she'd said all along, that she couldn't live the life he wanted of his wife, one of solitude and loneliness?

He looked around her room. A vase of flowers still sat on the table, and someone had tied back the curtains, so that the morning sun streamed through the room. The floors were shiny and clean, the wood gleaming, a cozy fire in the fireplace, the furniture dusted and comfortably arranged.

Dunskey House was no longer a house, but a home. Or it had been, until Thea had left.

Everything felt empty. Alone. Bereft. His heart beat as usual, but each beat was an ache, each thought an echo of what was.

And in looking at the home Thea had made, and feeling the emptiness of it without her, he realized all he stood to lose. If only she'd waited — But that was not her way, was it?

He squinted, listening. Had Thea taken Lance and Jane with her? If so, that could be to Conner's benefit.

He knew what he had to do. It was a gamble, and it might not pay out, but he had to try.

He threw her pillow to one side and roared, *"Spencer!"*

Conner grabbed his breeches from the floor and pulled them on, bellowing again. He was just looking for his boots when Spencer knocked on the door.

"Come in! Tell Ferguson he's in charge of overseeing the final repairs."

"But you wanted to do that to make certain they were perfect —"

"She's gone."

"Ah. You already know, then? She left at dawn with the squire and Miss Simmons."

"I thought as much."

"We are to chase after her?"

"Yes, but there's something I must do

first. Have a horse saddled for me, and one for yourself as well. A mon is coming to the docks today at ten. We must meet him."

"What's this mon have to do with the miss?"

"He may weel have the answer to my dilemma."

"And then?"

"And then we ride after Thea."

"But how will you find her, sir?"

Conner smiled grimly. "Och, Spencer. Miss Cumberbatch-Snowe may be hard to predict, but her accomplice is nae."

Spencer nodded thoughtfully. "Then there's hope."

"There's always hope." And Conner would die before he'd admit otherwise. "Come. We've work to do."

31

The streets of Staithcorn rumbled with laden carts and braying mules, dust swirling into the early-evening air, the scent of coal smoke and sea mingling with that of fresh bread. Thea watched from inside the inn as people rushed by, all with a place to go. *And someone to go to, no doubt.*

Her eyes grew damp and with a muttered curse, she pulled out a handkerchief, then dried her eyes and blew her nose.

It had been ten hours since she'd left Conner, and the ache in her heart grew by the minute. She knew that one day, this would be nothing more than a memory. Or so she hoped. Right now, she felt as if she'd carry this hole in her heart for the rest of her life.

A brisk knock sounded at her door and Alice's curly head appeared. "Awake, are you? I thought you might be." She stepped into the room, carrying a tray.

"I didn't request tea."

"No, but I thought you needed it."

Theodora hoped her eyes weren't red from her tears, and she managed to say, "You're turning into quite the lady's maid."

Alice beamed. "I do what I can." She set the tray on a table between two chairs at the end of the room, then patted the chair closest to the fire. "Come and have a drop of tea while I find a gown for you to wear to dinner. This is a proper inn, it is, and I was told you have to dress to eat in the parlor."

"Really? It doesn't seem that fancy to me." Theodora sank into the chair and picked up her tea, cupping the warmth between her palms. "I'm surprised Lance found such excellent accommodations."

"That's because he's still following Mac-Leish's itinerary."

"Good God, does he still have that?"

"Aye. And the way he's going, you won't get home for days, for he's drawn the longest route he can between here and Miss Jane's house." Alice opened the portmanteau and pulled out a gown of blue silk, and another of delicate cream. "Which one, miss?"

"The blue one, please."

Alice carefully replaced the cream gown, shooting Theodora a long look from under her lashes.

Theodora put down her cup. "Out with it, Alice. You might as well say whatever you came to say, or you'll burst. I can see it in your face."

Looking relieved, Alice dropped the gown on the bed. "Fine, I'll say it. But you might want to put a mite of whisky into that tea before I do."

"The tea is fine as it is, thank you."

Alice blew out her breath with such a gust that her brassy curls fluttered. "It's the squire and Miss Simmons. They are —"

"In love. I know. I've known for days now."

Alice sagged against the bedpost. "Good lord, you know!"

"Of course I know. They've been quite obvious about it."

"I was *wondering* how you didn't see it. I thought maybe you didn't want to, so —" Alice eyed Theodora with a critical eye. "So it's fine with you?"

"Completely. The squire and I decided days ago we were not suited."

"Then who are you suited for?"

Theodora's laugh held a tinge of bitterness. "That's the question, isn't it? I thought there was someone . . . but it didn't work out."

"I know who that someone might be. I saw how you looked at him, miss."

Theodora's face heated. "As I said, it didn't work out."

"Perhaps, in time, things will change."

"That's unlikely. But I don't wish to speak of it anymore."

"Yes, miss, but —"

"No! Not one more word!"

"Very well." Pouting, Alice reached out to adjust the curtain, pausing as a commotion arose in the inn yard.

"What is it?"

Alice peered into the yard. "It's nothing. A horse and —" She stilled.

Theodora took a sip of tea. "And what?"

"A mail coach or the like. It's nothing. Drunk people. A monkey. Just all sorts of things."

"A monkey? I want to see —"

Alice slammed the curtain closed and swooped across the room. "You can't. It's gone."

"Already?"

"Yes." A firm hand grasped Theodora's elbow, while another took the teacup from her hand. "Look at the time! You must change for dinner."

"We've hours before dinner."

"Lud, no. Didn't the squire tell you that dinner had been moved up?"

"No, he didn't."

"Men. They never pay attention to the details, do they?" Alice picked up the gown she'd laid out for dinner and tossed it back into the wardrobe, and then flipped hurriedly through Theodora's other gowns. Finally, Alice pulled out a green silk ball gown and placed it on the bed.

"Alice, I can't wear that. It's far too formal for dinner, and besides, it's very low cut. I'd be too self-conscious to sit down at dinner in it."

"It's what you're going to wear."

"No, I'm not. Alice, what's going on? Are you drunk?"

"Yes. That's it. I'm drunk. But you still must hurry, miss! The clock is ticking and you don't want to keep the squire waiting, do you?"

Theodora tried to argue, but Alice had a pert, ready answer to every protest. The maid worked with lightning quickness, chattering so much that Theodora was prevented from asking more questions.

And so it was that Theodora found herself dressed in her best ball gown of green silk, her hair pinned on her head in a pretty if extravagant manner, and almost shoved into the private parlor where she found herself surprisingly alone. "Alice, where's the squire?"

"Late, obviously. He *and* Miss Simmons. I'll go fetch them."

"But —" It was too late; Alice was gone. *That's it,* Theodora decided, staring in bemusement at the closed door. *As soon as I get home, I'm calling the doctor and having that girl examined for madness.*

A noise in the courtyard pulled Theodora's attention to the window and she went to peer out. Where was the monkey Alice had mentioned? Surely that was —

"Lass?"

The warmly accented word rippled over her and set her heart aflutter. Heart in her throat, she slowly turned around.

Conner stood before her, as handsome and seductive as he'd ever been. His swashbuckling coat and sword were gone, though, replaced by a sober dark blue coat and a pristine white cravat held by a sapphire pin.

She wasn't the only one who'd dressed for this meeting, and surprise shook her. "I . . . what are you doing here?"

His gaze raked over her, lingering on her mouth, and then lower to the décolletage of her silk gown.

Suddenly, Alice's actions made perfect sense. *That little wench! She dressed me like a Christmas goose in a wasted effort to entice Conner back to my side.*

Theodora would have words for that girl, but for now, she had to deal with the fact that she felt almost naked, and that Conner was far too appreciative of her exposed neckline. She fought the desire to cross her arms over her chest and instead said in as cool of a tone as she could find, "Why are you here? We said our good-byes."

"I never said good-bye," he said evenly, although she caught the hurt in his blue gaze.

It stopped her, that flash of pain. Had she been unintentionally hurtful, leaving in such a way? She owed him a final word, if so.

He took a breath. "Come. Let's have a wee dram." He glanced around, looking relieved to see a decanter and glasses resting in a cabinet near the door. He poured a measure into the glasses and then brought them over. Raising his, he said, "To us."

She'd started to lift her glass, but at this she lowered it. "Conner, we've already been through this. It isn't going to work."

His gaze warmed. "Yes, it will."

"It can't."

"Och, but it can. But before we begin, I owe you an apology. I was wrong about everything. Every last, bloody thing."

She opened her mouth, and then closed it. What did one say to an apology like that?

He gestured to the settee. "Please sit down; I will nae keep you long."

She put down her glass. "This will only make it harder —"

"*Please,* Thea."

She couldn't refuse the plea in his gaze. "Fine." She perched on the edge of a chair, smoothing her gown over her knees.

His gaze heated, and for a second, her breath caught in her throat.

She thought he'd say something, or perhaps kiss her, but instead he picked up her glass and handed it to her before he claimed the seat across from hers.

She cupped the glass between her hands. "How did you know we'd be here? We didn't — Oh. MacLeish's itinerary."

"Aye. I would have been here sooner, but I had to sell a few things."

"Oh?" She looked at him curiously.

"Four ships."

She blinked. "You sold your *fleet*?"

"I sold that one, aye. And in return, I bought a merchant ship. A large one, as pretty as the day is long. And that's what I came to tell you. Thea, lass, I cannae do everything you wanted, but I'm hoping you might meet me halfway. I'm giving oop my privateering papers in exchange for a merchant license." His jaw firmed. "It will cost me a pretty penny, but I'll make it back, and then some."

"I don't understand. You . . . you didn't do this for me, surely."

"Aye, I did — and also for myself. I wish us both to win, lass. And by win I mean be together for the rest of our lives, to have a family, and happiness. For I've discovered that my happiness is tightly wrapped to yours."

"Conner, that's —" She put down the glass of whisky, her hands shaking. "I don't understand. Even as a merchant captain, you'd be gone all of the time."

His eyes gleamed. "That's where you're wrong, lass. *We* would be gone half of each year."

She blinked. *"We?"*

"Aye. I bought the new merchant ship today. *The Solution,* she's called. 'Tis a big ship, with a verrah large captain's suite. And before we set sail, I'll have it outfitted with every luxury you can imagine. You'll have silver, guid linens, a wardrobe, and a maid, too."

"I see. So we'd sail half the year. And then?"

Her gaze locked with his and he had to fight the desire to pull her into his lap and kiss her until she couldn't breathe. "The other half of the year we will be at Dunskey, setting her to rights, making a home. We'll send our retired sailors to work the farm; they'll need a place to live once their sailing days are over. As will I."

"I . . . I never thought about sailing with you."

"Neither did I, for sailing with a privateer would be too dangerous. But a merchant ship, that's another thing altogether." He leaned forward and said in an earnest tone, "We could do this, Thea. I'll spare nae expense to make it comfortable for you."

She gazed at her hands, which were clasped in her lap so tightly it would take a wedge to part them.

Conner watched every expression, every flicker of emotion that crossed her expressive face. When he'd stepped into the room, her beauty had hit him like a punch to the heart. She was wearing an almost scandalous gown — the green silk clung to her body, the décolletage curved tightly around her full breasts. He ached anew for her, but refused to make a single move that might send her away. This was his last chance, he knew it as sure as his heart beat inside his chest.

His gaze traced the delicate line of her cheek and throat. She was so damned beautiful, and he loved her so much, he couldn't breathe without her.

She looked at him now, her eyes dark. "We'd be together all year round."

"Every day. I fear you'll grow tired of me."

A ghost of a smile touched her lips. "What if we have a family —"

"*When* we have a family. I've thought of that, too. We'll hire a captain to oversee my route and I'll take only short trips, nothing beyond Calais. That will slake my need for the feel of the ocean beneath my feet, but will keep me on land long enough to make a *home*. With you."

She gave a shaky laugh. "You've thought this through."

"There is no other woman for me, lass. Life withoot you isn't life at all."

Her eyes filled with tears, and she arose.

Conner held his breath as she came to stand before him. Her voice was soft, breathless, and trembled with desire. "Very well, Cap'n."

"Very well, what?"

Laughter softened her voice. "I agree to your parlay."

For an astounded moment, he could only stare up at her. And then he was standing, and she was in his arms. He covered her mouth with his, lifting her until her feet no longer touched the ground.

Theodora's eyes burned with tears as she melted into him, kissing him back as passionately as he was kissing her, holding him as tight as she could. She couldn't press close enough to him, soak in his scent enough, *feel* him enough. "Enough" didn't exist where he was concerned.

It never had.

She could feel the pounding of his heart, feel the desperation of his hold, and she held him just as tightly, her heart just as wild, fighting happy tears.

After what seemed like forever, he sighed, setting her back on her feet and flashing his lopsided grin. "I'm a happy mon, Thea."

"You're also wealthy, because now you've won your inheritance."

His arms tightened about her. "The Campbells can have the lot. *You* are all I want, now and forever." He rested his forehead to hers and whispered, "Withoot you, I'm a ship with nae crew. A sail with nae wind. A mon with nae heart. I love you, Thea."

She placed her hand on his cheek. "And I love you, Conner."

To her surprise, he dropped to one knee before her. "Thea, love, would you marry me and come sailing with me? There's spices to be had in the Orient, cotton and furs from the Americas, and diamonds and precious woods from Africa. You've but to name a place, and I'll take you."

She laughed and tugged him to his feet. "How can I say no to that?"

"You cannae. And when we're done, we'll come home to Dunskey. It's where our children will play, and our grandchildren come to visit. It's where we'll grow old when we cannae sail any longer." He cupped her face between his hands. "On land or sea, I'll be by your side. There can be no bigger adventure than that."

Joy rushed through her and she slid her arms around his neck. "Yes, Conner, yes — a million yesses!"

EPILOGUE

The wind filled the sails as *The Solution* danced upon the waves. Conner rolled the charts and handed them to Spencer. "Return them to my cabin when you go."

"Aye, Cap'n."

Ferguson, who was overseeing the coiling of a rope by a sailor who'd mistakenly thought to do it in a shabby manner, looked up. "To France, Cap'n?"

"Aye. We're to pick oop barrels of wine and deliver crates of embroidered silks for the French court. They cannae get enough of Belgium's best."

"And then?"

"And then we're to pick oop a shipment of olive oil and Madeira from Spain and carry them to London." Conner patted the manifest tucked in his belt. "We stand to make a pretty profit this trip. Quite a haul, in fact." Anna would be proud of him. He glanced up at the sky, smiling at the sun-

470

shine beaming between the sails and sparkling on the dancing waves. *You were right, Anna. As usual.* He couldn't help but feel that she smiled a bit wider at that.

Ferguson stuck his thumbs in the pockets of the faded silk waistcoat he'd taken to wearing. "If you'd told me a year ago that we'd be fat merchants on a fat merchant ship, lining our purses with gold in an honest manner, I'd have called you a liar!"

"You do nae seem to mind the gold," Conner said.

"The gold helps," Ferguson admitted.

It was amusing to see how well his men liked their new venture. It had been a full year now, and Conner had never been happier. During the warmer months, he and Thea took to the sea. During the winter months he kept the ship routing up and down the coast of England, where he and Thea were turning Dunskey into a warm and welcoming home.

A flash of blue caught his eye, and he turned to see Thea on deck, her gown fluttering in the wind. She was speaking with some of the other passengers, most of them male, as the women seemed to find the constant wind difficult on their hair.

But not his Thea. She walked boldly, absorbing the rhythm of the deck beneath her boots, her hair blowing about her face. *God, but I love that woman.*

And she loved him.

He grinned and said over his shoulder, "Ferguson? Mind the helm."

"Aye, aye, Cap'n."

Conner leapt over the railing and landed on the deck a few feet from Thea.

She laughed as he joined her. He tipped his hat to the admiring gentlemen she'd been conversing with, took her arm in his, and started walking down the deck.

"Where are we going?" she asked.

He glinted a grin at her. "To our cabin. My staid merchant's heart longs for the embrace of his lady wife."

She leaned against him, smiling into his eyes as they entered the privacy of the narrow hall. "You, sir, are many things, but staid is not one of them." As she spoke, she slipped her hand to his hip and then around to his —

His body leaping in response, he caught her wrist with a chuckle. He loved her more now that he'd sailed with her, now that they'd argued over where to put the shelves in the new library he'd fashioned at Dunskey for her, now that they'd awakened in each other's arms day after day. Their life was just beginning, and each day was an adventure. He didn't miss his old life at all. But this — He pulled her into his arms and covered her mouth with his. This, he would have missed very much.

After a long moment, she broke the kiss, breathless and flushed, then grabbed his hand and swiftly pulled him toward their cabin. "I've things to discuss with you, my lord." She twinkled at him over her shoulder. "Things best discussed in private."

He grinned and let her lead the way.

He finally understood the beauty of the word "home."

For home was wherever she was, and she was in his heart.

ABOUT THE AUTHOR

Karen Hawkins is a *New York Times* and *USA TODAY* bestselling author of many wickedly funny historical romance novels set in Regency Scotland, including the wildly popular Maclean Curse series, the enchanting Hurst Amulet series, the funny and charming Duchess Diaries series, and now the romantic Oxenburg Princes series. Karen is also the author of two sassy contemporary romances set in the little town of Glory, North Carolina.